YOU'RE A BIG GIRL NOW

NEIL GORDON is the author of four novels: *Sacrifice of Isaac*,
The Gun Runner's Daughter, *The Company You Keep*, and
You're a Big Girl Now. He holds a Ph.D. in French Literature
from Yale University and is a literary editor at the *Boston Review*
as well as Professor of Writing at The New School and
Professor of Comparative Literature and Dean of
The American University of Paris.

NEIL GORDON

You're a Big Girl Now

PICADOR

First published 2014 by Picador

This edition first published 2015 by Picador
an imprint of Pan Macmillan
20 New Wharf Road, London N1 9RR
Associated companies throughout the world
www.panmacmillan.com

ISBN 978-1-4472-2792-2

1 3 5 7 9 8 6 4 2

A CIP catalogue record for this book is available from the British Library.

Typeset by Ellipsis Digital Limited, Glasgow
Printed and bound by CPI Group (UK) Ltd, Croydon, CR0 4YY

To big girl

Leila Ili Gordon

with all the love in the world

JACK SINAI, 87, RADICAL LAWYER,
DIES IN MANHATTAN HOME

The New York Times, November 21, 1995

Julius Aaron Sinai, a civil-rights lawyer known for his appearances before the House Un-American Activities Committee, died in his Manhattan home on Saturday night. He was 87. The cause, announced by his son, Daniel Sinai, an author and professor at Columbia Law School, was pancreatic cancer. Mr. Sinai had been diagnosed within the past six months and had refused treatment.

Julius Sinai, known as Jack, first gained prominence for his defense of Hollywood Ten defendant Dalton Trumbo before the Hollywood hearings of HUAC, for which he was dubbed by Senator Joseph McCarthy the "most dangerous lawyer in America." His numerous politically charged defenses included members of the Black Panthers, the Puerto Rican separatist group The Young Lords, and Black Liberation Army defendants in the 1981 Brinks Robbery Trial. He appeared three times before the Supreme Court, where he was known to Justice Thurgood Marshall as a "regular customer."

Citing his Spanish Civil War service in the Abraham Lincoln Brigade and his subsequent Dies Committee classification as a "Premature Antifascist," McCarthy attempted unsuccessfully to have Sinai's passport revoked in 1951, a defeat widely thought to have been the beginning of the senator's decline in power.

But Jack Sinai was best known as the father of the '60s radical Jason Sinai, a fugitive of the Vietnam era, who disappeared as a member of the Weather Underground after the accidental bombing of a Manhattan townhouse in March, 1970. Four years later, Jason Sinai was implicated in the Bank of Michigan robbery in which a security guard, Hubert Krosney, was killed. With his alleged partners Mimi Lurie and Sharon Solarz, Jason Sinai is one of the last "Weatherman" fugitives remaining at large.

Seven months prior to his death Jack Sinai had been awarded the

Medal of the Legion of Honor by the government of Spain in recognition of his "heroic wartime service to the citizens of the First Spanish Republic," during the Spanish Civil War and "a postwar career incarnating the noble ideals of the International Brigades."

In a statement announcing the death, Daniel Sinai explained that his father had concealed his illness for fear that his fugitive son would attempt to make contact. The Sinai family, Professor Sinai explained, had been under police surveillance for most of the twenty-five years since his brother's disappearance.

In addition to his sons, Jack Sinai is survived by his widow, the painter Eleanor Singer, an adopted daughter, Klara Singer of Tel Aviv, and two grandchildren.

JASON SINAI, WEATHERMAN FUGITIVE, ARRESTED IN MICHIGAN

The New York Times, October 29, 1996

In a dramatic operation involving mounted police and helicopter surveillance, Jason Sinai, the last remaining fugitive from the radical anti-Vietnam group Weatherman, was arrested yesterday in the northern Michigan woods, the Travis City FBI station announced today. Sinai had been the object of a six-week-long Federal manhunt, and was attempting to evade police in the dense Michigan forest north of Travis City. Mr. Sinai, the eldest son of the famed civil-rights lawyer Jack Sinai, who died last year, was arrested on charges of aggravated manslaughter stemming from the 1974 Bank of Michigan robbery in which a guard, Hubert Krosney, was killed.

The manhunt began in upstate New York when, following the equally dramatic arrest of co-conspirator Sharon Salzburg, the *Albany Times* revealed that Mr. Sinai was living under the name James Grant. Grant had been practicing as an attorney in Saugerties, New York, a small town next to Woodstock, where he was raising a 12-year-old daughter. Among the dramatic revelations of the story was that Grant had been married to the actress Julia Montgomery, the daughter of former U.S. Senator and current ambassador to the Court of St. James Robert Montgomery. A year previous to her husband's capture, Julia Montgomery had entered a rehabilitation facility in England, and was reportedly suing Grant for custody of their daughter.

After the revelations of the *Albany Times*, Grant—Sinai—had gone on the run, after succeeding in leaving his daughter Isabel in the custody of his brother and sister-in-law, prominent lawyers Daniel Sinai and Margaret Calaway. Speaking from their home in Martha's Vineyard, where they are currently fighting an extradition suit for Isabel Sinai/Montgomery, Daniel Sinai said that his brother was innocent of the manslaughter charges, and that they would continue to use the protections afforded by the commonwealth of Massachusetts to protect their niece from extradition to England.

While Isabel Sinai's future remains a question, her father's arrest marks one of the final steps toward closing a chapter of American history. Only Mimi Lurie, the last remaining Weatherman fugitive, is still at large. Ms. Lurie's whereabouts, according the FBI Travis City field office, remain unknown.

MIMI LURIE, LAST REMAINING '60S ERA FUGITIVE, SURRENDERS IN OHIO

The New York Times, October 30, 1996

In yet another of a stunning series of events following the manhunt for Weatherman fugitive Jason Sinai, who was arrested two days ago in a dramatic capture in northern Michigan, Mimi Lurie surrendered herself in an Ohio police station yesterday to face 25-year-old charges of robbery, aggravated manslaughter, and evading arrest.

In a statement released to the press by her lawyer, Gillian Morreale, Ms. Lurie declared that she was surrendering in order to clear her co-defendant Jason Sinai from charges of aggravated manslaughter in the 1974 Bank of Michigan robbery. Interviewed by *The New York Times*, Ms. Morreale said that "Mimi Lurie's testimony will show that Jason Sinai was not present at the Bank of Michigan robbery, nor involved in its planning." This claim will be supported, she went on to say, by Sharon Solarz at her upcoming trial.

Daniel Sinai, Jason Sinai's brother and lawyer, speaking to the press from New York, went on to say that the exculpation of his brother will ensure "that his daughter, Isabel Sinai, will not be subject to extradition to England," and that Mr. Sinai will continue to vigorously contest his ex-wife's attempt to gain custody of their child, born while Sinai was living under an assumed identity as James Grant in Woodstock, New York.

Ms. Lurie's surrender closes a chapter of American history stemming from the war in Vietnam, when a group of self-styled revolutionaries named themselves "Weatherman" after a line in a Bob Dylan song and conducted a campaign of bombings designed to force the Nixon administration to end the war in Vietnam. But public attention, in the coming weeks, is likely to be more focused on the continuing drama of Jason Sinai and his attempts to retain custody of his 12-year-old daughter in a continuing legal battle with his ex-wife, the actress Julia Montgomery, which brings to the public stage a pantheon of American left-wing royalty. If Mr. Sinai is indeed exculpated by Mimi Lurie's testimony, it is likely that Ms. Montgomery and her father, ex-Senator and current Ambassador to the Court of St. James Robert Montgomery, will find themselves facing a much larger challenge to their custody suit than previously thought.

Meanwhile, Isabel Montgomery is being held under legal protection by her uncle, the prominent left-wing legal scholar Daniel Sinai, and his wife, civil-rights attorney Margaret Calaway. Daniel and Jason Sinai are the sons of yet another prominent left-wing attorney, Jack Sinai, dubbed by Senator Joe McCarthy as "the most dangerous lawyer in America." Jack Sinai died last year at 87, shortly after receiving the Medal of the Legion of Honor from the government of Spain for his volunteer service in the Abraham Lincoln Brigade during the Spanish Civil War.

Our conversation was short and sweet
It nearly swept me off-a my feet
And I'm back in the rain, oh, oh
And you are on dry land
You made it there somehow
You're a big girl now.

—BOB DYLAN
"You're A Big Girl Now"

PART ONE

Chapter One

Isabel Montgomery

March 4, 2011

Riyadh, Saudi Arabia

1.

It was an amazing series of accidents.

Riyadh to London, six hours late for my connection to the States.

It is midnight already when the airport lights recede below and then give way to the sweep of desert from the city to the sea.

Nothing that could have gone wrong hasn't. I am going to miss my connection in England. I have just screwed one assignment, thoroughly, and I am going to lose another because I am so late. Fortunately, I don't actually have to think about it now, because I am about to spend the night in Heathrow on a molded plastic chair, staring at planes parked on tarmac as I am parked on plastic, and I can think about it then, all night. Particularly so because no sooner have we overflown Tel Aviv and put the Med below us than I find in my pocket and digest, rather than waste, a good gram of pitch-black, nearly liquid Afghan hashish—"tribute from the brave Mujahedeen, my love," Crown Prince Ibn Saud Cuntman had told me when he gave it me—and by the time I get settled for my night in the airport I am going to be very, very high.

With this inventory of what a fucking *terror* it all is—when I am pissed off, I tend to think in Momma's voice—I hit my wine again and try to convince myself, okay, this is bad, but at least it is as bad as it gets.

But the thought doesn't seem to alleviate the free-fall in my stomach, so rapid that I wonder at it.

In a minute, I understand.

See, I am not really at the bottom.

Not yet.

To get all the way there I have to realize not just that I have a 5,000-word article due to the *Guardian Weekend Magazine* in a matter of hours and I don't have the material I need; not just that I have missed my flight to the central event I'm covering for a *New York Times Magazine* article; but above and beyond all this I have to understand suddenly, inevitably—and this just as the first tendrils of hash-induced anxiety are reaching up into my womb—what it means to me now that I am wearing a *miniskirt*.

And then, there it is: not just rock-bottom but rock-bottom at a time when I have a whole sleepless, stoned night to think, long and hard, about how I got here.

1: First I got fed up with Crown Prince Cuntman, the days of waiting for minutes of interviewing, his long fingers on my knee, his office bottle of Glenmorangie, hidden in actual Biedermeier in a desert tent that took a crew of twenty to pitch and cost as much as a house in the suburbs of Detroit every time he decided to race his camel in the sand.

2: Then, when we did finally talk on the record, I meticulously disproved his denial of support for sharia as concerns divorce and the veil; argued over his refusal to acknowledge contracts with Halliburton; expressed amazement at his disavowal of state ties with Iraqi Islamists. Of which each point was a mistake not because I was wrong—in each I was right—but because it tended to make the Crown Prince irate, and when the Crown Prince became irate, that tended rather to imperil my status in his horrid little country.

Most purely self-destructive, though, was 3: my refusal, on my last day, to cover my head during my final audience with the son of a bitch, because although it did piss him off, which was good, it also got him to cancel the interview, which was not.

And finally, 4, once my credentials had been revoked; once I had been escorted back to Riyadh in one of the Humvees that had carried his son's Xboxes and flat-screen TVs out to the desert so they could amuse themselves while communing with their bedouin souls and been taken to my hotel room for the five-six hours before my plane left, late; finally, when Prince Cuntman's bodyguards came knocking at my door to escort me to the airport, it was a serious miscalculation on my part to have put on a miniskirt, just to piss the fuckers off further, because—and this is what I realize as we drop out of the sky over London toward the tarmac; this is what makes my stomach sink as, finally, a wash of realization of my own utter idiocy comes over me like the sad little film of rain streaking the plastic window of the plane—I will not only be spending the night in a molded plastic chair in the airport, but I will be doing so in a *miniskirt*, and that means the whole night I will have to worry about keeping my legs crossed every time I fall asleep.

If I ever fall asleep.

Heathrow circling below, the engines decompressing, wheels coming down with that little whine that announces that the inevitability of arrival is upon you, it seems to me that these bad decisions, these bad mistakes, are all there is to me. My little bad-girl act, my brash luck and fine connections that have let me muscle open so many doors over the years, has grown thin, extremely thin; this time my editors, my publishers, my employers are going to see through me, right through me.

And because I'm here, because I'm right into it now, contemplating, as I exit the plane, a night with tightly crossed legs in a molded plastic chair, being stared at by sexual psychopaths, hungover from the couple-three bottles of first-class champagne I'd downed to cover how stoned I am in anticipation of the airport bars being closed, unable to smoke, I could at last—this night—perhaps make some sense out of the amazing series of wholly inexplicable events "of which," to misquote Eliot, "my life was constituted." I could think about how much I drink, how much I smoke, why I am, at twenty-seven, single. I could think about why I have been on assignment for four years straight and written, over that time, three hundred and twenty thousand words of instantly disposable journalism rather than a book. I could think about my father—no doubt, I would think about my father. And I could think about how, normally, I wouldn't have to think about any of this, because there's a pill for that. Only, unless I wanted to do a Janis Joplin, I couldn't take one tonight because I am too fucking drunk, and I have to stay too fucking awake, legs crossed, in a molded plastic chair like a fucking Airbus 380 sitting, idle, on tarmac in a North Atlantic spring in the middle of the fucking night, because like a fucking idiot I am wearing a fucking *miniskirt*.

But aren't you just a laugh a minute? That's what Momma used to say to me when she drank. *You're just the funniest little girl in the world, aren't you?* Because no sooner have we deplaned than an amazing series of accidents begins to occur.

Off the plane at Heathrow, I run to the transit desk and am trying to keep from erupting while a bald, bookish little fellow asks for, guess what, a flight to New York, and when that's a no, then a flight to anywhere that changes to New York. I listen with interest, biting my tongue, as he strikes out—no coach, no business, no first-class— and then settles for a hotel coupon and flight the next afternoon. When I step up to the counter, I wait for him to be out of earshot, then I ask for an itinerary that stops over anywhere and finishes, not in New York, but in *Philadelphia*, and I find that guess what? A flight to St. Louis has been shockingly delayed, and there's a single first-class seat available—see why I didn't say anything to the bald guy? —and that, furthermore, from St. Louis there's a direct flight to Philadelphia, putting me in with more than enough time to drive to Washington Square Park in New York City, which is precisely where the *Times* expects me to be in just under twenty hours.

Fucking Philadelphia, man. Sometimes I think my whole career has been based on understanding that when all else fails, you can fly in to Philadelphia.

And yay! First class! Even my miniskirt turns out to be a help: it gets me right back through security after I get my bag, skipping the whole line, feeling the guards' eyes on my ass as I run from security right back to the gates, and down the corridor, and watch the steward close the door behind me as I slip into the empty seat in the first row of first class and take the immediately proffered flute of champagne.

All I need now is a car. When the stewardess isn't looking, I get out my iPhone and get avis.com, which wouldn't you know has availability right out of the airport in Philadelphia. On screen I scroll down to a Chevrolet Aveo, the least expensive car in the Avis Philadelphia stable which my contract with the *Times* specifies I am to take. And I am about to take it. Then I pause the transaction.

Because a moment of clarity has come to me, suddenly and without warning, and what it is, is, I don't *want* a subcompact rental. What I *want* is this little Mitsubishi 3000GT Spyder that my phone has somehow scrolled to, even though that took six screens, each requiring a movement of my thumb.

And at the thought I understand suddenly that I am *not* spending the night in a molded plastic chair in Heathrow. I have *not* missed my next assignment. And that, far from having screwed up my last one, I know *exactly* how to write the Prince Cuntmuscle thing—his name morphed subtly as we took off—because the whole article, the whole fucking article is not about him, it is about me—about the whole trauma of trying to be a woman in his horrible country; about the endless difficulty of trying to get him to tell the truth; about the lie after lie he seems to believe as he tells them, sipping his scotch in Saudi—and so the forced exit from the country was *exactly* what I needed to finish it. And, finally, I understand that I am going to have the motherfucker, lead to peroration, ready to *file* by the time we overfly Greenland because it is a walk in the god damn *park*.

With that thought, I reserve the Mitsu.

After all, Momma drives the GTP V6, and she will want to know whether to upgrade.

As for the *Times* and their expenses?

Fuck the *Times* and their expenses.

And, while I'm at it, as for you who were so enjoying watching me, beautiful woman and spoiled girl that I am, finally, get mine?

Fuck you too.

I was a man, you'd be applauding me.

The plane levels into its cruise over the North Sea; the seatbelt lights go off; I pour a glass of champagne from the bottle I made the first-class steward leave for me and open up my laptop.

I have this itty-bitty thing to write for a few hundred thousand Britons and, the strong, sexy, throb of the Afghan hash filling my veins, perfectly modulated by the bottle of champagne now sitting on my seatside table and ready to be replaced, anytime, by this stunning girl working the first-class cabin, I—as my American friends would say—am good, really good, to go.

Once this girl in Paris whined to me, *"T'es tellement m'en fichiste toi,"*—"You don't give a fuck about anything!" Then she left me alone in her little *chambre de bonne* on the rue des Abbesses, high above Sacré Cœur.

She meant it as a complaint.

I heard it as a compliment.

I launch iTunes and hit shuffle and who do you think comes on? None other than Bowie: Major Tom.

But what I don't know is that all the while I'm doing what I'm doing, or what I think I'm doing, something else is going on. An amazing series of accidents is preparing themselves, one after another, and at the end of them, that quality that so frustrated that pretty little girl in her *chambre de bonne* high above Sacré Cœur, that *m'en fichiste* quality that had served me so well, is about to be taken away forever.

And I don't know, yet, that I will never be happy again in quite that same way I am happy, that flight from London to St. Louis to Philadelphia, floating in a tin can, high above the earth, writing a piece of journalism that is accomplished and fluent, at the height of my powers, right through in one draft, and then sitting back and, looking out into the border of space, sipping my champagne, high as a kite.

Planet earth is blue, and there's nothing I can do.

2.

So, as for Washington Square Park, New York City, to which I turn my attention the moment I have finished assassinating Crown Prince Cuntmuscle, I believe what happened was something like this. A couple-three weeks earlier in the offices of the *New York Times Magazine* someone brought up at an editorial meeting that a march was being planned from Zuccotti· Park to Washington Square on March 6, 2011, to commemorate the Occupy Wall Street movement. It appears that the call is out to Columbia, NYU, the New School, the new SDS, Radical Students Union, the Confederation of Catholic Activists, and the like, for a huge mobilization, a march up Sixth Avenue, finishing with a rally in Washington Square.

Right. So there's a whole bunch of talk about that, and it gives birth eventually to the idea of publishing a "What's Left?" article. The editor who picks it up is Stephanie Delacorte and somehow, God knows how, she makes her case. Maybe she is impassioned and sincere: *Obama brought back a* Left *in this country, and maybe Palin's fought it back, but it's still there, and we need to report on it.* Maybe she is cynical: *Worked last year when* New York *did it.* Maybe they have a computer that tells them that no one's done such a piece in *n* months and so there's no market saturation. Or maybe it's pure opportunism: outside the annual protest against the School of the Americas at Fort Benning, there has not been a major left-wing mobilization in this country since Occupy Wall Street was raided by the police, and that makes it a rare peg to hang an article on—especially this year, which is an election year, in which it seems more than likely that we'll get another four of Obama, given his extra-ordinary unwillingness to do anything that might piss off the one percent and the inability of the Republicans to find anyone to run who is not, in fact, a bozo.

But since no one cares, not the slightest little bit, about a left-wing mobilization, they figure they have to generalize the article up the wazoo to make it relevant to anybody in their demographic. In other words, they can't report simply on the protest itself, seeing no one cares but the people who are already there, making fools out of them-selves—and who even knows how many there will actually be—so they have to make it the symbol for something, such as a "What's Left?" article. What could it be about? They do their homework with assiduity—Google played the major role, one suspects, magazine edi-tors being what they are today—and come up with the following. In March, the Occupy protest—note, they're already calling it a protest. Then in April, the annual Spanish Civil War Veterans Memorial, once again in New York. And finally, November, the School of the Americas Protest down in Fort Benning, Georgia. That's a cool series, What's Left, "The New New Left," one person covers them all, what say?

It's a strong argument—especially in an industry in which com-missioning an article entails no obligation to publish it, or pay full price for it, and so they're all suggesting names, as editors will—Philip Gourevitch. No, Kai Bird. No, let's ask Amy Goodman, she never writes. How about Jon Stewart? What about Amy Wilentz? What about *Sean* Wilentz? What about Arundhati Roy? God, too bad Hitch is dying, he could nail these guys to the wall. Or, get this, what about Christopher Buckley!—when someone—I imagine some kid just out of Yale—pipes up: what about Isabel Montgomery?

"From the *Guardian*?" The idea's so resoundingly stupid that Stephanie Delacorte actually stops talking for a moment. "Mont-gomery covers the Mideast, dear."

She has this soupy, phony English accent and now, it thoroughly shuts the kid up. So they resolve to assign George Packer, and move on. But later, Delacorte's going over something with the Yale kid in her own office, where her ignorance can't be seen by others, and she says:

"Why did you suggest Isabel Montgomery?"

The assistant knows his chance when he sees it. "Because she's a pedigreed lefty. Her real name is Sinai. Montgomery's just her mom. She's Jason Sinai's daughter and Jack Sinai's granddaughter. Her aunt is Maggie Calaway and her uncle's Daniel Sinai from Columbia."

"Is that right?" The editor looks at the kid. "How do you know this?"

He shrugs. "My dad was in SDS."

The editor understands. "I see. Think Montgomery would want to do it?"

"I can find out."

Or something like that. The result is that the kid calls his dad, his dad calls Uncle Danny, and Uncle Danny speaks to his wife Maggie, and Maggie—who is the single member of the family I stay in touch with, seeing she's the one who picked me up in a hotel room when I was eleven the fuck years old and had been dumped there by my outlaw father, on the run from the FBI—calls me, and when I—who might have actually to engage in a moment of introspection if I stop working—say I'm interested, Aunt Maggie calls Uncle Danny, Uncle Danny calls the dad, the dad calls the kid, the kid tells Delacorte, and Delacorte—smoothly muscling the kid aside—borrows another assistant from another editor to call me.

That's how it goes, see. I've met enough like me—Thai Jones up in Albany, Chesa Boudin and his brothers in Chicago, the Gold girl in Temple Mountain, my half-sister Beck—to know it's the same for everyone. We're this weird little breed, the children of a certain group of self-styled radicals who held sway, for a few minutes in the '60s and '70s, over the imagination of the American Left. If I ever write a book about the Weather Underground—and if I do so, I will be joining the multitude, because there's been an even dozen in the past ten years—that will be its title: *The Imagination of the American Left*, and it will catalogue the myths of which we, the children of Radicals, are such a prevalent example.

And so because my father in a University of Michigan cafeteria in 1969 decided to listen to this prick called Billy Ayers and join a faction of SDS that would later bully and steal and cheat to take over the organization and become Weatherman; because he then engaged in various shenanigans including planting a variety of what we would call, today, IEDs—improvised explosive devices—in various spots around the country that had made him what he was, that is, an over-privileged, spoiled young white male; because he then spent a quarter-century living under an assumed name; because, finally, he conspired to bring not just national but international attention on himself when he at last decided to surface, a plan that included leaving me in a hotel room to be picked up by an aunt whom I had never met—because of all that a phone rang in Bahrain where I was prepping my trip to Saudi and a voice said: "Can you hold for Ms. Delacorte," and next thing I am booked to travel to Washington Square Park, New York City, to cover what was promising to be the single largest Left-wing mobilization in the country since like 1974, for the *New York Times*.

3.

And so therefore—as Uncle Joe, whom I am soon to meet, would say—it is 6 a.m. now and I am clicking my heels down a sun-flooded corridor into Philadelphia airport and each step is taking me closer to a moment that is going to transform my little-bitty sense of myself, of who I am, of what I do, beyond anything I have ever imagined.

But I have no clue. Prince Cuntmuscle is done and ready to file the moment I find a wifi connection and my Mitsu 3000GT, twenty-two hundred a week as opposed to the Aveo for four, is waiting at Avis and the last little electric buzz of the Afghan hash is in my blood like a tiny warm orgasm. And God bless airports, don't we just come out of the off-ramp into the terminal and witness a Chili's open, first thing you see, and aren't they just claiming to serve breakfast burritos but just look at that well-stocked bar which is open for business and finding takers and where my laptop, perched on the bar, is in reach of an ambient wireless connection?

True, it is seeming like the finest place in the world to me just now as I order and down a straight shot of Irish whiskey—oh, how I love gentrification, because they have a single-barrel Red Breast here—and log into my VPN and file Cuntmuscle, four thousand words, fact-checking notes and photos, and aren't you just the most consummate little girl reporter? Just like Tintin.

Except Tintin wouldn't be going again on a shot of Irish at 6 a.m., would he now? Tintin wouldn't be hitting that and then an ice-cold Heineken and then sitting back in his bar seat feeling heat spread through his stomach, his breasts; Tintin wouldn't be thinking on a wave of drunkenness that everything has come together, just right, once again, would he?

On the other hand, just like Tintin, I am the consummate professional, aren't I just? No sooner is cuntmuscle.doc off into the ether than, on my laptop on the bar next to me, is the research Little Lincoln—how I call him, anyway, my long-faced research assistant in London—has so ably gathered for me in a single folder on the screen: *New York Times* articles on the Occupy Movement; clips of TV coverage, appropriate chapters from a little bibliography of historical sources about American activism since Vietnam, Jim Miller's *Democracy is in the Streets*, Gitlin's *SDS*, and all the autobiographies, published or unpublished: Billy Ayers, Cathy Wilkerson, Mark Rudd, Howie Machtinger. A cake walk. A fucking sleigh ride. I am almost done with the research already, sitting here at the bar. I mean after all. We were weaned on these images, on this story, a certain kind of us; we sucked it out of the tits of our weepy-eyed wet-nurse, this, Woodstock, March on the Pentagon, Democratic Convention, the mother's milk of the pathos of the American Left. There you go. That's the book right there: *The Tits of the American Left*.

Bet you thought I was going to say, *pathos*, didn't you? *The Pathos of the American Left*. Now there's the title, isn't it just? You can just see it in that clunky cover type on the *New York Review of Books*, can't you? *The Pathos of the American Left*, reviewed by Theodore Draper.

Only I'm not writing it.

Know why?

Because I don't give a fuck.

This is just an assignment for me. I only took it to avoid doing something more meaningful. That I'm familiar with my father and his bullshit doesn't mean I care about it, or him. In fact, I doubt that I've spent more than six months with my father, and that only because I had to, since, at thirteen, I insisted on going to live with my mother. The way I see it? I hit this Irish one last time, I shoot up to New York, I check into the W Union Square and then stroll down to look at the protest, I kill some time, grab some authenticating detail—tie-dyed shirts and Birkenstocks, one assumes—and then stick around to grab a quote from some speech. Then I see who I can find to spend the night with in my suite at the W, which will have a minibar, and in the morning I get the fuck back to the airport. The only possible delay is if there's some real violence, and I should be so lucky. Write the thing up on the flight to London, then talk Momma into going somewhere nice, somewhere sunny with many clothes stores, not a hard sell to Momma in any season but particularly after the rough work of shopping the fall collections which will have left her weary.

For a couple minutes I click through the photos the assistant sent me of my interviewees. The organizer of the march is this guy, Patrick Douglas, a lefty lawyer, nice-looking guy of thirty or so with an open face. But so was Crown Prince Cuntmuscle nice-looking—and he owned two billion dollars' worth of hotels from Mecca to Miami. Still he was about to be drawn and quartered in the *Guardian*. These little folk with their little gathering in Union Square? These half-baked heirs to a failed tradition of American radicalism; this new generation of shitheads who, once again, was organizing penny-ante demonstrations while the machinery of government, the military, trillions of dollars of the Federal Reserve, the combined powers of the mightiest nation in human history, was held by their enemies? I was taking them *downtown*.

The fact is, I don't only think in Momma's voice, but in Sinai's sometimes too.

Especially when I'm being an asshole.

Laura Whitehorn, when I met her once at the national LGBT convention, over coffee, she says: "He may be your father, but Sinai's an asshole. Always was, always will be."

Me too.

Then I lean back from my laptop and kill the Heineken and put on my earphones and hit shuffle, which bless its heart goes to U2, and I close my eyes and feel just how good it is going to feel to be in New York, that city of blinding lights, how wonderful it has been, the amazing life that brought me—my neon heart, my Day-Glo eyes—to this city lit by fireflies where they're advertising in the skies.

And I am, still, unaware of the most amazing event of all, the one that is about to change everything.

Because what I don't know, as I float on my morning buzz, is that none of these accidents have been quite so amazing as the fact that unbeknownst to me, while I am watching over this most beautiful of airports in this most beautiful of worlds, feeling the inexorable satiety of addiction; unbeknownst to me, while cuntmuscle.doc—wonder what the editorial assistant who downloads that will think of the title?—uploaded in my email program, I made a serious mistake.

Not miniskirt-sized.

23

Big, super-duper, major mistake.

In fact, two.

The first was that I leave my email program open after cunt-muscle.doc has sent and, thus, let my mail come in with that fucking little chime showing there's new mail and its horrid seduction and now, when I open my eyes, U2 loud in my ears, before I can think, I look at my email and see there is a letter from Sinai.

The second is that I read it.

Once for six months I had Sinai's email removed by my spam program.

Never would I open a letter from him right when it came in.

But because of this amazing series of accidents, I read it, then I read it again.

And then, all of a sudden, I am no longer drunk. I am no longer drunk and I am no longer high and what is more suddenly, from all around me—the Chili's logo, the McDonald's sign, the Hudson News, the flat-screen TVs showing CNN—all the color has drained out of the world.

Sinai is dying.

I suppose it's some sort of vascular thing. A blood-pressure drop, something like that. Or it's the booze. But for a moment, all around me—all around me—the world is turned to black and white, like the screen of an old TV in a movie, only still high def, like reality, and for a moment, everything stops.

Sinai is dying, but I'm not going to tell you about it. In a way, it wouldn't even be accurate to. Because I'm not thinking about my father's impending death, all that's in my mind is Laura Whitehorn: "He may be your father, but Sinai's an asshole. Always was, always will be."

And before I know it I have downed a third Red Breast and a second Heineken and suddenly not just drunk again but very drunk, very drunk indeed, I am able to slam shut my computer, pay my bill, and walk in my miniskirt right out of the terminal, the neon glowing in the periphery of my eyes, my feet strong and steady and a huge confidence in my heart.

I get my Mitsu, set the GPS, lower the top, and gun toward the airport exit, feeling the engine. Avis, turns out, has the non-turbo SL, which unlike the twin VR4 is only truly good if it's rented and you can abuse it. Before I pull out of the airport, I take a laced Marlboro from my pack—one of the six I had meticulously loaded with a little sliver of Cuntmuscle's Afghan hash—"tribute from the brave Mujahedeen, my love"—before I ate the remaining gram on the airplane, what seems to me, now, a million years ago. And by the time I'm speeding up the 95 through a landscape of budding trees, under a blue east-coast sky of high clouds, I have so successfully forgotten Sinai's letter that I even find myself singing to the random song that's shuffled up into my ears although, when I realize what it is I am singing, I stop myself and turn on the radio. It is, see, the first couple lines of that Dylan song:

> *Our conversation was short and sweet*
> *It nearly swept me off-a my feet*

4.

Tell me that it hurts less when your father is dying if you hate him. Tell me that it's not our fault we come from these goddamn people whom we never can leave alone. I was thirteen the last time I spent a full week under the roof of my father. I am twenty-seven today and if the time in between has been anything to me, it's not because I went to Cambridge at sixteen and graduated at nineteen; SOAS at nineteen and graduated at twenty-three with a Ph.D. Not because by twenty-five I had a byline in the *Economist*, not because I hold visiting appointments at LSE and The Monterey School of International Studies, but because in all that time, all that time, I have stayed the fuck away from my father.

Now look at me. Coming up through Jersey in my Mitsu 3000GT, driving drunk and stoned at not eleven in the morning, and under the veneer of all that drink and all that dope there is something growing in my chest, or rather shrinking, for it is hollow in there, hollow, and so is my stomach, like I have been reamed through, through and through, asshole to throat.

These fucking people.

Sinai is dying. What a fucking kick in the ass. Sinai at what, sixty-five, seventy? *It's called multiple myeloma, baby, it's been with me for years, and now its time has come.* And even this pisses me off. With you for years? How the fuck many years? Since I was ten? Since I was twenty? *I've more or less exhausted the treatments, and it's time to face up to it.* Oh, treated are we? In and out of hospital, getting chemotherapy, passing out with anemia, losing the rest of your hair? And the reason you don't tell your daughter is what? *I'll stay up in Woodstock for a few more months—see the fall up here if I can. Then Molly and I will move down to Papa's house in New York so I can be close to Danny and Maggie and Rebeccah and the kids for the winter, and I expect that before spring, one way or another, I'll be more or less done.*

Uh huh. So that's the way it is, is it? Danny and Maggie and Rebeccah and the kids, gathered around his bedside while slowly, bravely, he wastes away. Cooking, kidding, caring. Getting close to death, with love. Making those brave little jokes you make, waking at night to change his catheter bag, cooking delicious little meals—high-fat now, we're not worrying about cholesterol any more!—and every now and again, just every now and again, slipping out into the hallway to let a couple tears fall, just a couple tears, on the shoulder of one of the other brave ones there with you, doing it right, seeing Sinai off.

And where is Sinai's daughter in this? Where am I, the only one of his kids he brought up, his daughter and heir? Where am I in this happy little scenario of bravery and love?

Oh wait, funny girl. Remember? You're the one who's been ignoring his letters for two decades and only seeing him when his wife Molly, whom you love, guilts you into it. And he's been writing you those letters for two decades, now, hasn't he? Once a day, every day, for the entirety of your life. So maybe you're not in this little cozy club are you, gathering around the dying Sinai, holding his hand, smoothing his brow, watching him go. But you're still the only daughter he raised, and you're still the first to know.

Baby, I didn't want to tell you this by email, but you didn't give me any choice. And I wanted you to know first. Molly knows, but nobody else, and I won't tell anyone else until I hear from you so please, please baby: get in touch.

Aha, get in touch, will I? And why? *I don't know what you're going to do, and I won't try to dictate your choice. All I can say is that this fall is your last chance to hate your father, there, in person, and I hope you're going to take advantage of it.*

So. Fuck. For a long time, there, there is darkness. The road under me, the car humming, the music blasting, and for a long, long time there is darkness, a feeling hard and harsh and all-encompassing through me, empty, reamed out, hollow.

Such a long time that when I am able to think again I am approaching the Holland Tunnel, into New York.

5.

And don't all plans just belong to God? Just like Prince Cuntmuscle liked to say, quoting some piece of Iznik kitsch framed in his living room and worth, no doubt, more than your house. Everyone knows what was about to happen that March 6, 2011, in Greenwich Village, New York.

Did the protest organizers know—as I, alone of the journalists who covered the event, did—that the protest fell on exactly the anniversary of the deaths of my daddy's little buddies Diana Oughton, Terry

Robbins, and Teddy Gold at 18 West 11th Street, in Greenwich Village, New York, when they blew themselves to pieces trying to make a bomb intended for human targets—the Fort Dix NCOs' mess—their little way of protesting the war in Vietnam.

Really, it was amazing that I was there at all. Not only the accidents I already told you about, that brought me to New York to learn that my father was dying, but the others that happened when I got there.

Nothing, for example, that happens would have happened had not W Hotel lost my reservation, or Little Lincoln never made them, or the *Times* canceled them so they could put me in a Holiday Inn in Queens, or whatever, and so I have to go down to the Soho Grand.

Nothing would have happened were I not stoned—although that is arguably not accidental—and am so anxious to avoid thinking about Sinai that I'm afraid to nap, that I just dump my bag, take a shower, smoke a joint, drink a mini from the bar while dressing, gather the tools of my trade—my iPhone and a pack of Marlboro Lights—and leave early for the demonstration, which is due to begin at 3:00.

Nothing would have happened but that because I am early, I decide to walk, and because I am coming from downtown, my route takes me through Soho to Washington Square Park, the demonstration's destination.

Because, see, it is because of all of this, because of all these things that started happening a billion years ago in Saudi fucking Arabia, I happen to be the only person to see that every entrance to Washington Square—Fifth Avenue, Macdougal Street, University Place, 3rd Street—is closed by checkpoints, which you will argue is perhaps not that unusual in post 9/11 New York, but that those checkpoints are manned not by men in blue but by United States Marines in full battle dress and that, moreover, each checkpoint is deploying the signature twelve mounted video cameras of a PVI Array, some seven checkpoints, some eighty-four cameras, each wired into a central CPU housed in a mobile satellite unit and thence to the NSA.

This stops me in my fucking boots.

This is enough even to forget Sinai.

I am on Thompson, coming up from Soho, next to NYU Law School when I see the PVI arrays, and instinct makes me step onto the side of the street. A fully-deployed Patriot Vector Identification Array for this? In Sadr City, maybe. In fucking Kabul, maybe. In Washington after an Al Qaeda chatter intercept.

But a domestic protest, functioning under city permit?

I wasn't sure that a PVI array had *ever* been domestically deployed for an act of legal dissent.

I am high, and so a little tachycardic, but as I peer out from beside Bobst Library, watching an advance group from the organizers—white vests and arm bands, holding clipboards—come through, eating hotdogs from a Sabrett cart, walking unheeding through the checkpoint, unaware that if they weren't so fucking clueless their hotdogs would be congealing in their very stomachs, and fucking should. And as they pass through they are waving gaily at the cameras making crystal clear just how totally fucking dumb they are.

Not me. I stop and watch this display in horror. By noon tomorrow, I assure you, there is going to be a Homeland Security file opened for every single person here, name, face, Social Security number. Briefly, I wondered what kind of muscle they would bring into effect. NSA metadata mining for sure: email, cell phone, social media. Airline records into every area airport (and I bet *they* would include Philadelphia) of course, matched up against the video documentation with face-recognition software. E-ZPass records from the highways in and out of town—transponders could be set up to identify cars even if they're not using E-ZPass. Those two, alone, when compared with the PVI arrays, would capture the identities of a huge majority of the protestors, and data-mining of relevant search terms on email and telephone would bring their match rate up to the 98.9 percent that had become, in the ten years since 9/11, an industry standard. Each picture would drop into a relational dbase with fields for fingerprints, address, passport, police record, occupation. In a crowd like this, the program could flag 80 percent for further data-mining: bank, credit cards, taxes. In 70 percent of the hits, depending on the quality of the health insurance, it would also go for medical records, and synch with commercial databases that contain things such as likely sexual preference.

And all this, I'm realizing, as I watch the cameras—the tell-tale twelve cameras, each hooked up to a computer that it takes successfully to run the identification algorithm at the heart of PVI—I'm thinking, in some shock: they've got PVI out for this?

But if you're thinking that I'm thinking this with outrage over this abrogation of First Amendment prerogatives, think again. I don't give a fuck about First Amendment rights. First Amendment rights are not in my brief. My observation of the surveillance, the collection of authenticating detail down to the make of the cameras and the dress of the camera operators? Strictly professional exactitude, I promise you. Strictly what I need to put five descriptive paragraphs and a conversational panel—overheard at the Occupy protest—into my article tomorrow which I will write on the plane home to London.

Or so I'm telling myself. Because, in fact, as I circle back down to West 3rd Street then trail up Mercer, avoiding showing myself to the PVI cameras, looking down the cross streets to get an idea of what's going on, a totally different plan is taking place in my mind.

As I make my way up Mercer, and then—a few blocks north of the Square, well out of reach of the PVI deployed on its northern perimeter—over on 8th toward Fifth Avenue, which is closed and lined with police, I try to pin down what's bothering me about this. Besides, that is, the obvious. And after a time, the question materializes: does the NYPD really have this kind of electronic muscle available? And if so, why?

Did I tell you I am a regular little Tintin? Did I tell you I am the consummate scoop artist of the century? I place a telephone call, one single telephone call, to a Washington DC area code, and by the time I see the sea of people—forty thousand at least—pouring into

Washington Square from the south, I see that I didn't know it, and the *Times* didn't know it, but a little piece of American history is going to be made today. Don't ask me who I called, or what she told me, but I am so sure of myself, that in seconds I am on the phone with my editor at the *Times* telling her that this is no longer a magazine story, and then I'm waiting while she speaks to her editor, and then I am speaking to her editor and then, on verbal agreement that he will be settling with my agent as I work—I am suddenly *very* expensive—I am on special assignment to the national news desk at the *Times* covering the day for tomorrow's front page.

Life is this amazing series of accidents, and the most amazing is that I am, this March 6, 2011, reporting the piece of journalism that is going to win me the Porter fellowship.

6.

Now I don't need to tell you anything else about that day. You just go read the damn article: March 7, 2011, *New York Times*, page A1. And the days following. When the *New York Times* was defending itself against a suit brought by Homeland Security; when I was named as a defendant in the suit; when I got to spend a charming vacation at Beacon Correctional, an interesting time during which I met Judy Clark.

None of that is what I want to tell you about. What I want to tell you about is how after the day I learned my father was dying—the day after I had, *alone among the American media*—interviewed *not* the forty thousand odd (and I mean *odd*) protesters who duly filed up 6th Avenue to Washington Square, but rather the *policemen and soldiers* making up the security; after I had sourced and confirmed—Little Lincoln spent that night up in London, let me tell you—that the entire security operation was running out of the NSA under direct presidential order—see the phone call I made to DC, that's called *an anonymous source*; after I had reported, documented, and written the whole thing, filing it at 2 a.m. on a computer in the *New York Times* newsroom; after that, as I spun back to my hotel in a taxi driven by a young Mr. Khan from Islamabad, sipping from a bourbon mini I had artfully concealed in my pocket, damp with grime and smelling—I have little doubt—like an ammonia-pickled onion; after we went down 7th Ave, hitting every light in the way that will happen in New York on the big avenues, when there's no traffic, say in the early morning or late night, and no people, but all the city is still on, lights and subways and buses and cars—*oh you look so beautiful*—and for a moment you feel like you are in a place that is not some aberration of late-stage capitalism, nor some grievous insult to the environment, but the place it once was where everyone, everyone in the world, escaped to be free—after I had spun down to Soho, spent like I cannot tell you, needing a shower, needing a fucking *douche*—what should I see sitting outside the Soho Grand, just as cute as a little pumpkin?

I see a black Humvee, with blackened windows, sporting a short-wave antenna, and without a thought, without a second thought, I tell Mr. Khan to drive on.

I am not so tired any more. I smell just as bad, I'm sure, but I am not so tired. And I do admit that I am scared.

But being scared doesn't count. It's what you *do* while you're scared that separates the men from the boys.

After all, you don't need to be a hero to know that there's only one thing to do when you are under surveillance by a big black Humvee sent by the NSA, you don't need to be an ace reporter, a regular little Tintin like me.

Here's what you got to know when you're under surveillance: first, and most important, you want to *avoid* that the people looking for you know *where* you are. This is a key move in escaping capture, perhaps *the* key move. And if you have been in a position, as I have, of nobody knowing where you are in the first place, well then you go to plan B: you *avoid* giving up that advantage.

Having accomplished that, there is one single move left to you: you get a lawyer.

For the first, then, I get it done in one smooth move by requesting that Mr. Khan drive on, past the Soho Grand, and on downtown, leaving the black Humvee behind us. So far, so good.

And for the second there's no sensible course but to call my Aunt Maggie.

When you are scared, and in imminent danger of arrest, there's rarely a course as sensible as calling my Aunt Maggie.

Not the least because when you call my Aunt Maggie, even at six thirty on a Monday morning, my Aunt Maggie answers on the second ring in this sleepy voice softened by the fact she is lying in bed, answers directly and is, instantly, awake.

"Hey, my lovely. Where ya?"

"New York, Mag."

"Are you?" A little pause while she connects the dots. "Of course you are. You're doing that piece for Stephanie Delacorte. How's it going?"

"Um . . . in a variety of unexpected directions." It's funny how reluctant one is to introduce one's own sordid life to others. I say, carefully: "The short version would be: it's going very well. But very well in a direction that requires me to get in touch with a lawyer."

"And what part of 'going very well' requires a lawyer?"

"The part where you use an anonymous source to break a national news story and then find Homeland Security parked outside your hotel."

My Aunt Maggie didn't need a lecture on the status of the First Amendment in 2011. "I see. Can you name your source?"

"Can I? Sure."

"Will you?"

"Of course not, Maggie."

Any major lawyer would tell you the same. When the demon is at your door, or at least at your client's door, first thing, you secure the client in a place where she cannot be apprehended, then arrange the representation and then, and only then—when you have privilege—find out what happened. So Maggie doesn't ask any more.

"I see. Okay. First of all, you can't go back to your hotel. Come here. Or wait. Danny, wake up." This last to my uncle, voice off. "Go look out the front window and see if there's surveillance."

That tells you something about my aunt and uncle, and what it tells you is, that the years that Sinai was underground, they were constantly under surveillance in the hope that he would contact them. Maggie doesn't bother to talk while she waits. I can see her, in bed, her round, freckled face, once amazingly beautiful, framed by red hair. I hear Danny's low voice. In response, she says.

"Uh-huh. Well, lovely, it looks like there's rather a preponderance of black Humvees here, too. That might not have to do with you. Worth watching us too. I mean, during a protest. But let's think."

Now it is about 8 a.m., and poor Mr. Khan has been driving me around the Financial District, and—at least by the look of the back of his neck, which I have been staring at for hours—getting rather irate, and I'm listening to my Aunt Maggie and Uncle Danny going back and forth about how I cannot go to a hotel because they'd surely get credit-card records, and about people whom I could stay with who might not be under surveillance, all with the kind of tinny quality in the sound that makes me think they are now in their kitchen, making coffee, until I hear Maggie say and my heart, just like that, jumps instantly into my throat.

"The safest place is Bedford Street."

And Uncle Danny pauses, then says: "That's not so dumb."

And Maggie says: "They probably don't even know we still own it."

And Uncle Danny says: "But how's she going to get in? We'll be followed if we go meet her."

"Uncle Joe can let her in."

"Let me call on the cell, see if he's home."

And this, at last, is when I get my voice back.

"Stop."

"What, dear?"

"Wait."

"Why, dear?"

Really, even I wouldn't have suspected it. At the words themselves, *Bedford Street*, my heart had gone from one side of my chest to the other. I breathe deeply in, then out, and then in again. "Because there's no way on God's green earth I'm going to stay at Bedford Street."

But this is Maggie I'm speaking with. She says: "You know you sound exactly like your dad?"

"Yeah yeah. 'God's green earth,' I get it. I'm not fucking going there."

She has her *I'm speaking to an infant* voice, which I hate. "No, darling. Not the expression, though it is your dad's. More the flying in the face of reality, the incredible, inappropriate stubbornness. The self-righteousness, the adamant overstatement. The apple doesn't fall far, my darling."

I pause on this for a moment. Until I remember that they don't know yet about Sinai dying. Then I pause some more. And finally, I find my voice.

"God damn it, Maggie."

"The taking-everything-so-personally. Jesus, *you* called *me* for help, Izwizz. I'm *helping you*."

I don't have an answer for that, so I don't say anything while, in the background, I hear Danny talking to someone. Then I say: "My dad's not there, is he?"

"Where?"

"At *Bedford* Street, Maggie. Christ sake."

"No, no. Woodstock, dear."

Then there's more talk and Maggie says, "All right, darling. You're in luck. Uncle Joe will let you in."

"I don't *have* an Uncle Joe."

"Joe Igneri, stupid. The next-door neighbor. Jack's old friend. I can't believe you don't remember him. He'll come in through the back garden and open up for you. You remember the way? 22

Bedford, just off of 6th, runs east from 7th. Ring the bell at the gate under the stoop."

It was an amazing, amazing series of accidents. My whole life has been, and will be, but never has there been nor will there be an accident more amazing than that one which had me, not forty-eight hours after wheels-up in Riyadh, the day after I learn that my father is dying, pulling up in front of my grandfather's house at 22 Bedford Street, walking to open the little black gate to the basement under the stoop.

And you know what?

I am actually so clueless, so stupid, so delusional as to try to convince myself that, boy, this is a sweet little perch, a townhouse in Greenwich Village, you can't buy a house like this for love or money, wonder where the closest liquor store is, I'll just settle right in here, won't I, and order up some bottles, cop a loose joint somewhere, a half gram, a dime bag, whatever's going, pick up a hippy girl from the New School, wait for Maggie to make it go away.

Aren't you just the funniest girl? That old glass-half-full child, aren't you just?

Chapter Two

Isabel Montgomery

March 7, 2011

New York City

1.

Okay, so it is March 7, 2011. Early in the morning. I know that something strange is happening to me, but haven't you been paying attention? Something strange is always happening to me. And if it isn't, well then, I make whatever is happening strange by frontloading it with masses of THC or whatever else is going. Given: I don't have a clue how strange this one will be. Given: I don't give a fuck.

This has been going on for a very long time. The fucking decade has been a steady series of strange things I don't give a fuck about.

This is just one more.

The house is a four-story brownstone on a block which, at this time of a weekday morning, is apparently sending half the corporate lawyers in the city to their offices dragging half the private-school students of the city behind them. Is this what it was like fourteen years ago, when last I'd lived here? Oddly, it's easier to see what it was like when my grandparents moved in, in the forties, because I've read about it. No doubt, Cy Twombly's studio was next door and Martha Graham lived in a cold-water walkup around the corner. This much I know: the price of any one Sub-Zero refrigerator in any one kitchen on the block would have bought Willem de Kooning a decade of paints.

Mr. Khan pulls off, leaving me alone on the sidewalk, feeling bereft. The house stands out, somehow, from the block, in a way I cannot put my finger on, so I cross the street and look some more. Through the big parlor floor windows you can see a wavy image of a well-furnished living room all the way to the back windows, which are filled with the branches of a huge tree. That it feels as if it houses empty rooms is true, but it's also not quite it. Then I get it. It's not the house, it's the windows themselves: wood-sashed and single-paned in hand-blown glass: thus the wavy image. All the other windows on the block are renovated, double-glazed, and as clear as lenses—also, all the other windows on the block are shaded, hiding their interiors.

Jesus. This place is a museum. Or a mausoleum. But it's also the mausoleum or the museum that, at this hour, is my best bet for a) not getting arrested and b) getting a drink—if I can actually get my ass inside.

What a fucking dilemma, girl, and don't you just fucking deserve it? Couldn't you just laugh your head off? Years of therapy and I could say that it is this house and all it represents from which I been fleeing since, at thirteen, I made them send me to live with Momma, and yet here we are.

And then with that little shiver to which I am growing all too rapidly accustomed, I think, also, that this is the house to which my father will come, in a few months, to die.

And with that thought, I come aware of the fact that I am a girl who has not changed her clothes or washed in days, standing alone on a street, hands shaking and likely with a look in my eyes like a wounded deer, about to bolt.

That from where I stand here, there is nowhere to go.

And that if ever I want to release the hold of anxiety on my stomach then I had better move one foot in front of the other and go inside.

Ha, ha, reread that last line. It tells you, in rather starker terms than I care to, what this is really all about, doesn't it?

*

I ring the bell, as instructed, not at the main entrance up the stoop but at the little iron gate under the stairs. There is a stage wait and then appears a tiny little man, a dwarf nearly, or so I thought until I saw how bent over he was, a grizzled little person, immeasurably old. He greets me as if he's known me all my life, and I am unsure what to make of that, until I see his expression. That makes me think that he knows more about what is going on here than I do, and so I step in and follow him into the kitchen while he chats about my aunts, uncles, cousins, of which last category I recognize virtually none of the names.

"You don't remember me? Well, I remember you, missie. Last time I saw you, you were this high. *Meerskeit*. That's what your grandmother called you. Weird Jews, calling their kids ugly. Superstition. Thought God would take you if she complimented you. Weirdness from the old country. Just like my grandma, dressed in black her whole life, even though her husband's death was the best thing ever happened to her, that old bastard. You were her favorite, you know that?"

Did I know that? "No. I didn't know."

"She loved you. She loved all of you, but you were special. Her lost one. Remember the day she died? That was a black day here, a black day."

"Not really. I must have been . . . away then." For some reason I found myself unwilling to say where.

"Ah yes, you were living with your mother. She's the only one of all of you I never met. No regrets, on that one, pardon me."

I'm listening to him, but I still have time to notice all the things I remember: the linoleum floor, the '50s fixtures—stove and refrigerator—the huge window out to a backyard where a massive leafless tree sits against the blue sky—I immediately feel the texture of its bark and the damp wood of a little bench underneath—and then we are up what seem to me to be a set of servants' stairs. When we pass by a book-lined living room, I experience the uncanny. I stop for a moment and remember the silence, bathed in soft sun and leafy shadows of the big tree in the garden. It is a chestnut, I remember, and was higher than the house even then. I look around and find something of which I don't have a childhood memory, but which I am now looking for specifically: the liquor cabinet. Then I follow the man up again past a coffin niche into a floor of bedrooms, and then up one more time, all the while he is talking away:

"This is where Beck stays when she's here. Should be about your size—Maggie says you'll find some clothes here to fit. Rebeccah. Your . . . sister, do I get that right?"

"Half-sister." I answer mechanically, a girl with a British accent, arrived out of nowhere, carrying nothing, and too tired to explain. "I met her once. Is no one living here?"

"Christ, no. No one's lived in this house since your grandmother died. Beck stays here sometimes, but your Aunt Klara, when she comes from Israel, likes to stay at the Yale Club. Girl never fails to invite me to dinner there. And of course your dad likes to stay here. But it's been two years and more since I seen him last. Still, I help keep up the house." The emphasis of this statement was not just of fact, but of intent, or determination, as if the odds against which he keeps up the house—notably, that no one lived there—are well understood.

And so on. While he talks, I'm asking myself what I really do remember here. There's that faint sense that I know what's coming—the staircase, the landing. And the smell here in the back of my throat—oil paint. What did I spend here? A hundred nights over five years? I shut my eyes and remember lying in Granny's bed with her in the morning, the dry feel of her skin, the flannel of her nightdress. I open them and see the tree outside the window. I shut them and see Granny's studio, an easel stained with oils.

What I do know, though, is the family mythology. Molly, Sinai's wife whom he met when he was underground after he packed Momma off to rehab; Molly, whom even Momma kind of sees as my real mom, made sure I did: every year when I came, kicking and screaming, for a summer month in the States, she spent that month indoctrinating me: pictures, letters, books. One of those weird family things, seeing Molly herself was and is a staunch Republican, a Vietnam widow, and mother of a Marine lifer, and the Sinais, from the moment my grandfather shipped out to Spain in 1935, have been red, through and fucking through. Cosmopolitan, East Coast, Liberal elite: despised by T. S. Eliot and Spiro Agnew alike. Jews, don't you know; I'm one too—at heart—even though Momma is Church of England. It was one of those things, that Molly made me learn the family history, just like she made me have a bat mitzvah, though she's no more Jewish than Momma. I only did it because it was Molly. Probably it was Molly's summers of studying family history that made me become a reporter.

Anyway Sinai's parents, my grandparents, Jack and Eleanor, lived here for an historic fifty years, from the year after WWII ended to 1995, the year he died: rare birds, both, American-born Jews, second and first generation, respectively. It was an expanse of time long enough to make it home for three generations: Jack Sinai and Eleanor Singer's huge family, first, who had transplanted a Lithuanian shtetl, neuroses and all, here after the Civil War and whose second generation of patriarchs—Jack and Eleanor's parents and uncles—survived into the '50s before dying or moving to Florida. Jack's father was the black sheep, a Bundist, anti-Zionist, and Jack himself was red from the moment he heard of Eugene Debs. And then the generation of their children, among the multitude of doctors, lawyers, stockbrokers, and other rip-off artists were the oddballs of Jack's kids: Sinai and Danny and their adopted sister Klara, who were born in the '50s and grew up during Vietnam, and who so notably inherited the long, moving legacy of the Bullshit of the American Left. And then, finally, the next generation, which, on the Sinai side at least—the Singers had dozens and dozens of kids, none of whom I knew—consisted of my half-sister Rebeccah, whose mother is Weather Underground legend Mimi Lurie and who, thus, has been known to make sentimental lefties burst into tears at twenty paces, my cousins—Uncle Danny and his wife Maggie Calaway's kids, and then, of course, me. Only the older of Danny and Maggie's kids knew my grandfather, though she doesn't remember him, but all four of us knew Eleanor, my grandmother, who lived ten years after her husband died.

Myself, I loved her.

But the little man is still there, and so I turn from the window.

"And, if I may ask: who are you?"

"Me?" He laughed. "You just call me Uncle Joe. Everyone else does. I live right next door. Have for nearly fifty years. I take care of the house for your family."

That tells me something, but not enough. Does he work for Danny and Maggie, or is he a friend? It seemed important to know, from the viewpoint of security, at the least. "You were . . . a friend of my grandfather's?"

"Yes I was. For sixty years and more."

"Childhood friends?"

"No, ma'am. Do the math. Your grandpa and I, we met on a cargo ship, on the way to France. And you know what we did then? We walked across the Pyrenees to Spain. That's how I met your grandpa."

For a moment, now, he regards me critically, favoring his left eye which, I now see, is bright blue. "Okay, missie. You look like you might want to get settled now. You call me if you need me—the number's on the fridge."

Standing at the window, listening to Uncle Joe's receding footsteps on the stairs, I can feel the bulk of this house weighing upon my lungs as if I were underwater. I breathe carefully, in and out, looking intently at the naked chestnut, as if it matters. I can see there are tiny buds on its branches, leaves in utero, the leaf, waiting to join the blossom, growing from the bole. Great rooted blossomer. Fuck me, how can we know the dancer from the dance? I actually say the words, aloud, trying to relax my diaphragm against the sense, suddenly that I cannot breathe, cannot breathe at all.

But I don't give a fuck about the tree, you know that. It is yet another legacy of the Molly Sackler Catskill Mountain Summer School that I can name trees, and it is just that I am so fucking over-educated that I can quote Yeats. And it is because even having had the good sense, at thirteen years old, to insist that I leave my father's house in Saugerties and live with my mother in England, I am still infused, imbued, with the pathos of the American Left, title of that seminal study I will never write and which, therefore, will never be well reviewed by some predictable contrarian in the *Nation*, so much so that now, suddenly, for a long moment, I simply hold my breath. Once I was researching a piece in the British Library and Lord Zuckerman was referenced in something, so I'm going through archives, and a copy of *IF Stone's Weekly*—for twenty years the bible of the American Left—falls out. The typeface alone reduced me to tears. So imagine how I feel now. Imagine how I feel now at the nerve center of generations of neurosis from which I am descended. Imagine how I am feeling now, at the symbolic center of all these people, all these people, who made me what I am and who are all, now, either dead or dying.

I will be dreaming I saw fucking Joe Hill in a moment. Alive as you and me.

Do you know, I'm actually clueless enough not to understand my asphyxiation?

Instead, I think: That's all bullshit. Instead, I think: In reality, all I'm fucking doing is standing here, body as tense as a spring, waiting for Uncle Joe's footsteps to recede fully down the stairs, trying not to think, and why? Because I'm badly needing a drink. And when at last his footsteps are gone, I slip off my shoes and follow him, softly: down again past the third floor of bedrooms, down the first few steps of the staircase into the huge living room—the stairs are well founded, super well: there's hardly a creak, and on the carpet runners, the bare feet of a slim person—such as me—can be without sound. At the bottom I stop and listen carefully. In the living room, down the servants' stairs, I can hear Joe in the kitchen. I cross, feeling the rough kelim under my feet, and carefully, so there is no noise, open the glass door of the liquor cabinet. In front of me are staggered rows of scotch, bourbon, vodka, all good—Johnny Blue, Glenfiddich, Stoly. I skip these and reach far in the back where sits a bottle with a black cap. This I extract, slowly, carefully, and am more than a little pleased to find it is a liter of Turkish raki, nearly full as odd liquors like this will tend to be. In normal houses, that is. Any house I am, a bottle of witch hazel is likely to be empty by lunch. Standing there, I open the cap—it sticks, as if it has not been opened in twenty years— and pour a hit down my throat, reborative, hot, life-giving. Then I close the bottle and, closing the cabinet, make my bare-footed way upstairs again.

Now I can breathe.

I pause on the stairs and put another shot of raki into my stomach.

Now I can breathe my ass off.

Now those lungs of mine in my strong little chest, under those beautiful little breasts, which, that reminds me, one of these days I must find someone to touch, now these little lungs of mine work just fine, just fine.

This time, in the bedroom, hitting the bottle, I step out of my pants, my underwear. I put the bottle down and peel off my shirt, my undershirt. To say that I smell is an understatement. But so is it, I note, to say that I am looking rather fine. Naked, I pick up the bottle and look at my reflection in the window. Saudi, and my liquid diet there, has been good to me: I am slim and taut, with little boyish hips and—this time of month—tiny breasts, no more, surely, than one-ten which, at five-three, is just where I want to be. But—I come to my senses—I'm also just where whoever may be watching from across the back yards wants me to be, so I kill the light, then open the window and, the chill air on my skin, smoke a cigarette. I drink from the bottle. Then I carry it into the little bathroom—ceramic bath, round toilet, black and white tile on the floor, full-length mirror in an oak frame—and, balancing the bottle on the end of the tub, step into a hot shower.

After which, I suppose I go to bed, because when I open my eyes to the beep of my iPhone telling me that it is shutting down for lack of battery, it is eighteen hours later, four in the morning, and I am naked in pitch blackness, wondering why I haven't charged my iPhone, then remembering that I am not in my hotel, where I left my charger, but with no idea where I am.

2.

Though blackness is a big word, too, isn't it? Above me, on the ceiling, big shadows of the branches of the chestnut move slowly in the huge silence of the empty house. Beyond them the sky of flat cloud is lighted by what must be a fairly sizable moon, of which I cannot remember the phase. For a long time I lie there, floating on the surface of a huge depth of emotion, like when Dadda used to take me to swim in those rock quarries up in Maine when I was a kid, old slate and granite quarries that were hundreds of feet deep when they hit water and now, when I swam, I was aware of two, three hundred feet of teeming blackness below .

But I am no fool. I am no fucking idiot. It is for only a moment I lie there, watching the shadows of the branches sway; a moment that I lie there watching shadows on the ceiling of a room in the house in which my father grew up, even if that moment seems to last forever. For only a moment I lie there and feel the blank blood in my veins, empty of alcohol, free of THC, and think of the million mistakes of which my life is constituted, all culminating in the huge, overwhelming mistake of my presence here, in this room, now, tonight.

But, see, I am no fool, so I only do this for a moment. In just a moment I will get up, and out of bed, and away from all this.

But first, just for a little second, I will lie on the surface of this depthless bed, in this tall house, watch these shadows of the chestnut in a gusty March wind outside, and, just for a moment, feel the black distances of water below me, hundreds of feet, swimming with fear.

And then I am standing, then padding my way down the stairs: third floor, second floor, straight to the liquor cabinet, and genuflecting, naked, in front of its open door as I arch my back and pour a long shot of warm vodka down my throat.

I gag, and I swallow.

Then I carry the bottle down to the kitchen and put it in the freezer to cool.

So this Uncle Joe is some sort of a saint. In the kitchen there is coffee, milk, sugar. I make coffee in a little espresso pot, then I drink it. I make another pot, and drink it, then another, hitting the vodka once or twice in between. The last coffee, I carry through the kitchen and into the dining room, and through the dining room into a little book-lined library.

You can see, here, the trunk of the chestnut through a huge window, its branches outlined in front of the lighted clouds from what, I can now see as I come right up to the window and crane my neck, is a three-quarter moon, amazingly bright. That makes sense: it had been barely gibbous when I left Saudi. The light switch is right next to me and, when I throw it, the moon disappears and in its place, in the window, is, suddenly, my face.

But why would I look at my face? Why would I look at the face that takes all the delicacy of Julia Montgomery's, its high cheeks, its depthless green eyes, its full mouth—remember, Momma, before she decided to start shooting cocaine, had acted for Martin Scorsese and posed for Avedon—and dumps the Sinai nose in its middle? True, this professor once said to me, in college, that that nose, it was the difference for me between pretty and beautiful, and she was, herself, a very, very beautiful woman. Then she put her tongue down my throat. But that was then, and this is now, and now is four in the morning in New York City, where I have been brought by an amazing series of accidents; now I am before a mirror, not a lover, and all I need to do, all I need to do, is turn away. Anyway, my blood is filled with only some of those things I like to stock it up with—nicotine is still missing. I close the blind on the big study window. Then, naked, I pad back upstairs to my room to get my smokes.

3.

Rebeccah Schulberg—my half-sister Beck, born to my father and Mimi Lurie when they were underground and, in a move that would turn out not to be an aberration in their interesting little lives, but something of a habit, abandoned so that they could pursue their little careers as radical criminals—was in fact more or less my size, though with bigger boobs, judging by the bras in the little wardrobe. Of course, she had bred—or so I'd picked up somewhere—so her tits would be bigger. In any case, I don't wear bras. I find a not bad little T-shirt by Karan which, if I rolled up the shoulders, is wearable, and a pair of chinos which, after I meticulously take in the hips with safety pins, fits pretty good. It's only now, for some reason, that I notice how cold I am—the little silver radiator under the window is only warm, not hot, and it is early March—so I add on a cardigan and a pair of socks, which gives me a college girl dyke look which in turn makes me feel a little sexy. Anyway, fuck it: no one's going to see me now, and I'm in New York and sooner or later I'll get to my luggage and/or credit cards and in either case go spend some money on clothes over in the Meat Market where the shops, I am reliably informed by years of reading Momma's *Vogue*, are now to be found.

This time I explore the house a little more carefully as I descend. This top floor has four rooms, all bedrooms, all impeccably made, with floors in wide plank pine liberally covered with kelims, of which none are new. One of these rooms, I suppose, was Sinai's, one was Uncle Danny's, and one would have belonged, after she came here from Israel, to my "aunt" Klara, adopted by my grandparents at eleven, who now never talks to her siblings, for reasons I've never understood. Or, for that matter, given a fuck about. If, though, you're expecting that Sinai's room was filled with Filmore East posters and anti-war memorabilia, no way: any trace of the childhood inhabitation of these rooms had long been removed: they are tidy, pretty, and empty of personality, which is a disappointment, because had they been the childhood rooms of my dad or uncle, I'd likely be able to find some way to get high. There are, however, quite a few framed photographs: Sinai, with long bangs over one eye, sitting on a stoop in a denim shirt, squinting into the camera; Danny and Klara on the beach at what must be the Martha's Vineyard house, a black dog with a white nose, standing straight and staring at the camera, his tongue hanging out one side of his mouth.

The third floor has the master bedroom, and while it, too, has been denuded of personal effects, I remember that this was Granny's room, and this the bedspread, and these the paintings on the wall, of which two are large abstracts of a style I believe to be called Abstract Expressionism and one is a large, naturalistic vision of an overgrown garden gate, likely by my grandmother. Also on this floor is an artist's studio, smelling very faintly of oil paints, which is evidently built over an extension because it has lead-glass windows and skylights through which, had the lights been off, I would have had a splendid view up into the chestnut. Then there is a small library with a couch that, I can see, doubles as a guest bed. The books on the shelves are jacketed and, I have no doubt, firsts. I look only briefly at the shelves and catch these names: Fuchs, Dahlberg, Sanford, Farrell, Greenberg. Clement, I mean.

Down one more flight, the living room, as I say, occupies the whole parlor floor, and now that I understand the extension at the rear of the house that allows the studio to exist, I understand why it is so big, perhaps fifty or sixty feet deep by twenty-five wide, an immense piece of New York real estate, immense enough to have two staircases descending to the garden floor: one, a more modest continuation of the grand staircase I had just come down; another a small spiral descent, no doubt directly into the kitchen for the servants. Likely, I thought, the room had once been divided, with huge pocket doors in its center kept closed to define a dining room on the street side. Visitors would have been meant to come up the stoop and enter a corridor that ran next to a huge formal dining room, leaving their coats with a maid. Now, however, the corridor had been taken down to open the space entirely, the doors were wide open, and the only divisions in the room were made by the groupings of furniture and rugs. Why this was so, I understood when I went down, this time, not the servants' stairs but the main stairs, which came out, on the garden floor, to the right of the kitchen into a dining room of which I find I have no memory whatsoever. It's huge: could easily seat twenty-five, set right back against picture windows out to the garden in which grew the massive chestnut. I pause for a moment here, shocked by the sudden stillness of the room, a stillness as if made more impressive in implicit comparison to the noise that must so often have filled this room over numerous dinner parties.

There is also an entrance to this room by a set of swing doors to the kitchen, which I do not remember seeing earlier, from the other side, while making my coffee. I go through to the kitchen, pause to hit the vodka, which is slightly more potable now, from the freezer. Then, on reflection I backtrack up the guest stairs and come back down the servants' set to the kitchen. Now I can see how I missed the swing doors, which are removed from the main work space. The only explanation is that I wasn't allowed to use the big stairs when I was a child, or that I didn't want to. In any case, I have no recollection whatsoever of their existence. Further, another door altogether, from this vantage, is more immediately prominent: a small one that leads into a book-lined lounge with a television.

This feels more familiar. The television is a Zenith and perhaps forty years old. There is a large abstract painting on the wall signed "Carton," another signed "Golub," and a charcoal nude signed "Soyer." There is a framed Hebrew document, ornately inked and dated 1948 which, from somewhere unknown in my memory, I suspect to be a marriage contract, and then verify, because Hebrew is one of my languages. I stand for a moment, breathing in the musty smell of the room. Then a memory strikes and I turn. Behind me, yet another door leads off, and when I put my hand on the knob a vivid picture strikes me of lying on a bed next to a window, staring up at leaves. I open it. I find myself in a small study lined with legal texts. A large window gives out onto the garden. The lights turn on with a toggle switch. The room is carpeted in yet more splendid Turkish rugs. A couch—bed, really—sits under the window, but the window is still too dark to see outside. A huge oak desk holds a lamp, a dial telephone, and a squat, nearly round plastic television which, in due course, I realize is an antediluvian Macintosh. This, I look at for a while, feeling something which, in turn, I come to understand as a deliquescence. I feel slightly ill; and I feel so because somewhere in my stomach I understand that I am in a room belonging to my dead grandfather which has been left empty and intact for a long time. I squat, then, and look under the bed; then I check the surfaces of the desk and bookshelf. Everything is spotless: this is a room that is maintained impeccably, no doubt by Uncle Joe.

Feeling better, now, I find a power button on the Mac and it actually whirrs into life and begins to boot. While it does I examine the ports and find there is a USB. This is good in so many ways, I hardly know where to start. For one thing, I can charge my iPhone. I run up the stairs, literally, and down, like a kid at Christmas, and hook my iPhone into it. It leaps into life, and as it begins to charge, I click through the antique desktop icons. Now I can see that this was not my grandfather's Mac but Uncle Danny's, no doubt from when he stayed here during my grandfather's death. Or mostly, anyway. It was also my father's, or sort of: an ancient version of iTunes launches itself in response to my iPhone being plugged in, and a dialogue box asks me if I want to sync with "Sinai's Music." I click through a bit— Band, Bowie, Dylan, Fitzgerald, Mitchell, Sinatra, U2—got most of it from Sinai already—and launch a track from *Ziggy Stardust*. Then I click yes on the sync request, and consider the ensuing dialogue:

"Are you sure you want to replace 'Izzy's Music'? This action cannot be undone." I think for a second, then click yes: my music's all backed up on iData anyway, I can merge again later. While the music loads, I get even more ambitious, and find my way into the system settings. It appears that even those days they understood the concept of display mirroring, so I set my iPhone up as an external boot device, and tether the internet through the cell connection. Then, when the music import is done, I reboot and, to my immense satisfaction, the Chrissie Hynde wallpaper from my iPhone comes up on the ancient glass screen. Now I got me a computah. And I am just getting on the web when an explosion shatters the silence and I jump clear out of the chair.

It is an incredibly loud noise and it goes on, and on, and on. Then, as abruptly as it started, it stops. Then it starts again. Heart bursting, I finally understand it to be coming from the dial telephone which, later when I turn it upside down, turns out to have an actual *bell* in it with a mechanical ringer. And in order simply to stop the noise, I pick up the receiver.

You'll say this is not a smart move, and you'll be right. It's a rare mistake for me, but see, the noise was so fucking loud. Anyway, I am lucky: it is Aunt Maggie on the line, and as if knowing how much I am already blaming myself for answering, she begins to talk right away.

"Izzy? Maggie. I've been trying your cell, can't get an answer. Where are you?"

"Sorry." I am finding my voice. "Sorry, my cell was out of juice. I'm just charging now. Ummm . . . I'm on the ground floor in a little study."

"You're in Jack's study?" My aunt is laughing her surprisingly deep laugh. "That telephone must have scared you out of your skin."

Now I smile, a little. "Minor heart attack. I'm young and strong."

"I bet you are. Can't wait to see you. It's been what? Six months since we were in Rome?"

"God. Something like."

"What is it with you? Leave some stuff for someone else to write."

"I'll think about that."

"Now listen. The news is good and bad. The bad part is that you have in fact been subpoenaed. It's the internal specs of the PVI array—specifically, you published that they're hooked into the Pentagon satellite system, which would violate Separation of Powers, if true, and make someone in the West Wing prosecutable. Did you know what you were saying, doll?"

Doll. That's Sinai speaking. I wonder, suddenly, if it came from Jack. I pause, then speak carefully. "I knew I was reporting that they'd violated Separation of Powers, yes. My source is good."

"Can you name him?"

That gives me pause. "Who?"

"Your source, doll."

"Oh. Her. It's a her. No, I'm not naming her."

"Well, they say she must be from the Pentagon, and that means she's treasonous. They'd have to, wouldn't they? Now they want her. You're subpoenaed, you have to show in court, and if you refuse to give the source you will be jailed. I'm representing, the *Times* is co-counsel. You're super-duper covered."

Super-duper. I note that. And I note this, too: you'd have expected me to be pretty uptight at this point, no? Jail, blah blah? Dimly, it occurs to me that I am on the front page of the *Times* this morning and I haven't even looked. All I've done is explore this strange house I find myself in. Tintin? Not so much. Even now, I find my eye straying down the bookshelves in front of me, which I now see contain things other than legal texts. There is a large number of leather bound portfolios filling one long shelf, one of which, as Maggie talks, I open. "What's the good news? That I'll be in a woman's jail?"

"That I'll get you out in a couple-three days. This won't stand up, not even in a New York state court. But it will take a few days. So for now, I recommend you stay put while I negotiate a surrender."

"That's wonderful. People actually pay you for this?" A *couple-three*. I know that one. Sinai said it, and I knew it to come from my grandfather, 'cause when he was interviewed for a movie called *The Good Fight*, he said, at one point, that he had taken *a couple-three bullets at Cape Tortuga*. The portfolio is surprisingly heavy, and I have to stand to get it. But I find that you can cradle this receiver between your ear and shoulder, and thus use both hands.

"Very funny. For the moment, they have no idea where you are. Stay put. Let me get your stuff from your hotel meanwhile."

So I am stuck in this mausoleum for a few days. With a full liquor cabinet. Suddenly, in a flash, I remember that I had once dBased a marijuana delivery number in New York. The portfolio is tied with a thick ribbon, in a bow. I leave that for a moment, launch my address book and search "delivery."

"Please do, will you? Soho Grand. Be careful—there's some dope in a pack of cigarettes." *Delivery* doesn't hit, so I try *service*.

"Dope? Boy, like father like daughter, hey? Okay, doll. Uncle Joe was meant to buy groceries, did he?"

I answer in a raspy voice. "Yes. He keeps up the house." Nothing for *service*. I try *pot*.

She laughs. "He's an angel from heaven, that man. You okay? You going to be lonely?"

Bingo. *AAA Pot*, an 800 number. And aren't you just the little undercover operative? Christ sake, listing my dope dealer under *pot*. Talk about the purloined letter. I can just imagine the intake cops at whatever prison they sentence me to scratching their heads over that. Heads? Underarms, and hooting, because unless they're fucking apes, they are going to be tracing that number in seconds flat and adding drugs to their little shopping list of Izzy Montgomery's prosecutable crimes. I cover the mouthpiece of the phone to laugh a little. That done, I go back to worrying the knot on the portfolio, which gives suddenly and completely. "Lonely? Did the *Times* say they're honoring my contract?"

"Yes, of course. Oh—I spoke to your editor. He said to give him three thousand words background on PVI by closing tonight."

"Well then. Who has time to be lonely?"

"Okay, my lovely, you keep busy, and I'll keep in touch."

By now, the portfolio cover is open, showing a number of photographs, which I spill out onto the desk. Childhood pictures mostly of people I don't recognize. Then I hit one of Sinai, at maybe sixteen, his long red hair combed down over one eye. Then one with Danny, looking up at his big brother with shining eyes. I put these two out on the desk, and go on looking: my grandmother, in a painting frock, and one of my grandfather, walking next to a river, perhaps the Hudson, on a brightly lit day, looking up in surprise.

The people who made me who I am. I watch these for a while, smoking a cigarette. Then I turn back to the portfolio and sort through the rest of the pictures.

Only, it's not only pictures. Below them, I find a set of light blue airmail envelopes, a type of paper called "supercalendared," very brittle at the edges now, with age, and typed on a manual typewriter. The first is postmarked in 1956 in Mexico, and addressed to Jack Sinai, Esq. I open it, gingerly: I dealt with paper before when I did a *New Republic* piece in the British Library, the one where I found the copy of *IF Stone's Weekly*. In the envelope is a folded letter signed in hand by "Dalton," addressed to Jack, and directing him to go ahead and take the "1,200 weekly for *The Brave One*." All of the envelopes are the same. But now, my ear suddenly is filled with a horrible, deeply offensive beeping, and I realized that the telephone receiver is still under my ear. I hang it up, close the portfolio, and pick up my iPhone.

Enough wasting time.

First things first. First, get some dope delivered.

Second, check my email and get to work.

But before any of that, I cross over to the bed by the window, lie down, and look up into the bare branches of the chestnut going right up to the sky and remember a magical world of green watched from a silent refuge in a huge, strange house by a tiny little girl.

4.

And aren't you just the consummate professional? Aren't you just the intrepid girl reporter? By noon I am spread out on the big kelim in the living room, with the antediluvian Mac all set up and glowing, my iPhone getting the web, toggling between websites and databases and taking notes and emailing sources and plying my trade like a motherfucker, three thousand words background on the PVI by closing tonight. I've blocked the GPS on my iPhone so I can't be tracked, and have installed Tor on the Mac so I have some encryption, and having done that, not only Skyped in lunch, but dope too, which is why I've also got a little saucer serving as an ashtray with a loaded cigarette sitting on the window sill, letting up a cheerful little flag of pot smoke out into the wet spring air.

Earlier, after I called the number I had for the pot delivery service in New York, a motorbike messenger had shown up at the door under the stoop. I sat him down at the little Formica table on the linoleum floor and counted out a couple hundred of my dollars from the ATM in Riyadh, then he weighed out twenty-four—misdemeanor quantity in New York—grams of green weed, "New York State of Mind," he called it, and promised it was organic. We sparked up a little taste, and while he toked he looked slowly around from under his helmet, then looked me up and down.

"What is it you doin' in this museum, girl? Ain't you ready to come out and play in like the twenty-first century? You too hot to hide."

I thought about that, hitting the J, which was wet from his lips. Then I said: "I don't play with your kind."

Surprise darkened his face. "You shitting me."

"Men. Stupid."

"Ah, that what you mean? That cool, that cool." And with my two hundred dollars and the promise to return with anything else I might require—coke, K, ecstasy, acid—he took his leave.

Stoned, I got busy. I muscled the antediluvian Macintosh up to the living room, jacked in my iPhone, got online. I searched the neighborhood restaurants, then ordered Chinese delivered from a place round the corner, then went down and found a wine closet in the kitchen, which took some searching, but was well worth it, cause it appears that someone had laid in a collection of American pinots from which I chose a '96 Russian River vintage that cost $75 even then, the color of a translucent ruby, and ate while I worked.

And aren't I just the proverbial rolling stone, gathering no moss? I went right at it and started reporting a straight-out history of the PVI, three thousand words, including the lawsuits that were filed to limit it when it was first unveiled after 9/11, and the Supreme Court ruling that denied its deployment in Times Square on New Year's Eve the year after, and how therefore, shocking, it was that Homeland Security had used it again in New York.

After a couple hours, though, I find myself, instead of reporting the article, googling "Dalton" and "Mexico" and "Sinai" and I come up with a page in a book by Griffin Fariello about the Hollywood Ten screenwriter Dalton Trumbo, whom my grandfather apparently represented while he was blacklisted and living in Mexico. Coincidentally, the Fariello page is part of an interview, my grandfather talking about how he bought his house on Bedford Street on what he earned from representing Trumbo before the blacklist.

Trumbo, dude. Thank *you*, brother. From me and my four cousins who one of these days will own this fine place.

And that makes me more curious. I go downstairs to the study and pause, looking at the wealth of paper in this little room. There's work to be done here, I find myself thinking. But what work? I got an article to write. Upstairs again, I focus on the PVI piece for a while. For a while. Because soon I find myself standing and staring out the back window to the garden. There's late spring afternoon sun out there, and under the shadows of the chestnut, a gardener is working, apparently, planting bulbs in a flower bed. I watch him for a time, his back curved over a little trowel, working with deliberate, very slow movements, and I'm idly wondering how he got there before I realize that it is Uncle Joe. Then, as if I actually know what I'm doing, I go back down to the kitchen, open a fresh bottle of pinot, pour two glasses, and carry them out into the garden.

It is kind of as if we have an appointment. At my approach, the old man leaves off his work and we sit, together, at a little iron table. His first sip of the wine is more a draught—a long, deep draught—and he exhales loudly as he puts it down.

"Well thank you, missie, but if you pardon my saying so, that ain't wine. I'll bring you some of my own next time."

"I'd love that. Joe, can I ask you a question?"

He answers immediately. "That's what I'm here for, missie."

And that, of course, gives me pause. "What do you mean?"

"Oh . . . All you Sinai kids. Always going backwards. You'll see. Now what's the question?"

"Well . . . how you knew my grandfather?"

"Like I told you. Met him on the way to Spain. Don't talk to me about Spain. Can't stand it. He got me my house, you know that?"

"No. I don't really know anything about him."

"That right? Well, after Spain they won't let him go back to the war, right? Bastards. Premature anti-fascism, right? Me, they don't care: I'm wop trash and they're drafting every wop man who can stand on two legs, six weeks' training and to the front. Cannon fodder. Nearly every house on the street has a death—remember, we're four, six families to the house in those days. Some more than one. And me, I can read maps, I can handle artillery, I can judge distance. Me, I'm back in Europe by 1941 and I'll tell you something, young missie, you are looking at a man who participated in the liberation of Paris. But Jackie? Don't even talk to me about Jackie. He's got command experience too. But he's also got a fucking college degree, and that means he's too suspect to kill Nazis, right? Not only him but the FBI agents following him, day and night: strong young men, all of these young men here, none of them over there, while over there the fucking world is in flames. When I come home? I'm still a wop draftee. I got the GI Bill but that's not what wop draftees do. I go to work for my father, over on Sullivan, Igneri Electric. One day your grandfather calls me, says, Joey, the house next door to me is for sale. I'm buying it, you're taking it from me for cost."

"Now, I'm living in a flat over on Sullivan; a rental. Third-floor walkup, railroad apartment, wife, three kids, we didn't care. It's what, '56? '58? My father had just died, but he never owned nothing but the business. I say, Jackie, how am I going to pay for a Village town-house? He says, I'm taking your note, Joey. And you're putting your money into the business. I say, Jackie, what are you talking about? He says, Joe, this isn't your little Village anymore. The prices here are about to skyrocket. You mark my words. You take this house now on my note at a hundred large, you'll retire to Las Vegas on the sale in thirty years. Hundred large, Christ sakes. My house was valued at seven million last year. For me, Jackie says jump, I say, how high? I did what he said and you know what? Forget about the house. The house, fine. Split it up—did the work myself—I put three kids through college on the rental units and lived like a king in the garden apartment. Still am. The house? Forget about the house. But get this: altogether, Igneri Electric made more than Jackie ever did. Italian electrician in the West Village? These people. I got twenty people on payroll, by the end of the '70s. Central air, security, Jacuzzis, two dishwashers, two ice boxes, each the size of my house on Sullivan. Lap pools in the damn garden, excuse my fucking French, missie. Lap pools in the garden! You couldn't charge them enough. When Danny bought his place on the Upper West Side, you know who took his mortgage? I took his mortgage. Straight three percent, on a hand-shake. Paid me every single penny in five years. I tell you, Italians, Jews? Like this. Used to be, anyways."

"So you've lived next door since the late '50s?"

"That I have, missie. Next to Jackie, every step of the way. Lived our lives together. Raised our kids, worked our jobs, lived our lives."

"And your kids are still there?"

Now the old dude pauses, and hits the wine again, another deep draught. "No. That's the difference with you Jews. You all never leave home, even after you've left home. We never managed to do the family thing, did we? Uncle Joe's children? You'd think Jersey was a foreign country. Watching you all? Your uncle, your aunt. Even the girl, Rebeccah, and that ass of a husband of hers. You know I came to your family, what they call it, seder? Every year. You know how to honor your elders. Wish we knew that. Wasn't till my grandchildren started circling around the company that I even started hearing from them. Well, they didn't get the company, did they now? No sir. You know who got the company? Erick Jefferson Jr. got the company. Thirty years his father worked for me. We saw Erick through Brooklyn Tech, Brooklyn College, and then into the business. Know what he's doing with it now? Just did Susan Sarandon's place up in Nyack. Know what color he is?"

"Black?"

"As the ace of spades, missie."

"How come I've never heard of you?"

"Well, you haven't exactly been around, have you now, missie? Oh, I know all about you. Isabel Montgomery. I'll tell you something else, missie. I know what you're doing here."

"What I'm doing here?"

"Oh, you'll find out my girl. You'll find out, sure as the sun is coming up tomorrow. You don't know, Uncle Joe's not going to tell you. Tell you what. Of an evening, you come over to Uncle Joey's garden and I'll show you what red wine is meant to be. Not that crap your grandfather drank, California, Washington State. I'm talking the real thing, made from my grapes, in my cellar. You promise me, now, okay?"

"Okay. I promise you."

And that seems to be it. Uncle Joe goes back to his planting and after a moment or two I go back in and read the correspondence with Dalton Trumbo in my grandfather's study. It is not chronologically organized—it does not appear that my grandfather was a very methodical person, although he was certainly a pack rat—so it takes some time to divide out by postmark into what turns out to become three piles: one of Trumbo's letters from Los Angeles during the Hollywood Ten trial; another from prison in Kentucky, where he clearly served his contempt of court sentence after he and his nine comrades declined to testify before HUAC—perhaps, I am thinking, they will let me serve mine there after I refuse to name my PVI source; a third from Mexico.

By now I've given up all pretense that I'm not smoking in the house, and am exhaling big lungfuls while I stand at the oak desk, shuffling paper. Next, I give up all pretense that I'm not snooping. It is, after all, my chosen profession. There are ten or so of these big green portfolios, and the one on the very far left opens on a birth certificate, Julius Aaron Sinai, August 30, 1908. The last one, I already knew, covered the '50s. Then I open one of the desk drawers. This thing is a fucking rat's nest: credit-card receipts, photos, newspaper clippings. The receipts range through spring and summer of 1995, and I think about that for a while. Then I go back upstairs to the Mac, and get my grandfather's obit from the *New York Times*.

JACK SINAI, 87, RADICAL LAWYER, DIES IN MANHATTAN HOME

The New York Times, November 21, 1995

Julius Aaron Sinai, a civil-rights lawyer best known for his appearances before the House Un-American Affairs Committee, died in his Manhattan home on Saturday night. He was 87. The cause, announced by his son, Daniel Sinai, an author and professor at Columbia Law School, was pancreatic cancer. Mr. Sinai had been diagnosed within the past six months and had refused treatment.

Julius Sinai, known as Jack, first gained prominence for his defense of Hollywood Ten defendant Dalton Trumbo before the Hollywood hearings of HUAC, for which he was dubbed by Senator Joseph McCarthy the "most dangerous lawyer in America." His numerous politically charged defenses included members of the Black Panthers, the Puerto Rican separatist group The Young Lords, and Black Liberation Army defendants in the 1981 Brinks Robbery Trial. He appeared three times before the Supreme Court, where he was known to Justice Thurgood Marshall as a "regular customer."

Citing his Spanish Civil War service in the Abraham Lincoln Brigade and his subsequent Dies Committee classification as a "Premature Antifascist," McCarthy attempted unsuccessfully to have Sinai's passport revoked in 1951, a defeat widely thought to have been the beginning of the senator's decline in power.

But Jack Sinai was best known as the father of the '60s radical Jason Sinai, a fugitive of the Vietnam era, who disappeared as a member of the Weather Underground after the accidental bombing of a Manhattan townhouse in March, 1970. Four years later, Jason Sinai was implicated in the Bank of Michigan robbery in which a security guard, Hugh Krosney, was killed. With his alleged partners Mimi Lurie and Sharon Salzburg, Jason Sinai is one of the last "Weatherman" fugitives remaining at large.

Seven months prior to his death Jack Sinai had been awarded the Medal of the Legion of Honor by the government of Spain in recognition of his "heroic wartime service to the citizens of the First Spanish Republic," during the Spanish Civil War and "a postwar career incarnating the noble ideals of the International Brigades."

In a statement announcing the death, Daniel Sinai explained that his father had concealed his illness for fear that his fugitive son would attempt to make contact. The Sinai family, Professor Sinai explained, had been under police surveillance for most of the twenty-five years since his brother's disappearance.

In addition to his sons, Jack Sinai is survived by his wife, the painter Eleanor Singer, an adopted daughter, Klara Singer of Tel Aviv, and two grandchildren.

Correction: Due to an editing error, the number of Supreme Court appearances made by Jack Sinai was incorrectly reported as three. Mr. Sinai appeared five times before the Supreme Court.

November 21, 1995. I go back to the drawer, and look at some of the receipts. These would have been my grandfather's last few months, and in fact, down at the bottom of the drawer, the last dates are in late summer. At the very bottom, I discover two other things. One is a newspaper clipping. The other is a small stack of thousand-dollar bills.

The newspaper clipping is from the *Times*, dated April 16, 1995, and has a headline "Radical Lawyer Honored for Wartime Service in Spain." The subhead reads: "Jack Sinai, Communist-era backlistee and Spanish Civil War Veteran, receives Spanish Legion of Honor Award at annual Veterans Memorial." And the picture is the one I found earlier: my grandfather, walking next to water on a bright spring day.

This time, I look more closely, leaning down under the light of the lamp. He is walking on a promenade next to what must be the Hudson, because you can see the Colgate Clock across the water, in a tweed jacket and blue denim shirt. He has a full head of white hair and, in the flat morning light, an expression of great gravity, and was clearly walking unaided, some six months before his death.

I go back upstairs now, and work on the *Times* piece a little. A very little. Then I smoke by the back window for a while. Then I finish the last glass of the Russian River pinot, which now, having opened up some, justifies the price amply. Then I go back downstairs and take the pictures of my grandfather, my father, my uncle, and my aunt and pin them up on the bulletin board above the desk.

For a while I watch them, plagued by the sense that there is someone missing. Something deep in my memory, some memory, some
mystery. I go back to the portfolio, and leaf through the pictures,
until I find one of Danny and Maggie, at their wedding. This strikes
a chord, for in it you can see, already, the strange, attenuated tension
that has always existed between them. I consider the picture for a
while. Then I go back to the other photographs and search until I
find one more: a woman with vivid black hair, a red mouth, and
brilliant eyes. Klara Singer, graduating from college in Yale blue.

The whole lineup is on the bulletin board now, and for a long
time I examine them, my elders and betters. Then I open some of the
other five drawers. Each is full of paper, and I'm able to see quickly
that the dates run backwards by drawer, roughly by half-decades, to
the '70s. I go back upstairs, write a couple lines for the *Times*, then I
roll a joint and smoke a little. Then I go back downstairs and open
the rightmost of the green portfolios. The final document is a letter
on Lawyers Guild stationery, with an address of 5 Beekman Street,
and signed *Lenny*. So the portfolios cover Jack Sinai's life through the
'60s, but the huge desk has, unfilled, the next thirty-five years of his
life. Thinking about this, I go back through the dining room from the
study, into the kitchen, and back to the little wine closet. This time I
go for a Washington State vintage, an '82 with a deep ruby hue. I pop
it and pour a taste, thinking it will need to breathe, but this thing is
so smooth you could take it for acid indigestion. Upstairs, with a real
pour, I google "Lenny" and "Lawyers Guild" and come up with a hit
on Leonard Boudin—aha, the famous civil-rights attorney, father of
my father's old comrade Kathy, jailed for her part in the Brinks
robbery until a few years ago, and that after surviving the townhouse
bombing in 1970 in which three of her friends died. I read about him
for a while, then I carry my wine back down to the study and read the
letter, dated February 23rd, 1970, more closely. *I don't know what the
kids are up to, haven't heard from Kathy in a few weeks. But whatever
they're doing, it must be better than doing nothing, and Jean and I are
staying hopeful.* February 23rd.

That makes me pause, seriously. Cause when you think of it, in a couple of weeks, of course, on March 6, Kathy Boudin will be walking out of the smoldering townhouse, naked, deafened by the blast, and into ten years of life as a fugitive that would culminate in her twenty to life sentence for the Brinks Robbery. I leaf through some more letters—my grandfather and this guy were close.

And then I have an unexpected thought.

They must not have known if their kids were in the explosion.

I pause on that, then say it again. They must not have known if their fucking kids were in the fucking explosion.

That must have been some few nights for them, that week in March, 1970. Right about now, in fact, but forty years ago.

Wonder if any of the lefty fuckwits marching on Washington Square the other day thought of that. Thought of Jack Sinai, or Lenny Boudin, Teddy Gold's momma, or Diana Oughton's, wondering if their kids had just blown their asses off.

That thought seems to have carried me through the next few minutes, because next I find myself in the living room again, pouring another glass of wine. And while I drink it, at last I come to a decision.

Now, don't ask me to explain why I'm doing what I do next.

Who the fuck knows why we do anything?

All I know is that what I do next, even in a life like mine, governed by coincidence, filled with madness, is very, very strange indeed.

It is five o'clock in the evening. First I google the Apple Store, and see that the Soho branch is open till ten. Then I go back downstairs, only this time in my shoes, and find that little pile of money again. This time I count that there are ten bank-fresh one-thousand-dollar bills. Out of curiosity, I check the dates: all before 1975, and I know, suddenly, with certainty that this was a safety stash, meant for Sinai when he was underground.

How do I know?

Because I know.

Sinai's father had kept a safety stash for him while he was underground, and I know, because it's just the kind of thing that Sinai would have done for me.

Sinai, whom I had now treated like the piece of shit he was for a good fifteen years, had never once done anything but offer me everything he had.

That shithead. And his father, I knew with certainty, had done the same for him.

And now his father is dead, and he is dying.

Ain't that interesting? Ain't that just so fucking compelling and riveting and meaningful that it takes a strong liver and a sedulous effort to forget it, one day at a time, day after day after day.

And my poor grandfather, my poor grandfather never lived long enough to give this to his son, did he, because he died while his dear son was still a fugitive?

Well, in a way it was mine, by rights, wasn't it?

Not that I cared.

With the cash, I let myself out the front door, leaving it open behind me—I had no keys—and catch a taxi to the Apple Store in Soho. Ten thousand turns out to be enough for 27 inch LED display, a 1.8 gigahertz MacBook Air, and a scanner with a scaleable paper handler. I pay cash, haul it all to a taxi, bring it home, pour a glass of wine. Then I set it all up in the living room. When I am done, I go back downstairs and, in six trips, bring each drawer of the desk up to the living room and upend it on a different part of the kelim, around the computer setup, making six piles of paper which, moving clockwise, brings me roughly from the '60s to the '90s in my grandfather's life. I find and hack—easy, if you have a copy of Warlord, which I do—a neighbor's WI-FI connection, download my copy of iData from the cloud, get the scanner's OCR program in sync, and set up the record and field structure of a new iData database called "Jack.Sinai". I roll another J, pour another glass of wine, put on my headphones, and cue up Sinai's extensive collection of Pink Floyd, and began running paper through the paper handler.

Usually Little Lincoln does this but, of course, he is in London.

5.

Comfortably numb—very, very much so—I go to sleep sometime early Wednesday morning, then get back up and get back to it. Now, whatever the fuck it is I'm doing, I'm doing it like a dog with a bone. A stoned dog with a bone, that is, and a first-rate collection of pinot noirs and hard liquors—I even find a bottle of Red Breast—to help.

On Thursday, my Aunt Maggie calls to tell me that I've been indicted, and that I'm going to need to surrender, and also that the *Times* want their PVI piece. I ask her how long she can delay, and she says they want it now, without any delay, and I say no, I mean the surrender, and she says oh, not long. I spend the day working, and by Friday morning have two of my six piles scanned, OCRd and dBased. Friday afternoon, Maggie gets the idea of claiming that I am a foreign national, because I am traveling on a British passport. That has to go up to the State Department, and gets me through two more piles. Also she has a bike messenger deliver a letter from the *Times* inquiring about my piece. By now, the living room of my grandfather's house is looking somewhere between a Chinese restaurant after New Year's and an Irish bar. I work the *Times* piece for a while, and manage to file something serviceable in between running the scanner. On Sunday, my piece runs, and the *Times* reminds me, through Maggie, that in April I'm covering the Veterans of the Abraham Lincoln Brigade commemoration for the magazine. I ask Maggie to tell them that I'm on it but that I need a research assistant with a laptop and scanner. Also on Sunday, London files extradition papers, but the weekend is here so fuck them. Monday, I agree to surrender if I can take my computer to jail with me. As we're talking the minimum security in any case, this is quickly granted. I finish scanning the last pile of papers from my grandfather's desk and begin, now, on the portfolios, which have already been edited down and go much more quickly. On Tuesday we manage to get the surrender delayed for the following Monday and the research assistant arrives with a second laptop and scanner. Working together, we finish the entire job by about 4 a.m. on Friday. Then the research assistant, who is a woman of about twenty-three, just graduated from Brown, and I polish off the rest of my New York State of Mind as well as two more bottles of my grandfather's very fine pinot cellar, and probably would have gotten it on, twenty-three-year-olds being what they are, had we not fallen asleep on the living-room floor instead and, in the afternoon, I turn myself in at the Federal Building.

Except for one thing. I have one more encounter with Uncle Joe. On Monday morning, before I leave for my surrender, I'm in my grandfather's study and there's a knock on the window. Startled, I look up to see Uncle Joe standing there with a bottle and two glasses. The bottle is unlabeled, and the glasses are the kind you usually use for water. I go around to let him in, and start to take him upstairs. But rather than following me, he goes on and into the study, and I end up following him there. When I come in, he's already seated, and pouring very red wine out of an unmarked bottle into the two water glasses.

"I understand you're turning yourself in today."

"Yes." I'm surprised. "How do you know?"

He taps the side of his nose. "Uncle Joe knows. Try this, missie. This is wine. Give you the stuffing for what's ahead."

It is blood-red, viscous, and extremely strong. I sip a couple times and repress a gag. Then, like him, I drain the entire glass. This, clearly, is the way this wine is meant to be drunk: it descends into my stomach with a deep red glow.

Delicious.

He clearly finds it the same, because he pours another two right away and downs his. I, for once, uncharacteristically, leave my glass untouched. When he's finished drinking, he pours himself a third, and looks around the room—the piles of paper, the computer, the bulletin board of family pictures.

"This is where Jack and I used to spend our time. His favorite room in the house. Became mine too."

Then he looks at me. "You finding what you're looking for, missie?"

"Hard to say. I don't know what I'm looking for."

"You think?" His eyes are on the bulletin board again. "I'd say you're on the right track."

I don't answer this one, because I don't know what to say. In any case, I don't need to, because he goes right on.

"After he died, everyone and his brother wanted to talk to me. *Times*, *New Yorker*, TV. The survivor, right? Old comrade in arms. Oh, I talked to them I told them what they wanted to hear. But no one knew the truth. Not then, not now."

"The truth? The truth about what?"

"What it did to him. What it's done to you."

"What do you mean, Joe?"

He is into the third glass now, his gaze on the bulletin board, his eye absented. For a long time he sits like that, holding his glass.

"Oh. The price you pay. No one understands. We killed people, you know. Both of us did. Then we lost to Franco. Then you come home and try to make sense of what you've done."

He drinks off his glass and I pour him another. Waiting.

"The Good Fight. My ass. I did it differently. For me, when Spain fell it was all over. All our hopes. Put my family first, my business. Never told my kids a thing. I never even voted again. Jackie couldn't give it up. Of course what could I do? An electrician. I ran a good business, helped the folk who worked for me. It was all over. But Jackie, he never stopped. All his life, all his work—it was all about Spain. I think, he couldn't have killed those people for nothing. He couldn't bear to have. So he keeps fighting the good fight. But there's a price. That's what he doesn't know."

"Price?" He doesn't answer, so I top up his glass and wait.

"Price. For all of you." And at this his gaze comes back into focus. He fills my glass, toasts, and we drain them. "For you all. Jason of course the most. See, he didn't mean to have that effect on Jason. But not only Jason."

At this, he gets up, here, and walks to the bulletin board, fingering the family photos. "Klara. He lost her, too. Danny and Klara, what a pair they were, growing up. Then Maggie, her heart broken. All of them. None of them were untouched. Beck. Born and given away, while they were underground. So there's her life too. And now there's you."

"Me?"

"You, missie. You weren't born when Jack went to Spain. But everything you were going to be was. And now you have to figure out what to do about that."

At the courthouse, the business happens quickly. Aunt Maggie arranges for me to surrender in judge's chambers in the State Supreme Court, but it appears that I need to be brought there by the police, so I get to do something kind of fun: walk into the local precinct with my lawyer and give myself up. Maggie shows up at the Bedford Street house around two, which gives me almost enough time after Joe leaves to hide the empties and clean up a bit. Almost. She has some fairly dry comments to make about how prison might be good for me—either that or rehab. I had showered, dressed, and packed a bag according to prison regulations, as communicated on the web; I'd also backed up my iData dBase and packed my computer. Maggie is a little shorter and rounder than when last I'd seen her, but those shocking green eyes of hers are still shockingly green, and her hair, though lighter, is still red. She was in her late thirties when I first met her, and one of those unusual woman who are sexier at forty than at eighteen, and though I am not myself really Jewish—

just my father—I am close enough to understand that Maggie's particular beauty—her maiden name is Calaway—made her a very rare bird indeed in the Sinai clan. Anyway, she chats away as we take a taxi to the 6th Precinct on 10th Street, where they are waiting for us. I am duly booked, digitally fingerprinted, iris-scanned, photographed, and—to my surprise—cuffed; then we ride in a cruiser to State Supreme Court and go up the front steps next to that huge *Beati Qui Ambulant in Lege Domini* graving on the church, which always gives me a laugh. Lege domini, my ass. This also, is fun: the press had found out, so there are photographers, and the pictures will make more than a few front pages—you can see them yourself, if you want: March 19, 2011.

The only person who doesn't see the whole thing as kind of a lark, unfortunately, is the judge, His Honor Nathan Aronson, who quizzes me for nearly an hour. He is a squat little fellow resembling nothing more than one of those old-fashioned fireplugs, an impression heightened by his very red face. But he's also uncomfortably smart. *Do you think it right that government employees should reveal classified information to the press?* Yes, your honor, I do. *Do you not see that you are posing a serious security risk to our country at a time of peril?* No, your honor, I don't. *Do you understand that PVI is a vital security tool in the war against terror?* No, your honor, I think the war against terror is a stage show only equaled by the Cold War. *Oh, so you are able to judge these things better than your elected officials? Ms. Montgomery? Counselor, inform your client that she is required to answer me or I will hold her in contempt.* Could you repeat the question, your honor? I was daydreaming that I was talking to someone who understood the Constitution. (Sharp elbow to the ribs, here, from Maggie.) *Ms. Montgomery, this is your last warning. I asked if you think you are able to judge issues of state security better than your elected officials.* Well, yes, your honor, I do. My elected officials are representatives of a government, unfortunately, rather than representatives of a constituency, because this is the degradation of constitutional democracy over the past fifty-sixty years. But since you ask—forgive me, your honor, may I finish? Since you ask, I consider *myself* the representative of a constituency. It's called the Fourth Estate and our founding fathers, your honor, offered it protection under the very First Amendment to the Constitution—the same Constitution that puts so many limits on your powers, even today, in order to protect me, the *accused*, from abuse by the state. Your honor. I was elected by the millions of people around the world who have read, and trusted, and believed in my reporting, because that's what a free press is about, your honor, and we still have a free fucking press in this country, your honor. And aren't I just the impassioned little orator? Aren't I just the last damn defender of the faith? A Sinai, through and through. I leave, finally, to be taken up to Beacon Correctional Facility—Minimum Security—with a second contempt of court charge.

Perhaps I will start a collection.

And so now it is evening, and I am in a little concrete room decorated rather in pink by my cell mate, a genial middle-aged woman serving the end of a term for procurement. She's a pleasant enough person, and happy to give over the little desk by the window to my use, which is fine, as there's a window with a view of lawn and trees—you can walk out of this place, if you want to, which, surprisingly, turns out to be part of the punishment—and a nice, hard-backed chair. She also, it turns out, sleeps like a dead whale, because neither the light of my computer nor my typing disturb her one bit. How could they, given the astonishing noise of her snoring?

On my screen, running right across, are fingernail scans of the photos from the Bedford Street study, and I can click on them one by one to enlarge them. Danny and Maggie, looking uncomfortable at their wedding which, I can see now, is a casual affair—Danny in a dark suit, Maggie not even in white.

Klara Singer, graduating from college in Yale blue, her wide lips brilliant red and her black eyes watching the camera with suppressed excitement, as if the whole world were waiting for her.

Sinai—Dadda—got two pictures: one as a teenager, sitting on a stoop in sun, one eye looking out of a sweep of red hair; another from what must have been the late '90s, with Molly at Colgate Lake, a handsome middle-aged couple in swimsuits: a bald muscular man and his pretty, slim, well-kept partner.

And last the picture of my grandfather, walking next to the Hudson River in his herringbone tweed jacket, one hand, his right, in his pants pocket.

It is on this one that I pause the longest.

He is looking at the camera in something that could be called surprise, was almost surprise. And I am spending a long time thinking about that. It is surprise, but that of a man who is accustomed to being surprised by cameras—is that possible? Can that much be read into his expression? Or is it just a trick of the light—is he squinting? Where is the sun? What time of day is it?

Of course, there is no way to know that. Of course. Feeling frustration, I vow to get my mind back into the game—I have a piece to prep for the *Times* on the Veterans of the Abraham Lincoln Brigade memorial, and from now on it's what I'm going to work on.

I slip out of the room, now, and down the hallway to the door out to the lawn, where I light a cigarette and—you were probably wondering about this—sip from a bourbon mini, available for ten dollars a pop from a guard called Myeashea who has already taken fifty dollars from me, and is virtually assured of the same again tomorrow. I turn my face up to the sky for a moment, watching the stars, then shut my eyes. I say to myself: it's just a photograph. Then I open my eyes again, take a couple double-drags from the cigarette, put it out, and walk, quickly, back to the room. I wake the computer, then blow up the photo of my grandfather and look, not at him, but at the water. Aha. Clearly it is high tide: the water, textured by a breeze, is lapping at the very edge of the walkway.

Bingo. I go to the NOAA website—National Oceanographic and Atmospheric Institute—and search, find, and download tide tables from 1995. I scroll down to the Battery, and find high water was

11 a.m. Then I search, find, and download solar declination tables. These are harder to read, much harder, and require some research as to how they work. Still, by early morning, about three or so, I have figured it out.

The Hudson was on his left, so he was walking north. It was 11 a.m., thereabouts, because the sun was high in the sky, heading for its apogee, and *behind* him. The photographer was therefore north of him, shooting into the sun, which can only mean one thing: it was not a posed picture. Otherwise, the photographer would have put the sun behind himself. Now how did that happen? Maybe he asked my grandfather for a shot, and my grandfather said no. Maybe my grandfather had a reputation, and the photographer knew there was no point in asking. Thus he'd taken the opportunity that presented itself and shot the image against the sun before my grandfather noticed he was there. No doubt he'd shot several frames, and in the one that got printed, my grandfather was looking up with an expression of surprise, and annoyance, tempered by the fact that he had been so surprised, and annoyed, so many times before.

By now, I've been at my desk for a couple-three hours straight. Madame—which is how I've come to think of my roommate—has been snoring musically; my neck is aching, and my blood is screaming for nicotine. Still, I stay outside only long enough for a smoke and a mini, then I'm back. Now, next to the picture of my grandfather, I launch my iData dBase.

But I don't go to anything to do with my assignment for the *New York Times*.

Instead, I go right back to the beginning, the very first document in the very first green folder.

It is a birth certificate from Mt. Morris General Hospital, August 5, 1906, in the name of Yankel Aaron Sinai, 5 pounds, 4 ounces, born on the stroke of midnight.

Seeing I don't know what I'm doing it is, it seems to me, as good a place to start as any.

6.

I cannot blame my Aunt Maggie for the fact that my couple-three days in jail turns into three-four weeks.

I want to, but I can't.

For one thing, the actual original charge—refusal to name my source—was indeed settled in a couple-three days, not because of Maggie's fine legal work, but because my secret source turned out to have much more of a sense of obligation to me than I had had to her, when, just after we had told each other we loved each other, I had promptly left to cover Operation Cast Lead for the *Economist*. In effect, she lost her job at the Department of Defense in order to get me out of jail, which was, when you think of it, moving.

I am moved. More than that. I find it sexy as hell, and more than a few of my nights in jail, listening to the Madame snore, are spent imagining just how I will show her how sexy I find it.

For another thing, it is my fault—my second contempt charge— that I was there for so long, for His Honor Nathan Aronson was a vindictive little bastard and made me serve out nearly the whole charge.

And for a third, I didn't actually mind being there. I met Judy Clark, who had been transferred from Bedford Hills to serve out the end of her seventy-five to life in something a little kinder than she had known before, and Judy, who had known my father and his little band of brothers well in the day, had a lot of interesting things to tell me. I had a lot of visitors. Danny and Maggie came often, and I spoke to them at length—at real length, as you will see later, and learned a great deal from them and about them. So did my half-sister, Beck, and her whackjob husband Ben, who may be about the biggest dork I've ever met but whose work I knew well—he's the reporter who smoked out my dad in the first place—and they, too, had a lot to tell. So much that I started recording them all and running their interviews through WordRec and then dBasing them right along with everything else in Jack.Sinai, just like I would an interview.

And then, I had my work. In four weeks I had catalogued and read every piece of my grandfather's study and I knew, I felt, his life just about as well as he knew it himself.

So to speak. I have a lot to say about that.

And finally, let us bear in mind the fact that Beacon Correctional Facility is a fairly pleasant place to be, at least, the minimum-security wing. Everyone wears these orange jump suits which can be quite flattering. My friendly local guard, who made a close to a hundred dollars for every day I was in jail, kept me in bourbon singles and even, a few times, baked me some marijuana brownies. There were plenty of cigarettes. And last, but by no means least, was this girl from Miami who had performed an act of civil disobedience at the School of the Americas protest and was serving six months. She was interesting, seeing my original contract with the *Times* had me covering exactly that same protest in a few months, and in fact, she was more than interesting, she was delicious, with a funny twisted smile and white-skinned shoulders that sloped down into what may have been the most perfect pair of breasts I've ever seen, incredibly and increasingly perfect, like a story, as you slowly unzipped her orange jumpsuit and let yourself see, ever so slowly, more and more of them, and we made each other climax many, many times during those three weeks which, after my long term in Saudi, was more than a little welcome, more than a little.

Downside: I put on some weight.

It was a fairly remarkable series of accidents, you'll admit, and one that, in the end, I came to think of as just what I needed. Nor was I in any way uptight. The only thing I cared about was that I be out by April 15 which was, I knew, the date of the annual commemoration of the Abraham Lincoln Brigade at the Borough of Manhattan Community College—the exact ceremony to which my grandfather had been walking along the Hudson, that day in 1995, the last spring of his life.

It was also my next assignment for the *Times*, but I didn't think about that. I planned to be there, and I will be honest, if I had had to, I was planning to walk out of the jail for it.

See, by then I knew a great deal about that day. I knew a great deal indeed—including that, on April 15, 1995, I had been there too.

Which perhaps explains something.

Perhaps.

Explains why, over my four weeks at Beacon Correctional, I did not fulfill my contract for the *New York Times*, did not write an autobiographical piece about my life as the daughter of an icon of the American left—yeah yeah, I got it: *Daughter of the Left: my Life as Jason Sinai's Daughter*, my agent is upgrading his kids' summer plans at the very name of it—but instead catalogued my grandfather's study, following each name from each piece of correspondence—Dmytryk; Sanford; Odlum; Scott; Kazan; Schulberg; Dassin—through labyrinthine google searches, through encyclopedias and histories, through police records and memoirs; why, I spent hours each day on Skype with Maggie and Danny and my half-sister Beck and Ben and Molly, even going so far as to contact Mimi Lurie herself, Sinai's first love from the days and Beck's mother, not to mention all kinds of other members of the cast of characters from the historical soap opera of the Sinai family, some of whom played very obscure parts indeed.

The thing is, April 15, 1995, was turning out to be a big day. A day when very, very many more things happened than any of the people involved ever understood. Anyone, that is, until I began looking at that photograph of my grandfather, and trying to understand what was behind that look in his eyes.

Tintin had nothing on me.

Sinai even FaceTimes me, his face popping up, though he could not know that, next to the picture of his father and watching him—his thinning face and hair, his unexpectedly blue eyes—for the first time I can see the resemblance.

"Doll, what are you actually up to?"

"Hi, Daddy. How are you? Everything well? I'm fine, thanks. Great to catch up. Sorry you're dying of a disease you kept secret from me for the past ten years. Speak soon, okay?"

"Sweetheart. Mimi says you called."

"Aunt Mimi? That lovely old lady in Michigan? Sure I call, regular as clockwork. I like to check up that she's taking her Geritol and seeing her doctor regular and all."

That made him laugh.

"Okay, doll. Now tell me."

I did, in a way—not that he got it. "Dad, is it right that we were at the Veterans of the Abraham Lincoln Brigade Memorial in 1995?"

Now there's a long pause—long enough for me to launch WordRec and route the call right into it.

"How do you know?"

"Does the name Walt Arden say anything to you? Or Bradford Flanagan? They were there."

"Ye-es. How do you know about them?"

"Know *about* them? I *know* them. I've got about ten hours of tape on them."

"Jesus, Iz. What are you doing? Investigative journalism on your own life?"

Now it was me who paused. I hadn't quite put it to myself that way, and that he did perfectly illustrates why my father is such a pain in the ass.

"Listen, Pops. I'm asking the questions."

And Sinai sighs this little sigh of his which he has been sighing at me all my life.

"Yes, I took you there. I wanted you to see my father. It was perhaps foolish."

"Perhaps?"

"Well look. Imagine my position."

And he was off, like always, he talking, I listening, and as I was listening, I was running through my iData transcripts from Walt Arden, and Bradford Flanagan, and filling in details, and making notes.

Watched, of course, by the picture of my grandfather, looking in annoyed, unsurprised surprise at a camera on the walk next to the Hudson River, flood tide beside him, sun behind.

And, Jesus Christ, I am understanding as Sinai talks, me in front. Yes, I'll explain.

On April 13th, His Honor Nathan Aronson exercises his benevolent discretion, in response to the seventh petition from Aunt Maggie, and commutes the remainder of my contempt sentence.

On April 14th, after promising Jessie to be up during visiting hours over the weekend, which I of course know I'm never going to do, and bidding a fond adieu to the Madame as well as introducing her to the idea of sleep apnea, and leaving a generous tip for my Myeashea though I have paid her a clean twenty-five hundred dollars by now, I walk out into a Hudson Valley spring day, the sky a depthless blue, the trees coming into life, and find Uncle Danny waiting to take me back to the city—to be precise, back to Bedford Street.

And on April 15th, at 11:00, I am walking next to the Hudson River, the spring sun declined just behind me, the neap tide lapping the edge of the walkway, the river pregnant beyond belief.

In a few minutes I will go on up, as my grandfather did, to the Borough of Manhattan Community College where the 75th Annual Veterans of the Abraham Lincoln Brigade commemorative ceremony is about to take place.

When my grandfather had gone, he had been one of a couple dozen or so surviving Lincoln Brigade members.

Today there were of course almost none left, but there would be four generations of their descendants.

I cannot know where exactly my grandfather was photographed. But at a certain point I stop and turn in a slow circle, watching the path, the water, pregnant beyond belief, the Jersey skyline, the Statue of Liberty, New York Harbor, the Verrazano Narrows with the span of the bridge, and the buildings of downtown New York among which, to be accurate, I have to try to imagine the World Trade Center, which my grandfather would have seen. Then I close my eyes and breathe in, deeply, feeling tweed on my arms, Bay Rum aftershave and pipe tobacco in my nose and mouth. I turn my face up to the sun and pause, for a long time. Then slowly, holding the rail, I go on.

I think of my son, whom I have not seen in twenty-five years.

I think of my wife, with whose life I am about to change for the last time.

I sing to myself, softly, the line from that Bob Dylan song the kids so loved:

> Our conversation
> Was short and sweet

Then I open my eyes again and slowly, one hand in my pocket, the other on the rail, move north.

FBI Agent Walt Arden is sitting on a bench just a few yards to the north.

My son, whom I will never meet again, with his daughter whom I will never know, my granddaughter, is about half a mile further on, walking south, seeing the World Trade Center for the first time.

In a moment, Bradford Flanagan will stop me and make my heart launch into a tattoo of beats.

See, I know all this. And after I go to the VALB ceremony, I will follow my father and my own self, in my mind, back up the 87 to Saugerties while in reality I will follow my grandfather's footsteps back to the haunted house on Bedford Street, crack another bottle from my grandfather's first-rate collection of vintage pinots—fuck it, wine was made to drink—roll a joint and light a cigarette and, on the kelim in the living room, launch and get back to work not on the article that the poor *New York Times* is expecting from me, but on the one I am, in contradiction of all the rules of professionalism, writing instead, and which you are, if you are still with me, about to read.

And every now and again, as this night goes on and I grow drunker and drunker, I will go down to my grandfather's study and steady myself by holding the desk and close my eyes and breathe in, deep into my lungs, the smell of his life, which began to end on this day sixteen years ago and which I no longer believe, not in any serious way, is different from my own.

Hour by hour. At 7:00 was when my grandparents sat down to dinner at a restaurant called Grange Hall in the Village. Uncle Danny and Aunt Maggie dropped them off at nine, then drove home with their single child—they only had one, then—up the West Side Highway. Maggie was pregnant. My grandfather and grandmother sat, as they always did, at the kitchen table for tea and a debriefing of this amazing day—just where the Rasta from Triple-A Pot and I sat— but my grandfather didn't tell her what was really on his mind. As usual, my grandmother went up to bed, and my grandfather to his study. He spent a few hours there, alone. Two a.m. was when, at last, he raised himself from this desk and went up to tell his wife what he had learned, just that morning, from Dr. Holmquist.

There are lots of things I do that Tintin would not approve of. I drink like Captain Haddock, smoke like General Alcazar, take the kinds of drugs that he spent books eradicating in mysterious suks and ports and illegal freighters, and as for my sexual proclivities, well, we all know Tintin never had sex but if he did, it would not have been with boys.

Or come to think of it, would it? That's actually a good question.

But one thing that's sure is that Tintin, brave little Tintin, would never have abandoned an assignment for the *New York Times Magazine* and, instead, written a piece with no future and no genre that could not possibly get him anywhere but into trouble.

7.

And as for this piece, let me just say one or two last words about it before you read it. May I?

As for this little opus on which I am about to immolate my entire career—and note, note that my career, apart from retail therapy with Momma and a series of stunning women in many different countries of whom some I have sex with and some I fall in love with but all, repeat all, I leave, is really all that I have to show for my nearly thirty years of life, my education at SOAS and Cambridge, my bylines in the *Guardian*, *Harpers*, the *Economist*, and now, the *New York Times*; note that my career is really the only thing onto which I can hold, increasingly, by the nails of my fingers—but as for this magnum opus, the opus suicidus, this is what I have to show for my illustrious little career; this is what I know.

I know that on April 15, 1995, a Saturday sixteen years ago, my grandfather Jack Sinai walked north along the Hudson River promenade in downtown Manhattan, a man of eighty-seven with a full head of white hair and, in the flat light, great gravity, walking unaided in a tweed jacket and open-necked denim shirt.

Sometimes, it seems to me, it is the only fucking thing I know.

The river was on his left, on high tide and, this early on a Sunday, textured by wind and undisturbed by wake. I know this.

I *know* this. I can see the proof of it, right in front of me, sitting here in my grandfather's study, staring at my computer. I can read the tide charts, the weather reports, and the declination tables of the sun. So this I know.

And this I think.

Above him the sky was marine blue, brilliant, with a delta of distant birds coming back north for the summer.

I think it because so it looked, this morning, when I walked there myself, on the neap tide with the sun behind me to the south, and as I looked up and around, feeling the scratch of tweed on my arm and the smell of Bay Rum in my nose, this is the sky I saw. High above, I saw a delta of geese, so distant as to be translucent, and far and away in my mind I thought, exactly as my grandfather would have thought, of a day nine years earlier when my Uncle Danny and Aunt Klara walked out on Hammonasset Beach, up the Connecticut coast from New Haven, and saw just the same delta of migrating geese etched nearly translucent against a sky of marine blue.

Now let us talk about accuracy, just for a moment. Let us take this question by the horns.

You will say that my grandfather may have made that connection—indeed, I know that Danny had already told him the story of that day on Hammonasset Beach, and what it meant later, to Klara, to Maggie, because Danny told me he did—but that there's no knowing that he saw birds. To which I answer: true. True, but trite. We don't know if the birds were there. We do know, however, that they *could* have been. We know that in 1995 there were still migrating geese in North America; we know that the evolutionary shift that, as global temperatures rose, made a portion of the species non-migrating, had not yet occurred, so if he did not in fact see them—as, nine years earlier, Danny and Klara, in fact *did* see them on Hammonasset Beach—that it really doesn't matter, because my grandfather's eyes were directed down, focused with such concentration below the surface of the water, as if on a submerged object, or a fish, that when a young man approached he had to ask twice—"Excuse me, are you Jack Sinai?"—before my grandfather looked up.

So let's let that be enough for the birds. Maybe they were there; maybe they weren't. Maybe he saw them; maybe not. But whether or not he did, he *could have*, and the detail is authenticating, and so helps us set the scene for what he did see.

The point here is one of truth, and if you're going to fuck me up every goddamned time about *facts*, then I'm never going to be able to tell you the truth.

And if you care so goddamned much about facts, well, as for what he did see next, my grandfather, there is no doubt about it at all, because while I was at Beacon Correctional, when I tracked down and interviewed Bradford Flanagan, the young dude who had just approached my grandfather, that day in 1995 on the Hudson River promenade, he told me that when my grandfather did look up, so slowly did his attention refocus that he, the young man, thought he had done something wrong.

And this, this I admit that I believe, but note this: I believe it so strongly that I am no longer prepared to admit to any difference between what I believe and what I know.

What I know and believe, and know and know, is that young man was wrong. My grandfather's reaction had nothing to do with any offense. Why should he be offended? Just a few minutes ago, he'd even managed to be reasonably polite to a *New York Times* photographer who photographed him without permission. On the other hand, to be approached by a young man today was a very particular experience for my grandfather. What the young man noticed, in my view, was a very particular hesitation caused by that fact that, in the instant between hearing the words—*Excuse me, are you Jack Sinai?*— and raising his eyes to the speaker, my grandfather had careened between two emotions, as strong as he had ever felt, each the polar opposite of the other.

See, he thought that the man in front of him was his son, my father, whom he had not seen in twenty-five years.

The first was to say to himself, "I knew it!"

The second, just as certainly: "It couldn't be."

With the first thought his heart, eighty-seven years old, leapt into a dangerous tattoo of beats.

With the second, it must have seemed to contract slowly, painfully, to something even smaller than it had ever been before.

Okay, you will say I cannot know. Fine. Fuck you, but fine. That's what I *think* my grandfather was thinking. But as to the meeting, I know about it for sure. Not just because of interviewing Brad Flanagan, but because my grandfather, in the months before he died, had FOIA'd the FBI records and thrown them in the drawer of his big desk for me to dBase sixteen years later, and they revealed that three separate detectives, that sunny spring day on the Hudson River waterfront, were right there with my grandfather, each one taking careful notes, and although they were redacted heavily, I read those notes.

And I know one other thing.

I know that it was, in the event, my grandfather's first thought, not his second, that was right, that day and, of course, I know it because I had Sinai telling me it on tape and in transcript from when I was in Beacon Correctional.

He *knew* it.

And, in fact, it *could* be.

My father was right there, right there.

And so was I.

Chapter Three

Jack Sinai

April 15, 1995 ·

New York City

1

I knew it. Today of all days. Jack Sinai was due, in a short hour, at the annual Veterans of the Abraham Lincoln Brigade celebration, where he was to receive a medal that meant perhaps more than a whole life-time of honors: a Legion of Honor award from the government of Spain. It meant a great, great deal to him. To be recognized by the post-Franco government of Spain? And that, at the annual ceremony honoring the surviving members of the Abraham Lincoln Brigade? It was amazing to him as it was to all the brigadistas, a final, breath-taking surprise in the long series of amazing experiences that had been their lives since they shipped out, each one, to fight in a hope-less cause in 1937.

But for Jack, it also meant something far beyond the honor. It meant nothing less than that this day, this precise day, his eldest son Jason was going to come home for the first time in twenty-five years. For Jack, every moment since the award had been announced had been filled with mounting anticipation, not of the ceremony, but of seeing his son.

It was, he was convinced, simply meant to be. His son had been in hiding for twenty-five years, and in twenty-five years there had never been a better time to make contact. The award had made the *New York Times*, front Metro page on a slow news Sunday: there was no way Jasey hadn't seen. Jack would be surrounded by crowds: at the ceremony, at the reception afterward. Progressives, ex-Communists, Chomskians, anarchists—there was even a rumor that Robert Redford was going to be there. Never would there be an easier day for Jason to blend in.

That Jack Sinai was coming from his astounding conversation, earlier that morning, with Dr. Holmquist only made it more perfect.

I knew it.

But just as quickly: *It couldn't be.*

It couldn't be. Next to the glittering Hudson, against the floating of his heart on a warm wave of belief, the knowledge had to fight to make itself heard. *It couldn't be.* Surely Jack was being watched, right now, even more closely than he had been for twenty-five years. Surely surveillance was heavier than ever on days when it was likely his son would make contact, days like this. Jason knew that. Jason would know that there would FBI agents, or Federal marshals, or bounty hunters poised right now around him, especially now that he was in the news. *It couldn't be.*

Still, as Jack disengaged his attention from the river and raised it to the source of the voice, it was impossible for him to divest his expression of hope—a childish hope, one that in an eighty-seven-year-old man was nothing short of ridiculous.

And of course the voice turned out not to be the commanding one of his son, his beautiful, broad-shouldered, handsome son whom he had not seen in twenty-five years, but of a total stranger.

"Excuse me, are you Jack Sinai? My name's Brad Flanagan. Congratulations, sir. I'm coming to see you receive your medal . . ."

It was a freckled, middle-aged man wearing a Red Sox baseball cap and a plaid red hunting jacket and holding the hand of a brown-haired girl, perhaps nine years old, an utter stranger, a slightly ridiculous one in comparison with Jack's twenty-five-year-old image of his son.

2.

Because, see, Jack Sinai was right in thinking that today was a particularly appropriate *and* a particularly dangerous day for his son to make contact. He was more than right: he was kind of prescient. So much more happened that day than Jack ever understood, so much more than he ever could possibly have imagined. In fact, no one really understood the full complexity of what you were going to encounter that day: not Jack, not his son Jason, not Walt Arden or Brad Flanagan, though each was to play such a big role in that complexity.

So on one hand, Jack was profoundly right in understanding that his son had both strong reason to be at the ceremony, that day, and strong reason not to be.

And on the other hand, Jack was wrong: his son had no plans whatsoever to make contact with his father. So in a sense, it *couldn't* be. And yet, what he *knew* was also right. Because in fact—in fact, now, not the fantasy of an eighty-seven-year-old man who had just learned he was dying—five, six city blocks north on the Hudson River promenade, his son was standing, one hand holding his daughter's hand, the other shielding his eyes from the sun as he stared, aghast, at the World Trade Center.

Of course, as Jack thought, Jason had never been near the West Village neighborhood where he had grown up since, twenty-five years earlier, he had gone underground. Therefore, he had never seen the Twin Towers before.

Each time they came into view, as we walked south on the water, he stopped, shaded his eyes against the southward sun, and stared up at the incredible bulk of buildings, massively ugly, depressingly utilitarian, harrowingly close—for the tenth or twentieth time since we got there, he felt a strange vertigo and moved me behind him, as if the towers were about to fall.

Then he shook off the thought. Fuck it, the fucking things had been there since the mid-seventies. It was only he who had never seen them.

Plus, he was going to scare me. Holding my hand—his eleven-year-old daughter—he tried to turn my attention to the water, to show me the hulking Staten Island Ferry, out in the harbor, and the Statue of Liberty.

But the towers loomed above him, just over his shoulder, like a threat.

So Jack was both right and wrong, which makes sense, in that Jack's insight into criminality was correct only insofar as it went. Yes, a fugitive needs to stay far from the people and places that could be presumed to be important to him. But Jason Sinai, over his twenty-five years' exploration of the archeology of deception, had come to operate on another plane of analysis altogether.

Jack was right to think that his son would be there. Where he was wrong was in understanding why. What Jack didn't understand, and couldn't understand, was that in the architecture of deception, the layers upon layers of calculation of odds and imagination of impossibilities—the art and craft by which the law is broken—there comes a point when you had to think beyond the logic of simply not getting caught.

Take, for example, the fugitive's obvious strategy of simply avoiding the places where you could be expected to be: the places of your childhood, your friends, the familiar places where people like you gathered. In Jason's opinion, the law had become increasingly able, every year since he had assumed his fugitive identity as James Grant, to read *negative* evidence as well as positive. In Jason's opinion he was as suspicious for what *he did not do* as he was for what he *did*.

Was it, for example, noteworthy to some data-mining operation, some random surveillance of the sort that any criminal-defense lawyer could attract, never mind a civil-rights lawyer and social activist called Jim Grant living in Saugerties, New York and sharing not only many convictions with the notorious '70s fugitive Jason Sinai but many physical characteristics also—was it possible that some surveillance operation would one day find it remarkable that Grant not only never took the two-hour drive down the Thruway to New York City, but that he never, ever appeared at any of the rallies, protests, lectures, or gatherings which a lefty lawyer could reasonably be expected to attend?

In fact, Jason Sinai thought, sooner or later it would become possible to read an exact profile of Jason Sinai in those very places where James Grant *never* showed up.

So he had decided in his twenty-five-year meditation on deception, the twenty-five years during which he had, less than a hundred miles from the home of his father, lived as James Grant, small-town lawyer in a little town tied to Woodstock by the hip. And therefore, increasingly over the past five-six years, he had quietly ventured to the city every now and again, to a lecture at the 92nd Street Y or Town Hall, to a party at the *Nation*, to a rally or a protest. If nothing else, just to create an electronic trace—E-ZPass, cell phone—of his presence.

But never, ever had he deliberately gone anywhere he knew his father would be, such as the Veterans of the Abraham Lincoln Brigade ceremony, and certainly not the VALB ceremony today, when his father would be the center of attention.

Anyway, he didn't mean to go near his father. He meant to take a place with me far in the back of the audience and, from his vantage, watch. Even now, he was, with me, his eleven-year-old daughter, hiding out next to the water while his father, he assumed, was waiting in whatever passed for a green room at the Borough of Manhattan Community College.

But there are certain spaces in our minds that will always be in perpetual doubt, particularly when there is something we want. In fact, when Jason Sinai dressed that morning to come to the city, he had put on a corduroy sports coat, unusually presentable for him, and a baseball cap. As if, without admitting it to himself, he did not want his father to see how bald he had grown. And so just at the moment that his father, a few blocks south, is thinking, *I knew it*, Jason, a few blocks north, strolls, dressed for a meeting he knows can never happen.

That is us: our voracious little selves, always babies, no matter how we grow, always crying for more.

9:45. Jason checked his watch, then with a nervous, somehow petulant look up at the towers, he began to walk south. What he wanted was to get to the Borough of Manhattan Community College auditorium ten minutes late. Like that, he'd be finding his seat just as the lights went down, when all eyes were turning to the stage. That gave him time to take a little walk south along the Hudson, a promenade built long after he had last been here but which, with its easy view of people behind him, couldn't have been better for his purposes. So he'd walk a little further south, show me a little more of the city, spend some time, as the man said, watching the river flow.

3.

"Mr. Sinai, you defended my father, William Flanagan, in the New Bedford's Carpenter's Guild, in 1953. Do you remember?"

Flanagan, Flanagan. Standing before the young man, Jack searched his memory and came up blank. Somewhere, sometime in a totally forgotten past, he had defended a Mick called Billy Flanagan and now this was his boy. So.

It didn't faze him. Meetings like this. Other meetings, other places, had in fact been much, much more unlikely.

Once, in the '80s in Santa Barbara, he'd been approached by a young woman, a second cousin it turned out, to Marguerite Roberts, whom Jack had represented before HUAC in 1951 and who even then no one in the world remembered. Roberts had just died, and her cousin had held his hand between both of hers and cried while she thanked him.

That had been a strange one.

Another time on the subway heading for Columbia, as was his

wont, on the local so he didn't have to change twice, he'd been stared down by a patrol cop, perhaps thirty, implacable, from Sheridan Square to 116th Street. Leaving the train at 116th Street, when the boy shifted barely to let him out the door, he'd said—more to give him his chance to express himself than any other reason—"Don't tell me. Your father was on the job in Nyack, right?" He meant that his father was on the same police force of which two members had been killed during the Brinks Robbery in 1981, along with a Brinks guard, and Jack had helped represent Kathy Boudin, an accessory in the robbery. The boy didn't miss a beat although Jack had thought, in retrospect, that he could read, in the boy's eyes, the conflict between how he had been raised and what he said next, which was: "You bet, asshole." No surprises: his entire life after, when letters arrived at his office with a Nyack postmark, he forwarded them to the FBI, unopened.

And another time—this one, during Reagan's first term and by far the strangest—on a crowded street someone had handed him a photograph of a Yiddish-inscribed gravestone, which he slowly sounded out to read *Chaia Sinai*—his grandmother's grave in what was once a Lithuanian shtetl. There was a pebble precariously balanced on the headstone and the photograph was recent. He'd looked wildly around after the man, who had disappeared. Later, when Jack learned from the FBI who had sent it—an NKVD officer, Jewish, whom Jack had known in Spain as a Soviet soldier before the fall of Madrid—he had thought, God, could such a person really have survived not only the Spanish Civil War but all the way through to the '80s? Purges and putsches? Could that brown-eyed, troubled boy, the cruelty of his role fitting him as badly as his shabby uniform, now be an NKVD functionary of enough power to have this strange letter of greeting delivered on the streets of New York, in the diamond district—where Jack was on the way to lunch with a state judge at the Harvard Club—no less? That letter, at the end of the Cold War, had cost him a week in front of the House Committee on Intelligence, closed door hearings: only the fact that he had so promptly reported the contact had kept him from a more serious kind of subpoena.

There had been many such meetings in Jack Sinai's long life, and now, this brilliant April morning—standing next to the Hudson River in Tribeca, the glàssine water heaving under morning sun, not yet disturbed by the wake of morning traffic: a chance encounter with the son of someone he had known years before and long forgotten.

Jack watched young Flanagan with a falling expression, wondering how to get away.

This day, of all days, when he had to be free, and alone, so he could be found by his son.

It wasn't the boy's fault. Above the roar of his irritation. It wasn't the boy's fault, to want to talk to him like this. Following the *Times* article Jack had received telegrams of congratulation from Minnesota to Moscow. What would be surprising would be if Jack were *not* recognized by someone like young Brad Flanagan here.

And still it was a real effort to bring his attention to bear.

It was as if he had to reassemble, piece by piece, his whole present tense. The sun-flooded spring day next to the Hudson; the delta of distant birds high above; the reason he was making his way north through Tribeca. The fact of being accosted by the Flanagan boy before him, the child of a union man he had defended half a century ago and who, thus, now thought he had a claim on him, and, with all that was so huge in those facts of his day, the even huger news that Dr. Holmquist had announced that morning.

> *Our conversation*
> *Was short and sweet*

From nowhere, the verses played in his mind, a song Jason used to listen to.

Well, two conversations. The first was short. This one, judging from the eager, shy expression on young Flanagan's face, was threatening to be very, very sweet indeed.

4.

Of the three FBI agents on surveillance of Jack Sinai, that day, only one really understood who they were looking for.

This one, Walter Arden, was from Ann Arbor, and in Ann Arbor, the Bank of Michigan robbery, where in 1974 Jason Sinai's break-away gang from Weatherman had participated in the murder of a cop and sentenced themselves to lives as fugitives, was the stuff kids grow up on. Walt was a baby in '74, but his own father was on the job and never did they go to the Briarwood Mall without that he stopped in front of the bank to show his son where Officer Foley fell, a .32 cal-iber bullet having ripped through every vital organ in his torso. Well, the Bank of Michigan was, as an English professor at the U. of M., Walt's college—and Jason's, as it happened—had put it, "dead letter"—or, as police said, "leads were cold, perps were old"—by the time Walt joined the FBI himself, in Detroit. Except for law enforce-ment, that is. For law enforcement, whether in Ann Arbor at the Bank of Michigan or San Francisco at the Park Police Station, when radicals kill a cop, there is no such thing as a cold case.

And the FBI is national, not local. So when Walt's elders and betters found out how much he knew about the BOM murder, they'd several times seconded him to investigations that touched on Weatherman, such as the aforementioned Park Police Station bomb-ing in San Francisco, the only other unsolved fatality from the Vietnam days. That one, he'd interrupted the middle-class lives of ex-Weathermen to take depositions in New Mexico, in Chicago, in Los Angeles. And now, for four months, he'd been seconded to the FBI office in Albany, New York. Luckily, he was not yet married—luckily because he was mobile enough for the assignment; luckily because Albany was a college town. Even better, Skidmore College was just up the New York Thruway, and Skidmore had a dance school, which meant two important things: horny girls, gay men.

In 1995, Walt was having a good spring.

*

This is why Walt Arden was sent to Albany Station: the Bank of Michigan robbery had been carried out by three Weatherman fugitives, all underground since the townhouse bombing in 1970: Jason Sinai, Mimi Lurie, and Sharon Solarz—this was, remember, before Jason was proven innocent. They weren't the most visible fugitives, nor the most famous. But they were the most notorious, so much so that they'd even been repudiated by the self-styled Weather Bureau itself after they had, led by a fucked-up criminal vet called Vincent Dellesandro, shot and killed a cop in a holdup at the Briarwood Mall. Dellesandro was caught some months later—turned in, we learned later, by Mimi Lurie herself. They were after all, even Walt knew, hippies, and they must have been utterly shocked by finding that their little games with guns had actually taken a life. But after that: dead letter. The leads got cold, the perps got old. Not even the slightest whiff of a clue. They disappeared so thoroughly, so completely, that although until '80 or so there were teams of agents on the case, in the past ten years the total man hours put into their pursuit were virtually all Walt's, and could be counted on a handful of pay stubs.

Until last year.

Last year, a few months before, routine surveillance of a suspected dope grower in a little Catskill town called Saugerties had suggested that Sharon Solarz had been in touch in touch with him. A blip on the radar, but more than they'd had in a quarter-century and, indeed, the lucky break that was going to lead, within the next year and a half, to Jason Sinai's surrender, as the dope dealer was represented by none other than Jim Grant, which led to the discovery of his true identity as Jason Sinai by an enterprising reporter from the *Albany Times*, who used, oddly enough, negative evidence in making his identification. Which was when my father abandoned me in a hotel room downtown so he could go on the run. It was an elaborate and successful enterprise: he succeeded in leaving me alone only as long as it took for my Aunt Maggie, whom I had never met, to come get me. Only, before she got there, the police did, and when she did get there, she found them in the process of apprehending a dangerous twelve-year-old child at gunpoint. I expressed, I believe, my high level of culpability by crying.

Anyway, as soon as the name Sharon Solarz came up, Walt was seconded to Albany Station. And while there, he'd taken the trouble to come downstate and meet the New York City agents who were still detailed to the surveillance of Jack Sinai, routine coverage, occasional really, whenever there seemed to be some steepening in the curve that Jason may make contact.

When he read about the Spanish Medal of Honor, Walt had contacted his friends downstate, and they paid him the courtesy of inviting him to join the day's surveillance of Jack Sinai.

Now, dressed in a jean jacket, a Yankees cap, and carrying a well-thumbed copy of Chomsky's *Manufacturing Consent*—he'd read the fucker, too, though to make it looked well-thumbed had taken him a couple hours of abusing the book—he watched as Jack Sinai was approached by a young man. And although briefly his heart had picked up at the encounter, quickly it slowed again. This guy was a weedy little fellow with bony wrists sticking out of his plaid sleeves and a tennish-year-old girl at his side, significantly younger than Jason could ever pretend to be. Worse yet, he was shorter and bore no resemblance to any of the possible computer-generated projections, all in his pocket, of Jason Sinai's appearance as a middle-aged man.

In any case, if he wanted to listen, it was time to rotate. He called the pattern into his sleeve, then stood, ambled slowly past the old man, catching a word or two of his conversation with the weedy guy—*housing court*. Perhaps ten feet past, he leaned idly against the railing and opened up the book to read, for all the world another lefty killing time before the VALB ceremony. A big lefty, admittedly: Walt stood six-five in his running shoes. A well-coiffed lefty—he wore today a blond hairpiece with a luxuriant pony-tail that neatly hid the earpiece of his radio. And a bulky lefty: his wool-fringed jean jacket concealed his Kevlar vest, radio, handcuffs, spray-can tear gas, night-vision scope, and nine-millimeter Glock.

Meanwhile, colleague number one from the New York Station, Michael Robbins, moved south along the walkway and sat in his seat, while colleague number two, Richard Numeroff, detached himself from the river view and strolled south.

And right about this time, Jason Sinai, accompanied by his daughter, ambled past the huge space of the Winter Garden, hands in pockets, alternately watching the surface of the water to the right and casting worried glances at the unbelievable, massive square towers to the left, heading south.

5.

"Mr. Sinai, you represented my father, William Flanagan, in the New Bedford's Carpenters' Guild, in 1953. Do you remember?"

William Flanagan? Billy, his friends would have called him. Briefly, Jack cast his mind's eye inside, but could not bring back a face. He could remember the New Bedford defense—carpenters' union vs. a phalanx of red-baiting forces that ranged from local thugs to the FBI, around the time Jason was born. His house in Martha's Vineyard came from them: he'd bought the plot, and the construction was payment in kind. But Billy Flanagan? A blank.

Billy Flanagan's *bairn*, however, in his Red Sox cap and plaid jacket, remembered him. The Irish. They would not only not forget, like the cops and their families up to Nyack had never forgotten, what had been done *to* them. They would also never forget the kind of thing that Jack had done *for* Billy Flanagan's father and his mates in the union. But the boy was speaking.

"Congratulations, Mr. Sinai."

"Why thank you." Somewhere between disappointment and frustration, he found his voice. "Are you coming to the ceremony?"

"Yes sir." The young man spoke earnestly. "Read about it in the paper last week. It would have meant a lot to my father to be here too."

"Your father is no longer alive?"

"He passed over the winter."

The young man looked as if he were about to cry. The girl, holding the young man's hand, was looking up at him—as Eleanor would say—across the twentieth century. For a long moment, Jack watched her absently. Then, aware he was being strange: "And what do you do?"

Shy, with a look that told Jack he was witnessing a profoundly important moment in this boy's life, the chance to pay homage: "I'm a defense lawyer. In the housing court."

Oh, so it was this kind of thing. Old Billy Flanagan, evenings over a glass of Bushmill's, had liked to tell his son about the lawyer who stood up for them at the height of the red scare—*A Jew he was, but so was Joyce, now wasn't he? And as fine a man as ever stood up, a grand friend of the working man*—and the boy had grown up to be a lawyer. And now he, Jack, was about to receive an accolade. Some thrived on this—Bill Kunstler, for example; and so—in his way—had Lenny Boudin. Jack had never cared for it. Long ago, he had tailored a response. With a nod, he held the boy's thin arm, thinking that it made sense: it was not likely that he had gone into his father's profession, or his union, with arms like that. "That's very good work. I'm very pleased to hear that."

"Really? It just sometimes seems like such a total waste. Housing court's busting at the seams. This damn country. The rich get richer, the poor get blacker."

Evenly, in the same mendacious tone, Jack answered. "Isn't that the way it is."

"Don't you ever wonder what's the point?"

"Oh no." Jack was lying smoothly now, without second thoughts. Youth had stages, hope and disappointment, and to a young man in his thirties, thick in the first experience of the latter, there was no question how you responded. You lied. Later, in his fifties, he may learn a more durable, more informed, equally futile hope. And even later, there is something else—something stronger, a passage beyond judgment. Then, and only then—with the rare comrade who has lived long enough, and well enough to make that passage with you— you told the truth. Not now. He had decided this question long before. "No, I never think that at all. We've made tremendous strides in American law; in international law, in every arena. Sure, there are setbacks. But look at tort reform, gay rights, freedom of information. Look at the International War Crimes Tribunal. Look at the EU. And look at your own court—it may be imperfect, or overwhelmed, but it's not corrupt, and at least there's redress for tenants available and paid for by the government."

Brad Flanagan was listening, so eagerly that it made Jack wince with guilt.

"You feel hopeful, then?"

He hesitated, tightening his focus on the child. But this young man didn't want to know the truth. This young man was in mourning, for his father, for his father's time.

"Absolutely I feel hopeful."

Holmquist and Flanagan: two exemplary conversations, one short, the other sweet. Later, Jack Sinai couldn't remember how he and the boy had parted company. They must have talked more, because later that night, much later, when he was telling his news to his wife, a conversation neither short nor sweet, he knew that the boy had gone to BU and Northwestern, and that Northwestern was forgiving all his loans because he was just finishing ten years' work in the public interest. But he could not remember how they had said goodbye.

All he remembered was that after a time he came to himself again, pulling his gaze from the surface of the Hudson River, the glassine surface under morning sun, high-tide slack water not yet disturbed by the wake of morning traffic, with a line from a song his eldest son had used to listen to in the old days, a sweet, nasal-voiced singer: "*Our conversation was short and sweet.*"

Two conversations. One short, the other sweet.

6.

The short conversation had been that morning at his doctor's office at Beekman Hospital. A week earlier he had had a routine checkup. On Monday his doctor had ordered X-rays. On Thursday he called again and asked Jack to come in with his wife.

Jack had declined to panic. At eighty-seven? To be summoned by your doctor and told to bring your wife? This was not an emergency. It was an appointment, long scheduled, again and again delayed.

And he would not be rushed. His days had already had been choreographed hour by hour to leave himself open to an approach from Jasey. That meant being out and about and in public as much as possible in the kind of places where Jasey could evade surveillance. To make it easier, he planned—as they say—to "clean his tail" several times every day, doubling back through public spaces with multiple entrances; taking long taxi rides and watching behind for followers; going to movies and leaving, while the room was dark after the film started, through the emergency exit. Odd activities at his age. It pleased him to think that Jasey, following him, would understand. It was a form of communication.

A morning, however, in Beekman Hospital, speaking to Dr. Holmquist, would be a total waste. He would not be approachable in Beekman Hospital.

On the telephone, all the while downplaying the urgency, Holmquist had insisted, finally agreeing to a Saturday morning appointment: he had to be in the hospital that morning for rounds anyway. Jack had listened to the young man—Holmquist couldn't be more than forty—lying. He just wanted to be sure to see Jack before he, Holmquist, left on vacation. Then he contradicted himself utterly: Jack should be sure to bring his wife.

Jack didn't even listen: what mattered was that Saturday morning was the least likely time of the week for his son to make contact. Streets are too empty on Saturday mornings; there is no crowd to disappear into.

*

Of course he'd known what the doctor was calling about. Of course he'd had to go. Politeness demanded it. But he had not brought Eleanor—the suggestion itself was a characteristic impertinence of young Dr. Holmquist. In the morning he'd arranged to meet her later at the Spanish ceremony with Danny and Maggie, and let himself out in to the chill spring air. As if an act of defiance, he had walked downtown to Beekman. Eighty-seven years old, and he still swam every day during the summer in the pond at Hancock Beach—admittedly, no longer in the ocean. Later, thinking back, that walk had a slightly surreal quality. "Unreal," Jason would have called it in his druggy slang of the day.

The spring morning was so dry, and so chill, and the morning light from a still weak sun so long, only the naked trees gave the lie to the impression that it was autumn. In what he later knew to be bravado, he did not even think about Holmquist. Rather, as had happened all week, his mind reverted to imagining the contact with his son. This time he let play the scenario where they went to Wolff's Deli, sitting across from one another over bagels and lox, talking all morning as if the twenty-five years since they last had met was known, was understood. He could smell his son, the whiskey-rich odor of tobacco, the sweet fresh sweat of a young man. He could feel him, the smooth strength of his straight back and strong arms.

But then this scenario was interrupted by the nagging reality. How could they talk all morning when he was due at VALB at 11:30 and he was wasting half the morning with this idiot doctor? The thought made frustration rise in his belly, and it took all of his eighty-seven years to remind himself that it was all just imagination anyway.

That it seemed so inevitable? That was only because of longing.

The conversation, when it came, was very short. Holmquist was nettled that Eleanor was not there. Nonetheless, the facts were very simple. He had a lesion in his lower right lung that had spread to his liver and entered his lymphatic system. This was very bad news. Worse was that his pancreas was affected. Holmquist illustrated this with a little plastic model of the human body. Immediate, and very aggressive treatment was required. A course of radiotherapy and chemotherapy would be followed by a series of operations. Probably the whole lung and a portion of the liver would go. Following would be further treatment. Jack was to make arrangements to check into the hospital immediately.

But Jack had stopped listening when he heard the word "pancreas." He watched the young man sweating through the conversation as if from a distance. He should, he remembered feeling, help the young man out. Then he thought, perhaps, when you are being given a death sentence, you do not need to feel compassion for your executioner. Or perhaps you do.

Our conversation was short and sweet. Out in the street, in the blinding early sunshine, the empty downtown avenue on a Sunday morning, blocks away from his own father's law office, the line of the song had come to him for the first time. Holmquist had been unwilling to let him leave without an escort. But the one thing you got from the life Jack Sinai had led—a life that had included taking a couple-three bullets at Cape Tortuga and being left for dead in the Jarama Valley—was not being afraid of reality. Anyway that same folk singer had also said: *He not busy being born is busy dying.* Now there was a young man's perception. Should have been: *He not busy dying is busy making a living.* The thought made him smile.

And yet, he didn't feel like smiling. And he didn't care that he was dying. What he cared about was his conviction, his moral certainty, that today he would be in touch with Jasey.

Now it was sure. Now it *had* to be today. The realization came to him factually, a certainty, logically correlate to Holmquist's announcement. Tomorrow Jack would checking into the hospital, who knew for how long? It would be incredibly difficult for Jasey to visit him in the hospital, impossible really. That, clearly, was why the universe had arranged for Jasey to make contact today.

And the universe *had* arranged that. This incredible day. The depthless blue sky, the sun south over Staten Island, that high delta of distant geese coming back north, so high as to be nearly translucent, the mass and glitter of the huge, heaving river. Walking north now, slowly, through the brilliant spring morning, the ebullient expectation that had animated his week took hold of his mood again. Now he had something else to discuss with Little J.—how lucky, because his younger son Danny would be no help. Danny would fall to pieces at the news. In what was ahead Jasey, however, his strong, smart, stand-up son, would be an incredible support.

And then he was walking along the river, his eyes directed down, as if searching for a submerged object, or a fish, and a voice was interrupting him, *Mr. Sinai, you defended my father, William Flanagan, in the New Bedford's Carpenter's Guild, in 1953...*

I knew it. It couldn't be. Another conversation. Another false alarm. Young Brad Flanagan, his eager face, meeting his hero. Wanting to mourn his own father with Jack Sinai, who had inspired his father, who was dying. And Jack, shocked that such a demand was waiting in the wings, even now, even today, waiting in the wings, unable to say no.

7.

And as for Jason Sinai, he walked south along the river, holding my hand, squinting against the sun over Staten Island, the Colgate clock on the Jersey shore, the heaving, pregnant surface of the neap tide, quoting Whitman aloud—*Flood-Tide below me! I watch you face to face; Clouds of the west! Sun there half an hour high!* But in his stomach he felt anxiety swell, just like the high tide. 10:45. He had fifteen minutes to kill before starting for the Borough of Manhattan Community College. This would get them there just late enough to find their seats after the lights came down. Their seats were stage right, last row, next to the emergency exit. He'd found the plans of the auditorium at the Department of Educational Services website: BOMCC was part of the State University system. But how much further south could we walk? Already, I was complaining of tiredness.

So he broke one of the rules of his life and bought me a warm pretzel from a Sabretts guy—perhaps the second time I'd had white flour in my life—and a bottle of water; then we sat on a bench and while I ate he closed his eyes, tipped his face into the sun, and let his mind go through permutation after permutation of fear.

As soon as his eyes were shut my father's anxiety took shape in an image. He saw himself dressed in sandals and a T-shirt, perhaps a denim jacket in this season, his red hair thick and framing his face, a cigarette between two fingers. Like that, he understood something about what he was feeling. It was not his normal, adult fear of capture; it was the anxiety of adolescence, angst rather than fear, existential rather than situational. That's what New York did to him, and only New York.

Once, traveling from Penn Station to Riverdale he found he had actually gotten out of the train at 72nd Street and walked west to the West End Bar, only realizing, when he found himself in front of a Borders Bookstore where the bar used to be, that it was twenty-five years since Jason Sinai had last sat there with Teddy Gold, that Teddy was dead, that he was a middle-aged man in a beige linen suit over a blue shirt, and that his name was Jim Grant.

Now he fixed himself in his awareness of the present, as if to insulate himself from the city's influence. He was a forty-nine-year-old man called James Grant, a lawyer from Saugerties, New York, right next to Woodstock. He was born in Bakersfield, California; came east to college in Chicago, where he had met his wife, now his ex-wife, the actress Julia Montgomery. He was dressed in a corduroy jacket, chinos, and a baseball cap from Modern Apizza in New Haven, where he had gone to law school. He was in New York today to bring his eleven-year-old daughter, Isabel, to see the Abraham Lincoln Brigade celebration service, while there were still brigadistas left to see. He was in New York today to make sure his daughter heard, once, the International sung by Europeans who had sung it when singing it had meaning. And when he was done, he would go home to Saugerties.

Now the sun was warm on his face. Such a familiar sensation. A form of mindfulness. To become aware, specifically aware, of who you are and how that is different from who you are. The sun warm on his face; my hand warm in his. The anxiety ebbed, going out with huge exhaled lungfuls of river air.

And that was when he opened his eyes and found himself looking at his father, not fifteen feet to the south, staring into the river, and his heart went dead in his chest.

For a long moment my father froze. His father was standing, evidently finishing a conversation with a man and his daughter and then, when they took their leave of him, turning his gaze to the surface of the water. Then his father was alone. He could have walked up, and touched him.

But twenty-five years' training, twenty-five years of never looking back, never resting, the habits of twenty-five years came to him, woodenly, automatically.

"C'mon, honey. We best get our seats while there are seats to get."

"Aw, Daddy. I'm still eating. And I'm so tired. Can't we wait?"

There was no question, of course, of anything like that. Holding my arm gently, Jason Sinai stood and together we moved—myself unwilling, he wooden—off up the promenade.

And therefore not seeing that behind him, not ten to fifteen feet, Jack had, still with his gaze on the water, turned right and begun to walk, following the river, a dozen steps behind.

8.

"C'mon, honey. We'd best get our seats while there are seats to get."

Walt Arden, leaning against the fence, facing the water with Jack

Sinai just a few yards to his left, listened to the voice of the girl and her father as they walked away from their conversation with Jack Sinai.

"Aw, Daddy. I'm still eating. And I'm so tired. Can't we wait?"

"Later, baby. We got to go in now."

"You're mean."

He didn't even look back. He knew who the man and his daughter were—the same ones who had just been in conversation with old Sinai. Knowing that—putting together the details in a way that kept you from even having to look—was what made surveillance, rather than a science, an art.

It was while he was thinking this, with satisfaction, that Walt became aware, with a slight shock, that Jack, too, had just walked past him, heading north. In the same instant, Numeroff's voice sounded in his earpiece. *We're moving, boys. Pattern three. Three* was Walt on tail, Michael leading, and Richard trailing and calling changes. Walt stepped away from the railing, deliberately not watching as Jack passed. Richard stepped forward into lead. Walt didn't see Michael step back, but heard his whispered voice in his ear—*In position all. Let's roll it up and move it out.*

And so they went, turn by turn, up the side of the river under the shadow of the Twin Towers, in the riverine light, Walt behind Jack Sinai, Jack Sinai behind Jason Sinai, and Jason, with me, behind Brad Flanagan: a procession of people walking north, some not looking forward, others not looking back.

Chapter Four

Isabel Montgomery

May 6, 2011

New York City

1.

Okay, so you want to know what I'm doing. You're not the only one.

Uncle Joe, to name one example.

Although he seems, sometimes, to know more than I do.

For the next two weeks I work in my grandfather's study at his desk, only I've moved my computer in here and moved the antediluvian Mac to the closet, and also have sent away for a little Bose minispeaker system which—with the help of the Rasta dope-delivery dude, who has taken to hanging around after his dropoff, and who turns out to have, in addition to a surprisingly textured critical vocabulary for pinots, a very useful set of handyman skills—I think though he's still hoping to do me—I've installed and is blasting Billy Joel—Sinai is a corn dog, I swear, as you gathered when I told you there was Sinatra on this playlist.

The fact is, over the past two weeks, I have had human contact with exactly two people: the Rasta dope-delivery dude and Joe. I've got absolutely no problem with either. The Rasta boy is an unending source of interest, not just his sedulous efforts to do me but also his commentary on the world—the kid is a Chomskian anarchist, at heart, and smart as a whip. As for Joe, I got sick of this uncle-family-kindly-caretaker crap pretty quick; this dude was only pretending to be an old-school Soho wop. In fact he is a man who has thought long and hard about the near century of his life, and that thinking may have been fueled by copious amounts of his home-brewed wine, but it wasn't in any way marred by it, and truth be told, even misanthrope that I am, I don't get to see him half as much as I want to.

Oftentimes he is just not around, and when I go out into the garden—in which Joe's bulbs, which turn out to be tulips, are pushing up, and the branches of the chestnut tree are dusted with fine green—and look over at his house, the garden apartment is dark and the cast-iron garden chairs are tipped up against the table. The upper three floors, the Yuppie families who live there are doing their thing—having cello lessons, trying to get appointed to their private-school boards of trustees, getting in SAT tutors, or heating up their Garlands, but Joe's little garden apartment is dark and locked, which I know, because I tried the door more than one time. I don't, and never will, have any real idea of where he goes, although I imagine that he is simply withdrawn into an interior room with a bottle of red, and as I think that I can feel the heavy interior air, the dark furniture, the dim lights.

Wherever, it is never more than a couple-three days until I see him outside the window of my grandfather's study, carrying a bottle and two glasses, hear the back door open from the garden and feel his foot crossing the floor toward me.

At first I don't quite get it, and I turn from my obsessive documentation, if that's what it was, of the VALB ceremony of April 15, 1995, with something close to annoyance. What did I think? That I was humoring him, I guess. That there is nearly a century of pain in this old man, but I was not sure that his upkeep of the house was enough to justify being called on to listen to it. Deep in his wine—which is what made me think that the days I didn't see him, he was in his cups in some windowless room in his house—his eyes lose focus, and for long moments he would be seeing something not there.

But I am a smart little girl, aren't I just? Soon, I realize that something else is going on.

First off, although I have not come to share his contempt for Washington State pinots that pulse mellow with ruby and cost in the thirties and forties per bottle—yes, I checked—and rivaled, as far as I was concerned, anything coming from anywhere between the Loire and the Rhône, Beaune included—Bordeaux, I'm not saying—I had come to appreciate the viscous fermentation experiment that he conducted in his basement, which, as the French say of their Beaujoulais Nouveau, *se boit comme l'eau et monte directement à la tête*. See, I like things that *monte directement à la tête*—as you may have noticed—and there may have been a half-century between me and Uncle Joe, but on the subject of inebriants that *montent directement à la tête* we were strictly contemporaries.

And second off, it didn't take me long to realize that when Joe began to talk, I had better have a pencil poised—or, more accurately, a Bluetooth keyboard in my lap. Because when he did start to talk, his eyes still absented, he wouldn't notice the fact that my little fingers never stopped moving, and that never a word he was saying went unrecorded by WordRec.

And here's the strange thing.

It didn't matter *what* he was talking about.

It was all—all—to the point.

Such as—and I quote:

"Your grandpa and I? We was kids, we had met in the street, we'd have beat each other to a pulp. But we'd nevera met. His type, come down to Little Italy? He'd not have gone south of 110th Street, not alone, and wisely so. And me, go to Mount Morris? Not without brass knuckles or a lead pipe. Down here, we were bare knuckles. But they were *Harlem*. Remember, we're talking the '20s. Say what you will, those Yids were thugs. Still . . ."

Long silence while Joe's eyes abstract, and I wait patiently. Then, emptying his glass suddenly and holding it out for a new pour (I had become bartender long ago):

"I remember one. Iggy. My uncle—my mother's brother—was out in Sheepshead Bay . . ."

But I am not willing to get lost.

See: it's all too precious.

"One what, Joe?"

A moment of incomprehension. "Yid. I remember one Yid. Only one I ever met without beating the hell outa him, or getting the hell beaten outa me by him. Until I met Jackie and his crew of Reds, of course. But that was way later."

Silence again. "Thought you said Yids didn't come to Little Italy, Joe?"

"They didn't. But we left, sometimes, missie, believe it or not. I had an uncle lived out in Sheepshead Bay. My mother's brother. Those trips, oh boy. We'd catch the train at Chambers Street. City Hall? Like a castle floating up into the sky, it was to me."

It happens that I, too, like City Hall, because I once was interviewed on WNYC up in the tower of the castle itself. So it is with feeling that I say: "Still is."

"You should have seen it then. Chambers Street was like the fucking Champs-Élysées to me, missie, and I've seen the Champs-Élysées, in fact, I've marched the fucking Champs-Élysées. Going down there was like going to Europe for me. Then the train out to Sheepshead Bay, it was an El in Brooklyn—you know, elevated over the Gowanus Canal? You know it?"

And the thing is, it is important to him to know if I know it, because through those piercing blue eyes, when they focus, Joe is learning as much about me as I about him—or more.

"No." So now Uncle Joe knows I have never been into Brooklyn. I'm hoping he won't also learn that I've never taken the subway.

"I see. Suddenly you're shooting by Erie Basin, and you can barely see out to the Verrazano Narrows. That monster bridge wasn't there then. And then you shoot past neighborhoods of free-standing houses, with front yards, which I had never seen before. And then, oh boy, suddenly we'd be next to the ocean. Only times in my life I ever saw the goddamn ocean was in Brooklyn, till I shipped out with Jackie."

"And the Jew?"

"OK, the Jew. Well. Little scrawny kid lived down the block from my cousins. Never dared come near us, we was little, but later—in high school—one day . . . I don't know."

A long silence, while Joe stares at nothing. Then:

"One day, I don't know, we start to talk somehow. Maybe he had some smokes, I don't know. And this scrawny little Jew, he changes the world for me. Iggy was his name."

"How?"

Joe looked up, now, smiling.

"Let me put it this way. He taught me the International."

Bingo. "I see."

"Stupid, tiny little Jewish kid. Never told nobody about him. Forgot, in fact, all about him for years. Then I'm at a Daily Worker rally in Union Square, like '36, and there's this City College student, thin as a rake, handing out pamphlets. Fuck me if it wasn't Iggy. After, we get a beer, and you know what he told me? He was leaving the very next day for France. Died in the fall of Madrid. It was still months before me and your grandfather. Months."

See what I mean? It was all good stuff. I never found out what Iggy was short for, but I managed to get his last name and some months later, by the purest chance, met him again in a book by another wop called Ben Morreale.

Sometimes I would get him started with a question, which worked, because I never got the answer I was looking for. Like this one, right out of my notes:

"So where did you and my grandfather meet?"

"Meet?" His blue left eye hard on me for a moment. "Well, strictly speaking, I heard him speak at the Daily Worker rally in Union Square. Same one I met Iggy. Then we met on the way to France. But it ain't where we met. It's what we did."

"Meaning?"

"See, missie, everything we did, was for you. You know what we really, truly, thought? We thought we were building the International. The future of peace. The world that would be completely different. And what do we find when we get home? I should have known when the Stalinists came into Spain. We all should have known. We thought we were destroying the old world. But fuck me, there it was again, the moment we got home. *That* was the problem."

"That the world didn't change?"

He stares at me know with a moment of incomprehension. "No, missie. Of course the world doesn't change. That's just the way it is. People who mourn that, they're stupid. The problem wasn't that we thought it could. It was that he taught his children to think the same thing. It was the regret of Jack's life. That he taught Jason to hope the way he had hoped. That's what you got to understand, young lady. Not all this crap about New York in the '30s."

I thought about that one for a long, long time, and went back to writing, and thought about it some more.

And then I came back to it, albeit obliquely, and when I did Joe was right there too.

"Every century is a tragedy, Joe."

"There you go, missie. Now you're talking. And it's just where you're wrong. Ours was unique. Till you get that, you get nothing."

But like I say, I had been thinking about it.

"Joe, there are tens of thousands of combat-scarred veterans from Vietnam to Iraq. Don't tell me that Spain was worse, or World War II, or Korea. You didn't have Tony Molinari from over on Thompson Street coming back from Germany having inadvertently shot up the Jaibaji family's Sunday outing because old Abu Ali didn't slow down fast enough at a checkpoint and thus lost Ali, Nahla, Umm Ali, and Teta—the whole goddamn Jaibaji family, daughter, son, mother, and granny—to a twenty-two-year-old from Little Italy, who, in turn, lost a leg, an arm, and an eye to an IED planted by a teenager, and then went home and started thinking about three of his friends who were killed by mistake by a friendly fire drone missile and then decided to shoot up his local bar."

"Missie, you don't know what you're talking about."

"Oh come on, for Christ sake, Joe."

"Missie, you are wrong in so many ways I hardly know where to start. No, you shut up a second there, young lady. Lemme remind you a couple-three things. One: I was in Normandy on June 6, one-nine-forty-four, okay? Two: In 1945 I was seconded to the British 11th Armored. You don't know what that means, do you?"

"No, goddam it, Joe."

And you believe it or not, but if you don't, I got it recorded, so just fucking ask me.

"I bet you don't, young missie. And I bet you something else."

"What?"

"That you've never even *been* on the New York City subway because you always take *taxis*."

See what I mean?

"Why were you seconded to the British 11th Armored, goddamn it Joe, and what does it mean?"

"Well, have you?"

"No. I've never taken the subway because I always take taxis."

"Um hmm. Well I was seconded to them because by then I was a map-man, and no one knew lower Saxony like me, and what it means is that I was at the liberation of Bergen-Belsen. So don't you fucking talk to me about atrocity. Atrocity is *not* the issue. The issue is that we didn't come home having fits about it. We didn't even *talk* about it. *Why* is the issue, and the answer to the question *why* is what I'm talking about. The precise, exact difference between these boys coming home from Eye-raq and us is that we *believed* in something. We had *hope* in something."

"Oh fuck that, Joe." "*Fuck* that. A: Your goddamn 11th Armored, just like every other part of your Allied armies, fought the war against the Germans and tacitly let the Germans fight the war against the Jews for them. B: Half the rocket scientists working for the Wehrmacht went straight on to jobs in the US. C: the real war your fucking army of doughboys was fighting was the war against Stalin, only, they didn't bother telling you that, did they, cause they didn't want you to know that *they* didn't give a fuck about the Nazis, about you, or about whatever you believed. They had eyes only for Moscow. Believe? *Hope?*"

"Yeah." He drinks some wine with every appearance of satisfaction. "Exactly, missie. That's what I've been trying to explain to you. That we was wrong. But you keep not getting it. I'm not talking about our suffering, I'm talking about yours. Because the fact that we were wrong didn't stop us from believing because we were too fucking stubborn, and too fucking stupid, and that's what we did to you."

"What does that *mean*, Joe?"

"What does it mean? It means what happened to Jasey, and Danny, and Klara, and Maggie. Don't you see? It was *our fault*. We fucked up their lives. And now they're fucking up yours, and that's *our fault* too."

"Every goddam generation has people who hope."

"No. Not any more. Not the way we did. And not the way your father did. That was the last of that kind of hope, only, we were so full of it that we had to try to make our kids feel it. Me, who's going to listen to me? My son's a stockbroker. But Jackie, his kids listened."

And at this I felt, for the first time in a very long time, discouraged.

"Oh, Joe. Then what the fuck am I doing here?"

"Oh, girl, don't get discouraged on me. You're way too brave for that."

Brave? I know I look brave. But I don't feel brave, I feel lost. For a moment I considered saying that to Joe. Then I said:

"I don't feel brave. I feel lost."

"I know you do, girl. Joe knows that better than anybody."

"What do I do?"

He pointed at my bulletin board. "Exactly what you're doing."

On the bulletin board were the pictures of my family with, now, a multiplying number of Post-its with what I assumed were cryptic notes: "Passover 1996," "Danny's Yale Graduation," "The night grandfather died."

"I don't understand."

"Listen, missie. Families die. That's natural. Jackie died, Eleanor died, and soon enough Uncle Joe's going to die too. Then you get a little break, maybe, if you're lucky, before Jason and Danny and Maggie die. But families also get destroyed, and when you come from a family that's getting destroyed, you only have one choice."

"Which is?"

"To find out what's killing it."

With that encouragement, with that shot in the fucking arm, with that fucking Bronx cheer, I go back to work. And now it's May 6, and fueled by Uncle Joe's endless talk and the Rasta-boy's endless substances, I've gotten to the very end of the chapter about the VALB ceremony that you've just finished reading, and I'm just writing that last sentence about some of us not looking ahead and others not looking back, which I thought a good one, when I feel a hand on my shoulder and I jump out of my fucking chair.

2.

When I land, I turn to find Maggie, highly amused, standing there in business clothes and holding a briefcase. I turn down the music.

"What the fuck, Maggie. You serving me or something? You look like a goddam process lady."

She looks briefly offended, and actually steps out of the study to look at herself in the hall mirror, then comes back in and takes off her jacket.

"Well, I happen to think I look like an eight-hundred-dollar-an-hour lawyer who does a boatload of pro-bono, which happens to be what I am, but whatever you say, Ace. Now tell me, what exactly are you doing to Jack's study?"

At first I'm not sure what she means, but then I kind of see the place through her eyes, and she has a point. My grandfather's papers are everywhere—the desk, the bed, the floor—liberally interspersed with glasses and wine bottles. A cigarette is burning in an ashtray. Visible also is a bag of New York State of Mind, a little vial of pharmaceutical speed—Focalin, if you must know—and on the bulletin board next to the desk, the same bulletin board that Joe looked at, all the family pictures, and so forth. All of this Maggie takes in, which is bad enough, because the little worry that has been percolating at the back of my mind—what my lovely family will think about what I'm writing—is suddenly right in front of me, huge. And then, to my extreme discomfort, she sits for a moment to look at the text you just finished reading. When, at last, she turns, it is with a quizzical expression.

"What is this, Izzalah? You writing Jack's biography?"

I give it a moment, wondering if a lie might do. Then: "Not exactly."

"Then what, doll? Who said you could go into Jack's papers?"

She scrolls back on the screen and reads again for a moment, and as luck would have it, hits the exact line I was afraid of her seeing, about Danny and Klara on Hammonasset Beach.

"Jesus, Izzy. Is this why you've been harassing everyone from here to Sunday with questions?"

Finally, I find my voice, though in the event, it's not the voice I meant. "Stop it, Maggie."

"Stop what?"

"Stop quizzing me. First off, I don't need anyone's permission to go into my grandfather's papers. They're not fucking copyrighted and he's my grandfather, not yours. Second off, stop yelling at me."

"I'm not yelling at you."

"Yes you are. You want to know what I'm doing? I'm writing. You want to know what I'm writing? Then fucking take the time to read it." I reach over her, hit print, glower for a moment while the printer does its thing, then toss her the manuscript, and storm upstairs to the living room to sulk.

During which sulk I pour a substantial hit of Glenlivet, and am deep into it when, twenty minutes later, Maggie, considerably calmed, comes in. Again, she surveys the room with an expression by no means devoid of judgment, only this time, she is visibly restraining herself from comment, though whether she's being restrained on the state of the room or the state of the now decimated liquor cabinet, I cannot tell. In either case, she pours herself a drink and sits across from me.

"What are you doing, Iz?"

"That all you have to say?"

"What is it you want me to say?"

"How about, shit, girl, that's some fine fucking writing."

Silence.

"How about, way to go, Iz. Finally writing yourself out of that 'instantly disposable journalism' I've been telling you to get away from for the past n+1 years."

Silence.

"How about: At last. Iz, baby, you're writing the book you're meant to write!"

Finally, in a quiet voice: "What do you know about Danny and Klara and Hammonasset Beach?"

But I'm pissed. Defensive? Maybe. But pissed. "Not as much as I'm going to, that I promise you, Maggalah."

"Christ sake, Izzy. What is this, you're a reporter."

"Precisely."

"You reporting on your own family?"

And just like that, just like that, I start to cry.

Fucking baby.

Fucking *girl*.

"You fuckers with all your secrets. How the hell else am I supposed to make sense of Sinai before he dies?"

Which is all I have to say. Everything, just like that. Big, mean Isabel Montgomery. War reporter. International correspondent. Maggie is concerned enough not to listen to the last part of that sentence; she's out of her chair in a second, and in another, I'm way deep in her arms, sobbing my ass off, and she's not saying another word, not another word, just holding me and holding me and for a long time, in the living room, we stand like that.

Finally, at the tail end of my tears, sniffing. "You treat me like the fucking bad-girl orphan of the family. Bunch of goddam Jews with your little inbred language. How the fuck you think it feels."

"Iz, I love you. I've always loved you. Eleanor loved you. Danny too. Molly too. Even your father, no matter what you say. You're the apple of our eyes, you know that. You're our hero."

"No I'm not. Even Beck and that dork Ben know you more than I. I'm the weirdo little runt of the litter."

"*You* are? You? I'm the shiksa of the family, girl."

"Bullshit. Don't be ridiculous. Jack loved you. Eleanor loved you."

"Okay. Okay. It's not that simple. But okay. It's good. What you wrote is good. It's really good. It's like you were there. It's like it happened to you. I believe it. I don't know how on earth you did it. I knew you could write. Where are you going with it?"

"I don't know yet. I need you to speak with me. I need to speak with Molly. I need to speak with Danny and Klara."

A silence. "And our privacy?"

"Fuck your privacy. There's been too goddam much privacy for too goddam long in this goddam family."

I step back now, and now, I know exactly what I am going to say.

"I'm serious, Maggie. Thank you for the hug. Thank you for saving me when I was a baby. Thank you for everything. I love you. I really do. But that's my position."

A long silence. Then:

"So where next."

"The VALB ceremony. That night. When Jack learned he was dying. It's the heart of the story."

She considers. "I was there at VALB. And the dinner after. I know he spoke to Eleanor that night. But I wasn't there for that."

See? That's love. The real thing.

But this was work.

"Thank you."

"Then?"

"Then the night my grandfather died. Molly and Daddy, up in Saugerties. When Molly spoke to Sinai about her husband."

"I don't know anything about that, love. I don't even know what you mean. Molly was married before Jasey? I don't know *anything* about that."

"You will. And then I want to know about Hammonasset Beach in 1986 and then Passover of 1986."

Now I thought she was going to cry. "You going to speak to Klara? In Israel?"

"Yes. No. I'm going to speak to Klara in the '48 territories of occupied Palestine."

She let that one float right on by. Remember, she's a *Dissent* type. But she said: "You're going to publish this?"

But I was adamant. "If anyone will print it."

"What are you, the avenging angel? You going to leave us anything?"

I felt bad, but I felt sure, also, and for the first time in a long time, I felt like myself.

You may say I only feel like myself when I am being cruel.

"So? Do I have it right?"

A long sigh. "Yes, you have it right." Maggalah shot her drink, like an Irishman, and stood up to leave, looking old, looking like an old woman practicing hard, unconditional love. "When you're ready tell me, and I'll tell you about the dinner after the VALB ceremony. Then if Molly will speak to you about the night Jack died, and if Klara—in *Eretz Isr'ael*—will speak to you about Hammonasset Beach, I'll tell you about the Passover after. Fair enough?"

Now I really felt bad. "I'm ready now."

We cried a little more.

And then she began to talk.

Aren't you just the fucking consummate little professional. Aren't you? Cry for a story?

I've done so much worse.

Molly Sackler once told me that my father had changed identities so many times that he could often not even remember the person he had been last. It was by way of an explanation, when I was fifteen; I didn't understand it then and I am not sure I understand it now. As for my mother, by 2011 her memory had become as permeable—more precisely, semi-permeable—as her sinusoid capillary membranes, the osmotic porosity of which she had by then been testing for years, usually with fine white powders.

Not me. My problem is precisely the opposite. My problem is that my girlhood sits so close to the present that I feel trapped by it. In this I was, as you'll see, more Molly Sackler's daughter than either of theirs.

What I remember, I remember. And I remember that auditorium of the Borough of Manhattan Community College, in April of 1995, exactly. I can shut my eyes and see the orchestra, a descending sea of the backs of heads to the stage. I can see it: the stage itself, empty, with two wooden chairs in profile, stage right, facing a lectern on stage left. I can hear it: the murmur of the audience as, greetings finished, it settled into its places, the lights flashing once. And I can smell it: the musty smell of coats, all bathed in a heavy suspicion of something I recognized but could not name, the smell of the coat closet in Molly's rarely used formal living room. This last detail confirms for me that it is actually the VALB ceremony where my grandfather received his award that I remember, because Sinai remembers wondering about the same smell, only he could name it: camphor, and later, came to understand its source.

We found our seats in the last row of the orchestra, stage right. Here our view of the lectern was not great, but in retrospect I understand that the seats allowed my father a view of the entire audience and access the emergency exit, next to him on the left. These were the seats he had reserved after finding a seating chart of the Borough of Manhattan Community College's auditorium on the web.

And this, a couple-three weeks deeper into the spring of 2011, most of which I spent on Bedford Street listening to Maggie talk, is what I know—*know*—happened that night in April, 1995, to my father, my grandfather, and to me.

Chapter Five

Jason Sinai

April 15, 1995

New York City

1.

Sinking into his chair next to his daughter, as the auditorium lights flashed, Jason Sinai felt he was breathing normally for the first time since he had seen his father. He saw himself as a boy, shy and safe, taken to the theatre by his family. From fifty years away he smelled the camphor of his grandmother's coat at a matinee on Broadway, smelled it far within his nose, at his brain stem, with exactitude. Then, as had been happening to him more often recently, he wondered to whom that memory belonged: Sinai or Grant? Was he remembering New York in the '60s, which he lived, or Bakersfield, California, which he had invented? The invention was fact-based, researched, and precise. The problem was not that it was true, because it was. The only difference was that it was not real. It was like suddenly owning the memories of a stranger.

The lights flashed again, more slowly, and in the momentary darkness he felt inexplicably comfortable. So, then: he owned also the remembered feelings of a stranger, so what? Fugitives, too, had to become comfortable with middle-aged memory loss. But comfortable, for Jason, was always a word that demanded attention, because with comfort comes complacence, and so when the lights came back up he told himself to sit up, adjusted his hat and collar, checked on me and only then, when he was satisfied that there was no danger around him, did he lean back again.

On stage left, Victor Navasky was coming out now, taking one of three chairs behind the podium, followed by Henry Foner, a child-hood family friend of Sinai's parents, uncle to Eric, his childhood nemesis. From far away came the memory of his mother talking about him, "the Foner boy." Next was the actor Richard Dreyfuss. For a moment Jason was taken aback by his presence. What was Dreyfuss doing there? Ah, but wasn't Dreyfuss a Red Diaper baby? He was, Jason remembered, a man deeply imbued with his sense of his his-tory's pathos. Unlike Sinai, who was infused with a sense of its kitsch. The Spanish Ambassador, also a man in his middle fifties, resplen-dent in ceremonial clothes, was next.

Now what would these three make of Jason Sinai's presence there, if they had known? As the audience went silent, although the lights were still up, Jason found that he was able to catalogue their reac-tions with ease. Navasky: against. Navasky, from the younger end of the old left, would hold that Weather had stranded the Mobilization Against the War in '69, decimated it, and in the process given Nixon an excuse to demonize the Left under COINTELPRO. For a second Jason felt that the auditorium was cold. But then he reminded him-self, correctly, that Dreyfuss would disagree. Dreyfuss would be happy to be in the company of Jason Sinai: a romantic, the same quality that made him susceptible to the drama of his parents' story, would make him romanticize Weather, too.

Nor would he be alone. Jason reminded himself that many, many other people would welcome Jason Sinai's presence, likely a majority here.

And he was right, too. He was perfectly right there were more who sympathized with Sinai than who condemned. Even Molly admitted it, in the endless conversation about Vietnam that still characterized their existence together, although she said that this was because they don't understand the history, and on balance, Jason knew—and some-times, even, admitted—she was likely right. But the fact is, there is no litmus test of historical understanding for political conviction, is there? It's not like you have to know what you're talking about in order to hold an opinion, do you?

The train of thought was interrupted, but not stopped, when Moe Fishman, who now ran VALB in New York, stepped up to the lectern and in a few short phrases invited the Veterans of the Abraham Lincoln Brigade, those attending, to make their way to the stage. Throughout the audience, a stirring now accompanied the Veterans as they rose from their seats. And shifting his gaze away from the stage and into the audience, Jason found himself pursuing the same thought: he knew that many, many of these people had, in the day, been energized by the direct, simple expression of Weatherman, artful violence against the state, smart kids playing, successfully, with fire. Now, these years of dormancy later, many would see him as an avatar of their own best hopes from a time when they thought change was possible, a refreshing reminder now, when they accepted that it was not. And it was not only the old. Many young people, Jason knew, felt this way: both Ayers and Bernardine Dohrn swept the country on the lecture circuit, lionized by young folk who had no purchase in any existing movement for change. What movement was there, anyway? Anti-globalization? Radical environmentalism? The School of the Americas Protest? In each one of them, the romance of political violence was potent, had never gone away, never would.

This is what Jason Sinai was thinking, at first, as he watched the ancient Veterans rise and begin to make their way, through the audience, to the stage. Then, as he became aware of who it was he was watching, he stopped thinking, for a bit, altogether.

Aware not just of the Veterans themselves, although they were noteworthy, but of the rest of the audience. The many other veterans there, perhaps not of Spain but of the long, hard service in Europe or the Pacific. Others, of course, would be Dies Committee army rejects, "premature antifascists"—blacklisted for opposing Germany in Spain rather than in the US Army after the so tardy American declaration of war—Party members, Fellow Travelers. Some were in suits, others out of the mainstream. Berets abounded, some worn at a rakish tilt, many also sporting buttons referring to Vieques, or the Bush–Gore election, or—there must have been some union contest going on locally, because these were common—"You Can't Scare Me," and "I'm Sticking to the Union." An occasional magnificent head of white hair stood out among the bald heads. The women, in general, were dressed for an outing, some in clothes that looked as if they had not been out of the cedar chest since the year before—and thus the occasional whiff of camphor.

But contrary to his expectations, there were not exclusively old folk here. There was also a whole other dimension of the audience that was coming clear to him: the middle-aged, in fact, his peers. There were bald men of his own age, nearly comically resembling their bald fathers, women sitting shoulder to shoulder with their aged mothers, a few couples whom he thought he could recognize from Woodstock, or perhaps they just looked like the Sunday afternoon crowds crowding those streets. Now, as he became aware of them, he saw people of his own age everywhere.

And slowly it was dawning on Jason that that inventory of the audience, still, was incomplete. Because some of these middle-aged men and women were not there with their ancient parents, or even if they were, they were *also* there with their children. And their children ranged from infants to adolescents, even—and this dimension of the audience, as he watched closer now, was also coming clear to him—college students, many college students, some dressed in clothes, in fact, that would not have been particularly out of place at the University of Michigan in 1968.

Looking closer now—nearly squirming in his seat to do so—he was able to derive two important facts from the audience. First, that there were more middle-aged people there than could be attributed to sons and daughters of the old folk, and secondly, that there were more college students than could be attributed to the middle-aged parents. The conclusion of this estimation made his jaw drop: this event had drawn a crowd of people with no personal connection to the Veterans.

There were, Jason slowly realized to his astonishment, four full generations present here, from Veterans born in the first decade of the century to children born in the last.

To pay homage to the Veterans of the Abraham Lincoln Brigade? To honor his father?

True, there were only—perhaps—five hundred people here.

But—and here Jason mentally vowed to question this feeling more carefully later, perhaps with Molly's help—that was five hundred people.

Did that not constitute a community?

And now the veterans of the Abraham Lincoln Brigade in attendance today—most helped by children, many on canes, and some still amazingly spry—had made their way from the audience to the foot of the stage and Moe Fishman was at the podium with his black mustache, white curly hair, nodding and smiling happily and modestly before the applause, the movements—it seemed to those who did not know him—of a slightly addled old man, an impression that lasted just until Moe began to speak. *We are very proud of what we did in Spain, and equally, we are proud of all the activities we've engaged in ever since we came back from Spain.* The lights dimmed and Jason, listening, turned his attention from surveillance of the audience to the stage, watching his father's peers, realizing that, from his perch in the darkness, he would soon be watching his father, in the flesh, for the first time in twenty-five years.

2.

As the lights went down Walt Arden took his seat stage right, the last seat in the first row. Michael was in back, as close as he could get to the last row, stage left, and Richard stood up in the projection booth, empty today, watching out. Like this they had the audience within a huge triangle.

Walt's position, though, was key: only he, turning in his chair, or—when the lights dimmed—standing up and against the wall, could survey the faces of the audience. Which he did as soon as the lights went down and some old fool with a mustache climbed onto the stage and began to talk. *We are very proud of what we did in Spain, and equally, we are proud of all the activities we've engaged in ever since we came back from Spain . . . lifelong commitment . . . that we hope to pass on to future generations is the idea of commitment and activism.*

Walt tried not to listen. Proud of what the fuck, was his view, their role in the triumph of Stalinism? But that didn't matter. A good police officer was above his own involvement. These strange people, they only looked like they came from a different country. In fact, they were Americans, and in fact his role there was instrumental, not ideological: he was there to enforce a law and apprehend a criminal, if that criminal was stupid enough to show up. His eyes had adjusted to the dark; he began to divide the audience in quarters and conduct a first inventory of the faces, counting the areas where there were possibilities—middle-aged men—and beginning to draw a mental map.

Really, if this old fool was proud of a lifetime spent undermining his democratically elected government, of opposing his fellow citizens as they fought for their lives on foreign soil, of subverting the very constitutional processes which guaranteed him his freedom of speech and assembly so that he could wear his goddamned moustache and talk his goddamned bullshit, well, that was his prerogative. Walt's prerogative, however, was to catch Jason Sinai, and it was with a view to this, and only this, that he settled further back against the wall next to the edge of the stage, deep in shadow, and quartered the audience, and inventoried the middle-aged men in each quarter, and then, one face after the other, watched, and watched, and watched.

3.

This is what they were here for. Listening to Moe's introduction from his seat, center stage in the last row, clutching his daughter's hand, Bradford Flanagan, old Billy Flanagan's son, felt the old man's voice, clarion and believable, penetrate in his chest. *This—*this—*is what we came for.* And for the first time in this horrible year since his father had died, he felt something like okay.

This is what they had come for. To celebrate these men who, alone on the globe, during the few years that politicians maneuvered Europe closer and closer to war, were the only ones doing something rather than—like the powerless populations from New York to Paris, from Los Angeles to Peking, from Moscow to Miami, the whole world—watching with powerless fascination.

Brad closed his eyes. Since the winter in which his father died, he had felt only the dead. Now he put an arm around his daughter, felt her small shoulder against his chest wall, shut his eyes, breathed deep, in, out, and quietly, in the back of his throat, began to cry. His father's death had taken a massive toll on everything he cared about: his marriage, his finances, his friends, his health. He had been unable to work for a serious period, nearly three months, in which his wife supported the family and his daughter stayed with a babysitter. Finally he came at least part way out on Zoloft, which in turn left him nearly unbearably sleepy and fat. But even post-depression, this certainty that nothing good would ever happen again was proof to drugs. As if it were more than even a certainty. As if it were a mathematical conclusion. Until now. Now, sitting high up in the audience, for the first time in a year, that certainty began to shift. Brad pulled his baseball cap down an inch, and his daughter closer, and opened his heart, opened his heart, to the people in front of him.

Moe was finishing now—*there are fewer of us this year than last, but those that there are are strong of heart and hale of spirit, still on the barricades against fascism and inequality, and so like every year, please join me in welcoming my colleagues to the stage for the 60th*

Annual Veterans of the Abraham Lincoln Brigade commemoration.
And as they did every year the brigadistas, a dozen and a half of them,
stood to accept the huge, sustained applause from the audience, and
none more enthusiastically than Brad Flanagan, cheering for these
men in front of him and for the gift they possessed, the gift of having
once, purely, completely, done something of which they would never
be ashamed.

4.

A gift, Jack Sinai thought, watching these men from the wings, he
had never been able to share with his children, perhaps the only such
gift. Used to the potent narcotic of applause, out of sight in the wings,
even as the house rose for his comrades, he could think with clarity.
This gift they all had, this gift that was about to die. Money, property,
beliefs; all of these you could give to your children. But not this
kind of moral surety. And not only could it could not be inherited, it
could no longer be created. "The good fight" was an ethical category
that died in '39. The World War? Jan Karski spoke to Churchill and
Roosevelt in '43, eye witness to the Warsaw Ghetto and the camp at
Belzec, and Churchill and Roosevelt did nothing. What else was
there after the Nazis? Abba Kovner, his scheme to poison Germany?
Stalin? Now, what was it they were supposed to pass onto their children?

He rose now and moved into the folds of the stage-left wings, just
out of sight, and searched out his family in row G. There he was,
Danny, his handsome face with its natural authority exposed under a
broad, bare forehead, in a white shirt and black sports jacket, with
Laura on his lap. Next to Danny, Laura's seat empty, and then Maggalah herself, her shocking red hair standing out like a beacon in the
audience, her distance from her husband somehow emblematic of
the slight remove at which they, each busy with their own achieve-
ments, lived together. Or of something else. Jack knew a bit of what

had happened between Danny and Klara, when they were growing up together, at Yale in the '80s, and their walk on Hammonasset Beach, but only a bit—a suspicion more than anything else, and a suspicion—he had to admit—that he let lie because at heart, whatever had happened was his fault. Now Maggalah, his daughter-in-law, whom sometimes he was afraid that he and Eleanor loved more than Danny, was all grown up, a mother herself, and as an adult, she was hurt. She wore neither makeup nor jewelry; her skin was nearly alabaster under a fine sprinkling of freckles, and unless she was succumbing to middle-aged drift of her weight, which Jack much doubted, she was in the first couple months of her second pregnancy, still unannounced. Right now she was leaning toward Eleanor, clearly reassuring her mother-in-law. It was a role the young, strong woman took on more and more often, as if she sensed the family trauma that preceded her marriage to Danny which, Jack was reasonably sure, Maggie in fact knew nothing about. And why should she know what a surprise their marriage had been? That was, as Danny would say, a "no-brainer."

On stage, Jack knew, the microphone would pass down the line of the perhaps sixteen veterans present, each of whom would have the chance to say a word or two. Normally he would be one of them; today, his moment was held apart. First came Martin Balzer—"I'm glad to see all of you folks thinking the way that we did." Then Abe Verodin, taking the microphone from Martin, began what seemed to be a mid-length lecture on the history of the fight against fascism and Jack let his eye wander back into the audience. When the veterans were done, it would be his turn, and he needed to turn his attention toward what he would say.

But was he to say? After this morning? His eye rested on a middle-aged woman, handsome, sitting alone, next to an empty seat. What did he want to say? *I have a son your age. I haven't seen him in twenty-five years. I believe he's alive. I don't know where. You could be his wife, for all I know. I miss him so much.*

God damn it, he couldn't say that.

For one thing, he was determined to be short.

The problem was, Jack thought to himself, they—all of them out there—they needed it to be sweet.

5.

The wave of applause rolled over the audience when the veterans stood and, the audience rising in ovation, Jason Sinai found himself cut off from the stage, seated in a little hollow of standing people. Thinking of the irony of being here, a ceremony for which he would, twenty-five years ago, have had utter contempt.

He could remember it as far back as his adolescence, lying on his bed in the Bedford Street townhouse, listening to his father's voice, and those of his friends, arguing Israel, or Marxism, or Guatemala, or Czechoslovakia, out in the garden. It had enraged him then. The falsity of this need to feel that they had done something other than participate in a moment of history—a moment, furthermore, of a rank failure. They had failed to defeat fascism in Spain. They had failed to have the antifascist agenda even on the table in the greater field of World War II, in which they had been, most of them, promptly sidelined in any serious way. Even worse was the truth that no one dared pronounce: that they had been duped by the Soviets, used not only against their own government but worse yet by the Soviets against their own internal dissidents. The good fight. Fuck the good fight.

Now he smiled.

How easily he was able to feel the anger of his adolescence.

He stopped smiling.

It scared him sometimes.

6.

Which was, near as I can determine, precisely the minute that Walt Arden recognized Jason Sinai.

Not even he can tell you how it happened—how he accomplished, that day, what every best effort of every law-enforcement agency in the country had failed to do for twenty-five years.

See, Jason Sinai—like Mimi Lurie and Sharon Solarz—had built his phony identity in a time when birth and death records, both kept on paper, were not reconciled. You could assume what was known as a "dead baby" identity with virtually total certainty that the child's death would never be discovered. Everyone is always carrying on about how the FBI couldn't catch these college students, but how could they possibly? For Jason Sinai and his friends, it was like taking candy from a baby: all you had to do was go somewhere and search the town-hall records for the death certificate of someone born close to your own birthday, preferably in a distant location. Then you go to that location and copy their birth certificate, which was freely available to the public. From here? Driver's license, Social Security number, even passport—you could get any document you wanted. To catch Jason Sinai through a paper trail you'd have had to take every birth certificate in the country—he had picked James Grant's in Bakersfield, California, where he hadn't the slightest tie—within five years either way of his own birth, and then do a paper match up with every death certificate in the country.

Now, of course, it's all different. Then, without a paper trail, surveillance—of family, friends, known contacts—was the only option. But Jason—like Mimi Lurie, like Sharon Solarz—had never again, not one single time, ever contacted anyone he had ever known. Never. As for being recognized, to alter his appearance sufficiently to avoid recognition was a discipline, but one that he only needed until he had lost all his hair; that and a minor nose job had been more than sufficient. Friends? Not a single one from before the Bank of

Michigan. Family? But Jason, at nineteen, was not just *willing* to give up his family. He was *determined* to.

To catch Jason Sinai, after twenty-five years, required the simple, dumb coincidence of the one mistake in his career as a fugitive being combined with Walt Arden's extraordinary luck.

Walt, standing in the shadows of the stage, quartering and surveilling the audience while the brigadistas took turns with the microphone, realized two things. First was that he was not going to make a positive ID in this light. Second was that he didn't need to.

Why was because the shadow in which he stood was deep enough that he could literally not be seen.

And therefore he could, unobserved, mount the three steps leading into the stage-right wings which, because the lectern was all the way over on stage left, were entirely empty.

Moving very slowly, watching the audience for tell-tale moves of the head that would reveal that someone had noticed him, he stepped gingerly backward up the steps one by one until he was hidden, effectively invisible, in the stage wings.

Then he took out a night-vision scope.

Brilliantly included in his kit, this morning.

He mouthed the words *Thank you, Lord* and then, moving slowly, took out four computer printouts: the four artist's projections of what Jason Sinai might look like in his mid-forties. He lined them up at his feet and scanned them through the scope, then raised the scope to the first row of the orchestra, stage left, and scanned right.

Repeated row by row for the entire first quadrant, then second, then third, and then fourth.

And he would have repeated again for the balcony had he not, last row, stage right, next to the emergency exit, found him.

Really, it was incredible luck. Only the third artist's projection had any value, in that it showed Jason Sinai, aged twenty-five years, bald, and because he was bald, in a baseball cap.

Walt Arden's heart leapt into life. For a long moment he stared hard at the green image in the lens. Then he forced himself to look away. His heart was pounding nearly unendurably. It was a long suite of seconds before he could bring his attention back under control.

He gave himself a second look, very quickly. He wasn't looking for an absolute identification: he was looking for probable cause to question the man. It was a careful look though, and after it he decided to move. If he hesitated, he knew, he'd over-think the ID, doubt his own eyesight. If he was wrong, then he'd take the consequences.

But he wasn't wrong.

He was right.

And he knew it.

Gingerly, he lifted his mic to his mouth and spoke. "Gentlemen, I have a positive ID. Repeat, I have a positive ID. Jason Sinai is northwest in quad 4, the back row of the orchestra. He's in a baseball cap and is accompanied by a girl, perhaps twelve, perhaps his daughter."

Faint in his ear, Numeroff's voice.

"Christ on a fucking stick, is that him? I got him from here."

And Robbins. "Yes, *sir*, that's what I'm talking about. I confirm. I have a positive repeat positive."

Walt wasn't senior here, but like it or not he was walking point. "Go take a whiz, Mike, and when you come back, go to the back of the orchestra, northeast. Get Duane Street on the circuit while you're in there. Richard, hold your position. Let's wait till he moves—he's got a child with him, he must have to take a bathroom break some-time—these fucking old men are going to talk forever. Plan A is to take him out of the auditorium at intermission, plan B at his exit. Agreed?"

7.

It was agreed. In the bathroom, Mike radioed it in to the Federal building, four blocks away on Duane Street, and established a link to their local radio connect.

Within twenty minutes, the Borough of Manhattan Community College was cleanly, thoroughly surrounded.

Jason Sinai sat, smelling camphor, watching as one by one the brigadistas spoke to the audience, wondering where his father was, and feeling something he hadn't expected in the back of his throat, up where his spine entered his head.

Maybe it was the audience, so many people, so like him.

Maybe it was the college students, actual kids, coming to pay homage to the Abraham Lincoln brigadistas.

Or maybe it was the ancient brigadistas themselves, each one illustrating and indeed enlarging, because many were not Jewish, John Sanford's observation that in Judaism, it is the old men who are beautiful.

Whatever it was, the sensation running through Jason's throat and up his spine to his skull was one he had not felt in a very long time but which, as it happens, he was to have ample time to explore soon.

The sensation was tears.

8.

Jack Sinai, looking through the wings at his family while the brigadistas took their seats, heard rather than saw what was happening at the podium. Moe was talking, and Jack slowly realized that Moe was talking about him. A girl wearing a Che T-shirt was at his side, ready to escort him to the stage. He turned, thoughtfully, and straightened his jacket. He was too old, far too old, for stagefright. And yet that sharpening of the sense of the present, that emergency jettisoning of the extraneous—as the body draws blood in from the extremities during danger—was focusing him intensely on what he was about to do. Now the Spanish Ambassador, under a spotlight, was talking, and Jack found himself listening with mild curiosity. *It is my profound pleasure, on behalf of not just the people of Spain but of those, the world over, who honor the fight against totalitarianism, who honor liberty, who love freedom, to ask Julius Aaron Sinai, Jack, to the stage. Jackie, hermano: bienvenido!*

He watched his own steps out of the wings with super-real clarity, the girl in the Che T-shirt holding his arm. At the very edge of the stage he stopped her and, kindly, disengaged his arm. Then he was there. Standing in front of the handsome, larger-than-life ambassador and, while the ambassador recited an honorific that he did not hear, slightly dipping his head to allow to be placed the Legion of Honor medal around his neck.

Then he was staring over the audience, receiving the huge energy of their applause, a wave of noise that seemed to open and enter his heart.

This, too, was no surprise: he knew the amazing narcotic power of applause, and took what was happening to him for exactly what it was, pure pleasure, no more, no less. Something to drink in, to let bathe you in its heat, while it happened. Then, something to forget, because applause can also corrupt.

And it was a powerful force. The entire audience, perhaps five, six hundred people, clapping and roaring their attention. It eradicated doubt; it left you unable to feel pain. You felt it in your stomach and arms, not just your ears. Four full generations of Americans. He watched them with benign, warm gratitude, feeling—despite himself—a flush in his cheeks. From the balcony, a girl—college age—gave a long whistle, and a boy answered with a rock-concert shout from the orchestra. And the noise rose, if possible, a bit higher.

He was not going to give a speech, he knew that now. Just a few words of thanks, when the applause died, short and sweet.

But the thing was, the applause was not dying.

9.

Now what was this? The guy was *crying*.

Walt, trying to listen to Duane Street speaking in his ear against the roar of the applause, all the while watching Jason Sinai through the scope.

"Agent in the field, please advise. We can take the auditorium, or wait for exit and take him quietly. Backup is in position, either way. Please advise as to course of action."

Crying. Well. Nor was he alone: scanning left and right with the scope, Walt saw that there was high, very high emotion in the audience. It was the old dude on the stage, he supposed. Some kind of liberal sentimentalism. Their version of his own father's crying in front of the Vietnam wall. Should he tell Duane Street? But how would he explain it? Worse, how would they take it? He spoke up, loud against the clapping. "Duane Street, advise against any action. This audience could blow in a second. Emotion is high in here. The suspect is actually *crying*. I'd estimate at least a hundred college students."

That point did not need explaining: the possibility of a national scandal—a New York City Waco—was in everyone's mind. Robbins spoke up, and Walt felt a wave of appreciation in his stomach: "Duane Street, we have three sets of eyes on the subject. This sucker is as good as arraigned already."

There was a brief silence in his ear that coincided with a shift in the applause to yet another, higher decibel range as people began to rise through the audience. Walt listened, half to the noise, half to the silence on his earbud. No doubt consultation was occurring at the Federal building, and Walt felt his heart pound. These people were eminently capable of screwing this up.

"Agents in the field, you are advised to follow the suspect out of the auditorium and, if possible, make the arrest in the lobby or the street. Please confirm."

One after another, their soft voices: "Sir yes sir."

"Roger."

"Got it."

The last, breathed on a sigh of relief, was Walt.

10.

Dimly Jason Sinai realized that instead of quieting so his father could begin his speech, as if suddenly getting its second wind, the applause had grown, then grown some more. He dipped his head, surreptitiously, so I would not see, into hands and tried to wipe dry his eyes. Crying. Jesus fucking Christ. Then, instinctively, he took my hand and looked around, as if for danger. Here and there people were getting to their feet, then more people, and the clapping was still not stopping but growing, and growing, and a cheer was spreading, a huge, bass-pitched, open-throated cheer. On the stage, he saw the Spanish Ambassador take his father's arm, leaning over, saying something.

Jason had risen, by now, with the audience in its thunderous ovation. As if surprised to have done so. And standing, he found himself looking directly across rows of the audience at his father. He felt his breath stop in his chest. He was smaller, of course, and hunched, with none of the vitality Jason remembered: a very, very old man now. But his hair was full, shockingly white, and his gaze was direct and clear.

Jack Sinai, his father, clearly not quite understanding the ovation, was letting himself be led now to stage right, where two seats awaited him and the ambassador. He sat, and then the ambassador, moving slightly off and turning ceremoniously to face Jack Sinai, joined the applause.

What was Jack Sinai thinking? Probably something not far different from his son, who pronounced to himself, twice: Good God. Shocked not just by the standing ovation, nor by the occasion, but at the realization of how deeply they needed, these people, a reason to clap. How deeply they needed an occasion to hope. That slim, tiny little struggle over an enemy years and years dead—or not even the victory over an enemy, for they had lost in Spain, but rather victory over despair. It was that they were clapping for, Jason Sinai knew it, and perhaps Jack Sinai did too because, there onstage, slowly he began to recover his composure and to accept with grace this amazing accolade, not for him, he knew, but for something much greater than himself.

And then at last, at long last, the applause was fading, and the audience was taking its seat. The ambassador sat also. And now, at the lectern which Jack Sinai and the ambassador had vacated for their seats on stage right, a black woman in an evening gown had taken their place, and now the lights were falling, and the clapping silencing, until there was no noise at all in the hall except, when it started, the sudden pure soprano of the young woman, beginning to sing, pronouncing the words in a diction—and singing with a discipline— that revealed professional training, words that Jack Sinai had never thought to hear sung again:

> *Arise, you prisoners of starvation.*
> *Arise, you wretched of the earth*
> *For justice thunders condemnation,*
> *For a better world's in birth.*

For a long moment, listening to the girl's voice, Jason sat as if a spotlight had been dropped not on his father, but on him, stunned.

And then a new sound was added: a thin, high, reedy soprano, and Jason turned to the balcony to see an ancient woman in black standing also and joining the girl across the sixty years between them.

> *No more tradition's change shall bind us.*
> *Arise you slaves, no more in thrall.*
> *The earth shall rise on new foundation*
> *We have been naught, we shall be all.*

And from there, of course, in the way that will happen in crowds, the mood of the audience shifted suddenly, nearly instantly, and in one smooth motion, as if choreographed, the audience was on its feet again and singing together, open throated:

> *So comrades, come rally*
> *And the last fight let us face*
> *The Internationale*
> *Unites the human race.*

Unable to stop himself, Jason rose to his feet again, too, and as he did so, the house lights came up: someone had decided, while they sang, to light the audience. Staring at his father in disbelief as his father sat and watched out at the audience with an expression that defied description, but might be called amazement, a long, slow pan from left to right, coming ever closer, ever closer, until Jason, as frozen in the headlights, as if powerless to act, felt his father's gaze fall directly upon him, and stop there for a long moment before Jason, his knees literally giving way, sat.

11.

Jack Sinai thinking: no man should have to take this. It is just too much. The soprano had changed languages, but a huge portion of the audience was following her:

> *Debout, les damnés de la terre*
> *Debout, les forçats de la faim*
> *La raison tonne en son cratère*
> *C'est l'éruption de la fin.*

L'éruption de la fin. For God's sake. No man should have to take this, but especially no man who had had the day he had had. Onstage, Jack sat heavily in his chair, looking out at the audience, lighted now by house lights, watching the multitude—on their feet again, singing their hearts out—with the grace he could muster, nodding to the many, many people he knew there beyond the stage as the thunderous song went on, and on, and on: his son, Danny; his wife, Eleanor;

Maggalah and Laura, and behind them Raymond Hermann, an old fellow traveler from the Vietnam years, and up to the right young Alan McGowan, one of the very last to be blacklisted, in the '60s, and over a bit Ellen Greenberg, who had worked on Owen Lattimore's defense with him, and Harry Farmer from Defense and Aid, and Joe Salvatore from the Lawyers Guild, and Donald Black, Jasey and Danny's pediatrician, a Red Diaper baby himself, who seemed to be in tears.

But as the song went on, it was a face he didn't know that kept attracting his attention, directly across the audience now, from his new position on stage right. The face of a middle-aged man, nearly bald, with just the remnants of red hair under his baseball cap, in a corduroy jacket, not singing but silent, and Jack asked himself, why does this man seem so familiar?

> Du passé faisons table rase
> Foules, esclaves, debout, debout
> Le monde va changer de base
> Nous ne sommes rien, soyons tout

And then it came, slowly, like a sodden object released from the deeps rising with Brownian indirection to the surface.

I knew it!

Jack Sinai's heart leapt into life, an acceleration so rapid he was not sure he could bear it. Was he going to collapse? No—but his vision swam and for a moment, a long moment, he looked down at the ground.

He was, in fact, nearly scared to look up.

But then he did, and when he did, he found a hole in the audience where the man had been. Had he sat down? Jack stared and stared, not willing to lose the spot in the audience where, a moment ago, he had seen the face of his son.

12.

A slight panic had risen in Walt as the audience began to sing, then grown as it stood up again, and then blossomed when, watching Jason, he saw that the man's face had dissolved in tears. Why was that? What was this fucking song? What language was this?

> *Wacht auf, Verdammte dieser Erde,*
> *die stets man noch zum Hungern zwingt!*
> *Das Recht wie Glut im Kraterherde*
> *nun mit Macht zum Durchbruch dringt.*

Something about this noise, this high emotion, made him feel he was losing control. Should they take Sinai out? It was time for a decision. Smoothly, without a thought, he pivoted on his left foot into the backstage, out of sight, and pulled the night scope off his face.

He turned and experienced a brief disorientation when he found himself right behind Jack Sinai and the Spanish Ambassador. The girl in the Che T-shirt was staring at him in shock. Staring back, holding her gaze, Walt reached out his shield and held it up. He put a finger over his lips, *shh*. Then spoke into his mic, shouted really, over the huge noise of the audience singing, in English again, roaring really:

> *So comrades, come rally*
> *And the last fight let us face*
> *The Internationale*
> *Unites the human race.*
> *The Internationale*
> *Unites the human race.*

"Richard, Michael, I am made, repeat, I am made. Take him out now, repeat now, before the singing ends."

Mike's voice came back, nearly inaudible in the background noise. "Lost my view. Richard, you have a sight line?"

A long moment of terror for Walt. Then, thank God: "Can't miss him. He's standing, holding his daughter, in a baseball cap. He's crying his fucking eyes out. I'm heading up, can you see me? Follow my vector, come straight down and grab him from behind."

"Roger, I am moving. Walt, hold tight boy."

Staring at the girl in the Che T-shirt, as if his gaze were physical, Walt did more than hold tight. He held his breath.

13.

There was someone on the edge of the stage. There was someone on the fucking edge of the fucking stage.

In the dimness at the edge of the audience, Jason Sinai saw someone pivoting into the backstage, and every bone in his body moved to stand up.

Had stood up. Had grabbed my hand and started toward the emergency exit, like a skeleton clanking, toward the exit, all levers and ball joints, physics, no muscle, all will. All the while that the audience roared and roared:

> *The Internationale*
> *Unites the human race.*
> *The Internationale*
> *Unites the human race.*

14.

But what was this? Jack Sinai turned. In the corner of his right eye someone had jumped down a short flight of stairs from the stage wings to the audience, and began running toward the rear along the rail.

Singing had given way to cheering, a last, huge cheer, and Jack stood. There was something happening in the audience. He craned his neck, but it was impossible to see clearly into the standing audience. Two men were sweeping toward the emergency exit, carrying a struggling man between them. The man, in turn, held a child. The other man, who had run from the stage, was running toward them. Then it was all lost in the sea of people. What was this? Had anyone seen? It all happened so quickly, and apparently, no one noticed, because the thunderous applause went on, wave after wave after wave.

15.

Someone was running toward him, hard; the harsh feel of a large man's oncoming strength, something he had not felt for decades. Then, he would have responded with rage. Now, Jason Sinai slowed to face his capture. Two obvious cops, huge men, hands on holsters under their jackets, were coming toward him. In the corner of his eye there was a third, running up from the audience. For a moment, everything froze, suspended in the deafening applause.

And in a sudden second, he surrendered.

And then all sense stopped as the three passed him, converged on a man down the last row of seats, standing clutching, and lifted him bodily over the seat back. Then two, holding him by the arms, rushed him toward the emergency exit, his Red Sox baseball hat falling off his head, while the third lifted a child, a little girl, out of her seat and ran after them.

Brad Flanagan tried to shout, but one of the cops had a hand over his mouth; he tried to struggle, but in an instant they were out the door, his Red Sox baseball cap on the ground the only proof that anything had happened.

Jason Sinai, dragging me, moving on dead muscles, muscles paralyzed by the intellectual overriding of their irresistible instinct to flee, turned sharply left, crossed the auditorium behind the back row, stepping on the Red Sox cap as he went, and went out through the main exit.

In the hallway he stepped sideways into the bathroom, took off his jacket and cap and stuffed both into a garbage can. Now he rushed me to the edge of the lobby and stopped, watching a phalanx of agents bundling the man and his daughter out the front door into the street. Holding my hand, he turned left and strolled through the cafeteria to the courtyard exit, through the courtyard to West Street and then, and then, as soon as we were around the corner, began to run, free, still, so improbably, free.

Chapter Six

Isabel Montgomery

June 15, 2011

Martha's Vineyard

1.

My father will not know for years yet, unless what you are now reading is published before he dies—or unless, more unlikely, I show him the manuscript—everything that had happened that day.

My grandfather, of course, never knew.

Maggie, however, does, because I do show her the manuscript and she reads it in one sitting.

But not in Bedford Street.

She reads it on the porch of the Menemsha General Store in mid-June while I wait in Jack and Eleanor's—now my father and uncle's—house on the bay, where we'd gone in early June to spend a weekend alone. And while I wait, I sit on a rocking chair on the porch, hugging my knees and watching out over the pond.

There is a summer rain over us, today, coming down hard, patterning the surface of the pond with a million rings, which is apt. My earliest memory is of Momma taking me into the shallows of Colgate Lake, sitting me on her knee, my cheek against her wet bikini top, and showing me the rings that formed on the surface of the water when she dropped pebbles into it. Funny to think of Momma so young. Momma knew how to love when she was young. I know that, because I saw it once in Paris with some Nowhere groupies on four hits of some very fine acid, itself couched in 200 milligrams of

MDMA. The only thing was—and this I remembered clearly under the influence of the Medicine—I didn't understand her. See, I was focused on the sandy ground under the water, and for some reason I thought that the circles she mentioned were little silver bracelets— real ones—that were going to form and sink to the bottom, and with mounting frustration, I could not figure out why I could not see them. Under the drug, I thought to myself that that moment was, for me, the beginning of consciousness. Now, the millions of raindrops making millions of rings across the surface of Menemsha Pond seem only too apt a reminder of how entirely I had, all my life, misunderstood.

I never took either acid or MDMA again after that. Who the fuck wants to revisit the past when you're trying to get high?

I fucking hate being read.

This is the house that Billy Flanagan's union, the New Bedford Carpenters' Guild, built for Jack as payment for his defense work, and it is virtually unchanged since then, a memorial to Wakefield and Greene and Greene, midcentury populist modernism, linoleum floors, Formica tables, a breakfast nooke. It is beautiful and, to me, like a prison. No matter how clean it is, and it is a very, very clean place, it feels to me as if everything is covered with a light sheen of grime.

And this is the house to which Israel Singer, my adopted aunt's adoptive father, brought Klara when she came from Palestine in the early spring of 1969.

Sitting on the porch, watching the pond, I think of Israel Singer, in 1969 when he came to bring Klara to the States for a visit.

For a visit.

What a visit.

It was raining that day, too.

I close my eyes and imagine him, in the evening, walking gingerly down the sloped lawn, anxious not to fall. He had arrived that morning: Lydd—Ben Gurion Airport—to New York, New York by train to New London; then the ferry, trailing a eleven-year-old girl, his adopted daughter he hardly knew. Jack picked him up in his Dodge Dart; greeted him in Yiddish; then brought him home for dinner. When Eleanor met the girl, thin and gangly and tall, she was shivering and wet and Eleanor enclosed her in a long hug before taking her upstairs and dressing her, as it happened, in Jason's old jeans and a sweater—she was taller than Danny and Israel had brought virtually no clothes for her. After dinner, Jack and Eleanor took Klara and Danny to the Bite in Menemsha for ice cream, which may have been the first normal thing she had ever done in her life, and Israel changed into his bathing suit and picked his way, gingerly in the wet grass, down to the edge of the pond, the pond textured with the millions of little rings from falling drops. He limped from four toes lost during the winter of '44 in Bergen-Belsen. Jack's house was the only one on the pond, then, and no one saw him.

See, I know all this. I know all this. I know that his wife had died not six weeks before in the market-bombing in Haifa, where they lived, herself a survivor of Treblinka—I've read the death notice, in Hebrew, in *Yediot*'s online archives. They were childless, she had been sterilized in the camps, and had only had the girl for weeks, since the Jewish Agency had convinced them to take her after her own parents were killed in an ambush on their kibbutz in the Negev, and the children were all evacuated. Klara, anyway, had refused to stay on the kibbutz. When Israel went into the water he swam out for a long time, a very long time. The next morning his body was found by a fisherman in Menemsha harbor. The autopsy found fifteen undigested hits of Seconal in his stomach, and enough in his blood to indicate another fifteen had been metabolized. In his bag, which was otherwise empty, they found the empty container, prescribed by a shrink in Afula. That, see, is how Klara came to the Sinais.

I close my eyes and watch this. I feel the ache of phantom toes, lost to frostbite during the winter of '44, digging mass graves in shoes made of newspaper. I feel the wet grass against my feet, balancing down the slope, gingerly: I know I will break if I fall, and I do not want to go that way. I am dizzy, comfortably numb, as the first hints of Seconal titrate into my brain, and through the growing pleasure, I wonder for the first time about timing. How long will they be away? But I am at the water now, and I walk right into it, its textured, patterned surface of little rings under the rain. I swim out, slowly, on weak arms, not worrying about preserving the strength to get back to shore. Swimming to Shanghai, the sailors on the *Haganah l'Aliya Bet* steamer had called it, smuggling me to Palestine after the war; I remember it vividly. Then, when I can go no further, I turn on my back and close my eyes against the fall of the rain until slowly, slowly, I fall asleep. In my dream the raindrops, the millions of raindrops, turn into millions of corpses, tiny little corpses, thundering down from the skies, and the comfortable familiarity of Europe, Europe in the ruin it has meant to me, two thousand years of horrible Europe, washes through me: the smell of corpses, of garbage, of latrines and of gangrene. This is where I want to be, one last time; where I am meant to be—not that muddy, messy country next to the Med, but the ruined familiarity of Europe, and my thin body, as my lungs empty, lowers me in a headfirst backward arc into the ebbing tide out toward the harbor.

When Maggalah comes back, her Subaru grinding up the drive and into the carport, I am halfway through a breakfast beer.

Her hair is wet, glistening with rain, which I wonder about, as there was no need for her to have been exposed but for a moment climbing up to the porch at the general store. Her eyes are red at the rims, like she's been crying, and instead of her normal frown of disapproval, she cracks a beer herself, then sits next to me at the little linoleum table.

"This really what happened?"

"Precisely."

"Does Jason know?"

"Some."

"He nearly got caught that day?"

"Um hmm."

She hit her beer now, though just a tiny sip. "Would have been better if he had been, wouldn't it?"

I consider this for a long moment. Then, sounding more adult than I would have wished:

"No. It wouldn't have been. It would have been worse."

She thinks now, for a while. Probably about how Sinai did, in fact, get caught, just the year after the VALB ceremony, and how much better it was that way: exculpated, then, by Mimi Lurie's confession; able to resume his life and profession as Jason Sinai, reunited with his other daughter, my half-sister Beck. The only person for whom it was worse, the way it happened, really, was me.

But I don't have to tell that story now. That story has been told. What I need, now, is for Maggie to tell me about the evening after the VALB ceremony. Impatiently, I light a cigarette, and rather rudely, toss my iPhone on the table and launch WordRec. For a time we sit and listen to the rain on the roof. Then, at long last, Maggie gives in and reaches a cigarette out of my pack for herself and, in a small voice, begins to talk.

On reflection, though, I think that in some way more important than what they knew, my grandfather and my father didn't *only* miss meeting that day. Something else happened to them, too.

They certainly each thought very intensely about the other, that day, and did so under the same roof. You may say that makes no difference, because no communication actually occurred. But so what? This conundrum about communication, in my view, has always been a canard. In what did, in fact, happen during the months of his death, my grandfather may just as well have been speaking to my father daily on the telephone, so exactly did he do what my father needed him to. As for my father, say what you want, but I know for a fact—

149

for a fact—that in the months after that April Saturday in 1995, my grandfather was never out of my father's thoughts for more than minutes, and when he died, my father was all there, in body and—well, whatever you would call it when you sit shiva, as my father would be doing in a few months. So what more can a father and child ask of each other? Explain to me how things would have been different— what each could have asked of the other—had they actually met?

That leaves just me, and I was only a child. But now, years later when I come to find out exactly how much had changed that day, I feel more strongly than I can tell you that I am learning nothing new. Just the exact terms by which an awareness of change had come to me, one that I would have the rest of my life.

Driving back upstate that early spring evening in 1995, my father and I, watching the greening borders of the Thruway grow dark as the sun came down in the west and the Catskills came up in the north, I think we all knew exactly how much everything was about to change.

What we didn't know was how. And we did not understand, yet, that the change would come just months too late.

By winter, my grandfather would be dead.

Chapter Seven

Jack Sinai

April 15, 1995

New York City

1.

In the uproar of the ovation, no one had really noticed what had happened to Brad Flanagan and his daughter, and by the time the ceremony was over the FBI had totally cleared out. There had been the rest of the ceremony—Navasky, Richard Dreyfuss, more singing. There'd been the refreshments, surrounded by warm bodies in the packed college cafeteria, Jack's eyes constantly focused beyond his interlocutor on the possibility of his son. A cocktail was hosted at someone's Tribeca loft, and afterward, a long dinner at a Village restaurant, hosted by the Tamiment Collection at NYU Library, where Jack's papers would be housed after his sons' deaths: a long, drunken dinner at a table for twenty, ranging from young women with pierced noses and black clothes to old men in musty suits and black berets. That was one of the few perks of being on the left, Jack knew, the chance to be at table with the young.

The pleasure, however, was all visual. Eleanor and he had a running joke in which they assigned a date in the history of the American left appropriate to the level of political sophistication in any such discussion. This one, tonight, in which a particularly strident young woman with a crew cut was arguing the viability of domestic terrorism on global business and environmental targets, they agreed on with a single shared glance: 1970.

March 6, 1970, to be exact.

A particularly depressing moment in American history, and they had both, conspicuously to their peers although not to the young woman who was talking so much, stayed silent until someone with a bit more historical perspective, and tact, had directed the discussion away.

And after? They came out of the restaurant. There was rain in the air, the chill of an approaching spring rain. Looking up, Jack saw a half moon lighting the way for clouds moving in over Manhattan from the ocean. Under that sky they walked, Jack and Danny-boy with Laura on his shoulders; Eleanor and Maggie side by side, through the dark Tribeca streets and up to the Village.

They walked slowly, nearly aimlessly, the wind—revealed on the east–west cross streets—moist and smelling of the sea.

In front of the door to their house, Danny and Maggie took their leave. Jack thought the two were going to announce Maggie's second pregnancy. But perhaps they did not want to do it in front of Laura, and so they parted company at the door, the kids to their car and then up to the Upper West Side; Jack and Eleanor into their house on Bedford Street.

A heaviness had come to Jack Sinai as they made their way from the parlor floor down the back maid's stairs to the kitchen where Eleanor, in slow, practiced movements, put on the kettle for tea. Watching her from the table, he tried to weigh the feeling, which seemed an old one, distantly familiar, and to his surprise, the image that came to him was of a minor infidelity of his middle age, a woman who had kissed him once in a Chicago hotel. Now why would that image have come to him tonight, he wondered? Then he understood. It was because of the secret he was keeping from her now.

Still, he kept silent. They spent an hour at the kitchen table, drinking tea, Eleanor, her veined, aged hand on his, going over the evening with him, unaware that anything—everything—had changed. Jack had been on the verge of telling her about Holmquist. But it had been so long since they had basked, so thoroughly, in the potent narcotic of applause, so long since they had sat so peacefully here, in the kitchen, and Jack let her bask some more. Then he was going to tell her, but she'd risen to go upstairs, not to sleep but to read until he came up too, and he'd decided to wait until then.

And now it was heading for midnight and he had read the mail and still he had not gone up.

Rather he was sitting at his study desk in the yellow light of his lamp—lamp that had lit the same desk with the same yellow light for fifty continuous years—watching the branches of the ancient backyard chestnut out the floor-length window waving in the gusts of spring wind across, under the half moon, the dirtying sky of clouds.

It had been there as long as they'd had the house; had accompanied his children from birth to adulthood, its branches moving in wide, sweeping gestures across the window, and it was there now.

And then, out of all the day's impressions, from the morning with Dr. Holmquist to the award ceremony, what he saw was the young crew-cut woman at the dinner table, arguing a defense of political violence, entirely unaware of the effect her words were having on the aged couple at the table; unaware, perhaps, that these two interlocutors of the conversation she was monopolizing were the parents of Jason Sinai.

2.

March 6, 1970. The papers had been breathing sighs of relief that the '60s were over; Students for a Democratic Society had self-destructed in December of '69; the first three months of the decade had been nearly ominous in their quietude. Then, on March 6th in the morning, the Wilkerson house on West 11th Street had erupted in a long dynamite explosion that had shattered windows all the way down to

Fifth Avenue. Jack learned about it when Lenny Boudin called; the Lawyers Guild offices at 5 Beekman were only a few minutes' walk from Jack's office in the Exchange Building. He and Lenny had met out on the corner of Nassau Street and taken a cab up to the Village. That Jason, and Kathy—Lenny's daughter—had been involved with the Wilkerson girl was not in doubt: Lenny and Jack both knew her, as they knew Ted Gold, and Mark Rudd, and Brian Flanagan, and Harold Markson, and David Gilbert, and all the other SDS kids from Columbia who had come together in New York over the strike and occupation. There was every reason in the world to believe that their children had been in the townhouse, and they rode the taxi north in a silence so tense, you could hardly breathe.

The newspapers took days to catch up, but by midafternoon Jack was certain that the two women who had left the burning house after the explosion and begged clothes from the neighbor had been Lenny's daughter Kathy and the other one, Cathy Wilkerson—the neighbor was Susan Wanger and Jack had been able to get to her, discreetly, through a client, her ex-husband Henry Fonda. Even after he knew that his own daughter was safe, Lenny stayed on with Jack and Eleanor right through the night. By evening they knew—this time through a Manhattan DA—that two of the bodies had been identified as Diana Oughton and Ted Gold. There was evidence, however, that a third person had been there too. But the third body had been virtually vaporized by the blast—presumably it was the bomb-builder—and they had to rely on the FBI to identify it from a single surviving finger.

That shouldn't have been any problem: COINTELPRO had prints of the entire anti-war movement by then, and Jack had long been convinced that it had taken them not hours but minutes to make their identification of the final body. That they'd let parents across the country sit up all night in anguish was a policy decision. This was how they operated. Even in the '50s they had been implacable, brutal. It was their policy that required them to sit up that night on Bedford Street, so literally sick with worry that Jack had at a certain point, suddenly and without warning, leaned over and thrown up on the living-room kelim.

All through that night Lenny had sat up with them and later, when she came over with some food, so had Jean, who was still well enough to do such a thing. And it was not until 5 a.m., when Eleanor and Lenny and Jean had all dozed off in their chairs, that Jack, acting on a hope so slim that he had been embarrassed to pronounce it, even to Eleanor, had let himself out of the house into the chill dawn, in his shirtsleeves, and walked down to his office in the Exchange building.

There, on the twenty-second floor, he'd opened his office and examined the contents of the room. So enormous was his desire to find something changed that he could nearly not tell the difference between fact and fantasy, could not be sure of the simple forensic evidence that might reveal whether Jason had been there. Had someone been sitting in his desk, using the telephone? Papers seemed to have been moved, and a box of his cigarettes, Shermans, was nearly empty—had he left it so? The universe before the bomb explosion seemed so distant it was impossible to recall with any certainty. Finally Jack had opened the office safe, reached in for the little package Jason had asked him to keep there, a package—he'd assumed—containing documents necessary for constructing a new identity, and found it gone. That was conclusive: Jason was the only person in the world with the combination to that safe. For long, long moments by the open safe Jack had leaned his head against the surface of the desk. Now the entire office arranged itself in confirmation: the phone, the papers, the cigarettes. Jason had been there—after the explosion. So one kind of pain, which had lasted all night, ended, and another, which was to last the rest of his life, began.

It was the very next day that Jack gingerly placed in the safe in his office the little pile of thousand-dollar bills, in case Jasey ever came back, which a quarter-century later his granddaughter, whom he never met, found in his desk, and spent at the Apple Store.

3.

Now, in his study, at his desk, murkily lit by the ancient desk lamp and the big bulk of a Macintosh that Danny had bought for him and which he never used. It was, literally, book-lined. Next to the little bed he kept there, in the style of a Russian nobleman, there was a halogen lamp for reading, but he kept that off. On the floor was a rug worn thread-thin; a single easy chair, largely for the convenience of the cat. The ceiling was in stamped tin, the style of the house when they bought it in the early '50s with a windfall from work he'd done for Dalton Trumbo. That is, a windfall from before the blacklist: while Dalton was writing in exile from Mexico, Jack had of course discreetly handled his pseudonymous work and refused any commission.

Midnight gone. Jack was no longer at the desk. He stood by the window, hands in pockets, looking up. The moon was fully behind clouds that were thickening to rain, a black, wet presence, felt rather than seen, beyond the branches of the chestnut, lit now only by the light from Eleanor's window above him, where she lay reading, waiting for him to come up.

It would have taken Jason some time, had he been here, to recognize that expression on his father's face. It was one his father had learned long after his elder son left. Nor would Jason have recognized the shape of the body before him: Jack's elder son had only known him a vital, strong man—sixty-one when Jasey went underground. Now he was much shorter than the man he had left, rounded at the shoulders, bulkier. Still, as his younger son, Danny, would find, during the months of Jack's illness when he did considerable nursing, unbelievably strong. It was, perhaps, no longer a strength you could see.

In any case, Jason would not really have been able to see it. The room was too dark.

Beyond the study door, in the garden floor of the house on Bedford Street, the family room with its walls of shelved novels, the kitchen and dining room with its ingenious table that, when you fully unfolded it, seated thirty on Passover. Upstairs was the living room, a full parlor floor-through with both the grand staircase leading up and the maid's stairs going down to the kitchen; then two floors of bedrooms, three per floor, of which one was theirs—Eleanor lay in bed in it now, reading until he came up—and one was Eleanor's studio and the rest were empty save for when Danny and his family stayed over, as they would doubtless do, Jack found himself noting, for the next several months. Then, he thought with satisfaction, those rooms would again be full.

And with this thought, Jack realized that he had shifted his mode of thought entirely.

A moment ago, he had been reminiscing.

Now he was planning.

Ah, what a relief. To be in the future, of which you had control, rather than the past. Clearly there was no question of going to the hospital. Jack had decided this the minute Holmquist said "pancreas," though he had perhaps not admitted that he had decided it until now. He knew sixty-year-olds who had died from pancreatic cancer within a month of diagnosis, and that with every possible treatment. For Christ sake, the last time he had spent a night in hospital was with a bullet in his neck in 1937. In quick succession he saw hospital rooms, surgery, the half-consciousness of morphine, and although what he was seeing was a prewar Spanish infirmary, he knew that in no substantial way had anything changed, particularly the pain, the second-by-second experience of endless, unendurable pain. That, and the constant danger of infection. He wasn't going into such a place, especially not with his immune system knocked flat by chemotherapy, for God's sake. A final Passover; a few months of illness. They would jump to Israel right away, while he was still fine, and see Klary. Then, one day, he'd climb these steps to his bedroom for the last time and settle in. They had wonderful painkillers. He would have considerable control of their dosage. In his cupboard already were sixty-five tablets of Seconal, just like Israel Singer had used. At the rate he took ten huge Metamucil caplets every night, sixty-five Seconal would be in his stomach in minutes. Then you pump the morphine until you lose consciousness. That, as the kids say, was a no-brainer. And by winter he would be out at Acacia Cemetery, next to the Long Island expressway, next to his father, and his uncles, and his aunts and his cousins, all of those who had done what he was, in his turn, about to do—that is, die.

Telling Ellie he was staying home, that would be the hard part. There was no question about that. She would perhaps need a conversation with Holmquist before she understood. She was fifteen years younger than he, still in her seventies. Of course she'd get there in the end. Maggie could help, and then Klara. Until then, he could pretend he were considering treatment. Meanwhile, he could take Danny into his confidence.

That would be less hard. It was a good ten years since carefully, one step at a time, he had started treating his last son as a grown man. This shock, now, would be one for which he was prepared. He was, after all, nearly forty. Danny was an emotional person. But they would have a lot of time to talk; he would have many, many hours of talk to help Danny into this next stage of his life.

Then there was Klara. He would call the travel agent in the morning: they could spend a week, two weeks with her in Tel Aviv while he could. There are worse places to be when you're ill than Tel Aviv. In fact, there are not many better. Klara had not been home for nearly ten years, and would likely not come now: even if she could bear to come home: her work, for the Commerce Department, would not allow it.

Eleanor, Danny, Klara. As for himself, everything was in order. Living will, DNR instructions. There was a substantial estate. Eleanor, then Danny and Klary, would be fine. As for Jasey, when he surfaced he'd find not only his third of the estate, but every penny Jack and Eleanor had ever spent on Danny—high school, college, law school, summer camp, birthday—sagely invested in the '70s and quadrupled in value through the '90s, since Danny had taken over management of the money, all waiting. The only thing left undone was his papers, stuffed into the drawers of his desk. In the morning he'd go over to the stationers on 6th Ave—not the big new Staples, but the stationers that charged twice as much and had been there as long as he—and buy some of those big legal portfolios. He didn't need to do much. Sort them by decades maybe. That way, Danny and Jasey could make sense of them, if they wanted, before Tamiment got them after their deaths.

Now the sky was slapping the leaves of the chestnut with fat, gusty drops of rain.

There was only one piece of unfinished business.

Little J.

My father.

Now what could he do for Little J.?

The steps were as clear as one, two, three.

Give an interview. Say he was dying. Sit back and watch. One, two, three. Because as sure as there would be sun, somewhere, tomorrow, when Little J. read that he would come find his father. When Little J. read that, he would come find him. Without the slightest hesitation, Jack measured his son's awareness of the world, a man heading to fifty, perhaps with children, who had lived in regret for twenty-five years. As sure as there was a T in goddam Tennessee, Little J. would come to him then.

No matter what the danger.

No matter what the cost.

Watching the rain slapping the leaves, Jack traversed a long moment in which he told himself that he knew it, he knew it, he knew it.

And then, in a slow movement, he admitted to himself what he knew, had always known, to be true.

It couldn't be.

And he had to stop it.

*

It was the murder charge, you see. The preposterous murder charge. Jasey would never kill a person. Jasey would kill himself before he killed a person. But Dellesandro had, and accessory—given *mens rea*—was what they were calling, these days, a superprecedent: it was bedrock law. If Jasey were in fact there at the Bank of Michigan, which all evidence said he was, then he was accessory after the fact, and nothing in God's green earth was changing that.

The problem was that the Michigan Three—Jason and Mimi Lurie and Sharon Solarz—had not only gone underground in 1970 with the rest of Weather, but they'd then broken with Weather in '74 when the self-styled "Weather Bureau" had publicly disassociated themselves from the Bank of Michigan robbery. Up until then, from '70 to '74, while Jasey had been underground, it had been horrible, but less horrible. There was an actual network of communication; some kids—not Jasey, but others—even found ways to communicate with their parents, and parents found ways to get money to their kids. Jasey hadn't gotten in touch, not once, ever, but thank God Annie Stein had sometimes been more of a mother than an ideologue and had checked up on Jasey through her daughter and let Jack know, from time to time, that his son was okay. Then Annie had died, and that slim conduit of communication had disappeared.

At first they had kept up with some parents. Which ones, that's a secret they kept and which even he never found out: there are many more Weather fugitives than remain in the public eye, and some of those parents had sought each other out, desperate for any information they could get from each other, those horrific weeks when, like a ghastly fairytale, all their children had disappeared. Sometimes they'd help each other, get a chance to get some money to one of them for a medical bill; get news of a family death.

Then, like another kind of fairy tale, their kids came back. In the late '70s, when kids from Weather began to surface, he'd gone to them each, one by one. Everyone had told him they didn't know where Jasey had gone. Was it true? A ridiculous old man begging for help from the young, but he had scoured their faces to see. Some, clearly, didn't know. Others wouldn't have told him if they could. Some were unbelievably cruel, like the one from the Midwest, a beautiful blond-brunette girl with a law degree. He particularly remembered the look in her eyes, the tortuous glare of contempt of the young and powerful. He'd seen it in Spain; he'd seen it in Washington; he'd seen it in Union leadership; and he'd seen in it in Roy Cohn's saurian eyes. And yet, that same girl had gone to prison for eight months in the '80s rather than testify against her former friends, and had since then done wonderful work in environmental law. So people were complicated. It wasn't required to be kind to be right. He'd also seen that in Spain.

Finally, Annie's daughter—a girl sometimes capable, like her mother, of being kind rather than being right—explained to him that, in fact, none of them had known where he was, not for years. Jasey and his two partners had severed all ties from their former colleagues as early as '73, and after the robbery were in absentia kicked out of Weather. She had told him that on the Upper West Side, walking outside, just as Annie, with her experience in the Communist underground of the '50s, would have done, on the banks of the Hudson, watching that same damn river flow.

It was the murder charge, you see, that made this story so unendingly hideous. The others, even the few who served time, had come back to their parents, to their families. The Stein girl was a woman with a career and a husband, a house and two sons. Bernardine Dohrn and her husband lived in Chicago, both professors, raising their own two children and Lenny's grandson, worrying about private schools and SATs; Mark Rudd lived and taught in New Mexico. All of them had repaired the horrible injury to their own families and gone on to be wonderful parents themselves, even those who remained as adults what they were as children, that is, pricks. But Jasey was wanted as an accessory to murder. David Gilbert was serving seventy-five years to life for a murder of which he'd had no knowledge, just for driving the car. And there was no statute of limitations on accessory to murder.

It was pouring now, the skies wide open, the wind blowing the sodden branches of the chestnut, this way, then that. You were supposed to lose your children to puberty. Then you were supposed to get them back. An endless adolescence was a form of hell. But Jack, by the window, watching the spring rain, was convinced that it would have ended. If Little J. had been able to come back, Jack was sure that they could have found . . . found what? he asked himself. Found . . . a way across the '60s. He was sure that Jason, with age and time, would have come to understand the similarity between his father's experience and his own; would understand that the rejection of his father, the cruel rejection by the harsh New Left of the Old Left had been a personal act rather than a political one. Jack was sure that Jason would have come to see that what he and his friends believed wasn't the slightest bit different from what Jack and his friends believed—that the worker's paradise was inevitable, that the final fight was at hand to transform the world from the old to the new. *It's the last fight.* The last fight, for Christ sake.

Hadn't they both failed in identical ways?

And hadn't Jack walked away from his father too?

Hadn't he, too? Heading to Spain to a fight as insane as Jason's, at his age too, and never had he seen his father again either, because by the time he was back from Spain, his father was dead.

God. How he would have liked to explain. He had gotten to tell Danny, in detail. It meant something different to Danny. To Danny, it was bibliography; to Jason: biography. Jason would have had an entire other understanding of his father, especially of his father leaving his father. Little J. would have been able to travel to the depth of the experience, understand the full profundity of what his father had done, and the comparison would have helped because it would have relieved Jasey of guilt. Jack was an only son; a precious commodity in the New World, born in an age where children died at shocking rates. His father, at one year old, had been brought to New

York by his father's uncle, old Yankel Singer, then only fourteen—a fourteen-year-old and an infant crossing the Atlantic in steerage!— after his mother had died in a pogrom and his father was drafted into the Russian army. The primitiveness of that world! And Jack had, a generation later, left his father in New York without a second thought, buying passage on a cargo ship from Brooklyn to Biarritz and then walking across the border to Spain, the Bay of Biscay glittering below him on the mountain trail.

The deepest regret in his life, Jack thought, the single most horrific regret is that he couldn't tell Jason that; couldn't tell his son that he did not disapprove, he *agreed* with what he had done. He had to. Others could perhaps be contemptuous. But the same impulse that had driven Little J. into Weather had driven him into the Lincoln Brigade. Nor was it the slightest bit more stupid to have gone up against the American government in Weather than it had been to go fight Franco and Hitler with a couple thousand other volunteers, a tiny army of idealists backed only by a revolutionary government in the Soviet Union that the Wehrmacht, occupying the countries at its borders at will, had laughed at. So who was stupid?

Weren't there those who thought Churchill stupid, with his minuscule island-nation country, for thinking of opposing—alone, without America—Hitler? Was Ho Chi Minh stupid, or Castro, or Che, or Ortega, or Allende? Was Nelson Mandela stupid? Were that little group of wealthy Englishmen in the mid-1700s any different from this group, two hundred years later? What about the fact that everything they asked, every little thing Weather stood for, despite all their mistakes, despite all their cruelty, was proved by the march of history to be absolutely, word-perfect, right?

The intense pain of the experience had been that, from the beginning, Jasey and his friends had refused to allow him to help. To join their fight. Not for the first time, watching the rain's full fury pass and, the wind dropping, the sky set out to soak the earth, it occurred to him that they had done precisely what the Dies Committee had done: refused him the chance to fight. Senator Dies in World War II because of that pissy bureaucratic misnomer, "premature antifascist;" these young people because of their own pissy misuse of another word, "liberal." How a Spanish brigadista had failed their litmus test for radicalism, he was not sure. Of course, he had been the kind of Red they disapproved of: the Weather kids had been as orthodox as anyone, the POUM, the Stalinists. He'd been suspicious of the orthodoxy of the left even before Spain, as suspicious of the left as he had been contemptuous of the right. Then Trotsky had brought forward that possibility that had rung so true to so many, "Anti-communist Leftist." To true believers, heterodoxy was a serious crime. And just like the Stalinists in Spain, these young people were nothing if not true believers.

Intensely, more intensely than he could have imagined possible, Jack longed to talk to his son about this. So intensely, he could not distinguish the real impossibility of what he was wishing, he felt it impossible, to the contrary, that he would not see his son, and soon, within days, or hours, or minutes. He felt he had only to walk to the front door. *I knew it, I knew it.* Surely, surely now that he was dying, he would find a way to communicate with Jason, and Jason would find a way to come see him just as so many of the others had, and then he could tell his son everything.

How to do it? Nearly gratefully, his mind set itself on the details. One, two, three. A well-placed newspaper article. Jason would know him to be sick. Then some smart planning on his part. They could get out of town without being followed—he and Danny-boy could engineer that. Where should they go? Where would Jason go?

Jack, in his study on this spring night, thought like this for a long time. He saw himself and his son sitting in the saturated light of a Montauk diner. He saw them up at Mohonk, a weekend of talk. For a time he indulged himself before, with a huge sigh, suddenly, he let it all go away.

It couldn't be.

Ah, how long had it been since he had exhausted his ability to deceive himself? Years. Decades. He would never get to tell his son everything, never get to tell his son anything. He would never be able to tell his son that he did not disapprove of what he had done, that he admired him.

Because he would never allow his son to make contact.

Because if he did so, he could not protect his son, who was implacably hated by the law, from capture.

His son would make a mistake, come back, and be sent to jail for seventy-five to life, just like David Gilbert.

And therefore he could never let his son know that he was dying.

That was key. His son could never, ever know that he was dying. It would have to be a secret guarded in this house by his family.

All the more reason, Jack thought, for what he had decided.

See, after all, it couldn't be.

4.

So here he is, Jack Sinai, at the end of his life, a man of massive age, and he is in the company of his father, as vividly as if he were alive, and of his son, as vividly as if he were there. And he is thinking, I never really left my father anywhere. His father's example had come back to him with such vivid force when he had had his own children, and taken him through the endlessly ambiguous tasks of raising them with sure and kind humility. That old man with his smell of Bay Rum and cigarettes was there so often, long, long after he died. The real challenges of fatherhood are not those that you face when you are raising children, they are those that come after your death, the time when your own children are fathers and mothers and facing mortal danger, their fears for their children and of their own deaths, cancer, age, and the need to call on you for a kind of guidance that meant nothing when they were children, a guidance in how to give up children to adulthood and how to give up the self to age.

Outside, now, the torrent was coming to an end and beyond the chestnut, a moon-backlit sky showed that in the distance, the clouds were gone.

Oh, my Lord. There was no end to what they asked of you, demanded of you, these beings you created. You'd think that the act of creation would have been enough. In fact, there was no sacrifice was enough for them. Never enough patience, never enough money, never enough that you denied yourself to do what they needed, never sure that it was the right thing to do, either, and never, never, expecting any results. They have such a right, these children. The right to everything you have, and are, and wish for, and then some more, the incessant right of those you have caused to be born.

Jack didn't actually say that to himself though.

He may have meant it, but it's not what he said to himself.

What he said to himself, Jack Sinai, that night, as he made his way out of the study and up the stairs of his house, the house of his life, for the last conversation of the day, was something very different.

There was no point in waiting any longer. He knew what he was going to do, had known since the moment that Holmquist had pronounced the facts of his death. He must do it quietly, he reminded himself, secretly: it could not be in the news that he was dying, for that could make Jason try to come back.

He believed that, too. Quietly, thoroughly, and unexpectedly, Jack Sinai found that he knew throughout his being, as if he had just spoken to Jason on the phone, that if he knew, Little J.—an adult now, a man perhaps with his own children—would risk everything to try to come back.

Or was that just the foolish optimism of the old?

Perhaps, perhaps.

But at eighty-seven, you did not entertain that kind of thought.

It wasn't that you couldn't bear to.

You were at the Siege of Cape Tortuga; you can bear anything.

It's the people around you who can't bear you to.

Now was not the time to entertain philosophic doubts. For Eleanor's sake, sure, but Eleanor was an adult. It was for Danny, for

Klara. Maybe the thing that would make the two of them at last stop their stupid little self-exiles, the one from the other. Maybe the thing that would at last get them to get over what had happened to them, up at Yale, that day out on Hammonasset Beach. It was the time to lie, just as he had done that morning to young Brad Flanagan: lie about how bad it all in fact was. And above all, it was time to do it quietly, quietly, for Jason's sake, and so in this way it was not just for Danny-boy and Maggalah and Klary, but also for Little J. too. Yes, Jack thought to himself, yet another time that Jason is in my mind and Danny not. But then, it was now he must think very carefully, very centrally about Danny, because Jason was not going to be here for this, and Danny was. Briefly, before his eyes, Jack Sinai saw the crying face, that morning, of the Flanagan boy, and remembered his ersatz words of hope for him. But this was different. Then, he had been lying. This time, it was about love.

He rose now and turned out the desk lamp, went out the study door and—after closing up for the night—upstairs for the conversation he needed to have with his wife. A conversation—he thought wryly to himself—that would be neither short nor sweet. And so it was quoting Bob Dylan that my grandfather set out on his last act of fatherhood, dying for his family, just the way he had lived.

PART TWO

Chapter Eight

Isabel Montgomery

June 30, 2011

New York City

1.

By the end of June I have knocked out the chapter you have just read with the help of a steady diet of my grandfather's pinots and some timed-release Focalin, a drug usually used for ADHD but which is as pure a speed high as I myself could ever want, and which turned out to be in good supply from my young Rasta friend from AAA Pot Deliveries.

Maggie, of course, is all over me to read it, so we slip back up to the Island where a few days in a bikini under clear blue skies on Hancock Beach are so precisely what I need that I can even handle the lugubrious fatalism of Maggie contemplating the publication of the Sinai Family Saga, not that this is ever very likely to happen. But she is as good as her word, and for the ensuing days she tells me what she promised me she would, about Danny, and Klara, and Yale, and Hammonasset Beach—what she knows of it, anyway—and about Passover of 1996, and I am deep into it, deep into it, when Uncle Joe dies.

Just like that.

Maggie is sitting there on the porch in Menemsha, talking her head off, and her cell rings and she checks it, planning not to answer, but it is Danny, and he's calling to tell us that Uncle Joe has died.

You cannot—I swear to you—invent this stuff.

We're lucky to get Maggie's Volvo on the Oak Bluffs ferry the next morning—the Vineyard Haven ferry is full, but Kennedy's office, where Maggie knows an aide, intervenes—and we are in New York by midafternoon.

Maggie, I note, takes the 86 through Hartford, neatly avoiding the Long Island Sound coastline and thus Hammonasset Beach—though she does take the 95, rather than the Merritt, which adds fifteen minutes to the drive and condemns us to navigate the evils of the 95 which is charging, I note, tolls again—that enough authenticating fucking detail to convince you that I know how to drive from Woods Hole to New York?—but which allows us to stop in New Haven for a pizza and beer lunch—we go, like Sinai, to Moderna, fuck Pepes— after which she rather weaves down the 95 and over to the Hutch. We're in New York by three, and—of course—at Bedford Street where, it appears, a tribal experience is in order.

Oh, don't make me tell you about it. The Igneri clan is all there, and seeing Joe only ever had the garden apartment so he could rent out the other three floors of his townhouse to yuppies, they are all disposed variously in Sinai family beds, and I suppose they're nice enough people in their own way with their olive skins and their pretty kids and their endless dishes of manicotti, and their grief, I suppose is real, but it doesn't feel that real to me, it feels like they all thought Joe dead long ago, and all the while I'm either bustling around the kitchen with them warming up dishes of eggplant parmigian that, apparently, half of Little Italy has seen fit to cook for them, or I am huddling in my room and trying to stay out of their way and waiting for the day when we all troop out to Queens in a procession of limousines following a hearse from Racuglia Funeral Home where Joe's now unrecognizable corpse with a pink face, scrubbed and shaved, has been lying on view and consign him to the earth, and then troop back for another orgy of red wine and pasta and Muzzarell and baked artichokes and eggplants and olives and cannelloni and espresso and grappa and then, the women folk having, despite being impeccably dressed in Gucci and possessing the longest, brightest nails I have ever seen—as well as the biggest hair—scrubbed the entire house to a state of perfection, they all disappear in a roar of white SUVs and Maseratis and Camaros west to the Holland Tunnel leaving me, alone in the house for the first time, wondering what the fuck just happened and realizing, for the first time, that Joe is gone.

I try to get my head back into it for a while, only, I find myself not going to my grandfather's study so much any more.

In fact, I find myself avoiding it.

I am weak, depleted by the writing. The dope has turned on me, making me anxious and unhappy, and the booze, to which I turn for relief, is not helping at all. The only thing I've got going for me, in fact, is the Focalin which, I know, is going to exact a high price, and that sooner rather than later.

I'm also lonely. Jessie finished her six months at Beacon and came down on her way to wherever the fuck—Berkeley, Oregon, somewhere alternate. Outside of the orange jumpsuit, she turned out to be pretty whole wheat. Certainly, since I'd been out, she had not shaved her underarms, which turned me off: I am the girly kind of lesbian, not the dykey kind. I like my lovers to be hairless, preferably with some pearls or gold against their skin, and an ankle bracelet, and some diamonds, and smelling just so faintly of tobacco and alcohol, like your folks when you're a kid and they come home from a party.

Not for the first time, I realize that I have in some profound way invented a lover rather than discovered her, which, not for the first time, discourages me profoundly.

That's not a good thing, for me. To get discouraged.

Because once it starts, it goes on, and soon, as a shrink once told me, I have used a sort of psychic pathetic fallacy and invested my entire world with it. The lead-glass windows, the polished parquet and kelims, the chestnut tree out the window, weeping leaves, *the shadowy hazel grove.* Room by room, parts of the Bedford Street house start becoming closed to me. First the study, once the repository of a wealth of history that I had no choice, no choice, but to master, now become the place where my grandfather began the process of his impeccable death. Then the entire first floor, with its library of beautiful editions of forgotten books, each the highest aspiration of a long dead soul, utterly forgotten, Edward Dahlberg, Julian Shapiro, John Sanford? That it is all accessible on a computer screen turns out, in the end, not to make the slightest difference. Once, there was a literature masterable by a real reader. Now, the literature of our language is known only to scholars and that which survives in print does so at the mercy of editors of reprint series.

That means the kitchen is off limits to me, which puts me, in turn, at the caprice of local restaurants. But the only one I find myself using is the Corner Bistro, and how long can one live on bourbon and hamburgers?

Not long, I know.

As a palliative measure, although likely in error, I cut out the hamburgers.

I spend a lot of time in my grandmother's old studio, breathing deep the smell of oil paints which, like a ghost, was the one dimension of the past that would not quit this room. I am able to remember her precisely, a short woman, grown increasingly round with age, with a gaze that could shuck an oyster and who, I strongly believe, loved me.

But in time, I come to wonder whether it's time for a break from this house, as beautiful a crib as it might be. Momma, of course, is lobbying for me to return to London, and I do agree to meet her for a weekend in Marbella.

I do three things before I leave Bedford Street.

First, I clean the house, thoroughly, and destroy all the evidence of the debauchery of my stay, although I can't possibly repair the damage to the wine cellar or the liquor cabinet.

Second, I go shopping in the meat market, and buy myself a California wardrobe.

It feels good to spend money. Very good.

And finally, I invite the Rasta Dope Dealer for dinner, an act that apparently amazingly raises his hopes and libidinal level, until he realizes that it's just dinner—and, incidentally, a final chance for me to re-up.

I don't bother with dope, as I know I'll get a medical marijuana card in LA. What I do take is coke, Focalin, and some methamphetamine, all in good but concealable quantities. These I transfer into empty capsules then deposit them in pill bottles in the bottom of my toiletry bag, which I bring to the table so as to get the Rasta Dope Delivery dude to help me with my little arts and crafts after-dinner project.

When we're done, he pulls one more thing out.

"Here's one on me, baby. Two, in fact."

It's two plastic capsules filled with white crystal.

"What's that?"

"MDMA. Pharmaceutical grade. Almost impossible to get."

"Ah, baby. Thank you. I don't do X."

"I noticed that. Why is that?"

"Don't need drugs to make me think, dude. I do enough of that without 'em."

"Um hmm. Well, I tell you what, Ms. Izzy. First off, this isn't X, and it isn't Molly. You just hang on to these, in case you change your mind sometime. This is the real, real deal. I'm telling you."

With that, he takes a piece of scrap paper from his pocket, folds it into a little envelope, and draws a heart on it with a red sharpie, also from his pocket. Then he puts the two white pills inside, and puts the envelope into my toiletry bag.

So I fly to Marbella, first class, overnight, change in Madrid. But when I get to Marbella it turns out that Momma isn't there: she's tied up over some garbage in London—her father left her with a foundation—so I go to the hotel to wait for her to get in, thinking I'll spend a weekend and try to get over myself. But no sooner do I get to the hotel—Momma favors the Four Seasons—than this little guy tending bar convinces me to buy a gram of coke, and instead of lying out on the beach relaxing, I hole up in my hotel smoking coke in tobacco, which does me no good at all and which Momma must not have the slightest hint of or she will be back on the pipe for months, perhaps years.

The thing is, I am antsy there, and want to come back.

And what I want is not Momma, but Molly.

And what I want from Molly is to spend three-four days speaking with her, at least in part, about the night of November 18, 1995, the night my grandfather died.

This one, unlike my little visit to New York with Sinai, six months earlier, I remember vividly.

Here's something no one knows. Not even Molly. After Momma and Sinai split up—I was like eight, and we moved down to Saugerties, into the house kitty-corner from Molly's—I woke up every night just before midnight, nearly every night, and crept across the hallway to see if my father was in his bed, and if he wasn't, then waited until Molly's kitchen light came on, which it did, every single night at midnight. I did so very silently, so as not to alert the baby monitor they left on. Then I waited awake until Sinai crossed the lawn back to his own bed, and only then, only then, did I go back to sleep.

To this day I don't understand why they didn't want me to know they were fucking. I guess they thought it would make me uptight, Momma just having been dragged off to rehab and Sinai having moved me from the house in which I was born. Make me uptight? You got to be kidding me. Molly was the best thing ever to happen to me. That Sinai had the good sense to be sharing her bed—and that, furthermore, there is something to him, something I've never seen but that Molly assures me is there, that makes him worth her while? The only thing that's ever given me any confidence in him. Remember Laura Whitehorn, who told me that my father was an asshole?

Something else she said to me, once. She said, Izzy, you're not really gay. Your dad's just made you phobic of men. Well, not quite. The truth is, in my opinion, that sexual proclivity can originate not only on the interiorization of a person we hated, but also of one we loved. It's not just that Sinai made me phobic of men. It's that Molly made me love women.

Lying there in Marbella, in my room, waiting for Momma, what I long for is Molly.

And won't you just guess what? Don't you just know what happens next? It is an amazing series of accidents. The whole fucking thing is this amazing series of accidents. Because there I am, going downhill very fast in a hotel room in Marbella, when my iPhone beeps with a beep reserved for my always-on agent, and guess what he wants to tell me?

I cannot tell you the number of times this guy has called with an assignment that has lifted me off the bottom of my life like an egg on a spatula, just in time. Want to know why I've written three hundred and twenty thousand words—now three hundred and seventy, with the last two done—of instantly disposable journalism in the past four years? Because it's the only thing that's kept me out of the morgue. Want to know who made it possible?

And this time, this time, this glorious fellow, sitting in his corner office on Madison Avenue, has something better than even I, who believe in my luck, could have imagined.

"Iz? So I just got an interesting phone call."

"Oh yeah?" I'm sitting up, congratulating myself for smoking the coke rather than snorting it, because he would have heard it in the nasality of my voice in a second and probably, as he should have done years ago, dumped me out back with the empties.

"Yes. A place called Trident, in Los Angeles. It appears they've gotten a copy of an article of yours, and they want to option it."

"Oh yeah? How did they get it?"

Dead air. Then:

"I met the guy who backs them at a party."

"I see. In other words you've sold some piece-of-shit article of mine to a major film producer for some ungodly sum of money, even though you're a literary agent."

Dead air, of the kind that only he knows how to leave on the line. Five years ago, it would have made me nervous. Now I just listen.

"So do you want to hear the terms?"

"Sure."

"Six months at seventy-five thousand."

"And what did they offer?"

"Opening? Two years at fifty."

"Got it. And which piece?"

"That last one in the *Guardian*, Ibn Saud."

"Cuntmuscle? You got to be kidding me! Who the fuck wants that?"

I can hear him wince. "Iz, please. The Prince's ex-wife is a client of the agency. Remember? That's how we got you in there? It's a great story. Sexy reporter vs. rich Saudi Prince. Topical, important. You could see it on Fox Searchlight, you could see it on HBO."

"Okay. Tell you what."

"Um hmmm."

"Tell them they can have it if I write it."

Pause. "You serious?"

"I am."

"Want to hold?"

"I do."

There is a silence, while I calculate the time in LA, which is early. This poor guy is probably getting woken up. Then my agent is back.

"I can get one-seventy-five for a draft, forty-five per rewrite. But you have to be in LA."

This one, I don't even have to think about. "Fine, limit of two rewrites, and a suite at the Viceroy and a car. Car has to be a Mitsubishi V6 Turbo. Suite has to have an ocean view."

"Just a sec."

Pause—or what I will soon be calling "a beat."

"Done. They're ready to get you a ticket. Where are you?"

"Spain."

"Shit. I have to negotiate that."

"Don't bother. I'll get the ticket."

See, I'm already packing.

You've understood, right?

Because the last thing I do before I leave the room is shoot off an email that, before the door has closed behind me on the hotel room in Marbella, is making a little ching of arrival in an inbox in Saugerties.

Thirty-six hours later, fresh as a daisy, and the phone rings in my room at the Viceroy. I have slept, eaten, showered, and sobered up, and even my breath is minty fresh to hide that I've been smoking—tobacco, I mean—and I am hurrying down the hall into the lobby where there is a flash of sunlight from the windows and then I am in the thin, strong arms of Molly and her long body is against mine and the smell of her skin is filling my mouth and nose.

We have five days. Sinai doesn't know why she's here. She found a conference to go to during the day, but from four or so, she is mine. That's good, because I only get up at about two, wincing in the bleached Pacific sun, having talked till dawn and then, after she went to bed, working my way through the minibar and running her voice through WordRec—I am recording her surreptitiously on my iPhone which, magic though it is, still can't run a robust word-recognition program—and, as it converts into iData, running down her references.

Some on Google.

Some in my memory.

At first she is a bit suspicious.

"Iz, hon, what the hell do you want to know about *that* for."

We are in Venice Beach, eating at Joe's on Trident's dime.

And how do I explain?

I do not lie to Molly.

Much.

"It's my job."

She is watching me carefully, her eyes wrinkling around their black pupils. She is a woman who has lost a husband and son, and now in her eyes it looks as if I were receding over a hilltop, waving her goodbye. It's always as if I were receding over a hilltop, waving her goodbye. But what am I to do? I didn't ask God to make life the way that life is. I say, "Molly, I love you."

"Then don't ask me to do this."

We finish our dinner, talking about something else.

But later, after dinner, walking out on the beach, she asks again.

"Iz, why are you doing this?"

"I told you. It's my job."

"No it's not. Your job is writing what you yourself call 'instantly disposable' journalism. This is something else."

I don't answer for a bit, and when I do, I sound a bit adolescent. "It's investigative."

"Yeah, right. Investigative fiction, I'd call it."

"Well, that's legitimate."

"No, it's not."

We walk for a little bit in silence. Then I say the thing I meant not to, but which I know is the thing that will get her to help.

"I want to know how you all dealt with my grandfather's death."

"You know what we did. We mourned."

"Aw, Molly. That's not true."

"And how do you know that?"

I pause on this for a long time. I think of trying to explain it to her. That lies have an effect. That you can feel that effect even if you don't know what the lie is. That nothing is without a price. And when I speak it is in a smaller voice than I can remember using for a long time.

"When you are brought up by people with lies at the center of their existence, you suffer from that even if you don't know what the lie is."

"What lie? *What* lie?"

"Oh, Molly. You know what lie."

"Then so do you. Then why do I have to say it?"

"Because *I* have to say it. And I want to get it right. So you have to say it."

And there, on the beach under the approaching lights of the Santa Monica Pier, she cries, and I cry. When we finish, sniffing, wiping our noses on our hands, she finally says: "Did Danny talk to you?"

I play dumb. "No."

"You know, if you're really doing this, you'll need to spend time with Danny and Maggie, but also your Aunt Klara. I'm not the only liar in this family."

"I know you're not. I know you're not."

There's a silence. Then she spoke again.

"The thing was, I had never told anyone about Donny."

That's not a typo. She said "Donny." Not "Danny."

That's when I started surreptitiously recording her on my iPhone. We talk for a week.

And now, at last, I am alone in my suite at the Viceroy, watching out over the bland, blue Pacific, little choppy white tops, a sail heading in from Catalina, and iData is up on my big Macintosh screen, which I had shipped from New York, and in my mind's eye is the light of Molly's kitchen window across the little dirt road that separates our houses, the kitchen window lighting at midnight.

Only, now, for the first time, I know what's going on inside.

And I know what's about to happen inside.

I'm sorry, dudes. I don't want to bore you. No one is singing the International inside; no one is getting chased by the police, and no one is going to die.

But the drama of my life is playing out inside this house and to me, it is a story of the highest suspense.

I'm going, now, to tell you it. And I hope you'll give it a chance, because I've never cared quite so much about anything I've done with words before.

Chapter Nine

Molly Sackler

November 21, 1995

Saugerties, New York

1.

Now it is midnight in Molly Sackler's kitchen, very clearly so. If you didn't have a clock, you'd know it because her kitchen light just came on. You can see it: kitty-corner across the intersection of the two little streets that divided our houses. Not even really streets. Graded dirt surface, maintained by the county because there were more than three residents on them, but not so many more that they were prepared to give them actual names.

Molly's is a three-story Center Hall Federal, once the Grange House of the Bentley Farm, which Molly's grandfather was the last Bentley to work and which included much of what is now the nearby village of Saugerties.

In the day the house is white, green roof-and-windowed, on lush lawn, bordered by huge maples, carefully planted many years ago at a distance from each other that would allow them to grow spherical crowns. And this they have done, emphatically: these are stately, huge trees, avatars of season and incarnations of time, and in the day—drying into autumn, erupting into color, rustling on the breeze—they are mindblowing visions, poignant beyond belief.

But at night, as Molly herself likes to point out, all cats are gray. Or more exactly, this night, because there is a huge, nearly full autumn moon, all cats are duotoned, like the trees, between planes of absolute black and pure silver.

The house sits in a pool of silver lawn surrounded by the huge shadows of absolute black thrown by the trees. It is a kind of shadow that, for people of Molly's age, is always slightly kitsch because of a singer called Yusuf Islam, formerly known as Cat Stevens. She has, though, another reference too: the Margaret Wise Brown book she read to her son, and later to me. Therefore it is a view of a world suffused also with kind mystery: the rustling crowns of trees, the silver lawn on which are thrown moon shadows.

And then there is Molly's lighted kitchen window.

Molly wakes every midnight. Just moments ago she had pivoted to the side of her bed, swung her feet to lie flat on the weave of the rug, and turned her gaze right out the window to the big gibbous moon, a post-harvest moon, suspended over the turning leaves.

For a moment she could not place herself: this is her childhood bed and in it she has been girl, wife, mother, and lover.

But because there is this low, silvery moon, soon to be a full moon, she knows it to be late autumn.

And because she is awake, she knows it to be midnight.

And because of the thought that came to her next she knows that because she is not a girl and not a wife but a lover and a mother, then it is morning in Somalia, and she must go down to the kitchen, flip on the light, wake up the computer and get onto the web to find out if her son is still alive.

Morning in Somalia. There could already have been what the paper would call an "early morning firefight" or an "overnight artillery duel."

What the paper doesn't say is that every person involved—every person—in these scenic incidents is somebody's child.

Once, she admitted to J. that she hadn't slept through a night in thirty years, from the day Donny went to Vietnam. But that wasn't quite true. There was this one time she slept all night. One night shortly after they began making love she had put her cheek against the red hair of J.'s chest and, to her shock, disappeared till the birds woke her at dawn. She didn't tell J. that. And she didn't tell J. that if she woke up that morning rested like she could not remember being since childhood, she also woke up pissed. Pissed that after all these years of widowhood, she could still be so *dependent*. On a god damned *man*.

Thirty years of waking at midnight. Then she was sitting up for a husband, now for a son. One was worse, she knew which, but that didn't affect how she felt. Vietnam was years ago. Her son's death, in Somalia, in Iraq, in Haiti, in Afghanistan, was still an inevitability.

That is, a *threat*. Not an inevitability. She corrects herself, and — perhaps by way of penance — says to the Macintosh: "Leo is alive. Leo is alive."

Yeah, well. Years of therapy, and she could *call* it a threat. But she *knows* it as an inevitability. Somalia, with this philandering Arkansas cracker as Commander in Chief? This *civilian* draft-dodging shit-head? Leo could be killed a thousand and one ways. He could be beat down, shot at, knifed, bayonetted, blown up. He could be ambushed and paraded shackled through the street on international television. He could be dragged behind a fucking Jeep, every bone in his body smashed inside his cammies, then torn limb from limb by a crowd. Only American news would decline to play the video: the rest of the globe would go on the Internet, find a choice URL for a universe of scumbags wanting to see her son's living terror and brutal death. These things had happened to other mothers' sons. Other *American* mothers' sons. She is supposed to be comforted that he was piloting jets rather than Blackhawks. But the Federation of American Scientists claimed to have tracked a Stinger sale from an Israeli arms dealer in Pretoria through to its end-user in Mogadishu. The Israeli bought it from an Afghan, who got it straight from the CIA during the war. A Stinger could bring down a fighter plane — that's why we gave them to the fucking mujahedeen in the first place: to fucking shoot down Soviet fucking fighter planes.

"Fu-uck." She draws the syllable up and out, addressing the screen of her Macintosh, as if it didn't just feel like another person but could actually be spoken to.

"Ah, you goddamned machine." This is the next thing she says, some minutes later. The server is down, as usual, on the *Djibouti Standard*, first stop for real-time reporting on Somalia, at least in English. With the tips of her fingers she types in the address of BBC South Africa, URL of second resort for those intent on finding out if their child has been killed on duty in Somalia, nation-building for that fucking *liberal*—when Molly uses the word it is with the same spitting contempt as Jason, but with an entirely different meaning. During Leo's tour of duty in Desert Storm she'd relied on the Pakistani English dailies, or on *Al Jazeera English* or, oddly, on the *Turkish Daily News*, which kept a Kabul office. Tonight, the BBC has nothing. No good news, no bad news. The fact doesn't even slightly affect the anxiety that compresses her body. Five minutes of information, a night of insomnia. When Jason is there, sometimes she goes back to sleep around dawn. That is still far away. She reads her other email, answers a note from a parent at her school. She rises and finds, in the dump-everything drawer of the counter, the butt of a Marlboro Light, which she lights off the gas stove, holding her black hair, salted with white, back from the flame with one hand. She wears white flannel pajamas and, bending over the sink, you can see the obtuse curve of her hips to her waist: she is fifty, once an Olympic hopeful in cross-country, a woman who had had only one child and that much too young to hurt her body. Then she sits again, cigarette in the side of her mouth, one eye closed against the smoke, watching the computer screen with what seems like an expression of real skepticism as she clicks through to read the *New York Times*.

Which, of course, was when she is greeted, under the national headlines, with the news that Jack Sinai had died, in his sleep, six months after a cancer diagnosis.

"Oh, Jesus Christ." She turns from the screen and says it like this: Cha-*rist*. When she looks back, she finds she cannot refocus her eyes, and has to set the zoom to enlarge the type.

> . . . his numerous politically charged defenses included members of the Black Panthers, the Puerto Rican separatist group The Young Lords, and Black Liberation Army defendants in the 1981 Brinks Robbery Trial. He appeared three times before the Supreme Court, where he was known to Justice Thurgood Marshall as a "regular customer." ... But Jack Sinai was best known as the father of the '60s radical Jason Sinai, a fugitive of the Vietnam era, who disappeared as a member of the Weather Underground after the accidental bombing of a Manhattan townhouse in March, 1970.

Shock subsiding, she says to herself, well, that's the *Times* for you, singing in its most liberal voice. And, as always, getting it wrong. Best known as Jason Sinai's father? Outside of hippy dippy Woodstock —just down the 212 from her house—she doubts anyone in this country remembered who Jason Sinai was. Or cared. Whereas any serious student of American politics knew that Jack Sinai had appeared before the Supreme Court not three but *five* times, and, except to the twenty-five-year-old affirmative-action hire who wrote the obit for the *New York Times*, he was best known for that.

> In a statement announcing the death, Daniel Sinai explained that his father had concealed his illness for fear that his fugitive son would attempt to make contact. The Sinai family, Professor Sinai explained, had been under police surveillance for most of the thirty years since his brother's disappearance.

That makes her turn from the screen again. Did Sinai really think that? Well, that was wrong. Not even his father, not even his father, would make Jason Sinai surface, and she knows it because Jason

Sinai, who was right then asleep with his daughter in their house across the road in what had once been the carriage house to hers, was her best friend and, for the past year, lover.

"I mean, they're right in one way." She admits it to the Macintosh. J. longed—longed—to see his father. Particularly since seeing him on stage at the VALB ceremony. To learn that his father was dying would have . . . would have *swept him off his feet*. From far away, the Dylan lyric came to her. But lead him to make a mistake, like trying to surface? No way. In some ways, Molly knew, Jason had been mourning his father these twenty-five years. In some ways, Molly knew, he had never really given up the hope that he'd see his father again before he died. But to surface to see him, even for the very last time? She confides to the Mac, "It's his daughter, you see. To see his father? He'd have surfaced ages ago, even if it meant jail time, to see his father. But jail would mean he'd lose Izzy. So I don't know how the old man could be so *wrong*."

And then, suddenly, her mistake comes clear to her, so obvious it could only be the result of her shock. Sinai has not spoken to his son in a quarter-century. He could not have any idea that he even had a granddaughter. And at the realization it swept through her, through and through, what this old man had done, protecting the son who had ruined his life, even in his death.

For a time, this very early morning in late autumn, Molly is carried along that wave of emotion. When it releases her it is one o'clock gone, the moon fifteen degrees further across the sky, the earth fifteen degrees closer to the moment when it would show Saugerties to the morning sun, and she, Molly—she realizes with shock—is one hour closer to something she had never had any idea that she was going to have to do, never.

Before dawn, when I will awake with the rising sun, it is Molly's job to tell her lover Jason Sinai that his father is dead.

A little laugh now, involuntary, almost embarrassed.

See, there is a terrible irony in this for Molly. It's that, this is not the first time she's brought news of death. She's done it before, and it was the worst moment in her life.

The only possible comfort, at the time, had been that she'd never have to do it again.

2.

But that night in her lighted kitchen, that huge gibbous moon outside the window, Molly still isn't even close to understanding the enormity of what is about to happen.

Perhaps one day she will look back and see that, of course, everything was about to change for her, that night.

See, Molly doesn't know it but there's this little decision she made, in this same house, thirty years ago, that is about to bear fruit, and when it does, it will change everything. Really, it's incredible that she doesn't see, two moments of her life, thirty years apart, wrinkling time and meeting, like two folds in an origami bird, in perfect symmetry.

Lies will do that.

Lies will punctuate our lives like that.

Especially the lie Molly told, and has been telling, all these last thirty years.

Now, however, she has something else to think about. Now, she has a practical difficulty to surmount. And thinking about that, Molly purses her lips and whistles, low.

The conversation she is about to have will be neither short nor sweet. It is going to sweep J off his fucking feet. But in the morning, there'll be Izzy to deal with, and what could they do with an eleven-year-old girl while her father fell to pieces? Get a babysitter? Molly explains this to the computer: "Say I take her for early dropoff at school? Then where would I park J.? The second I leave him alone, J.'ll be reading the *Times* online—he has the damn newspaper up on the computer screen before he even has coffee."

No, it was clear, and what was clear was that sometime, sooner rather than later, she is going to walk out of her kitchen door into the moon-flooded, late autumn night, cross the unnamed road between her white clapboard house and Jason's, dappled silver and black herself as she walks below the duotoned leaves, let herself in the front door and climb the back stairs to his bedroom where she will wake him and sweep him off his feet.

She'll need to be quiet, firm, and, to some extent, removed.

She'll need to be almost clinical.

See, she has done this before, and so, she knows how much focus it takes.

Thirty years ago, she had driven, as the locals say, "up the mountain" from Saugerties to Tannersville to lie to Don Sackler Sr. that his son, her husband, had been killed walking point in Songh Be Province.

One o'clock. She considers the computer screen soberly, one eyebrow raised. When they slept together, this was when she left his bed. In this respect, her insomnia was useful: she could sleep against the hair of his chest for a couple hours, then go home, and Izzy never knew she had been there.

She thinks: let him sleep the REM cycle out. Wake him around two-thirty. Have coffee ready, breakfast. She remembers how hungry Don Senior, her father-in-law, had been after his short, private outburst, for which he'd left the room: she'd heard him from behind closed doors, sitting alone in the living room of the dead silent Onteora Park house. But as quickly as her mind touches this she pulls it away. Later for all that. Now there is refuge in the practical. She'll have to do it in his kitchen. Somehow have him composed by seven, when Izzy gets up for school. And be aware—of course—in case she wakes up during it all. Molly purses her lips now, taking resolve to be perfectly mindful of the possibility of Izzy waking up. To be ready to come out and take her back to bed before she could see her father cry. She will, she thinks, put him with his back to the living room and sit across the table from him, watching the door. But not yet. Two more hours of sleep before she changes his life.

No worry, after all, that someone else would wake him with the news.

The thought made her laugh, a little and without amusement.

See, no one else knows who Jim Grant, one of n-plus-one lawyers in the Saugerties telephone book, is. So no one else is going to have any reason to wake him in the middle of the night to tell him of the death of the great Jack Sinai except insofar as Jack Sinai could be said to be an inspiration—like Leonard Boudin, or Martin Garbus, or William Kunstler—for Jim Grant's law practice.

So she has a plan. Briefly, she wonders what else needed taken care of. J. has a mother, brother, a half-sister. As far as she knows, J. has not been in touch since 1970, when he became a federal fugitive. Need she contact them? Immediately, she rejects the thought. That was precisely how fugitives got caught.

How awful it felt to her, not to have family available. How unnatural. Like not being able to bury Donny because, according to the Marines, there wasn't enough of him to ship home. It felt like something else, too, something else unnatural. For a moment she sought, sitting at the computer in the lighted kitchen, the similarity. When she found it, she pronounced it before she could stop herself.

It was like having to lie about how Donny died, to his own father, to her own parents.

But there is no time for this, no time for this. She rises to go get dressed, to take a shower, to have something to eat, to get ready.

And still she finds herself, moments later, standing rifling through the dump-everything kitchen drawer, just in case the past fifty times she searched it she missed a cigarette, tears coursing down her cheeks.

Thirty years had passed since she drove up the mountain to lie to Donny's father about his son's death in Songh Be Province. Johnson was president. She wore her hair in a center-parted perm wave, owned a mini-dress. A paisley one. She remembered perfectly how it felt. The thought itself didn't upset her. Thirty years after your husband's death, you can be matter-of-fact about it. What weighed on her was that the other person she hadn't told the truth to, that was J.

She hadn't told J. the truth about Donny. It had felt like a betrayal too. Not because J. was her lover, but because J. was a radical, the kind of person, in the war years, Donny hated. And vice-versa.

It wasn't personal, and that was what made her feel so bad. It was political.

Of course, she hadn't told anyone else, anyone else in the whole wide world, the truth about Donny either, had she?

And why was that?

3.

Molly and Jason met nearly ten years earlier when Mount Marion school district had to hire a lawyer to sue the Board of Education on behalf of the Teachers' Union. The lawyer turned out to be this celebrated local liberal, Jim Grant from Woodstock, married to the actress Julia Montgomery, who wanted to take the case pro-bono. Had she been in charge, then, they never would have hired this caviar-left asshole with his starlet wife. Then, however, she had been a high-school French teacher, not the grammar-school principal, and had no say.

That turned out not to matter. He won the case, for one thing. Nor was that all. Because after months of working together on the law suit, it turned out they were both training for the Boston Marathon, and so they came to run together first sometimes, then frequently, then regularly. Grant never told her that he and his wife were splitting up, had in fact split up. She heard it one day in Aunt Lucy's when she ran into Betsy Pelliteri, a real-estate agent from up the mountain. She said Grant's wife was already in England rehabbing a drug problem the size of a house; that Grant, because the sprawling ranch he lived in on a hundred and ten acres in Woodstock belonged to his wife, was looking to move—and looking, now, as a virtually impoverished public interest lawyer, not as the husband of an heiress. Of course, she called him that night and offered him the empty carriage house, kitty-corner across the dirt road to the old Bentley Farm. So they became neighbors, Grant, his daughter Isabel, that is, me, and Molly Sackler.

And then it was the afternoon they came home from a run. Rain had broken out around mile three, they'd stuck it out five more. So they were soaked, and Izzy was in school, and they were on the intersection of the two dirt roads between their houses, in soft afternoon light, the rain sheeting down. There had been a sort of ecstasy in the run, shoes slapping against wet grass, the roadside passing field, house and tree, melting into the gray light, the body's machine hot in the wet air. And suddenly his lithe, long body, the warm working muscle, the rain-cooled skin, was in her arms, and his wet mouth was open against hers, and fatigue and heat and comfort and utter thoughtlessness, utter thoughtlessness, were pouring into her like water into a glass, the rain whispering shh, shh, shh, the light like a blanket, and just then, when all her strength and courage and age and desire were perfectly equal to what was about to happen to her, just then, he stepped away.

Mol.

Jim. It came out like: Ji-im.

Molly. I have to tell you something.

The long shh, shh, shh of the rain, near and far. What, for God's sake, is worth telling me now?

Who I am.

I know who you are. She was trying to say: and I know what I want you to do.

He said, no. You don't. I have to tell you.

So that was the love story. Like so much in his life, outsized. You did not have to know J. well to see that he lived very large: huge accomplishments, huge mistakes. Later, there was more. Later she learned about his whole life: how he was a founding member of Weatherman at the University of Michigan, how he narrowly missed the townhouse bombing on March 6, 1970 and went underground, how he escaped again after the Bank of Michigan robbery and created Jim Grant's identity from a dead baby's papers in Bakersfield, California, and went back to college, where he met Julia Montgomery, and married her and went to law school and finally came to live in her house in Woodstock and have a daughter with her. How after all the other fugitives from the '60s surfaced and resumed their lives, one even claiming his social-security earnings from his false identity, J. failed to, because of the murder charge; for fear of the consequences to his daughter, in fact, to his daughters, for my half-sister Rebeccah was born when he was underground with Mimi. Later Molly came to grips with the fact that J. was not only a person, he was also an icon, and being in love with an icon is a job. Now, there was just the contained heat of his body with its red chest hair drawing her, up to her childhood bedroom, toward him, less—now—because of its inherent attraction, although he was attractive, than because of the realization cascading within her of what he had entrusted to her, himself, his daughters.

And here is Molly, midnight gone in her kitchen, not lost in reminiscence, hardly. Aware, rather—shockingly, lucidly aware—of the facts before her, because now she turns from the hold-everything drawer, which is entirely devoid of cigarettes, and addresses the computer screen: "Naw, let him sleep till five. Don't give him too much time. Two hours till Iz wakes? He'll have to step right up to the plate."

Was that better? Evidently. Because right away, as if guided by remote control, she turns, walks to the sun porch and takes a barely smoked Marlboro Light from a pot of narcissi even though she had no memory of putting it out there. Lights it and, exhaling smoke, nods conspiratorially to the new green shoots of the plants, just emerging from their bulbs. "He can't handle himself by seven, he takes off and I wake Izzy. That's all. Tell her he had to go to work early."

So it was a plan. And this was a cigarette. She says aloud: "That is a plan. And this, man oh man, is a cigarette."

For a moment, on the flood of nicotine in her blood, she feels something like normal.

Then the rush passes and soberly she thinks that she is going to own Jason and Izzy a little more after this. Jason with his iconic, strange, secret life; Izzy with her lithe little spirit. In a serious way, they were going to be a little more hers than ever before, after this.

Another zone of vulnerability, as Tolstoy would say. Was she ready? Extend her life of sitting up reading the news to two more people? Have to worry about a daughter too? You worry about your son? Try having a daughter. Her father used to say that. She could see him. *Worrying about their physical safety? Just wait, young lady, till it's their emotional safety that's at stake.*

That it was a worry she knew so well, that added no value whatsoever.

The world of worry for your child, she knew, everyone who came to it was the first explorer, and discovered it anew.

And—pay attention now—the little truth that had just barely shown itself to her, the little thing she had neglected to tell anyone in the thirty years since her husband died, that inconvenient detail that, a moment ago, had shown itself to her in sudden glimpse of a realization as unalterable, inevitable—the lie—backed off.

As lies, if you try hard enough, will.

4.

How he cried. She had never seen anyone cry like that. It was like turning on a faucet. Inconsolable wasn't the word. She didn't think there was a word.

Waking, in his room, he was Jim Grant—a lean, middle-aged man, his warm body covered with still-red hair that had all but abandoned his head—waking to face another responsibility, another request for help, another demand. Waking he was, as always, in control; as always, instantly collected, open for business. He'd leaned up on an elbow in the black room, shaking off sleep, then swung his legs out of bed and stood up.

"Moll, Izzy okay?"

"All okay, J."

"You okay?"

"Everyone's okay."

"What's going on?"

"I need to talk to you."

"'Kay." Little J. No more questions, no objections. He stepped naked across to the bureau, slipped on a pair of underpants, then a bathrobe from the closet, and followed her out of the room. On the staircase she waited by the window while he checked on his daughter. Late November, the trees trumpeting their mad duotoned cacophony, the pregnant, hugely gibbous moon on the wax, dropping a silvery light over the street, and across the street, her home. Not that the night-time view from J.'s house had much mystery for her: she saw it too often. Rain was due that day, the paper said, but there was no sign of it in the moon-flooded sky. Still, it seemed a long time that she waited by the window, a long enough time that even she had to admit that the stillness, the absolute quiet of the street under the silvery fall of moonlight, the street her Royalist family had owned since Washington's army had driven them up the Hudson two centuries before, was a testament to something. For a moment she sought for what. The best she could do, though, was to how much they took the solidity of the world for granted, which, Molly thought then, was not quite it.

Later, she'd know otherwise. It was it, exactly.

And then Little J. was there, and she took him down the stairs, sat him at the kitchen table in front of a cup of coffee, just like she had planned, his back to the living room in case Izzy woke up, and instantly, he was a different man.

It lasted a full hour. Sitting at his table, serving him food, holding his hands. They read the *Times* coverage on the Web, the *Guardian*, J.

peering out from behind a mask of tears, Molly half perched on a chair she'd pulled up next to him, so she could keep him in her arms as he read. How he cried. He talked, he made the kind of wry jokes the grieving make, then he cried some more. And just as she was beginning to prepare him for me to wake up, as abruptly as it had started, it stopped. He stood up and, for a long time, let her take him in her arms, stooping slightly so he could put his face in her neck. Then he asked her if she could take care of Izzy for a couple of days. She was ready for all this.

"Little J., I do *not* want to hear you're going to the city." She was ready to say: *Your father was so, so careful to keep you from that*. She was ready to say: *You owe it to him to be careful*. She was ready to say more, too, much more—perhaps too much more. But he shook his head and answered softly.

"No, baby. It's that, I always promised myself that when Pop died, I'd sit shiva at Huckleberry Point."

Huckleberry Point was a rock ledge off Platte Clove that looked clear over the Hudson Valley. It was, she knew, a place J. and his father had camped, in the early '60s, when Jack Sinai first introduced his eldest son to the Catskill Mountains that would later be his home. She asked softly, "What does it mean to sit shiva?"

"It's like a wake. You're supposed to do it for seven days, at home, with your family. All your friends come to visit. They'll be starting today on Bedford Street."

Then he began to cry again, his sodden face against her neck, his body heaving with sobs, so much she thought this time he'd never stop.

Jason Sinai kept two bags ready under his bed in case he was discovered. One was a suitcase to disappear into the city, one a pack to run to the mountains. Now he was out the door with his pack in ten minutes.

He didn't trust himself to see his daughter.

That gave Molly an hour and a half to wait until she had to wake her. She spent it online, reading about Jack Sinai. It wasn't that she hadn't known who he was. She had. But the lefty pantheon of which he was a part was filled with luminaries who meant nothing to her. The attention paid to him in the papers was astounding. It seemed that Hillary Clinton was planning on attending the funeral. The *Albany Times Union* chimed in with an op-ed on entitled "Eleanor Clinton."

That the wife of a sitting president should even consider attending the funeral of an avowed Communist, a lawyer who defended the Brinks Robbery cop killers, and the father of notorious fugitive Jason Sinai is as much of an insult to the state of New York as was Eleanor Roosevelt's support for the Communists in Spain an insult to the people of the United States of America.

She nearly put her head in her hands. Such inchoate thinking. Jack Sinai was a Socialist, or an "Anti-Communist Leftist." The irony was that if he had been a real Communist, the Weathermen would never have forced J. to break with his own father. An article online from the *Nation* did better. *Sinai had been shocked to be rejected as insufficiently radical by the New Left, a shock that colored the rest of his life.* "These fucking lefties." She spoke to this computer, too, though it was a PC. "So busy fighting with each other that they don't even know who the enemy is anymore. And fighting over what? Fighting over words, words, words."

At seven she woke me, easing me out of bed, cajoling me downstairs to the breakfast table. She was aware that in some fundamental way she was lying to me and that this was something for which, one day, I may not forgive her. The thought tore at her as she looked at me as I was then: the auburn hair around the grave oval of my face, just turning adolescent, my rosebud mouth cherry red, still a child, a beauty mark on my right cheek. There was J., convincingly, in my nose, but I was, luckily for me, in every other way my mother's daughter, and it wasn't for nothing that my mother was, in her day, a starlet.

And me? I didn't find anything strange about Molly waking me, or about spending a few days in her care. Happened all the time, when my father traveled to court in Albany, to the mountains for a solo camping trip, to IMS on retreat. Molly waited while I dressed, then took me to her house as she herself dressed.

Now, with me on her bed, chatting, she stands just inside her closet, takes off her T-shirt, puts on a bra. Then she takes a light gray silk blouse off a hanger, slips it on, buttons it.

And then, without any pause, she unbuttons it, takes it off, puts it back on the hangar, takes off her bra. Standing topless in her jeans she leans over to a lower drawer and takes out a running bra. She puts that on, puts her T-shirt back on, then a sweatshirt. Then she steps out of her jeans and into running shorts, then sweat pants, and comes out of the closet, holding her trail shoes in one hand, gathering her thick black hair into a ponytail with the other.

Thinking to herself, There's just no way I'm going to work today. No way. What I'm doing is, I'm dropping Iz off, then I'm going the fuck for a run, and the run I'm doing is the full eight miles into Dutcher's Notch and back.

Not thinking to herself, however, that what she was doing was precisely, precisely what she did thirty years ago.

Drive up the mountain.

Deliver her news of death.

Then run the eight into Dutcher's Notch: four miles in, four miles out.

5.

It's foolish even to try to describe what Molly sees, that morning, when she approaches the Dutcher's Notch trail through the big meadows on the old Colgate property.

Greene County in late November.

The trees, as if launched into flame by the touch of the sun, dropping their scent in fine dust from the canopy of their leaves.

The sun itself, filtering, deepening, maturing, through the colors. The carpet on the trails, the hands of lost lovers, Apollinaire called them, dying on the ground. It is poignancy so profound as to be almost kitsch. And above the kitsch poignancy, above the deepening autumn light, the endless well of Catskill sky.

The Catskill sky. Molly's father had liked to call it "Small Sky Country," but not in disparagement. It gathered over you like a gothic cathedral, the horizon constantly cut by the line of mountain peaks. She'd been out West, seen real mountains, experienced the massive liberation of big sky and endless vistas. She hated it. This sky here was the sky of her whole identity, as if it contained all the moments of her life, risen and gathered there in the tip of its parabolic arch.

At nine o'clock Molly Sackler pulls into the little trailhead parking lot at the Dutcher's Notch trail, watching the vista before her, and feels her heart falter. She climbs out of her car, an Escalade, bought to protect Leo when, home on leave, he drove these upstate roads, mostly drunk. She runs her thumbs around the elastic band holding her sweatpants up on her waist, then drops her sweatpants to the ground and steps out of them, showing her running shorts, then begins to retie her shoes, one foot up on the running board, then the other. Very precisely, she sees her foot against the treaded running board of her VW Beetle, thirty years ago, very precisely she feels her shoelace in her fingers. And there it is again, deep in her thoughts, the image of an origami bird, forming in her father's hands, as he curves two paper edges toward each other, pins them with a thumb, then creases them neatly together with a nail.

Once again it is as if thirty years were folded away and hidden.

Once again, she puts on her red reflective vest, the same one she has been running in, hunting season, for thirty years.

And then she is running already, leaving the car door unlocked, as soon as her shoes are tied: no stretches, no warmup, no game plan to pace herself through the eight miles ahead.

Worse yet, she is running fast.

As if she were not a seasoned practitioner of the sport, but a child, running away.

Thirty years. One time J. asked her if she could remember being a girl. She had thought about this for a long time, wondering if she could tell him. How she had grown up watching everything that happened to her, girl and woman, float up into the parabolic Catskill sky and nestle there, always available, always there. It was so intimate to her, what he was asking. If Donny had lived, he may still not have known this about her, not after thirty years of marriage. But because he had died, and because she had been, these thirty years, alone, she did answer and what she said was this.

"You know how they used to pour sidewalk with rubber expansion between the squares? Remember? That white sidewalk in four-by-four squares?"

J. watched her blankly, shrugged.

She said: "Sometimes, I walk out behind Mount Marion. The sidewalk out back, around the playground? The same expansion joints are there from when I was in nursery school. I put my foot on it and I can see my Converse sneakers, size three."

He thought about that. "The rubber must be gone."

"The rubber was gone then, too." They were in her backyard, which had been her parents' backyard, and she said: "J., that's the thing about me. Maybe because I've always been here, you know? Eight years old? J., I can remember being *four*."

"God, that is unimaginable to me."

He said it with wistfulness, and she understood. It was like showing your new car to a poor friend. Everything was fracture and dislocation in his life, tectonic periods of time that ground against one another, much forgotten, much more lost.

And why was that? Now, running too fast on stiff legs across the meadows toward the tree line, she thinks, really, it isn't obvious. It isn't Vietnam, or being a fugitive, or anything. It's that he has no sense of common identity with his younger selves. How could he? He's had so little sympathy for them, rejected so much of them, judged them so harshly. And if reasons for this may have seemed obvious—his fractured life, the war, his long criminality—the real reason was beyond that. Not for the first time, Molly thinks: we are never turned into who we are by our politics. Rather, our politics are always an expression of who we are, whether we want this to be so or not. Her life, too, had been filled with dislocation: Donny's departure, his death, then both her parents, one after the other. What made J. who he was is not history, it is that he simply has never practiced the processes of rehearsal and remembering. Those totally interior processes that made continuity, they had to be *practiced*.

But perhaps to achieve that continuity you had to want to. She tells herself: perhaps you had to want to graduate from a child's life in to an adult's. Graduate, gently, the one developing into the other. Not be ejected, forcibly, too early, from childhood into adulthood, from identity to identity, life to life. And there, history *does* matter. You had, she thinks as she crosses the tree line into dappled shadow and goes on into the woods, to feel comfortable enough with your past to want to remember it. You had to *like* your past self. And you couldn't *like* your past self if you were brought up with the idea that every one of the past's hopes had failed.

Her heart sinks at the thought, and she picks up her pace, again, as if in punishment.

For a time she runs in silence. Then she finds herself thinking, how harsh it must be for J. to feel his father's death in all that abandonment, fracture. Like a cold muscle injury. As if at the thought, she stumbles over a root, fights to get back her balance. And when she does, she's thinking that even Donny's death had had a context, the context of the tens of thousands of other wives, daughters, girlfriends, mothers who were suffering the same loss. Fifty-eight thousand Donnys. How many Mollys—mothers, wives, lovers—did that make? But J. To spend twenty-five years away from your father and for him then to die? To J., this was just another nail in the coffin that held everything normal a person could want: his childhood, his family, his home gone, gone, gone in the bleak landscape of his adulthood.

The thought is shocking to her, and Molly finds herself gasping for breath now, running at her full capacity, still searching for her second wind. Who thought that shocking thought? Who felt that awful desolation? It was her, her, her. She says it to herself, nearly angrily, her feet slapping and slapping the trail, heading uphill, the long, slow uphill that started the run, *her, her, her*. Who was there, that day, bringing news of death to an old man? It is me, me, me, she thought, in the rhythm of her feet: *my* mind, *my* body, *my* cells, *my* genes. I *am* her.

But there was no comparison. Then, and now. Then, she was a child, arms and legs taut muscles over bone. Then, she wore her hair in a center-parted perm wave, owned a paisley mini-dress. Then she had been ruled by desire, skin alive to every puff of wind, this endless well of wanting; then she was vivid, acute, full with the romance of deprivation and satisfaction, needing and getting, staged again and again. They had been children, starving for each other, and then he died, just like that. Bouncing Betty, Bouncing Betty. And after— nothing. Blankly, her mind traverses thirty years, inspecting, coolly appraising. Had it been an empty life? It hadn't felt empty. It had been, perhaps, a lonely life.

They'd never have even met, she from slummy little Saugerties, long before the spillover from Woodstock made it hip, he from WASPy Onteora Park, the fourth generation to occupy the same mansion in the private enclave. Her breath was coming harder and harder as she pushed, nearly sprinted up the rise, perhaps a half-mile of steady climb. When her father learned that Donny lived in the Park he said, *I guess Sackler only sounds Jewish, right?* That was, of course, right. Such an odd comment it seems now, when everyone is Jewish: J., Izzy.

For an instant, running uphill, breathing very hard indeed, she is confused, and the slap of her step seems to call out then, now, then, now, then, now. But then she jumps a stream, long jump, and she is there again.

They married right after graduation, in All Souls, the stone church at the end of 25 that still services the mansions of Onteora Park. It was summer, the first summer after their college graduations. They lived in the guest cottage on the Sacklers' property. They played like children in the club house, the pool, the tennis court, the fourth of July party, the place her husband had grown up, summer after summer, with the friends he grew up with. In late August 1964 he took her to San Francisco, Monterey, Big Sur, Los Angeles. He left her at the airport, he to Camp Pendleton, she to fly home for her job at Mount Marion elementary. The Sacklers had invited her to stay: her summer at the clubhouse, on the tennis court, at the fourth of July party, her mini-dress—apparently—she had passed muster. But she wanted, while Donny was serving, to live with her own parents in Saugerties. That was one of the things she wondered about, afterward. Was there a feeling, even then, that her relationship with these people was tenuous, temporary, until Donny came home? If Donny came home? Was she another army wife, guiltily avoiding pregnancy until the big question, the question about their husbands' survival, came clear?

He was in Saigon by fall. They next met in Okinawa, a one-week leave. Nine days later he was dead. She knew he was dead a week after, but only she. And still another week passed before, when the official notice came, she drove her Volkswagen Beetle up the mountain from Saugerties, through Palenville, past Kaaterskill Falls, and Haines Falls, and right on 25 and into the big stone gate of Onteora Park, to the Sacklers' huge house overlooking the Blackhead range.

Of course she'd had to go alone.

*

On the Dutcher's Notch trail Molly crests the rise now, a half-mile in, her lungs bursting, her energy flagging, hits the long, wide trail that will sink for a half-mile, now, until it hits the edge of the Harriman Lodge's holdings and turns brutally up. She is aware how awful is her pacing: no stretching, no warmup, and running way too fast. But she pushes into the downhill, dangerous, rocky, speed unchanged.

It was 11 a.m. Only Don Senior was home. In his living room she sat him down and told him, as softly as she could, precisely what she'd been told that morning by two full-dress Marines who'd come to her front door. Donny had been killed walking point on a patrol in Songh Be. He'd stepped onto a booby trap—a Bouncing Betty, they called it—and died instantly. Old Mr. S had been very proper. He listened carefully, sympathetically, kindly, as if it were only she who was suffering. Then he went out of the room for a short time, perhaps minutes, during which she suddenly was convinced, convinced, that he was going to commit suicide: she knew he kept a pistol by his bed and a shotgun in the study. She rose then, half meaning to follow him, and had just opened the door out of the living room when she heard him, from the bedroom, make the sound she tried not to remember.

Because when he made that sound, suddenly and without warning, she felt worse than she had ever felt in her life. She turned back and went to the window and looked out at the thin fall day, the drying lawn falling to the stone wall, the drop of the valley over Tannersville and the peaks of Roundtop and Overlook under the low sky.

And then he made that sound again and suddenly all color drained from the view before her, all color drained from the world, or rather, all color drained from her range of emotion and the green of the lawn, the gray of the sky, went mute.

She knew that this is what Donny saw in the long, slow moments before he died. She thought, you were supposed to have three score and ten to prepare for this view. It was supposed to be our last view.

You were not supposed to see it at twenty-two. You were not supposed to. You were not supposed to. For a long moment, while Don Sr. made those noises in a far-off room of the house, the house Donny grew up in, she saw the world as she never should have seen it. When her father-in-law came back she smelled scotch and mouthwash on his breath. And when he spoke, his voice was very hoarse, which made her understand he had thrown up. *Darling girl. Darling girl. You'll always be a member of our family.*

She hadn't told him she was pregnant—she didn't actually know it herself, then, though she suspected. Lie number two. When, a week later, she heard from the Sacklers' lawyer in Manhattan that Old Mr. S had already emended his will to leave the Onteora Park house and membership to a nephew—*The Park bylaws don't allow membership to pass out of the families, my dear*—she knew she was pregnant, but didn't mention it. Later, when their lawyer contacted her with an offer to adopt Leo, she broke off contact with them altogether. She had let Leo know his grandparents, of course, but Leo had started refusing to see his rich cousins as early as twelve, or thirteen, and still—as far as she knew—had not touched the trust fund Old Mr. S had established. Still, she had called Old Mr. S, four years ago, to get him to say a word to someone at Quantico when Leo announced he was following his father into the Marines.

So much for righteousness.

She is deep in the woods now, past the Harriman inholding, across the East Kill bridge, climbing the long, rising spur up to Beaver Pond and Molly thought bitterly, Son of a bitch. Her breath is coming in sharp gasps, her heart pounding, even more as the trail evens out and her muscles began to drink oxygen again. Thirty years later, Old Mr. S. joining forces with that cruel uphill to torment her. It was always like that. The harshest thoughts come on the uphill. Then they leave you weakened for the rest of the run. Against the wish of her body, which already wants to rest, Molly picks up her pace. And, in the pain of running, manages actually to stop her thought; manages actually to get a break, lost in the ache of her legs, her back, the sharp work of her lungs, gasping, until, to her surprise, she rounds a corner and finds herself jumping hard to avoid tripping over the steps of the little bridge over the East Kill.

On the bridge she drops onto her knees, then rolls herself onto her back on the hewed wood surface of the bridge, thoroughly pissed. A beginner's mistake. Lost in bad thoughts, she'd been running too fast, and now, not even at the halfway point, she had run herself anaerobic. "Idiot, idiot." She hisses the word at herself while she waits for the pain in her back to fade and her breath to come back.

The thin line of sky showing through the dry leaves was white as often as blue, now, with big, high clouds blowing in on the wind, the promised rain coming in. Soon they would block the sun, and the high, tenuous autumn would step toward winter with the first rains. The thought makes Molly unaccountably anxious, and although she's not ready, she stands and takes off again at a measured pace.

A beginner's mistake: not to know your run and therefore, to pace yourself wrong. One that, she'd been amazed to see when they started training together, J. made constantly. Slowly she realized that it was because, before they ran, he got stoned, secretly—she was, then, a teacher at his daughter's school, and he wasn't about to light up a joint with her. He liked to run stoned, and that was why he never, ever, really knew where he was on the trail: between the THC and the endorphins he was constantly in a state of elated confusion. This was a huge disadvantage in competitive running: you had to know the track to devise a pacing strategy, and for the first several weeks that they ran the Colgate trail together, she watched him exhaust himself early and then, to his frustration, consistently ran out ahead of him.

One day he told her, driving up to the run, that he had a nickname in his family, for always reading the map on a road trip and finding ingenious shortcuts: the Navigator. Much later, he told her how, in what he'd called "the Underground," he'd used that as a code for a certain kind of payphone-to-payphone contact, an initial contact that buried, in code, served not for communication but as the modality to set up a future conversation. "The Navigator call," they called it: the call that gave directions of where to be for the next call.

And finally one day, having beat him on the Colgate run for the sixth week in a row, she repeated to him, with a shrug, a line her father had used, often, from his own Navy days during Korea.

"You know the expression, Little J., 'the navigator is always lost.'"

Jason was bent over, hands on knees. "The fuck that mean, Mol."

"Sailors say it. Because by the time the navigator's fixed a position, you've already moved to another? You know where you just were, but not where you are. That's you on the trail, buddy. You never know whether it's a climb or a sprint or a goddamned bridge because you're always lost."

That inspired him to run the trail straight for a month to figure out the stages.

But that was the thing. Even straight, it took J a huge effort to put the trail together into a continuous narrative. Everything was fracture for him, disconnect, and the stages of the run stayed for him forever different stories rather than parts of the same. In time, he came to follow her speeds rather than memorize his own. It allowed him, he said, to experience the thing he liked most about running in the woods: the fun of being lost.

The fun of being lost. The fun of being lost. The thought annoyed her so. Like everything he had done? Weatherman, and all? It was all fun. It was all the fun of being lost. Weather was a delusion, a self-delusion by a bunch of rich kids who thought they were underground. But all they ever were was lost, and when they were done having fun being lost that way, they went on to have fun being lost other ways: lost as adults, lost as parents, lost as runners.

Molly has never been lost. Never in her life. She's running uphill now, on her heels, hamstrings and gluteus muscles, minor and major, a boxer's run as she takes the wide climb, feeling the ill effects of her earlier profligacy with her energy, working very hard indeed. She has never been lost. She *comes* from Saugerties, for God's sake. Both of her parents were born and died here. The only time she ever left was to go up to New England for college—Dartmouth, on a track scholarship, where she met Donny. They came back after college to be married—nothing else made sense but that she came home while he went to war. Then Donny was killed on his first tour of duty, and the farthest away she ever went again, save tourism, was Albany for her Ph.D., which she needed when they offered her Mount Marion School, as principal. Now she lived in her parents' house, her childhood bedroom hers, her mother's kitchen the kitchen where she raised her son, and was principal of her own childhood school. Briefly she saw her life as leaving a trail of memories that rose slowly behind her as she moved on, to gather in the parabola of the sky's depthless blue. She tried to hold the thought, breathing very hard in the last hundred yards of the uphill, using a great deal of muscle to keep her speed up. But it flew away too, up into the sky, up into the parabolic heights of the sky, and she thought instead, "It nearly swept me off my feet." A distant line from Dylan. Memory was two-edged. Sometimes for weeks you could only remember the bad things. At the edge of her capacity, she increased her speed. Fifty yards. The runner's myth was that you could go through a wall, find a source of energy where you'd feel no pain. But the pain was a wall, and you could also halt before it. That's why it is all so high stakes, so high stakes. Real depression could result from that: days of wondering whether you'd run again. With a wresting in her attention that she could feel in her legs, she forced herself to count steps, seven at a time marked off on a finger, seventy steps times seven, then seventy more. It was so hard to let pain just be physical. It infected your brain. You could not tell the two apart, whether it was age, and exhaustion, and gravity slowing your step, making you feel pain, or if it was your mind, your mind, your mind, your mind. If only your mind could go silent.

And she crested the hill, her step naturally lengthening, and in the relief of the downhill across, now, the softly grassed path, for a suite of seconds, it did.

Molly's run is over now. Not literally, but in every way that matters. She'll hit Dutcher's Notch soon, turn around, and run out, the way she came in. It's virtually all downhill, the way out, and still she'll run on stiff, injured legs, badly, painfully, her eyes on the trail, her mind half occupied with reminding herself to lift her feet, to avoid tripping, worried about a fall, a real injury. Who'll pick Izzy up after school then? She'll think more, but her thoughts will be useless, and she'll know it: pure self-destruction, no insight, no value.

Just living, unattached, uncontrollable worrying.

Worrying about the sky, graying above her, lowering with the sudden, approaching rain.

Worrying about the wind, coming up in the trees, as if a huge hand were passing its palm over them, loosing dry leaves into the air, and dust, and scaring the birds from the branches, and carrying the distant howl of a coyote, bereft, waiting for winter.

Worrying about the afternoon, trying to hide her anxiety from the child in her care.

About the night, waking at midnight, the light of the computer screen, the kitchen.

About J., alone in the woods as the rain came in.

J., alone in the woods. She sees him, in the door of his tent, under the rain trap. He sits, arms around his legs, watching the darkness, saturated with rain. She hopes he hasn't gotten high. That will make it harder. J., for all he's done, is not equipped for the view before him, the world drained of all its color, the degree zero where every hope runs away. J., for all he is the rock of support for so many people, he's not equipped for what he's going to see, tonight, in the rain. It's not a view for the optimistic, for the hopeful. It's not a view for people who believe in things. It's a view for people like her, like her, people who hope for nothing, people who've lost everything.

Except she hasn't lost everything, has she? Not yet. Not until now, now, when she loses J. J., the last survivor, but it's not the Vietnam era, or the underground, or the '60s, that he's the last survivor of. It's that he's the last to come see that view of the world without color and know that everything he's ever hoped for was a ruse, a self-deception, a fantasy that can only be maintained until now and now, losing J, she has truly lost it all. In the falling light, in the gathering wind, in the chill of approaching rain, she finds she is hissing the word aloud with the shock of each step on the trail: "All of it. All of it. All of it."

At her car, in the parking lot, rain is just splattering the windshield. One o'clock, a late November weekday afternoon. Inside the car, the air rancid. She cannot open the window, because of the rain. For a long moment she sits, traversing the huge emptiness inside of her, an absolutely inaccessible, inscrutable emptiness. She puts her hands on the top of the steering wheel and then her eye sockets on the top of her knuckles. Furiously, she hisses: I am *not* going to lose everything, I am *not* going to lose everything. With a huge effort, eyes still against her left hand, she reaches down with her right and ignites the engine, then down again to put the car in reverse. When she is rolling backward and has hit the brakes, hard, the movement finally jerks her head up off the wheel. And only now does she flip into drive and pull out, very fast, down the road to East Jewett, speeding. She has no intention of passing in front of Onteora Park. She'll drive all the way through Windham to Catskill, then around and down the highway to Saugerties, adding some forty miles to her drive.

Besides anything else, it gives her an excuse to drive fast.

6.

It's gone midnight at Molly Sackler's house, several hours gone, and something is wrong.

It's that there's no kitchen light on.

You'd think the power was out. There is no light at all. Not the faint illumination of a night light; not the glow of the second computer screen in the upstairs study.

Is it a power failure? But the outside light is burning at his house, and that shows Jason Sinai that the electric is on in the neighborhood. Is Molly gone? Her car is in the driveway. But Molly's house, under the moonless sky, is black.

It is a fact so strange that Jason, crouching in the drizzling rain at the edge of the nameless dirt road between the two houses, checks his watch again.

Two a.m.

It's a fact so strange that without even going into his own house, he crosses to Molly's yard and lets himself in the front door with his key.

He is not surprised, not exactly. Two and a half hours before, Molly had missed checking in. When he was away anywhere, an 11:30 call to his pager meant all was well—for Molly, for Izzy, for him. An 11:30 call to his pager meant nothing had happened to Izzy, and no one had come looking for him. Out on Huckleberry Point, sitting in front of a hissing fire under the rain fly of his tent, Jason had checked and double-checked his pager, though he knew it received here: the Woodstock cell tower was in line of sight, across Platte Clove.

Their plan for this contingency was simple. Jason would run away. Run away and call in, the following morning, to a phone booth in Catskill—a straight call, not a navigator, and every day thereafter, ascending one hour per twenty-four save for the 10th and 21st of any month, which threw the schedule backward three hours, and keep calling, and keep running, until they had made contact and Molly had told him what was wrong. That there had been, say, an *America's Most Wanted* episode about him. That someone had been asking about him in town. That there had been a suspicious car on the intersection of un-named roads between their houses. Or that one of his failsafes—the toothpick bolted to his office back door that would crack if it were opened; the potato chip under the doormat by the back door—was reading wrong.

At Huckleberry Point Jason put the pager back on his belt and watched the fire for a moment. It was 11:35, and those five minutes seemed to glow like the core of the fire. Then, in a fluid motion, he rose and turned. His pack was hung from the bears in a tree on nylon climbing wire; in ten minutes he had struck the tent, dropped and packed the bag, doused the fire. Pack shouldered, he was following the path out by the light of a halogen flashlight.

One of two improbable things had happened.

The first was that he had been found, somehow, by some trail that led to him from his father's death.

The second, even more unlikely, he thought, was that Molly was asleep.

Either required investigation.

A strange lightness had floated in Jason as he came out through the misty rain, the woods black save for the circle of his flashlight darting up for trail markers, then down at his boots slapping the path of wet autumn leaves, the saturated black of the perimeter of his vision, the long reiteration of the rain revealing distance as the sound fell away into the woods, shh, shh, shh. He remembered the day he first kissed Molly in the sibilant rain and for a moment he felt the times between then and now touch up against each other, itself like a kiss. Then the present came back and he cried, suddenly and briefly. Just as suddenly he stopped. Then for a long time there was just the abstraction of flashlight and black night, the slap slap slap slap of the balls of his feet, the shh, shh, shh of the rain.

He had come out of the woods and reached his car around 1:00, not at the Huckleberry Point trailhead but down Platte Clove Road where he'd parked by the Bruderhoff's logging operation in the woods. Even then he did not approach directly. Rather, he circled through the woods, across Platte Clove Road and into the woods again, then out again and slowly, keeping to the tree line, up the dirt road to the parking lot.

No one was there.

In November, the 16—the seasonal road down to Saugerties—is meant to be closed, but he descended it anyway, in first gear and still having to ride the brakes, peering worried through the rainy wind-shield. Nor did he approach his house directly. First he went in to town, driving with his lights off, parked behind the theatre and walked through the parking lot and alley to the back door of the brick-façade colonial housing his office. He climbed the back stairs— raw wood, dry with dust. His anxiety was a thin, attenuated note high in his ear. With the flashlight, in the crack of the hinge he could see that the toothpick tip that he knew to be held down with a gunned staple was unbroken. He opened the door slowly with a key, went in, and reached down for the toothpick to check that it had indeed broken when he opened the door, which meant that it had done its job. Then he crossed to the front door, in the dark, and checked the tattle-tale there, and the one on the desk, and the one on the tele-phone, the latter two made with thread.

But no one had been there.

He left the office through the backdoor, regained his car, and crossed town now, still driving with his lights off. He parked down from the little crossroads near Molly's house and climbed out. Then he walked up the side of the unnamed dirt road until he could see, crouched down in the rain, and watched.

That was when, for the first time, he saw something wrong.

It was something for which he had no plan.

There was no light in the kitchen window.

For a long time he crouches and thinks. But really, there are only two things he can think of to do: go away or go in.

Jason rises and walks across the driveway to the front door.

Inside the kitchen, there is still no clue. On the table were the remainders of his daughter's homework. This, clearly, was an after-dinner activity, because the dinner dishes are cleared to the sink and a smell of thyme is in the air. The smell makes his stomach awaken: he has been fasting since the previous morning.

He climbs the dark stairs quietly, crosses the hallway to Leo's old room, and opens the door. I sleep here neatly in the bed, composed under taut wool covers. Next he checks Molly's room. So. It was against all his rules, but he was right not to run. As unlikely as it seems, Molly is actually asleep too, in total darkness. It is so remarkable, in fact, that Jason actually goes into the bathroom, shutting the door before he turns on the light, and checks the medicine chest. There's a little plastic vial of Lorazepam in there, but it's as full as last time he looked at it. Don't think he never counted the pills: numbers, for Jason, are a map of life. Anyway, it's his Lorazepam. Molly never took pills.

Reassured, he turns off the bathroom light, slips out of the bedroom, closing the door behind him, thankful for its solidity, for its even swing and quiet hinge, and goes back downstairs.

So, Molly didn't send the failsafe message because Molly has slept all night. The second time in thirty years. His surprise stays with him all the way through the leftovers of our dinner, which Jason now consumes with a full quart of milk. Then he turns on Molly's computer to read about his father in the papers, and this is what he is still doing when hours later he hears Molly's step coming down the stairs.

7.

Molly wakes at dawn, feeling bruised, as if a crowd of people had been haranguing at her, her dreams a loud memory. Her sleep has been black, syrupy, a sleep of resistance rather than rest, a stubborn refusal to face what lay ahead. With consciousness came the fact of having slept all night, an astounding event that she greets with sourness. Now she had broken a thirty-year habit of insomnia twice, and both were for the wrong reasons: once for that completion she didn't want, the other, now, an act of nearly childish denial. Sitting on the side of her bed, she also knew that for this second failure, she couldn't blame Jason.

When at last she rises, it is first to check Izzy, across the hall in Leo's room. Next Molly goes to check the web, not in the kitchen but in her study on her desktop: she wants to do this now; she does not even want to wait to go downstairs. Her heart stops, then pounds when she sees that two Marines have died in Somalia. She can barely focus enough to absorb that they were both ground force, so neither one was Leo. When she sees their names she shuts down the monitor and then leans her forehead against it until the adrenaline flood passes. Now the day, with its blank, metallic sunlight, its matter-of-factness, the tedium of pain. She goes downstairs slowly, her calves and ankles aching from the run yesterday. On the stairs she smells woodsmoke and stops. In the kitchen, at the computer, is J, reading.

She watches him watching the computer screen, still unaware that she is watching. The smell is the campfire he had come from. He is unshaven, his face pale. His T-shirt hangs loose on his shoulders and arms, the still-faintly-red hair on his temples curled and bushy. Normally, you look at J., you see the power of his wide shoulders and strong arms. Now he is hunched, thin, defeated.

Temporary. Watching him, her mind catches on the word, and the conviction comes to her from the other side of the night, from the afternoon before, that J. has come to say goodbye. For a moment, she detests him, purely and bitterly, a little paroxysm of hate squeezing in the pit of her stomach like an endocrinal process. She says, coldly, before she means to speak: "Where do you plan to go?"

He looks up, surprised.

"Plan? I planned to go to Chicago. But . . . I broke all my own rules. I just didn't believe it."

She takes a long moment to understand. When she does, horror floods her.

"Jesus Christ. The pager. I could have sent you to fucking Chicago."

"Um hmm." He nods: he has already finished with this. "You didn't, though, so it doesn't matter."

She feels sweat on her skin and such an awful feeling in her stomach that she has to sit.

"Only by luck."

"Everything's luck."

Now she looks up. There is defeat in his voice. Slowly, her awareness of him pushes away her awareness of herself. This suffering man. And he is not, in fact, leaving. Unshaven and small at the kitchen table, smelling of smoke and sweat. Later, she tells herself, she can do full penance for what she had nearly done. Now, she stands and rounds the kitchen table to where he is and puts her arms around his head, her stomach against his cheek, stroking his scalp. For a time she stands like this. Then he pushes her away gently, a hand on her stomach, and looks up at her.

"You slept all night."

By way of response, she pulls his face back against her stomach. Then she steps away again.

"I'm so sorry, J."

He puts his hand, or rather his fingertips, back on her stomach. "For missing the failsafe?"

She hesitates. "That too."

"You got me out before the worst of the rain."

"What were you thinking?"

He hesitates too, now. He doesn't really want to formulate this thought. He's too superstitious to admit that when Molly had missed the failsafe, he had felt confident nothing was wrong.

"That you had slept through midnight."

Molly shifts her weight now, and crosses the kitchen to the coffee pot. The sight of a pack of Marlboro Lights on the counter draws her up short. She'd bought it the day before, on the way home from running the Dutcher Notch trail. Stopped to buy gas in Catskill, and the pump credit-card machine had been broken, so she went in to pay. On the counter was a cigarette display and she thought fuck it. But she'd never have left them out, she'd known J. was coming. She'd have hid them. For the second time she thinks: fuck it, and lights one.

"Is there any news?"

He shrugs, then wakes the computer up to show an article from the *Times*. "*Times* says the memorial's next week at the Spanish Embassy. The obit notice asks for donations to the Veterans of the Abraham Lincoln Brigade in lieu of flowers. *Rockland County News* has an op-ed. Predictably."

Molly smokes, watching him. His tone is dull, his face drawn and tired. She thinks of him, watching the world without color, all night in the rain. She says:

"I think I know how you feel."

"How?"

"Like all the color's drained out of the world."

"No. I mean, how do you know?"

That makes her hesitate. He knows how. She said: "Because I've felt it too."

"Have you?" He stands now like a horse in a stall, moves to the window. "I don't think so."

"J." She hadn't expected him to be angry.

"No, I don't think so." And now she sees that he's not angry at her, but at himself. "Your folks didn't die alone. Donny didn't die alone.

Donny didn't die abandoned by his youngest son. Donny didn't die having seen everything he believed in his life turn to shit."

That surprises her. Because Donny died exactly like that, exactly. But she is still not planning to tell him that—or more exactly, she still doesn't know that she is planning to tell him that. What she says is: "Neither did your father."

"Yes he did. He died seeing everything he believed in fail. And I was one of the people who made it so. Donny—you told me yourself. He went to Vietnam to fight Communism. He believed in what he was doing, and died, just like he was prepared to, while doing it. And everything he believed turned out to be right."

Really, there is no point in this. He is lecturing, not discussing. He is recounting what he had been thinking about, sitting out at Huckleberry Point, when the vista drained of all color. She listens carefully, an ear cocked toward the interstices between words, where she might find what he had experienced. Then she answers.

"J., Jesus. They lost the fucking war."

"Right, and won everything else. The White House, the national agenda, the future. Don't talk to me about Clinton. Clinton's about as left-wing as you are, and you know it. You know there's not one serious issue you disagree with his administration on, and you've never voted but Republican since '68. My father? From the day Stalin came to power he saw everything he believed in fail. One after the other after the other."

"Fathers die. It isn't a defeat."

"His death was." He moves from the window again and to her utter shock takes the cigarette from her fingers and hit it. J., who once ate a non-organic stringbean, sometime in the '70s. But when he speaks, it is not exactly to her. "You think I don't know? You think I'm a fucking idiot. He loved us. My dad? He lived for us. There was a hole in the middle of his life exactly my shape. The color drain out of the world? *I* made the color drain out of his world."

Ah. A little puff of satisfaction in her belly. The incredible power of listening. So this is J. without hope. She never would have guessed.

For a moment, she watches with nearly clinical curiosity. And then she realizes that she would never have guessed, either, how much it hurt her. Never would have guessed how much she depended on his hope. His optimism. His mad optimism in the face of such steep odds.

He has carried her cigarette away. She lights another, and tries to think what to do next. See, you don't comfort Little J. Little J. comforts you, or me, or his clients, or his friends, or the fucking counterwoman who serves him coffee at a fucking highway diner he'll never be back to in his life. Little J. has a heart for everyone. But you don't comfort Little J. So she says, with trepidation:

"Little J. Fathers die."

But it is too much, even this, and for a moment she recognizes him again in the coldness of his response. "I don't know what you're talking about."

"Okay." She approaches him again now, takes the cigarette butt from his hand and, with hers, tosses them into the sink. Then she puts her arms around his shoulders. "Enough."

And then Izzy is there, having woken with the first light, and come downstairs, and because she couldn't even know that she had a grandfather, never mind that he died, they say no more.

Lies, lies, and lies. All happening so fast you cannot even comprehend them.

8.

But it stays with her. All that day. A Saturday under November rain, with Izzy to take care of. J starts a fire in the living-room fireplace. They play a round of cards. Maybe Izzy has that rarest of treats, and one she only had at Molly's: a half hour in front of the TV—but if so, it's just Bill Moyers, or Amy Goodman, a barrel of laughs. Molly feeds everyone, twice: breakfast, then lunch. After lunch, when the rain stops and the sky begins to rise, aided by winds from the south, they take a walk, tramping on the wet dirt of the nameless street outside the house, up past the only other resident, the sculptor who rented Molly's barn, and then up some more to where it peters out and becomes a trail, winding up to the meadows that were all that remained from the Bentley Farm.

Does the normalcy of this activity emphasize, for Jason, the bizarreness of what he is doing, playing with his daughter and hiding from her the death of a grandfather she didn't know she had? Not sitting shiva, not mourning, just carrying on, as if the worst thing in his life, the thing he had feared the most, has not just happened?

That night they have dinner in front of a W. C. Fields movie. Then, without any discussion, Jason sends Izzy to bed there, in Molly's house.

As if they live here now.

Jason comes in to kiss his daughter goodnight. Then he falls asleep on her bed with me for a time. When he wakes, it is well into the night. Downstairs, Molly is smoking in front of the living-room window, lights off, watching the moon rise, real light now falling on her face. She turns quickly, putting the cigarette out in a potted plant.

"Are you all right?"

He nods, by way of reply, and sits in an armchair by the fire. "You?"

She shrugs, and there's a pause. Then he says: "What's up, Mol?"

This time, she shakes her head. "I don't know. I feel awful for you."

Now he shrugs, and watches the fire. "Don't. I was waiting for this for years."

"Doesn't help."

"I know that."

He turns to the fire now, this time for such a long time that at last she speaks again.

"Are you going to tell me about it?"

"No."

"J."

"You've already been a casualty of Vietnam. You don't need to be one again."

She speaks in a neutral voice, as if making a contribution to an only slightly relevant symposium. "In what way is this about Vietnam?"

"Everything is about Vietnam. Without fucking Vietnam I'd have been with my father on the day he died. Maybe the moment he died."

"Your brother was there." She speaks neutrally again, watching him closely, nearly clinically. And when he goes on, again, she gets a glimpse at what he is thinking.

"I made his life meaningless. Without me he'd have been a great American jurist. I made him marginal. The father of a criminal. Then I left him to die."

"Bullshit, J." Now she has said it, for the record. She doesn't expect him to listen. Did he? For a long time he looks into the fire, and she thinks: I'm sorry. She looks up now to find him looking up, and she nods.

"J. You stay here tonight."

He considers this. "Izzy'll know."

"I know."

There is a long silence now. Then he says: "Okay."

She nodded again. "Okay."

"Should we go on up now?"

This time she turns around, to face him. "We should."

9.

It is midnight again.

You can tell by Molly Sackler's kitchen window, across the way, alight.

Or can you? Really, the moon is so bright and silvery that it's hard to tell if you're watching a bright electric light within or the very moon's reflection on black windows without.

Funny how in the presence of the absolute, all certainty is lost.

Wish my father and his fucking friends had known that.

This fucking light. This fucking window.

In fact, it's the moon you see. Last night's clouds are gone and the moon, forty-eight hours older than when Molly woke at midnight to the news of Jack Sinai's death, is full. So perfectly full you know it the second you see it. And so bright that you really could not—really not—a moment ago, tell whether it is the moon you see, on Molly's window, or a brash light within.

But that window, it was *not* a literary device. It *is* the moon you see. The interior light is off and the moon's absolute silver lies on the window like water. Molly Sackler is still asleep, lying in the absolute black that, during the huge November moon, is the only alternative to the absolute silver that lights the lawn and trees and the street with no name, outside, this little edge of the village of Saugerties under moonlight falling softly, softly falling, on the house and on the grounds.

What's more, this fall night, this moon declines so steeply to the south that, by 12:30, from down the steep fall of the lawn toward the woods to the south, it actually peers up under the eaves of Molly's house into her bedroom window, its bright silver light suddenly appearing in the far corner by the bureau, then beginning its slow creep across the room, throwing a deranged trapezoid over the bureau, the rug, the rocking chair and, before it leaves altogether, the bed where Molly sleeps.

Who knows? Without this moon, this could be the third night in thirty years that Molly sleeps till dawn. Everything has changed, so suddenly, so enormously, why not that also? She's exhausted enough—drained really. Ran two days in a row. Took care of Izzy. Dealt with J. That was not the exhausting part. What drained her was the realization that her life, as she was leading it, was no longer tenable. Maybe that is what her sleeping self has recognized: that everything might as well change, including the thirty years of waking at midnight, because of a lie she told thirty years before.

During the day, she could say to herself, as she had said to herself for years: we all have our secrets. J., if nothing else, had taught her that. She didn't even think of it as a secret. She thought of it as something she shared with no one simply because it was within her own legitimate zone of privacy. But sleeping, her lie weighed upon her now as it had not in years. Sleeping, it was no longer legitimate, or private. Sleeping, it was no longer even hers. My grandfather's death had changed all that. Or maybe it had never been hers.

So now, drained, she sleeps, the old argument falling apart in dreams. J. and Izzy, Leo, all of her students. The dirt intersection of the unnamed roads on what had once been the Bentley Farm. The cracks in the rubber expansion joints behind Mount Marion Elementary. Old Mr. S. in his mourning suit on the lawn outside All Souls, birds flying over him out of the south. A young woman cresting a grassy hill under the Catskill sky and waving her goodbye. *You stay. But across the open countryside the grass is waving its goodbye to you.* A line in a poem by Frank Stewart. Then the supermarket dream, the one she had dreamt when Kennedy was shot where a girl died in the supermarket aisle she'd been in when she heard the news, the cold aisle in the Grand Union up the mountain, and in a catch of her breath while she sleeps the understanding that it is that one, the girl who lost her husband, the one in the supermarket aisle when Kennedy died, the one Molly cherished so, that is dreaming and that girl's dream is the thirty years since of her life.

If only she could remember it when she awakes.

So she sleeps, on her back, arms around her head, hair spread between her arms.

The moon has crossed the Wakefield bureau, with its framed pictures of Leo, and her parents, and, in a tiny silver frame, Donny, just his face.

It has crept across the rug, throwing its big-headed shape across the pattern of, in this light, blacks and silvers.

223

It has crossed the rocking chair and done so, carved spindle to carved spindle of its complicated back, with such a fuss that to the side, over the carpet, the rocking chair has nearly knocked over the dresser with its distorted shadow.

And Molly sleeps.

There is a pause while the moon peers under the bed, for an instant, before it jumps onto the covers, like a kitten. Now it is too slow for our eyes to see it move. But at one moment it is on the border of the quilt's first interior border—duotoned black and silver—then our attention wanders, despite ourselves, and when we look back, the entire half of the bed is alit and on it Jason is lying face down, his bare shoulders visible, the moon creeping over muscles of his back.

Molly herself, as the light advances, is as if preparing to wake. The quilt shifts slowly with her breath, evenly. But is she still dreaming? I don't think so. I think she is returning, slowly surfacing, as the moon lights her face on the pillow, the dreams already forgotten.

In a moment they'll have gone, leaving only the disturbance of their passage, like the flicker of a fish's tail passing as a wave along the algae beneath, or a disturbance of the light.

The moon touches her eyes. She wakes directly and in a smooth movement, as if she had been waiting, sits up on her bed. Fully in the present, vertical in the silver, framed perfectly and casting, on the corner of the bed and the wall, an absolute black moonshadow.

For a long time she sits there, her hands, silver skinned, on the mattress as if she is steadying herself on a boat. Her hair, as if a living thing, has fallen, sleek and heavy, into place. Her face is utterly unarmed. Her eyes, stupid, are focused on nothing.

Molly knows she is on thin ice. She is on thin ice because her plan for J. is done. It was a victory and as so often in victory it had drained her, drained her. Now she is reamed with hollowness, reamed through and through, her chest, her belly, her guts. In this trapezoid of colorless light, a light that eradicates color, everything has been eradicated. It is not like the day at Old Mr. Sackler's house up the mountain in Onteora. This is different. This she had never felt before, but she is not surprised. It had been promised, this, though she had never fully believed it to be true.

Nor, she knew, would she ever experience this again. What she saw that day at the Sacklers', that was just a fact about life and death, non-negotiable, a knowledge of grief. This was different. This was something that, after you have experienced it, something had to change radically in your life, so radically that you have never to experience it again, and because one choice for that change was of course non-negotiable, it made anything, as an alternative, possible.

Even, in Molly's case, telling the truth.

Before the silvery light has moved from her body, Molly has risen and stepped out of its cell. She's naked, and it's cold, but she stops only to step into Jason's camping shirt, lying where he had left it on the floor, smelling of sweat and woodsmoke.

Downstairs in the kitchen, she does not even bother turning on the light, but opens the blind on the kitchen window, letting another of those moon-made trapezoids, like a crazed Noguchi design, into the room. By its light—better, luminescence—she wakes the computer screen which, in turn, lights her face. Nothing is in the news about Somalia: no firefight, no bombardment, no kidnapping or beheading or public parading of corpses. For a time she absorbs that, and when she stands, now, you think it is to go to the counter for one of those cigarettes she bought that afternoon in Catskill, to light one at the stove and then, watching out the window, exhale. But in fact, she doesn't. In fact, she leaves the cigarettes, turns on her heel, goes back upstairs, and then upstairs again to the third floor, the never-used floor that contains her parents' bedroom and the formal parlor, that looks over the black shadows cast by the maple trees over the duotone garden.

It is an orderly room, cleaned monthly by the maid, never used, smelling more than slightly of mothballs from the closet, where her mother's and father's clothes are stored. She has not been back here in six months, or more, and before that it was six months before, or more. So long that the sweep of her bare foot on the wood floor surprises her, both with its strangeness and with its familiarity: recent strangeness, long ago familiarity.

There's a window, over the backyard—a huge leaded-glass window, lit silver now by the moon—and in front of the window, a deep feather couch, all blacks and grays until she flips on the light, when it turns to reds and oranges. The slipcover was sewn by her mother, the couch purchased by her grandmother. In front of it is a rug, holding the moon's light in its center. On the rug is an oak chest, darkly stained, on which sit a vase of dried flowers. On the wall are paintings, one of which is a winter landscape by Jervis McEntee of a field of cows and, in the distance, a red barn—the dairy, when the Bentley farm was still a farm. And behind this picture, in turn, is a wall safe, which she opens to take out, from under a small pile of deeds, and passports, and bank books, and jewelry boxes, and old report cards, and legal papers, and backup Zip disks, and all the things that need to be saved, when a house burns, including a single blue airmail envelope.

Is this part of Molly's plan? Has she know, from the moment she sat down to think, what seems like years ago, of how she was going to tell Jason that his father, my grandfather, had died, that this was going to be the end of the plan?

Maybe if Little J. had let her, if he had not cried so, she would have avoided this. Maybe if he had not, suddenly, so profoundly doubted the very principles on which his life was based, she would have avoided this. As she has been avoiding it for thirty years. In other words, Molly is not doing anything she needs to do. She is doing something, now, only for my Jason. Something so huge that if Jason gets it wrong, Molly will be paying for this the rest of her life.

But she is already passing into the hallway now, closing the upstairs parlor door, passing the empty third-floor rooms, turning off lights as she goes, and going back down the stairs.

*

In her bedroom, the demented moonlight is directly on Jason now, as if imprisoning him in a painting by Salvador Dali. The symbolism is not lost on her; she even smiles, slightly, for a second.

She sits, puts her hand on the small of his back, feeling its warmth even through the covers, and rubs. But J. has not slept properly in days, and it takes more than this to wake him. The rub turns to a shake, and then she speaks his name several times into the hush of the room before, with a glacial movement, he turns to his back and rises on one elbow. The movement leaves his body in the moonlight, but his face in shadow. And quickly, Molly understands that if this is going to work for her, she must start, and finish, before the moon shifts more. And so, in an even, expressionless tone, she tells him.

"When Donny died, they sent two Marines in full dress. That's what they do. It was January.

"They came during lunch. To the front door, not the kitchen, where we ate. It was lunchtime, I was with my folks. I went to the door myself and when I saw who it was I took them to the sun room. I let them tell me their news. They said Donny was killed walking point in Songh Be Province on January 14, 1965. They said it was a booby trap, and that he was killed instantly. I asked if they'd return his remains for burial. They said there wasn't enough left to bury. Then they left, and I went to tell my parents in the kitchen, and everyone cried, and then I went up the mountain to tell Donny's father, and then I ran the eight to Dutcher's Notch, and then I found out I was pregnant, and then the rest of my life happened."

She is still talking to a headless body. But the moonshadow is not going to wait forever. She understands that. Already the light has crept up Jason's chest, showing the edge of the still-red hairs between his pectorals, and Molly goes on.

"But that's not how Donny died. A week earlier I had gotten this. It was airmailed from Saigon. You can see the postmark. Just dropped into a mailbox—nothing special. It had Donny's driver's license, and a picture of me. And there's a letter, in French."

Molly unfolds the letter now, a sheet of airmail paper, and places it on the cover. The moonlight is actually bright enough that she can read it—or rather, that she can remind herself of what it says, because whatever you say, no moon is that bright.

"It says: 'Dear Mrs. Sackler, I send you these few of your husband's effects, sorry that I can not send more, but a package will attract the notice of the army censors, and a letter will not.' This is good French, nearly poetic. Lots of subjunctive. *Il se pourrait que vous doutiez de la vérité détenue par un tel gouvernement – le vôtre de surcroît. Vous en auriez raison. Il se pourrait que vous souhaitiez connaître la vérité sur les circonstances de la mort de votre mari.* You can't really translate the subjunctives. It's like: 'It is possible that you doubt the truth of that which a government—above all your own—tells you. You would be wise to. It is possible that you wish to know the truth of how your husband died. The Marine Force will tell you your husband died fighting the good fight, perhaps heroically. I am sure he was a heroic man, and I'm sure he thought himself a good man, but that is not how he died. He was put to death by a sixteen-year-old soldier, one of the two who bombed the Quan Loc Hotel in Saigon on Christmas Eve. Your papers told you of the bombing. They may even have told you that two Vietminh soldiers infiltrated the Quan Loc Hotel. But they did not tell you that they conducted the execution of your husband, and they did not tell you why. They did not tell you what your husband's job was, an interrogator of our comrades, so widely despised that he is nearly myth; they did not tell you the horror that he, with his colleagues, rained down up on our country; they did not tell you how shocked they were at our infiltration of the hotel and our execution of this war criminal. And they did not tell you because they are afraid for you to know.

"Mrs. Sackler. In 1943 at the height of World War II Jan Karski traveled from the Warsaw Ghetto to America to tell President Roosevelt what was happening there, and no one would listen. Now you must do the same. Your country is going to lose this war in my country. Your husbands and sons and fathers are dying for nothing, nothing. Their deaths are meaningless. Tell them that. Tell them that they are dying horribly, and for nothing, because you can never, ever win.'"

When she finishes, the moon has finished its tour of the bed. It's climbing the wall now, at the most extreme angle possible through the window, nearly upwards. From the darkness in the bed, for a long time nothing comes, just Jason's hand on hers. Finally:

"Molly. A nineteen-year-old romantic wrote that in 1964."

Her voice is nearly conversational. "But he was right. And I didn't tell them."

"Everyone's right in hindsight. Except those who were wrong."

Aware of the absurdity of their position, each arguing what the other believes, and in a far part of her mind, she thinks, so this is love.

But she's crying too much to say any more, which is perhaps the right way for such conversations to end.

Molly thinks that her life will never move from this moment, this moment when thirty years of interior scaffolding collapse and for the first time since she was a child bride she cries in someone else's arms. She's wrong, of course, and you, if you've been paying attention, know exactly what's going still to come to her. Within the year Jason will be forced to surface, betrayed by his ex-father-in-law when he divorced his wife, then smoked out by a journalist in Albany, a journalist who does so well at his job that he also will discover the existence of my half-sister, Beck, and go so far as to marry her. She doesn't know that, and she doesn't know Jason's plan, which he has thought about for a long time, and which will work. That means that contrary to all she has always thought, there's no jail time ahead for Jason, which is lucky, because within ten years Leo will be killed in an embassy bombing in Kabul, along with his wife, and after Leo and his wife die Jason, who will be her husband, will be able to raise her two grandchildren with her.

At least for a while.

Then he will die too.

But she doesn't know any of this right now. Right now she only knows that for the first time in thirty years she is leaning her head against the chest of a man she loves and crying.

These massive symmetries, measuring your life. You only see them two-three times, no matter how long you live. These two moments of crying. Those two tasks of delivering news of death. Those two runs on the Dutcher Notch Trail.

But I don't think that's what's making Molly Sackler cry.

Do you want to know what I think is making her cry?

I think it's that girl who learned that the President had been shot while shopping in a supermarket in Kingston. That girl who drove her Dodge Dart up the mountain to deliver Don Sr. the news of his son's death in Vietnam. I think it's because now, thirty years later, she is realizing how she had given that girl everything, everything she wanted. A husband, a son. A house in the Hudson Valley. A career, a lover. And how different it had turned out to be, even when they were exactly the same, the thing you wanted and the thing you got.

"Of course, I disappointed her, too."

"What?"

Dimly, realizing she had spoken. She pulled her head from his chest and wiped her eyes, her nose, on the back of her hand. This wasn't what she wanted to say to Jason. What she wanted to say was what she said next, and it was exactly what she wanted to say, and had been wanting to say for years.

"We were never going to win the war. It was 1964, and already, everyone knew we weren't going to win. They walked right into his room, shot him in the head. They will have interrogated him, and tortured him. Then they blew up the hotel and drove away. The next day was Christmas morning. And the war went on for *ten more fucking years*."

"Moll. Take it easy."

"Donny knew it the second he got there. He told me so in Okinawa. He said the whole thing was a lie, from the Gulf of Tonkin Resolution on. It's exactly what he said, just like the guy wrote in

Ramparts: *the whole thing was a lie.* He said that the North Vietnamese were fighting for their existence, and they were never going to stop. He said Ho was a genius, and he could have been our genius had Truman not turned him down. He said the South Vietnamese, the folk he had to deal with? They were like gangsters. They were corrupt like fucking hoodlums. The war was like looting a shopping mall for them, everything free for the taking. He said that Johnson and McNamara knew it even back then. They were lying through their teeth to protect the war effort. In '64 Ho had an *eighty percent* approval rating in South Vietnam. Then two Vietminh drove into American-occupied Saigon, walked into Donny's hotel, tortured him, then shot him through the head. It was so leisurely, he took Donny's tags, his wallet, everything. Then he sent me a letter. You see the postmark? Saigon, December 27. He was *still in Saigon*, mailing a letter with perfect impunity, *three days later*."

"Okay. Enough." Now that she isn't crying any more, Jason has a hand on her shoulder, watching her from the remove of his arm's length. "Why did you never tell me this before, Molly?"

"Because you guys. You and your friends. You were so fucked. The way you treated those boys? I remember when we were in San Francisco, before Donny's intake, we went to the Haight? We wanted to cop a loose joint somewhere so we could fuck stoned? All Donny had was a military haircut—he was still in civvies—and just that, that alone, the haircut and nothing else, was enough. I had never heard anyone speak like that before in my whole life. To Donny! The last time he was on American soil. Fuck you. Fuck you and your friends."

"Molly, for God's sake."

She regards him coldly. "You want to know what I think, Little J.? Because if you want to keep going with me, you need to know. I think you were just as bad as they, and you know what? I think that if by some far out, impossible chance, one of you had ever gotten into any kind of position of power? You, Jeff Jones, Billy Ayers, Bernardine Dohrn, their sanctimonious bullshit? I think you'd have been as bad as anyone else. Probably worse. You'd have been another god damned martinet. You *were* a god damned martinet. Weather Bureau my fucking ass. You people would have been ordering invasions and executions by their second day in office, and you god damn well *know* it. Democratic process meant *nothing* to you. You stole SDS and if you could have you'd have stolen the whole fucking country."

Jason takes this, not quite with bowed head, but not far from. She was wrong, about some of them at least, although not necessarily him, nor the ones she had named. But that doesn't matter now. And when she was done:

"Why are you telling me now?"

"Oh." She moves away from him now, to the window. Most of the lawn is under the shadows of the maples, just the border of the garden still lit by the setting moon in the valley. She has to struggle to reassemble the present, to recapture the events and reasoning that explained why she was telling him this now. What all these differences all are, these things that have seemed, for so long, to matter so much. For a time it passes through her, one image after the other, all equally meaningless, Then, in the swirl of elements in her head, her mind catches on Leo, and then on me, and then she turns again from the window to J. and says, simply:

"It was time. You've been in mourning long enough. Now he's really dead, J. Really dead. I'm sorry you've lost him. I really am. I'm sorry like only someone who loves you, as deeply, as completely as I do, can be sorry. That you lost him then, and that you lost him now. I loved Donny, J. He was a dear, kind boy and I think he would have grown up into someone much like us. But he's gone now, and your father is gone, and the past thirty years are gone, and you and I, we have a lot of our lives yet and a child to raise, and we can't go on like this any more. We can't go on like this any more."

Her voice is raising, dangerously, at the end. "Okay. Okay."

"No, it's *not* okay. You have to promise, me, J. It's bad enough that I can lose you any day to a jail term. But you have to promise me that you're not going to fall apart now. You did what you did. Right, wrong, that's just noise now. You were wrong, I was wrong, who cares? The only difference was *how* we were wrong. Now you have to step up to the god damn plate and *not* fall apart. We have a child to raise."

And Jason answers: "All right. I hear you. I'm not going to fall apart."

My father says more things that night. He brings Molly back close to him again, in the now pitch-black room, at last convinces her to let him put an arm around her and, with a hand on her back, says many more things. Maybe he even convinces her to take one of the Lorazepams in the bathroom. He gets her to lie down, at last, and then lies next to her, perhaps with an arm around her neck, perhaps he even holds her tight against the red hair of his chest, and maybe they make love, maybe she cries again.

All that is what it is. I don't need to know about it. But I do know that after my father falls asleep Molly lies for a long time on the bed, eyes wide open, watching the last of the moon, from the western edge of its declination, cast its light nearly upwards now across the ceiling of the room. Of course, it isn't really upwards, it's just a trick of the fact that it's setting into the valley. The moon can't really throw light upwards into a room. But it seems like upwards, and when Molly finally rises, walks to the window, and looks out, the illusion is still there, as if the moon were sinking into the earth below her. She watches it set, watches it until it has altogether disappeared under the tree line, holding her arms, shivering slightly in the cold through the glass. Behind her, in the bed, my father gives a long sigh and says, in a normal voice, "Bedford Street." That's where, she thinks, his family is gathered now around his mother—his brother Daniel, the Columbia professor, his wife Maggie Calaway, the lawyer, their children. His adoptive sister Klara Singer may have flown in from Israel, where she works for the American Commerce Department Mission, a Clinton nominee. She knows all about them, a family of left-wing aristocrats, gathered to bury their dead, and then carry on his legacy of moral certainty. She knows more about them than just that: she knew what my father had done to them all, which was not, as it happened, what he thought he had done. He had not, for example, ruined my grandfather's life—Molly felt that strongly, throughout the hours my father had spent telling her about his father—but he had, she was fairly sure, ruined his brother's, a fact of which he was totally unaware. There are still two hours till dawn. She sighs, a huge sigh, and pads quietly to the door. First she will check on Izzy. Then she will check on Leo. And then?

Well, then, there is that pack of Marlboro Lights on the counter, and she could—and believe me, she would—smoke one of those.

Chapter Ten

Isabel Montgomery

July 12, 2011

Los Angeles

1.

In April of 1996, a few months after my grandfather died, my Aunt Klara was recalled from Tel Aviv to Washington for a series of meetings by Deputy United States Trade Representative Charlene Barshefsky, her boss.

This is a matter of record. A trained baboon could find it, and in fact one did, Little Lincoln to be exact, in response to a very broad query from me to find out what the entire family did that spring, so far as he could.

One of the things he found was that my Aunt Klara had been recalled to Washington, a fact not in itself remarkable. What was, however, remarkable, was something else that he found: that after several days in Washington, for the first time since she had left, ten years prior, she had come to New York, that spring. In fact, according to a footnote in a biography of Nathaniel Singer, my grandmother's first cousin, who served in Defense under Forrestal, Johnson, and Marshall, Klara attended Passover that year on Bedford Street, the first since my grandfather died—she had not, in fact, come for the funeral—and, according to my Aunt Maggie, the last time Klara ever came to the States.

Shortly after returning to Israel, she resigned her posting at Commerce and took on a professorship at Bar-Ilan University, where she eventually became a dean.

This, too, is a matter of record. And this, too, Little Lincoln found and synced to me from London all the while I was writing whatever it was that I was writing about Molly, whatever it is, that is, that you have just read.

Whatever it is, I emerged from writing it to find this fact in some of the ten gigs of data that Little L. had sent and, for a moment, so huge was my momentum, that I nearly went right into it. Why was she there? What was she doing? And what made her go to the seder?

Did it have anything to do with my grandfather's death?

But remember? I am the consummate professional. Molly was way gone, by then, her five afternoons and nights of talking having given me a couple straight weeks of writing at my perch over the Pacific, twelve, fifteen hours a day, such profound access into those days in November, fifteen years ago, that there are times when I rose, and lit a Marlboro Light, and felt my mane of black hair shaking down my back, and the weight of my breasts, and the strength of my runner's legs, and only with a real effort did I manage to see that it wasn't my body I was feeling, it was Molly's.

The difference meant increasingly little to me.

I wrote fueled by the minibar, and by the last of my Rasta's Focalin, and down in the lobby very early one morning, when the hookers were going home, I scored some pot.

Practically a health cure.

Then, when I finished, knowing I had just written the best thing I had ever written in my life, I had so much momentum that I had to stop myself from going right on to the Passover of 1996 and the last set of lies in my little family that I have to explore.

The thing was, I wasn't ready.

I didn't have the reporting, for one thing.

I just had what I was imagining, and even if, in my heart, I knew it to be true, that wasn't enough.

For another, I had the minor matter of the $175,000 I was being paid.

So I ventured out in the Mitsu V6—beautiful car, which I had so far driven once, from the airport—and went to the Apple Store at the Grove, where I bought a copy of Final Draft, on my own dime, as I did not think it wise to expense it and let my employers know that they had been paying my hotel for two weeks and I did not even have the software necessary to write a script. Then—and here, I invested the time to get a medical marijuana card from some doctor in San Fernando, requiring me to recall all my high-school Spanish—I set to work translating Cuntman into a screenplay, nuts and bolts work, organizational more than creative, and except for being annoying and a waste of time, a total walk in the park: Establishing—Night—Riyadh Hotel, blah blah blah.

See, I did not have to worry about it being good.

I knew that whatever I handed in, they would want to change, whether it was brilliant or terrible, because no matter how you slice it, everything you think about film people is more or less true—though the fact that they are dishonest, disingenuous, and designing does not, as it turns out, stop them from also being a great deal of fun—so I just tossed the thing together. Then, when their response, which was apt to be senseless, actually got back to me, I would get back to work to make it good. Only, I would make it good my way, and they would think it was they who had done it with their incisive notes.

Meanwhile, I tracked down my Aunt Maggie who, I vaguely remembered, had told me she was going to Paris. Upon investigation, I found that not only had she gone, but she was staying: Uncle Danny was taking a sabbatical while she, Maggie, spent a year seconded by her law firm to the International Court of Justice. And Aunt Maggie, when I reached her in the Hague, listened to my question with interest, and then told me that if I wanted to know anything about Aunt Klara, she advised me to go ask her. Which, don't you know, is just an invitation to a person like me. Source one sends you to source two for an answer? That is just an invitation: first to get the answer from source two, then to go back to source one and beat them to a pulp with it, because there is nothing more suspicious than someone who won't answer a simple question, even if it's your Aunt Maggie.

But aren't you just the little Puritan? Go to Tel Aviv in mid-July without an assignment? Travel without someone paying? My take for the year was already over three hundred thousand dollars, and it was hardly half over. But spend money on traveling to Paris and Tel Aviv to write something I was dying to write, and I needed to write, and which was turning out to be the best thing I had ever written? That did not fit my work ethic, not one bit.

So I cast around a bit for an assignment. But none of the stories being so predictably rounded up and printed by the global entertainment-information complex fell even remotely in my purview. And no one seemed to be looking for the burned-out daughter of a '60s burnout to write anything for them. I even drew a blank with the *Times*, who had been literally begging for a piece but who told me that the next thing they had for me was in November, the School of the Americas Protest in Fort Benning, Georgia. It seems that I could write anything I wanted for the *Times*, as long as it was about America, and as long as it was about my father.

Cuntman submitted, and too smart to expect a read within any reasonable span of time, I spent a couple days at the pool, reading Little Lincoln's research, wrestling with my conscience.

What turned the trick was the realization that from Paris, the flight to Tel Aviv was, like, three hours. And in Tel Aviv, I could find out why my Aunt Klara had come to New York in Passover of 1996.

Without quite admitting to myself what I was doing, I called the concierge in Paris and had Momma's apartment on Cherche Midi opened, then packed and flew over.

I toyed with flying coach.

Or not renting the spanking new Lamborghini that caught my eye when—purely by mistake—I went to the celebrity rental website at Charles de Gaulle.

After all, the whole thing is a tax deduction.

And it is only when I am safely seated next to a bottle of

champagne in the first row of an Air France first-class cabin that I launch iData again and start reviewing what Little L. sent about my Aunt Klara and her flight to America in April of 1996.

Know what I do then?

I arrive at Charles de Gaulle and walk straight over to my favorite place, the ticket counter.

This one is easy.

I buy a ticket to Tel Aviv.

I take the endless hike down to El Al at the very end of Terminal Two.

Security takes three hours. I actually end up telling them what my Parsha was at my Bat Mitzvah.

On the other hand, I virtually breeze through at Ben Gurion—a mere four-hour wait in the Arab Room, which beat the hell out of the Yemini Twins—Christians from London, here for a Biblical tour—who have been there already for six, or the stunning Palestinian-Texan journalist, who has been there for seven, or the Italian film maker, who held the record at eight and a half.

When I leave I pick up a modest Mercedes 300 series, the best car available at that hole of an airport.

The irony is not lost on me.

I check into the Intercontinental Tel Aviv.

And the next morning, in brilliant Mediterranean sun reflecting off of the white buildings around me, I climb unannounced the stairs to Klara Singer's address of record, an airy walkup on the third floor of a Bauhaus apartment building on Rothschild Boulevard, and ring the doorbell.

2.

Klara Singer in person turns out to be a woman in her fifties or so, with jet-black hair turning white and jet-black eyes which, as they focus on me through the open door, appear first defiant, then turn confused, and then, as if suddenly flooded with understanding, very sharp indeed. She wears a sleeveless black dress that sits flawlessly on her dark skin and, save for bright red lipstick, no makeup. A black jacket, folded over the back of a chair, and black espadrilles, on the floor next to an overstuffed briefcase, evidently make up the rest of her work clothes: it is nine in the morning, and she is about to go to the office. She is shockingly beautiful and, I had always assumed, from the fact that she was single, gay: as such she was a very, very convincing older gay woman. I'd go to bed with her in a second—she smelled great, too—Opium, I thought—were she not my aunt.

But then, she isn't really my aunt, is she?

I know—I have heard it so many times—that this fact is key.

What I don't know is why.

Yet.

Whatever she is, and why ever it matters, she looks at me with those sharp black eyes for a long moment, sharp black eyes that actually have me at a loss for words, no mean feat. When she speaks, her voice is deep and tinged with staccato Israeli diction, which surprises me: she lived in the States from thirteen to thirty.

"So. I understood you might be coming this way one of these days."

She stood aside and, as I came in to the apartment, looked at me appraisingly and critically.

"How?"

"How what?"

"How did you know I was coming?"

"Molly told me that you might."

"Are you in touch with Molly?"

"My sister-in-law? Of course. Have a seat."

I sit on a little couch—the décor is suited to the neighborhood, which is the largest collection of Bauhaus architecture in the world. The room is viciously clean, and sparely decorated with high-modernist furniture including, I note, a Kroll sideboard with, visible through glass doors, a collection of bottles. Klara, in the meantime, goes off to what must be the kitchen, where I hear her on the telephone excusing herself in Hebrew from work because *"akhyaniti hagia l'California"* — *my niece has arrived from California*. This is interesting to me, that she knows I am coming from California; interesting to me, and meaningful to me. Also interesting, incidentally, that she refers to me as her niece. We have never met. When she returns, it is in jeans and a white men's shirt, the jeans showing a slim waist and rounded hips, the white shirt showing full breasts. She is carrying a tray with little cups of Turkish coffee and little white biscuits.

"Maggie is your sister-in-law too."

If I expect her to be surprised, I am disappointed. "This is your grandmother's recipe, these cookies. You knew her, didn't you?"

"I did." I take the coffee, wishing it were a drink, and looking around—fruitlessly—for an ashtray. Noticing that, she rises and resettles us out on the little balcony from where, between two tall buildings, I can see the Med.

Settled, she watches me light a cigarette. Then she gives me a smile that, for its pure warmth—even if not for its beauty—was little less than breathtaking.

"Yes, Maggie's my sister-in-law, too. No, I haven't spoken to her. I guess that's what you've come to discuss with me, haven't you? If I understand correctly."

We regard each other in the sunlight for a moment without embarrassment—on either part. Then:

"I've been reading your work for a long time. You know you're regularly translated in *Ha'aretz*, don't you? The little piece on March 6th in the *Times* gave me a hint of what you're up to. Then I heard some chatter. Writing a book about the year of Daddy's death? What brought you to that?"

Daddy. That does take me aback. But she thinks of my grandfather thus, doesn't she? Again, I choose not to answer. No answer seems required. Indeed, she has turned to show me her profile as she looks out over the low rooftops.

"Well, I suppose she has her right." This she says to the distance. But then, as if waking up, she turns those honest black eyes back at me. "But why do you? What gives you the right? You're not asking me to tell you a political story."

I didn't understand. "I don't understand."

"You're asking me to tell you a *personal* story. It has nothing to do with whatever you're trying to write about."

Still, I don't understand, and I guess I show this with my expression, because she says:

"Surely, what you're after is a *political* story."

"Ah. Well, that's just it. I think it *is* a political story."

"How? I have a right to my intimate life. Surely that in itself is a political commitment."

I know that to be wrong. But as she says it, with such conviction, it is hard to formulate why, and I am trying—or better, trying to try—when she goes on.

"Maybe your father. Maybe even your uncle. I don't even *have* children."

An instinct moves me. "My uncle?"

And indeed, she says the name unwillingly. "Daniel. I don't have children. I don't have the same responsibility to you."

Israelis. Always the victim. I watch her for a moment. Then I rise, walk into the living room through the sliding doors to the sideboard, choose a bottle—scotch—and pour myself a drink into a heavy piece of crystal. I down it, and then come back and light a cigarette.

I hadn't expected to have to go here.

I don't know what I had expected.

"I have three answers to that, Aunt Klara. The first is that I dispute that your experience is personal, not political. The second is that I dispute that you have any right to your own experience. And the third is that I dispute that you have any choice."

Do I expect her to be shocked? As I told you, there is honesty in those eyes. I should add that the honesty is huge. "Okay. Let's hear the first."

I gather my thoughts. "Let's grant that the distinction is meaningful, which is not necessarily true, but fine. To say that your experience was intimate, and personal, is to say that it was not politically determined. Are you sure of that? That you were even in America was politically determined."

She interrupted me. "Historically. Historically determined."

"Well, I don't know what history is, but the decisions that resulted in your being in Israel, never mind America, were to a one political. Hitler's, Eichmann's, Stalin's, Roosevelt's, Ben Gurion's. You know that."

"Okay. That's an interpretation, but okay. It still doesn't change anything. I'm not talking about those kinds of events. I'm talking about interior events."

"Aunt Klara, I have yet to find a single intimate event in the Sinai family that was not politically determined. Not a single one. Jack's secret death. My father's secret life. Not a single thing."

This is indisputable, and although I know I've trapped her in a simplification, and indeed, that she's only accepted that simplification because she has already assumed the very maternal responsibility for me that she denies having, I am not going not to accept my advantage when she says next:

"Okay, *khallas. Khallas.* Number two."

This one is harder, and I resist the urge to go for another shot of the lousy scotch, although it seems fair enough to me that I should get one drink per answer.

"Your right to privacy is superseded by my right to understand the reality of my life. That's axiomatic. People have the absolute right to understand the truth of their lives, no matter what damage that does. Something happened during Passover of 1996. I don't need to know what it is to know that it casts a shadow over our family as big as a house. But I do need to know what happened in order to get out from under that fucking shadow. Then there's two logical correlatives. A: my very willingness to understand, and my talent, as a writer, to understand it thoroughly, as thoroughly as if it happened to me, grants me the right to know it. I'm sorry, but I believe that, and I believe it so strongly that if I ever have this argument again, I am going to raise it from a logical correlate to an axiom. And B: unless you are radically different from every other member of your family, the thing I need to understand is a lie. A lie that has been perpetrated, by you at least in part, which I consider a political crime and one in which you are implicated. What I need, and have every right in the world to understand, is how, where, and why you told a lie, because lies are always, always, always wrong, and the truth is always, always, always right. Fair enough?"

"No. Not at all. Not even remotely fair enough. But it's one of those arguments so tightly wound up with its own self-interest that it's virtually impossible to argue. And what, may I ask, is answer three?"

Now I draw a blank. "Three? I've forgotten."

"That I have no choice."

"Oh. Well, that one's simple. When I leave here I'm going to see Danny and Maggie, and there's no way on God's green earth they're not going to talk to me, so if you want me to get it right, you'd better also."

Below us, someone is shouting in Arabic for someone else to move a car. Then I hear a car start. The canopy of sky, above, is light gray, dropping this pastel light that had struck me on the street.

"So where do I start?"

I put my iPhone out on the table, and adjust the mic for the ambient noise of the city below us.

"With the trip you took to New York in 1996, in April, when you were recalled to Washington."

She laughs, but not as if she were amused. "You make that sound easy."

"Isn't it?"

"*Motek*, you have no idea what you're asking."

I let a little dead air hang on that one.

And then, fixing me in a gaze that, so direct, accomplished what some might call the Herculean task of silencing me, she begins to talk.

Five days later, I retrace my steps from Tel Aviv to Paris. I take a taxi into town, drop my bag in Momma's place—big greeting from the concierge, shocking view of leaden rooftops stretching over to the seventh—then I go right back out and take another taxi to the rue d'Ulm, a straight shot down Saint-Germain which, in the glories of early summer, with its wealth of retail, would usually be something like heaven for me.

But I am not here.

I haven't been here since I got to Israel.

Uncle Danny is at his office desk at Normale Sup, where he's spending his sabbatical, when I come up the stairs. He's in a light blue denim shirt and—I see when he comes out around the desk to kiss me—khakis, a light blue tie. American. I make a mental note to tell Maggie where to take him shopping. The jacket over his chair is black, and I don't need to see him put it on to know that it doesn't fit. He has my father's and grandfather's blue eyes, but only the remnants of blond hair around the edges of his bald head. The result is a surprisingly open face, a face you want to believe, and one that slows you down when you begin to appreciate the subtlety, the ambivalence, of what he is actually saying.

"So, Iz. You're on a mission without permission, aren't you?"

"Was permission required?"

"I hear you're taking no prisoners. The little avenging angel, aren't you?"

"Please don't call me little. And how did you know? You spoke to Klara?"

"No, of course not. I spoke to Maggie. Maggie spoke to Molly. Molly spoke to Klara."

My iPhone is on the desk.

"Can we get started?"

He is trying to look amused. But what he is about to do, there is no way to keep any ironic distance.

I own this motherfucker.

"Are you planning on interviewing Maggie again too?"

"I am. She said she'd take me down to the Sologne for a couple days when we're done here."

"Okay." He swivels now in his chair and looks out the window, over the little garden. "Where shall I start?"

"Passover of 1996. Then ten years earlier. The time you and Klara walked out on the beach at Hammonasset."

"You're kidding."

"No. I'm not."

And so he does. And when he is done, several days later, Maggie and I go down to the Loire, and talk for several more days.

And when she is done, this is what I know.

Chapter Eleven

Maggie Calaway

Passover, 1996

New York City

1.

In April of 1996, a few months after my grandfather died, my Aunt Klara was recalled from Tel Aviv for a series of meetings by Deputy United States Trade Representative Charlene Barshefsky, her boss.

She flew Tel Aviv–Washington overnight on a diplomatic flight carrying three bureaucrats from the State Department, her first time ever on a jet this small. Partly because they were civil service and she the subordinate of a political appointee, the fellow passengers on the plane did not talk: it would have required careful attention to Separation of Powers at a time all wanted to rest. The entire flight was in darkness. She did not sleep.

In Washington, she had just time to check into the Mayflower, undress, shower, and dress again before she was due on Capitol Hill. Later in the trip she would meet with Clinton; today she was booked on a round of visits to the offices of Congresspersons on Ways and Means, meet-and-greets to prepare for Barshefsky's up-and-coming push on a complicated offset deal. The deal was a lucrative exchange of Turkish steel and Israeli communications technology which, drawing on many American patents, required many permissions under the Export Control Act. In both Israeli and American industry circles it would be appreciated that the licensing of this deal would make possible, in the future, conversion to military applications. Thus the meeting my aunt would have with the President: the deal also required an executive order. This was not a part of her brief that pleased her and she was, during her days in Washington, somewhat more reserved than Barshefsky, whom she liked, had wished—so much so that in due course my aunt would leave Commerce for a professorship at Bar-Ilan University where she would later become dean. But Barshefsky didn't understand what my aunt's reserve was really about.

By six o'clock of that first day, notwithstanding either her exhaustion or the pressure she was under, my aunt was at the airport again, catching a plane to New York.

It was April 3, the first night of Passover, and she was going home.

The Delta shuttle climbed out of DC like a rollercoaster going up the initial hill, a short, even acceleration at fifty degrees off the vertical before leveling suddenly out into the evening sky.

Klara did not expect to be on time for the seder—she was never on time. She did not expect, either, to feel quite as awful as she felt, although she had expected to feel awful. This was her first trip home in ten years and she had not previously admitted to herself, quite as clearly as she did now, that she cared far less about that offset deal she did not support than about this trip to New York.

She had sat watching out the little window at the thickening evening and how, instead of the bland east coast sky, she was seeing herself, ten years earlier in 1986, standing on the chill edge of the Long Island sound, with my Uncle Danny, looking up at the sky.

2.

"Maggie, who's missing?"

While Klara Singer was coming up from Washington, Maggie Calaway leant to peer into the oven held open by her mother-in-law, understanding the gravity of the question in terms of the timing of the oven's contents.

"Just Klara, Ellie. Has she called?"

"Klara?" Eleanor Sinai was teasing the brisket with a fork, aged face tense with concentration. "Klara hasn't been home in ten years, and she likely won't even know she's late."

In the sudden, warm silence of the kitchen, Maggie touched her mother-in-law on the arm, though as to whom the gesture was meant to comfort, she was not sure. Jack Sinai had led and Eleanor cooked the family seder in this house for an astounding fifty years. This year, the first seder since Jack's death, Eleanor had left the bulk of the cooking to her daughter-in-law. That was a judicious move: Maggie was held up to wives all through the clan, always with the standard line about the only shiksa in the family being the finest Jewish cook. It did wonders for her popularity, as did her exotic green eyes and red hair; as did the fact that besides cooking and raising children she earned very serious money as an associate at Frankfurt, Garbus, Klein, and Selz and ran a study group at the Council on Foreign Relations. The funny thing of course was that this food was little different than what she had learned in her mother's kitchen in Wellesley, Massachusetts: brisket was pot roast, kreplach were dumplings. Now she stood from the stove, her face of freckles glistening from the heat.

"Ellie, I think we can leave the brisket fifteen minutes more. And I'm sure Klara will be here by then. Come upstairs now."

"But what can be keeping her?" Eleanor spoke anxiously, helplessly, laboring up the stairs, as if her lifetime of domestic authority had at last, before this crisis, collapsed. "Is she coming straight from the airport?"

"Yes, but apparently not from abroad. From Washington." Leaning close to speak into her mother-in-law's ear, Maggie negotiated her way through the crowded living room, where the vast Singer–Sinai–Levit clan had all arrived save Klara, to an empty armchair. But Eleanor's comment had been overheard, because when she rose Wendy Sobel—née Levit—drew her aside and spoke in a whisper.

"Maggalah, I hate to agree with your mother-in-law, but effing

Klara's spoiling the evening. The fact is, Freddy Singer's managed to get drunk."

"Has he?" Alone in the crowded room, the two women regarded each other, each calculating behind her eyes. "Christ, Wendy, who gave him a drink?"

Wendy nodded. "I think he got to my husband, that wimp. And right now, don't look, but Freddy's telling your cousin Diane—who, I assure you, is simply lapping it up—how his uncle Nat's seder will be the first real seder this family's seen in fifty years."

"Good God, Wendy. Go tell him Danny's doing the ceremony, not Nat. He's been up all night getting it ready."

The other woman laughed. "You think Freddy doesn't know that? Now look, let's make sure he sits between us. We'll keep him busy."

Maggie Calaway agreed, her eye still on her cousin, all sense of order fled. But there was no point in panicking now. She hurried back down to the dining room to change the place tags on the big table, set for twenty-five in china, silver, and linen. And when she was done, as if summoned by the dual worries of the brisket and of Freddy's drunkenness, she crossed through the den, where the children's tables were set, past my grandfather's study and through the open door to the backyard where, sheltered from the light under the massive chestnut, she fumbled a cigarette out of the pack she kept under a piece of bluestone and, hands shaking, got it lit.

She'd started smoking again after Jeremy to help lose the weight—or so she told herself, because now Jeremy was six months. Taking hungry drags, the cigarette burning too hot, she admitted to herself that all the weight that was going was already gone. The rest, which was there to stay, was not entirely unwelcome: full breasted now and round of hip where she'd once been slim as a boy. As for her face, green-eyed and pale-lipped, the gravity of age was welcome here too.

Through the living-room window she could see Freddy Singer, glass in hand, talking to someone. Calmer now, letting the ash cool on her cigarette while the first wave of nicotine washed waves of relief into her stomach, she told herself that drunk or sober, Freddy was not the problem. Klara was ruining the evening. Klara, who had not been home for the ten years since Maggie and Danny were married.

Maggie had heard about her at the family table: about her steady rise through Clinton's Commerce Department. Jack and Eleanor had visited her every year in Jerusalem after Passover, and often met her in the fall in Madrid, where Jack went every year to a steadily dwindling meeting of the brigadistas. The last visit had been a year ago, just after my grandfather's diagnosis, and even the Memorial, last Summer, had not brought Klara Singer home. Klara wouldn't be coming even now, Wendy Sobel had said, if it weren't for the fact that Eleanor had asked her to: this would be the first Passover in fifty years that Jack Sinai would not lead the seder, and Eleanor was not sure she could bear it alone. Nor, Maggie suspected, could Danny, especially since he had beat off Nat Sinai's challenge to lead the seder tonight. Without Big Jack Sinai and his moral authority, only Danny stood against the steady Zionist tide of the family. Klara, prominent in Peace Now, and who counted Ilan Pappé and Amira Hass among her closest friends, would be, Maggie knew, an enormous boost to Daniel.

But she was taking too long, far too long. Maggie Calaway took a last, hot drag from her cigarette, resolving to tell Eleanor that it was time to start the dinner: Klara or no Klara. She hurried through the drizzle inside again, washed her hands at the kitchen sink, and climbed back into the noise of voices and laughter, from upstairs, then crossed again to her mother-in-law, still in her armchair.

"Ellie, you know it's getting really very late."

"Yes, Mag. But let's let stomachs rumble just a little more."

"Are you sure?" The girl's green eyes were on her now.

"Darling, Jack waited ten years for Klara to come back to this table. There's no point in starting without her now."

And instantly, as Maggie watched her, Eleanor Sinai regretted what she had just said.

3.

The sort of thing old folk do, Eleanor told herself, angrily, stroking her daughter-in-law's hair in apology. She got confused: confused in what she said to whom, confused among the children of Danny's generation — sometimes, truth to tell, among Danny's contemporaries too, although many of them were nephews and nieces. Who were these cheerful people who seemed all to make endless amounts of money and live somewhere in Brooklyn, or in the suburbs? Jack would have died sooner than leave Manhattan. As for money, why, he had never put a penny in the market in his entire life, not until Danny took over the finances. But then, he had also never been willing to fix a legal fee, had he, taking on defenses purely for their ethical or political bearings, and that they had lived in any ease at all was only because of the prosperous few clients who insisted on making up for the many who had no resources at all.

And there it was again. My grandmother brought her focus back to Maggie like a sleeper waking, or a swimmer surfacing from the depths. The equality that had come to exist between her internal and external realities: she could become, literally, lost in thought, even in the middle of this crowd. With effort, she picked up one of the young woman's warm, strong hands, around her own with their papery dry skin, and made herself speak. "Maggalah, who is that man talking to Danny?"

The young woman looked over, her green eyes sharpening, her red hair flat against the round of her skull, like feathers. Not for the first time she saw her daughter-in-law as a sleek, rare animal; a prize Danny had brought back from the world. Imagine a woman like that interested in a Jewish man in the old days. Maybe a Greenwich Village bohemian, for a fling, or one of those rare WASP radicals drifting into the circles of the intellectual Left, in and then out again. Eleanor could not deny that in her daughter-in-law she also saw a trophy, a sign of the acceptance that Danny's generation took for granted. She watched, thus, her daughter-in-law, herself watching the man they shared, son and husband, as he stood, holding his own son on an arm and his daughter by the hand, talking to a slim, handsome man of perhaps forty.

"Now, that would be Joshua Raskin. Marcus Levit's daughter Miriam? Married Stephen Raskin, who was in the Reagan cabinet? Her eldest son."

"Is that Miriam's son? My God, I haven't seen him since they used to come up to the Island for summers. And what does he do?"

"He's in equities, somewhere. Or arbitrage. Goldman Sachs, I think."

"I see." The number of them on Wall Street, she could not understand it. Their actual professions were making money itself, nothing more, nothing less. But why did they do that? Her own children, at least, were not tarred with that brush, and that was only right: Danny and Klara and Jason—her eldest son, the one, as she put it, they had lost to the '60s—both had sat in this living room as children with Lenny Boudin, with Annie Stein, with Izzy Stone. In a little flash—a kind of flash that had become almost as familiar as the reality around her—she saw Annie, an unfiltered cigarette in her mouth, a cloud of smoke around her head like the argument she listened to with the detached frown of her interior process, sifting the concepts she was listening to against the complex Marxist theory by which she tested everything. God, the young of the family were so much less vivid than her contemporaries, so much less . . . *focused* than her peers, so sharply drawn by the hard battle they had done, not just in Spain and Europe, Mississippi and Washington, but in courts, in hospitals, in businesses, and for nearly all of whom the comparative comfort of their old ages had been a byproduct, rather than the aim, of their professions.

Then, in another little hypnagogic flash, Eleanor saw her husband's face as he sat at the head of the massive dining-room table, his gently sagging cheeks shaven clean, his black eyes sparkling as if showing, in anything he did, only a hint of his depths. To look at that face was to feel stronger. There were few such faces left, she thought.

Perhaps there were none. But how did they, these young people, live without them? Was that why they needed so much money?

All these thoughts Eleanor Sinai thought as she watched her shiksa daughter-in law in profile, absently stroking her feathered head as if she were not human but animal, while around her conversation rose and fell in waves. And in other circumstances, she would have kept sitting, stroking Maggie's hair, in the comfort of being solitary in the middle of family. Now, however, she had this child to attend to. And so she leaned over, putting her lips next to Maggie's, and said, quietly: "Maggalah, my love, you get the brisket out then, okay? I'll give you ten minutes, then I'll tell Wendy to bring them all down to the table."

4.

My uncle watched his wife rise and then turn for the stairs, at which his daughter Laura tugged free of his hand to follow. Stephen Raskin was regarding him with his black eyes, pitch black, they seemed, under black bangs and thick eyebrows. He was, Danny registered dimly, only becoming handsome now, in middle age. Danny was becoming somewhat less so, but he had been so much better looking to start with. Stephen knew that also, which was why he had already referred twice to the price of his house in Sag Harbor and the fishing boat he kept there. And yet Danny managed to nod attentively, smile agreeably.

At last Stephen moved on, and Daniel Sinai crossed the room to his mother, handing her his infant son and settling onto the stool next to the chair just vacated by Maggie. For a moment his mother was occupied with Jeremy, who fell nearly instantly asleep. Then she looked up to him.

"So, Danny-boy. Having a horrible time?"

He nodded and she smiled. He smiled, then, too, and said:

"Mom, I can't stand the thought of Nat Singer sitting in Dad's place."

"I know." And she did know, Daniel thought, watching his mother's gaze abstract for a moment. In this entire room, only he and his mother knew that in 1941 Jack Sinai had asked Nat Singer, who worked on Henry Stimson's staff, to intervene with the Dies Committee when they had denied Jack Sinai a US Army commission on the grounds of "Premature Antifascism." Nat had refused, and so Jack Sinai, with command and combat experience from Spain, had been denied a place in the war against Hitler.

"And yet—" and now Eleanor Sinai's focus was on her son again—"your father wouldn't have minded. You know that, Danny-boy, don't you?"

"Yes." Danny answered as softly as she had spoken.

"Good." Now her voice strengthened and she motioned for Wendy Sobel to come over. "Go on down to get the Haggadah then, darling. Wendy and I will get these people seated."

Surprised. "Is Klara here?"

"No dear. But Maggalah's brisket is going to be ruined if we don't get started."

Your father wouldn't have minded. Downstairs, in the quiet of his father's study, my uncle sat at the desk in front of the Haggadah and the notes for his seder on which he had worked for much of the night. And that was true too. The seder, for Jack, was—precisely—the one time politics was not personal: the one time each year when this entire family sat at his table, and liberal, conservative, or—the ultimate crime—neo-liberal, everyone was welcome. "Fundamentally, Dad," Danny had liked to say to his father, "fundamentally, you're a Shtetl Yid in a Brooks Brothers suit." It had been a statement with which his father had, he suspected, secretly agreed. But he had said, only, "Family is compromise, Danny-boy. Harmony usually is."

When my uncle had lost his ability for that compromise he could no longer remember. Sitting at the desk a suite of quick images passed through his mind: Nat and the Dies Committee; the family shunning his father after he was blacklisted by McCarthy; the FBI files Ron Jacobas got under Freedom of Information, which showed that Simon Levit had told the FBI that Jason Sinai—Danny's elder brother—had been with Ted Gold the night before Ted Gold died in the Weatherman Townhouse explosion. His father—year after year his father overlooked all of that. But in the living room today, Danny had witnessed a catalog of reasons he could not, had not for years, been able to do the same. Stephen Raskin coined money on Wall Street as a tobacco industry analyst. Ray Levit devoted his Yeshiva education and Harvard law degree to managing large real-estate holdings in Queens and Brooklyn, in constant battle with his low-income tenants. Larry Singer, pouring a drink for his cousin Freddy even though Freddy was an alcoholic, had done defense work for Oliver North. All of them—even the most liberal among the family—were resolutely Zionist, as if it were impossible to be Jewish without being so. Now, what were those ties that united him to these people—family, religion? Flawed ties, they seemed to my uncle, as early as when he was in high school, and he argued as much to his father, often, in the long series of words, carefully and lovingly put together, that comprised their relationship. His father had never argued the point back.

"I hear you, Danny-boy."

"But you think I'm wrong."

He could see him, his father's face across the table at Wolf's Deli, pausing in the search for words. "It's not that you're wrong. It's that I'm closer to the source. I have a connection you don't."

And now it was his father inspecting him. "You know, Daniel, this was the kind of feeling that made Little J. do what he did. And if you feel the same, I don't know what we're going to do."

Neither had Daniel known.

Soon enough, of course, they found out.

And now?

Danny lowered a cheek to the surface of the oak desk and felt the pain of grief as freshly as if it were never going to diminish, never going to go away. He could smell him, far in the back of his throat, the dry and slightly bitter smell of his Bay Rum aftershave. He could hear him, the low rasp of his voice, the hesitant chuckle, his long cough. His father and he had never touched each other, avoiding all physical contact, doing whatever had to be done between them with words: long strings of them, well and subtly put together. Now those words struck him as less in their sum than a small gesture of affection. For a long time he sat there, eyes clenched shut. Then he opened them to the dim light of the empty room.

There was so much he wanted to say to them. He wanted to tell them that his father's religion had been such an expansive one, such a generous one, and that now, in the rising tide of neo-orthodoxy and fundamentalism, it was an endangered one. He wanted to tell them that the Jerusalem of this night's ceremony had nothing to do with the real Zionism of the real Israel; that it was not an ideology but an idealism, a way of touching the divine, and that to turn it into a blue-print for political dominance was the death of the Jews because statehood corrupts and absolute statehood corrupts absolutely. He wanted to tell them that this people who sat at seder tables across the world, rich with food and family, were only truly the Chosen People if they remembered that only they, only they had escaped a slavery that existed the world over, and that to celebrate their unique escape—just as it was to mourn their unique victimization—without mourning the ubiquity of those who have no country to run to, that was an obscenity.

And there was more. He wanted to say that his father had never been wrong. Not when he fought fascism in Spain, not when he fought apartheid in Israel, not when he fought the totalitarian impulse that ran through American democracy like a melody. He wanted to say that his father had fought the tide for over sixty years, and nothing that had happened had ever proved him wrong: not Reagan's Cold War victory; not the resuscitation of McCarthy by neo-conservatives nor the abandonment of liberalism by Clinton; not the disappearance of any credible Left in America nor the stock market that was making the Left irrelevant: none of it proved his father wrong, none of it.

If he could say it? Somehow, it seemed to Daniel Sinai, that if he could say it, here, tonight, the growing uncertainty of the past ten years, the diminishing confidence with which he wrote, and acted, and thought, would all disappear. Nothing had meant anything since his father told him, just after Laura was born, that he was dying. In the year of his father's death everything had fallen apart: his work, his writing. His father had been everything to him, a catalog of human virtues, an exemplar of integrity, a monument to the highest hopes of the twentieth century, an encyclopedic store of information. The impoverishment of the world, without him, was astonishing. One by one, Danny found himself examining the institutions available to him—the fractious, ineffective argument of the *Nation*; the insider-ish neo-conservatism of the *New York Review*; the Liberal Zionism of *Dissent*; the careerism of his students at Columbia, pausing briefly in his constitutional law course in between lucrative internships at corporate firms; the incredible sway of money in New York of the '90s . . . It was as if not only his father who had finally died, but his father's world too.

And now? Now, standing at the window of his father's study—without even being conscious of having risen from the desk—staring out at the swaying, dripping limbs of the chestnut he had known all his life, listening to the footfalls of his family descending the stairs to the dining room where, in moments and under the disapproving eye of nearly the entire assembly, he was expected to lead the fifty-first consecutive family seder? Now, when the only things that survived the death of his father were the memories these people had of him? Now, what was he to do? Holocaust and heroism were what these people had come for: the Holocaust of Pharaoh and the heroism of Moses which they would sagely and with infinite self-satisfaction transform to the Holocaust of Hitler and the heroism of Ben Gurion, a neat moral lesson that justified all their comfort, all their conservatism today. And they wanted that lesson served with righteousness and brisket: a healthy dose of the former and several helpings of the latter. And if they did not get it, this fifty-first continuous seder at his father's table, they would not come back and this family would shatter like glass breaking on concrete.

For a long moment, holding his father's Haggadah in one hand, Daniel Sinai stared out the window into the backyard of his childhood home with its towering chestnut tree. The rain had passed, a rising spring full moon, lighting the sky from below the rooftops north. And to his surprise, suddenly, with an immediacy that belied the complexity of the present, he felt himself in another spring—not that spring, a decade before on Hammonasset Beach, when he had carried out another decision he did not understand with a hardness that even then surprised him, but a spring even earlier, the spring night when he was twelve when he'd realized, irrevocably and with certainty, that his brother had run away and was going to stay away for ever.

5.

There had been a camera-flash vision of Bedford Street under light rain when she got out of the cab, an eyeful of the brick townhouse dappled by streetlight shadow from the new leaves of the London plane in front, and then the door had swung open into the living room. In quick succession she saw orange light on the drapes over the big bay window to the garden, a Raphael Soyer she had not known she remembered, a woman she recognized as a second cousin, and then Eleanor was before her and all else ceased as she shut her eyes and buried her face in her mother's hair.

When Klara's vision returned there was a series of faces in staccato sequence, rendered super-really clear by the film of tear on her eye. There was a flood of talk, and then with what seemed to her abruptness—Klara had no idea that she was late—they had been called to table, and Eleanor, holding her arm tight, was leading her downstairs, pulling her down toward her as she talked.

"My darling, are you all right? You look so pale."

"I'm fine, Mama," Klara whispered back. "I'm tired. I've been traveling too much."

"I'm a selfish old woman to make you come here."

Tears came to her eyes with their recent surprising ease. "God, I miss him."

"My girl, remember what I wrote you. We've all done our mourning here. It's just for you that it's new."

"I know, Mama." With effort, Klara calmed herself, wiping her eyes with a rapid movement. "Danny's doing the seder, right?"

Now, despite the stairs, Eleanor Sinai looked up at her adopted daughter, her only daughter, with attention. "I believe so, Klary."

That was good. She didn't think she could have stood seeing that old fraud, Nat, in Jack's place. Now they were in the warmth and smells of the dining room, air rich with the meat roasted in wine and cloves, and she was looking first at the china and silverware, then the lace tablecloth before her. As if of itself her eye rose and sought out the Jacques Lipschitz, the Leon Golub, Ellie and Jack's Katubah, and that of each of their parents. And then Klara sat suddenly for a swoon was passing through her, a swoon of the purest unreality, a hot flush of finding herself entirely, completely, at home.

She held her adoptive mother's paper-dry hand, waiting for the dizziness to pass, watching Eleanor watching the family settle in at the table, her eyes and face alive with animation and interest that made her age as if irrelevant. Again she felt the heat of tears behind her eyes, and perhaps actual tears would have fallen had not she become aware of the silence that had descended on the table. Looking around, she saw that every seat was filled save the one at the head of the table, Danny's. The red-headed woman across from her, that would be Maggie—she had seen her once or twice at Yale, not more.

The infant in her lap would be Danny's Jeremy and the little girl running in to whisper something in her mother's ear, now that would be Laura and Uncle Joe sitting uncomfortably in an ill-fitting suit. But still, there was no sight of Danny, an absence that was evidently responsible for the sudden awkwardness at table—an awkwardness that, she suddenly felt, she had been aware of upstairs, too. And thank God for Freddy Singer, the only one guileless enough, or drunk enough, to break the silence—with gratitude, she heard Freddy's voice come from across the table where he sat in a cloud of booze.

"Klara, is it good to be back?"

Somewhere she found her voice. "It is Fred. Very good indeed."

"And where do you go in Tel Aviv for yontiff?"

"Oh, to a friend or another."

As if Freddy had broken the discomfort of her ten years' absence, several people spoke to her now, one asking if she ever went back to the kibbutz, another asking after distant family in Rehovot, and a third, still, a political question, which Uncle Nat, who had not been in Israel since '48, began to answer. And while he did she saw Danny come into the room, holding, she was glad to see, Jack's Haggadah, and wait politely for his uncle Nat to stop talking. For the briefest moment their eyes met. Then both turned their attention to Nat.

"I'm likely the only person in the world who can still remember Yankel Sinai's seder. Two, three hours, and he thought nothing of it. There were no separate tables or children's services in those days, either. Jack and I were the youngest, but if ever we said a word, well . . ."

"You won't see that kind of seder any more, Nathan Singer." It was Harriet Rosenthal, Eleanor's sister and the third and last remaining member of that generation speaking. "Now they have women's seders, gay seders, mixed-marriage seders. And you won't keep children still for three minutes without a computer game, never mind three hours."

"But can't these new things be good, Aunt Hattie?" Freddy Singer's voice, too loud and slurring its sibilant consonants, now held the entire table's unwilling attention. "I mean, can't Pesach be relevant to gays and feminists?"

Nat took it on himself to silence Freddy again. "It's good for it to be relevant, Fred. But only if it's still Jewish. Passover is about remembering the past, and the past doesn't change to suit the times."

But Freddy was not to be stopped. "Well, you may say so, Uncle Nat. But with all due respect, we came out of Egypt thousands of years ago. You old ones are only a single generation closer to Moses, which isn't that much. I think you can be Jewish and gay, or Jewish and feminist."

"Freddy's right, I think." In the shocked silence, Danny's voice sounded for the first time, and Klara looked directly at his face, which wore a strained smile. "You *can* be Jewish and gay. Or Jewish and feminist. In fact, you can even be Jewish and *Republican*. Now there's a fact that never failed to surprise my father."

Listening to this, Klara felt her neck stiffen. Danny was moving to his chair with authority, a solid man, heavier than she remembered but with wide shoulders and light hair in the open collar of his shirt. That gave the right impression: strong, reliable. She had seen him on CSPAN or Bill Moyers: a convincing, articulate, impressive speaker, a man of the Left. Slowly, she conducted an examination of his face. A net of wrinkles around the deepening eyes, the widening forehead under the receding hairline that divided his face. It was not bad: he was handsome enough to lose a little to baldness. It didn't scare her. She had expected that.

But then, which she had not expected, she suddenly saw Jack, just where Danny was, a slight sheen of moisture on his forehead as he looked around the table, a dimple in his left cheek that had never been there before, and the smooth-shaven skin of Jack's cheeks as they fell to his jaw.

A few people were laughing now, the tension just beginning to ease. And Danny, holding a hand out toward his Uncle Nat, went on in the same high voice.

"Which is why my father's seder was always so wonderful. Because he brought out in us the one, central thing that transcends all the difference between Jews; the essence of Judaism. And that, in turn, is why I'd like to welcome my uncle as he takes my father's place tonight to lead us, as my father did for the past five decades, through the story that defines us, gay, feminist, and Republican alike."

General approval murmured at the table as Nat took up the Haggadah.

And Klara, when her shock subsided, felt rise, in her belly, the long-lived acid of rage.

6.

Sudden silence fell as Klara stepped from the dining room into the library, the words of Nat's first *brucha* disappearing behind the closed door. Crazy patterns, cast by the moon through the big chestnut that canopied the back garden, played on the walls from the wooden-sash windows. Her eye filled with the reflection of that chiaroscuro on the gray casing of the old Zenith TV. Around it the bookshelves rose with paperbacks, the order of which she had not known she remembered—Iris Murdoch, Evelyn Waugh, D. H. Lawrence, Bertrand Russell, John Sanford, the collected Yeats, Joyce's *Dubliners* in the green cloth first edition Jack's father had bought the day of its US publication, and as if he were here in the room, she heard Jack saying: "The Irish are the lost tribe of Israel, of course. Or vice versa."

A dreamy, childish feeling. Like returning from summer camp after six weeks away, or a college year abroad. This house, in which she had come to live after her father died—that is, her first adoptive father, Israel Singer—had become home so quickly that sometimes she could not recall any specific locale from before. She had not known him well, her father: the kibbutz—a hardline Hashomer Hatza'ir community that housed children communally—made it possible for children not to know their parents well, and she, like several other children adopted by survivors, had availed herself of that opportunity. There was grief after his death, but as it faded—she turned twelve that summer, a wildly growing, curious child, come to live in America—she came to realize something fundamental: this place where she lived now, it was *infinitely* more interesting than the kibbutz, *infinitely* more complex. There were old things here, beautiful old things, books, mad paintings, polished wood. Nothing smelled of cows, or silage. In winter, little steel radiators glowed with a warmth that, unlike the kerosene heaters at home, ensured you were never wet, or cold. And there was virtually no credible threat of getting your legs torn off by a bomb.

Each detail of her surroundings must have found a corresponding lack in her for she absorbed it instantly: the rules of the new household; the mythology of her new family, the provenance and worship of the household gods. She memorized the locales of her new world as a baby its mother's features. She was, she thought, born to live here, and she became not just an American, not just a New Yorker, but a Sinai as quickly and thoroughly as her English became not just fluent but native.

As for her new parents, my grandparents, they had taken her in as if she had been born to them, immediately, without a second thought. When, not a year after she arrived, they lost Jason, then they made her theirs with all the depth of that loss. They sent her with Danny to Elizabeth Irwin, Yale, and Yale again for law school; they fed her, clothed her, nursed her through disease and nightmare, heartbreak and adolescence, with never a single word that made her feel less than entirely their daughter as much as Jason and Danny were their sons.

And Danny? Ah, God, Danny-boy. The whole universe had conspired in their friendship, the whole march of the century's history that had made them adolescents, sharing a house. Of course a great diffidence had existed when first she arrived, of course: an adolescent boy and an adolescent girl, they ignored each other for a time. The first day of her new school was their first time alone, unmediated by

Jack and Ellie. Without a word they had left the house together, walking side by side down Bank Street, shoulders occasionally touching, in silence. And only when they had arrived at Elizabeth Irwin, joined in a crowd of longhaired, smoking young folk in baggy clothes, negotiated a series of crowded, noisy hallways and come into a classroom did she realize that throughout it all, without saying a word, this disaffected young man with half his face covered by a fall of blond hair, he may never have said a word to her, but he had never left her side.

From then on, they were always together: days after school, evenings doing homework, mornings at breakfast. Winters in the Catskills and summers on the Vineyard. They were together at every party, every dance, every evening at home with friends smoking joints and listening to Mott The Hoople or David Bowie or Lou Reed or Santana, every day, it seemed to her, of the rest of her life: perfectly unacknowledged, perfectly unquestioned and perfectly unsexual.

And now, as she advanced through the room, at every step she felt dizzy with the room's familiarity, as if the instant before seeing, her eye supplied the image that it was about to capture. Outside the window, she caught a glimpse of the flagstone path to the back of the garden, and her mind supplied the moistness of the chestnut-shaded air, the smell of damp bark. She had meant only to step out of the dining room for a moment, a moment to quiet the anger that had swept through her with its peppery heat when Danny gave up the seder to Uncle Nat. But now tears were welling in her throat, so she went up the stairs, past the parlor, empty now, and up. On the staircase an image of herself appeared in a frame on the wall, surprising her with the picture of a long-haired, black-eyed girl, watching her quizzically from a quarter-century before. As if against a physical force she pushed forward, up, and into her old bedroom, now the studio in which Eleanor painted, and without turning on the light she moved to stand by the window to now, really, freely, fully cry.

What had ever tied her to this family other than the shared years in this room, in all the other rooms? Old Yankel Sinai's Mount

Morris apartment, Evelyn Singer's Kips Bay house, Jack's legal offices in the Exchange building which had been his father's, the Martha's Vineyard rooms with their sea-sodden vistas over Menemsha Bay? What had they ever talked about, Danny and she, other than these places, and the sacredness with which they had been invested by time, by the vast continuity, the accidental and unexpected continuity in a century of massacre? Then it had been an exchange of ideas, high concepts, nearly translucent, like the flocks of geese they'd see each year, late summer over Martha's Vineyard, faintly etched against the distance of sky. But in them had been their entire future. And then had come that summer in New Haven when they went to Hammonasset Beach and slowly, surely, he began to harden away. Years before, as early as high school, he had said to her, lying on the beach, watching a delta of geese pass overhead:

"You know, Klary, Dad's appeared five times before the Supreme Court?"

They had been on their backs on the beach in front of the summer house, watching up into the summer sky.

"Yes, Danny, I know he has."

"And you know what? When he dies, I'll be the last Sinai not practicing real-estate law, or dermatology, or trading bonds. Eugene Debs? Peekskill riots? None of those little shitheads in Larchmont even know why Dad wasn't in World War II. And none of them know why my brother is underground."

Klara remembered that well, for she, only a few years an American, had not known either. Jason, of course, she understood: the war was still on in Vietnam, then, and the country was still largely the country Jason had known. For the former point, later she checked it in my grandfather's interview for Griffin Fariello and learned about Jack's Spanish Civil War service and his ensuing Dies Committee blacklisting for that bizarre crime of "premature antifascism," the fact of having opposed fascism on moral grounds, before the war, rather than political grounds, during it. Then, considering Danny's deeper point, she turned one cheek to the sand to look at him.

"Okay. They're shitheads. So what?"

"So it's such a farce. We're like those Canada geese, you know? The kind that still migrate. And the rest of the family, they're like the other kind, the ones that winter inland on golf courses and parks up in Westchester or out on Long Island instead of flying south. A couple more generations, the two won't even interbreed any more. They'll be two separate species, and you can be god damn sure that we're the one going extinct first. That's what we are, Klary: a dying species."

She remembered thinking about that for a long time, not understanding, as she would not for a very long time yet to come, the difference between herself, adopted by camp survivors from unknown Israeli parents, and her American cousin who had lived, at home, in a culture populated by generations before him. Maybe, had she known my father better, she would have gotten it. As it was now, a quarter-century later, she still did not understand why she was the one at home in the house and he a stranger. Then, watching him curiously in profile, she had spoken into the noise of the surf: "You don't get it, Danny-boy. And neither does your brother."

"What's not to get, Klary?"

Patiently, she had said: "You see, it doesn't matter how different we are. Daddy and Uncle Nat; Peres and Sharon; Noam Chomsky and Henry goddamn Kissinger. There just isn't any other kind of goose for us to turn into."

It was the first thing of any importance on which they'd ever failed to communicate. Neither knew the damage it was going to do. Neither understood how nonnegotiable it was, that sense of loss that my uncle held in him, subjacent to everything he believed. Now the tears were coming as if wholly independent of her being, rolling and rolling down her cheeks. Was it the pent-up emotion of her return? Her return to mourn her adoptive father? She knew it wasn't. She knew she had not returned to America to mourn Jack. What faced her in America, what she had stayed away from for all these years, was something else. Danny had been the promise of happiness to her.

She had been meant to be happy. She had been promised that by all the death, all the death and dislocation that had come over her life like a spell cast by the war over her childhood in Israel: the gassing of her grandparents, the violent death of her birth parents, and then her adoptive parents, one after the other, like a curse. The Sinais were meant to rescue her, to graft her on to the continuity of this house, this culture, this country. Danny had been promised to her, it was their turn *to be this family*, just as Jack and Eleanor had had their turn. But in the end, it had turned out that it was the happiness that was the exception, not the suffering, hadn't it? In the end it turned out that Israel's capacity for horror and privation, that was the norm all over the world, and the happiness of this little enclave in history, America, was the exception.

Someone was coming up the stairs, or rather, down, and slowly, like a swimmer surfacing, Klara Singer's focus came to her image in the glass of the window, a middle-aged woman, thrice orphaned and never recovered, with wide, lost, nearly panicked eyes. And in her mind, she said, We loved each other, and I thought everything else was just words. But it was the opposite, wasn't it? There were all these words, words, words. And everything else was just love.

7.

Once Nat had launched into the seder, Daniel Sinai lifted his sleeping son out of Maggie Calaway's arms and carried him upstairs.

It was a welcome excuse.

Upstairs, in his childhood bedroom, a moon was above the rooftops to the north, throwing silvery light through the early leaves of the chestnut, and in this mottled luminescence Danny stood, rocking slightly on his heels. People would remark his absence from the table, he knew that. He also knew, though, that he didn't care.

God, if someone had told him that adulthood contained feelings this awful, feelings that made the pains of adolescence seem trivial, he simply would not have believed it. His teeth were clenched, now, and with an effort he relaxed his jaw. Only then did he put his son down under the quilt, roll him to the side, wedge a pillow next to his back. He turned on the baby monitor and clipped the receiver onto his belt. He planted a kiss on the inscrutable roundness of his son's cheek, just below his closed eye. He descended the stairs deliberately, his mind empty, to the third-floor landing. Then he turned and stepped into Klara's room, unsurprised to find her by the window, the rising moon casting bars of shadows through the branches of the chestnut.

For a time they stood in silence. They could not pretend, as they would have as children, that they had come to be together in this room perfectly by accident. Nor could he pretend, as he would have as a child, that she was not crying.

And then she was moving toward him, just allowing him a glimpse of her tear-covered face, and he opened his arms to her.

For a long time they stood like this, Klara crying hot tears that ran down his neck and under his collar, her body—thinner than he remembered, more bony—shaking with hard paroxysms against his. For a long time they listened to the far sounds of the family in the house below, their bodies together, belly and breath, in silence.

A long time during which neither of them saw, nor realized, that Maggie Calaway had come to look for her husband, and was standing at the doorway, looking in.

In her chest Maggie felt her heart, swollen with blood, leaking tiny beats as realization after realization cascaded down around her. They still did not know she was there. Then Klara, like a sleeper briefly waking, opened her eyes and saw her. But instead of reacting, as if it were all a dream, she simply put her eyes, again, against Danny's neck. And only after a suite of minutes did she, slowly and unwillingly, move away from Danny to the window. There was a silence, Danny standing helplessly in the middle of the room, Klara by the window. When, at last, Klara spoke, it was still as if Maggie were not there. With a lean of her head to the family gathering downstairs, she said in an expressionless voice something that made no sense whatever to Maggie.

"So, Danny-boy. This is you as the guardian of the species, is it?"

Her husband said nothing. And Klara, her voice hardening, went on.

"And it still is. One species. Isn't it?"

Neither did he, Maggie saw, seem to understand. "What are you talking about, Klary?"

"Your geese, Danny-boy. They still seem to be one species."

Now, Maggie sensed, he understood. But Klara spoke on, her voice rising, as if inflicting punishment for her recent exposure, as if for an audience.

"In fact, I'd say the gene pool's been strengthened, wouldn't you? What with the good, strong stock you've introduced. The Sinais should be thanking you. God knows the Singers should."

I think my uncle was shocked how wrong she was, and when he spoke, it was not to protest, but to correct.

"Klara. You don't understand."

She shook that off. See, she did understand. "Ten years with Jack. Eleanor still here. Maggie's as lovely today as she was in New Haven. And those *meerskeits* of yours, your Laura's the image of Jack. And you dare, you fucking dare, to have become an unhappy man."

"Klara." To Maggie, now, it sounded like pleading.

"Daniel, what the fuck were you doing, putting that idiot in your father's chair? What the fuck are you doing? Everything that means anything in the world is here, and you're *wasting* it."

"*Wasting*," she nearly shouted the word, and instinctively, Maggie stepped back. But not Daniel, standing miserably in front of the woman in rage.

"Klara. I did what my father would have."

Sudden contempt in her tone. "No you did *not*, Danny-boy. Your father kept that old fraud at bay for five decades."

"He was my father's peer. I'm his junior."

"Exactly." With the same contempt. "Your father was a mensch, you're a coward."

And now—at last, it seemed to my other aunt—he raised his voice. "None of this was my choice. None of it."

"No? What was your choice?" A shocking bitterness was in her voice now, so much so that Maggie found herself nearly shrinking away from the door. "What was your choice? To be the one who had to go live in that pitiful little third-world hole?"

"I did what I had to."

"Ah, as opposed to I, who did what I wanted to. Isn't it amazing, that we both could have gotten it so entirely wrong?"

What would he have answered? Maggie didn't know, nor would she, because before he could speak the hallway light, controlled from the floor below, went on, casting a trapezoid of light through the open door at which Maggie stood, and they both turned to her, Daniel with shock, Klara with a slow, impersonal inspection. For a moment, everything paused. Then, moving toward the open doorway, Klara spoke to my aunt slowly, clearly, and with infinite cruelty, as if ten years had not diminished by a fraction her hurt.

"See, Maggie Calaway, you should have asked me ten years ago. I would have told you then: he married you because you're a WASP, but don't be surprised, dear, when one day he dumps you for not being a Jew."

8.

Ten years earlier, on one of the first spring days of 1986, my Uncle Daniel and Aunt Klara had driven up the Connecticut coastline to Hammonasset and walked out on the beach. They walked cross-armed, patrician, as if they owned the place; shoulders touching and in silence, silence that had been cultivated over the fifteen years they had been each other's closest friend—a clear understanding that they were people whose communication only rarely required words—and a silence that it fell to Klara to break. This she did when she was first to notice, high in the light-flooded sky, a flock of geese.

"Well, there you are, Danny-boy. Life imitating art."

My uncle stopped and looked up, as she directed, to the tiny forms etched faintly against the blue, so far that they seemed bled of all substance. The tiny waves on the pebbles ebbed, paused, and in the domed silence he felt the distant sky pressing against the drums of his ears as if it, too, were waiting for an answer. More of their lives had been lived together than not, and almost all of that time together had been as Jack and Eleanor's only children. They had been to Elizabeth Irwin together, Yale, and now Yale again for grad school. Now they were nearly thirty: Klara a woman of full, red lips and black hair, her face above the black cashmere coat a combination of perspicacity and vulnerability far too adult to be pretty, arguably beautiful. My uncle certainly thought so. Danny himself, he was just losing the slimness that had been his effortlessly all his life, but still had his light expression and thick blond bangs. There was nothing similar about them: Klara had been adopted by Izzy Singer, too. That made my Aunt Klara and my Uncle Danny no kin, despite their familiarity, and, in turn, enabled what was about to happen.

When no answer came, she spoke again.

"But of course, those are geese, Daniel, not people. We know that because people don't fly. At least, the rest of us do."

Wordlessly, he conceded the point.

This was, after all, Klara.

It was, after all, a negotiation.

That afternoon, in the bedroom of her apartment on Linden Street, as if keeping an appointment made years ago, Klara Singer and Daniel Sinai made love. And in fact, like an old appointment, to each in its own way, it was without surprise. The solid weight of his body on hers, the scrub of his palms, calloused year round from his summer sailing; the short hair on the base of the warm, blood-bathed muscle of his neck. Nothing was unfamiliar to my Aunt Klara.

As for my uncle, he felt the breath of this quiet, tall, powerful woman against his ear. The whisper of her voice did not grow confessional, did not abandon its reserve, but grew thick, flushed with emotion, the fluent emotion of someone who felt a great deal of it. And then the weight of this slim woman's long body came upon him when suddenly, with surprising strength, she turned him, shifted her weight onto his and then pushed herself up, hands on his chest, arching her back and watching him from a face draped, now, with hair.

Nothing of what he was experiencing was unexpected, no more than the topography of beauty marks that lay on the olive skin across her breasts and stomach—he had always known they were there, or felt that he had. So much so, in fact, that little intrusive stabs of entirely nonsexual familiarity nipped through the sensuality of the encounter, like tiny fish feeding, tempting but alarming. For my uncle, Klara was as known as the smell of his skin, a sensation so interior that he had never really noticed it was there. Now, joined to that life-long awareness was the sense of a perfectly naked woman, golden-skinned, Mediterranean, skin to skin in the ripening fall of Atlantic spring light through her window. "*Haimish*," he thought to himself, lying by her, afterward, using the Yiddish word, "home-like," familiar. Then he pronounced, in wonder, Freud's weighted German word for the opposite: "*unheimlich*," "un-homelike," "uncanny."

Haimish. His grandparents had had an arranged marriage in Lithuania; his parents childhood friends from Mount Morris Grammar in Jewish Harlem to Bronx Science, married when they were both at City College in the early '30s.

Uncanny. Night after night, that week, Daniel woke hours before dawn, feeling the heat of Klara's naked body next to his.

And next, to each of them came an experience of rupture that would determine the future course of their lives. To Klara, it was as bad as any of her childhood, even, in some ways, worse, because she had expected never to have to feel pain like that again. To Danny, who had had a sheltered life, there was a reverberation with his only other experience of tragic loss, but much more faintly: his brother had gone underground when Danny was only twelve and, in fact, his disappearance had also provided Danny with some relief, because my father was an angry and often violent young man who did not like his brother. And yet, Danny could have no idea of how long this reverberation would last and how, ten years later, it would open a faultline that cut right through the center of his life.

That spring of 1986, in late May Danny and Klara together graduated from law school. The next day they were to drive home to New York where Jack and Eleanor Sinai were throwing a party in their honor. They spent that afternoon in Klara's bed in Linden Street, their last, as the apartment was already packed and movers would be coming in the morning.

Outside the window, by Willow Street Pond, a flock of squat geese waddled over the ruined grass, not the migrating geese they had seen coming north earlier in the season, but the kind that in the past decade of warm winters had taken to wintering up and down the eastern seaboard. Watching them from the bed, through Danny swirled all the shared afternoons of their lives: Vineyard summer afternoons or those, up at Camp Treetops, of the long Adirondack light; autumn days in the '70s outside Elizabeth Irwin; endless Sundays in the West Village home of their youth. He missed them, those afternoons, suddenly and with an intensity that he knew only she, of all the people he would ever know, would understand. And what would he have said, had she not spoken first? As if seeing through his eyes out the window; as if continuing the old argument that never stopped, she spoke from behind him, her breath against the skin of his shoulder.

"Tell me, Danny-boy. Where, in your Unified Goose Theory, does Maggie Calaway fit?"

And so he said nothing.

To say anything was to say it all.

Later that night, Klara left the graduation party without a word to her adoptive parents. It fell to Daniel to break the news that she was taking a Department of Commerce posting in Tel Aviv. This he did in his father's ground-floor study, late that night after the party, and left his father to tell his mother. The news was not all bad: Danny himself was settling in New York with a job at Columbia Law School, tenure track. The other news he had for his father was about a classmate from law school whom he had been seeing for some time and whom he had decided to marry. Which, that winter, he did. It was a solitary ceremony, just the two of them, although why it needed be so, my Aunt Maggie never fully understood.

Until, that is, the Passover after my grandfather's death, when Klara Singer flew Tel Aviv–Washington, and then, again, up to New York.

9.

Long ago they had agreed they would not fight until the children were in bed. Now Laura was in her lap, chatting excitedly, her head swiveling this way and that to watch the blocks passing, the cab as if floating up Eighth Avenue, the lights of the buildings, the buds on trees.

At home, Maggie helped her daughter into her nightdress while she chattered, overtired, excited, about Granny, cousins, dinner, the day off school, and why again could they not eat bread, Momma? Maggie answered her quietly, slowing her with the tone of her voice, easing her despite herself under the covers, dimming the light and lying by her, feeling the warmth of the child's rich experience of family ride hard against the horrible coldness of its reality. As Laura's breath slowed into sleep, the need to smoke came to her with force. She saw herself earlier that evening, sheltering under the chestnut while, inside, the party went on. Like the line from the Dylan song that Jack had liked to sing. And all this time she had thought it was

Klara who had been left out in the rain, herself who was on dry land. It was, it was revealed to her now, a cruel arrangement with which she had lived, unquestioning, for years.

He had put Jeremy down and was waiting by the bedroom window when she came in, standing, watching out at the heave and fall of the water in the river, the high light of the moon. She lay on the bed and lit a cigarette, an unheard-of indoor activity, and only after a long time, still looking out the window, did he begin to speak.

"Her father was my dad's first cousin. Her adoptive father, I mean. Israel Singer. He'd been at Bergen-Belsen. Klara was adopted from the Jewish agency in Israel, an orphan. Both her birth parents were Israeli, *yalids*, killed by an ambush at their kibbutz. Israel's wife, Monique Singer, was French and had been sterilized at Treblinka. She died in a market bombing in Haifa in '69. So Israel brought Klara to the States. My mother says he came here to deliver Klara. The evening of his arrival he drowned himself in Menemsha Bay while we were all having ice cream at the Bite. That was spring, 1969. Klara stayed with us."

"You were lovers."

"Never. Never in high school, never in college. We were so tied, like siblings. It was impossible."

"That's not true."

He understood her, and answered readily. "It is true. We became lovers in grad school."

"After you met me?"

"After I met you."

"When?"

"The last year. In spring. The spring before we got married. For a month."

A long silence while Maggie cried. When she could, she said: "Why didn't you marry her."

"Maggie. Because I married you."

"That's not right." Speaking through her tears, there was a logic as clear as the brilliant moonlight in what she said. "You didn't leave her for me. Marrying me had nothing to do with it."

Could she see him? Unable to answer, he nodded, and as if she had seen, she said: "You never told me you were lovers, and you've never told my why you left her. Is that not true? Is that not true?"

More surprised than scared. He had not ever expected to tell anyone this. He had never expected that anyone would have the right to ask.

"Yes."

"Jack and Ellie wanted you to marry." She said the words with a flinty tone, a bitterness that betrayed the depth of her loss, not just of him, but of his parents, whom she loved.

"Maggie. It was spring, 1969 when Klara came. May, June, July, August, September, October, November, December, January. March was the townhouse bombing. My brother disappeared then."

"What does that have to do with it?"

"It has everything to do with it. My parents had lost everything when my brother went. It wasn't just him. It was everything they had ever believed in. It was a whole way of life. Klary and me? We were supposed to hold it all together. We were supposed to get married and be the next generation of righteous Sinais."

My aunt Maggie thought about that for a long time, smoking in the shadow of the bed. When she spoke, it was, at last, a bit more quietly.

"Then why? Why didn't you?"

My uncle turned his face suddenly out the window, into the vista of silver light and absolute shadow and answered, now, without hesitation, as though he had known the answer for years. It was an honest answer, which in some ways makes it all the more tragic that it was, I am convinced, wrong.

"Because we lived an idyll. Do you understand? It was given to us to live an idyll."

It was not what she had expected, and her voice rose again. "What does that *mean*, Danny?"

But he went on as if she had not said a word. "Summers at the Vineyard, the school year at Elizabeth Irwin, our lives with my parents. We were surrounded by heroes, by people who were right. The sit-ins they took us to, the vigils—the Civil Rights movement, the anti-war movement. We were at home the way no one is anymore. But it wasn't life. We didn't know it. Maybe they didn't. It was an *idyll*. The world didn't work the way they thought. There was nowhere to go from there. Jason put an end to it. Running, hiding, sending messages of hate from a dirty, criminal dimension. Those cruel communiqués from the underground? They weren't about politics, they were about parents. They made a mockery of my father's life, everything he did. Everything was ruined after them. Then he became an accessory to murder. It was a dying world, and Jason killed it."

"That's not true. You had a beautiful childhood. You and Klara have *happy* memories."

"I know we do." He spoke as if soothing a child. "But it turns out that having shared happiness doesn't only bind people together. It drives them apart, too. It turns out that, to live with shared happiness after it's lost, it's better to do it apart."

Perhaps he did not understand what he had just said. Maggie Calaway, however, did, and she answered without the slightest pause.

"God damn you."

She stopped then for crying too hard, in the darkness, the tip of her cigarette lighting her wet face between sobs. For a long time they were like that, he at the window, she at the bed so long that her cigarette went out and gradually, her crying quieted, and perhaps she slept. He saw her as he had seen her those ten years past, her small freckled body, the light behind the green of her eyes, an aqueous green, like seawater under midday light. But my uncle stayed at the window.

Somewhere, some other family was in its flowering, perhaps in Ireland, or Iraq, all the while his dissolved like wood in water, crumbling with age, battered with tide. The little children at the seder tonight would no more remember their heroic grandfather and his heroic times than he himself remembered the Yeshiva bochers and shtetl storekeepers who had given their genes to him, and as for the principles of his life, never mind those of his father's, they already meant nothing. It would even be forgotten, what he had done to Klara, ten years before. As if holographically inhabiting the fall of the spring half moon outside the window, a vision came to my uncle of his daughter as she would one day be, a high-cheeked, shockingly pretty young woman. With real longing felt himself drawn into the thin moonlight falling over the Hudson. Then, as though there were an actual risk, he felt himself step back. There were the children, you see, and the vacuous hope that they would one day be happier than he. And then there was Maggie Calaway, whom he had married without loving, and to whom he had now to try to make amends.

Chapter Twelve

Isabel Montgomery

August 16, 2011

Monterey, California

1.

Look at me.

I'm as helpless as a kitten in a tree.

First Cuntmuscle and my trip to New York; then my exciting days being a girl reporter and, incidentally, going to jail; then I get to be in New York and the Island with Maggalah and Los Angeles with Molly and in between in Paris, Tel Aviv, all great fun, and really, when you think of it, the only actual thing I have had to do, the only actual act of commission, is to pack my bag and catch a plane, a move at which I excel, have long excelled, have done so many many times in my life to and from many many places, with and without many many people, and when I get where all I have to do is ply my trade—research, interview, interview, write: I could do it on an Etch A Sketch if I had to—and now, as I finish writing the piece of prose you just read about my uncle and my aunts, guess what?, oh guess what?

Yep, you got it: Trident calls up having finally—six weeks late—read my script—and mind you, they are paying six hundred dollars a night for my suite at the Viceroy—true, they think I'm in it, waiting for them, which is after all an actual job description in Los Angeles, "Writer wanted. Salary: six figures with huge benefits. Primary responsibility: waiting for producer. Qualifications: willingness to feel worthless"—and how do they feel about the script? It's beautiful, it's fantastic, we have Brit Marling's office waiting for it, and Dana Forrester wants to cast, and this is going to be a big deal, a really really big deal, only could you take on a little rewrite, just a few notes, yes the script's at the Viceroy now, oh no hurry, would a week be enough?

Tell me, would *you* wander through this wonderland alone?

Well, let us not exaggerate the coincidence. The call actually came more like a week ago, maybe two, while I was in Paris writing the chapter you just read and I left it on my iPhone—the message, I mean – till I had found my way through Passover of 1996 and then a day or two more while I slept off my last forty-eight hours of writing which was fueled by some very rough, very effective methamphetamine, all I could actually score in Paris where I have fewer connections in the gutter and rather more in the drawing room or, to be precise, the runway, as Momma likes to buy couture. And now, when my bags are packed and I'm ready to go, saying goodbye to my Uncle Danny in his office, I can hear in the timbre of his voice, in the tiny hesitations in his syntax, the depth of the pain with which he lives and which I now know all about, all about. Now. It is not just the speed, the work, the travel, the drinking, the drugs. It is that I am a tuning fork. I am the tuning fork of the Sinai family. You know it by now as well as I: they're the disease; I'm the symptom. I tremble at every minor note in the orchestra of their sadness, the Sinais. I tremble and never, ever will I be able to communicate it, and like Danny, it is going to die with me.

Note to self: never have a family. Because if you don't, then you don't have to leave them with the legacy of your suffering. Note to self: try to die unremembered. But that's not how it works, is it? Because you may never *have* a family, but you still likely *come* from one. And your family may last a great long time. It just ain't your choice. Continuity, belonging, it gathers in little pools on terrain formed by glacial movements of history. Once a shrink—one I was nailing, not seeing—told me that neurosis can be inherited over seven generations. I was fucking floored. You have a transient moment of nausea in a diner in New York when some fuck raises his voice at his daughter at a table nearby, then it passes and you lose your appetite. A century earlier your great-great-grandmother, a child in the mud of a shtetl, gets yelled at during breakfast by a Cossack passing on a horse, and you are fucking programmed to see pogroms everywhere.

And so on and so on. What do I know?

Just look at me.

I'm as helpless as a kitten in a tree.

But I get ahead of myself, all for the benefit of rhyme.

And we are supposed to be free?

You tell me: what *the fuck* is free?

Listen. Listen! You cannot *be free* if you are not *happy*, and happiness itself is a function of historical accident. Whether your life is one given to pain or happiness has *nothing* to do with you. If my little trip into the sad life of my family tells me nothing else, ever, surely it has told me that?

But aren't you just the little philosopher? Let's get our asses back to Paris, rue d'Ulm, and Uncle Danny, a little embarrassed—how about that little rhyme: embarrass in Paris? Come on, that's *good*—he doesn't know what I know, but he knows what I've been asking—the lighted window framing his face, says:

"Well, doll. I hope you're finding what you're looking for."

I think: Doll.

I say: "Thank you, Danny."

But Danny's my father's brother, isn't he?

He says: "By the way, what the fuck are you looking for?"

And I, I am my father's daughter. I smile appreciation. "Ah good point."

Outside the open window, over the little garden next to the rue d'Ulm. It is August, and already there is an autumnal hint to the light, though the air itself is still warm and tourists are still sweating on the street. And suddenly I don't feel like lying to my uncle.

Perhaps it is because I know now that he, too, knows how elusive is the moral high ground.

Perhaps because this latter quality, shame, which we share, is not a very common awareness in his family, which tends more, in its response to its own faults, toward righteousness.

And so I tell him. About Sinai. Dying and shit.

When I finish, there is a long silence, he watching me with a stunned expression, the noise from the street filling the office.

Finally, he says, "How long have you known."

I respond a bit curtly. "A while."

But here's the difference between me and Danny. I understand myself to be going through an experience with which he is familiar. After all he was hardly ten years older than me when Jack Sinai died. He, however, doesn't even dream the connection, and why? Because he's an idiot. Though, of course, I'm the tuning fork, not him. Anyway, it doesn't make any difference, because not knowing what they're talking about is never any reason for anyone to stop.

You can't stop anyone.

They just talk their asses off.

Soulful expression on Danny's face.

"I don't know your father very well, you know. He was gone for so much of my life. Then . . . then, somehow, he was always there between me and. . ."

I'm holding my breath here, and thinking, Please, please, say he was always there between me and Klara and now is between me and Maggie, but when he finishes he says:

"My father."

Idiot, I'm yelling in my head. *They let you in front of a classroom? They let you have kids? Get a fucking shrink.* But I say, "I understand."

There is another long silence, this time filled by a police siren passing by with that European whine dropping in pitch with the Doppler effect.

"You know, Iz, after . . . your father passes. You always have a home with us. Always."

And what a home, I'm thinking. It's like offering a hundred bucks and a pipe to a crack ho.

But what I say is: "Thank you, Danny. I better get my plane."

Los Angeles. A September afternoon. The job, of course, is a total rewrite, a month's work easy, and it takes me a couple-three days even to open the envelope containing the script.

Even here, a chill light hangs over the Pacific, a slight sterility of sun and wind and ocean void that lets you know that the summer is on the wane.

Standing at the window, I make a serious mistake, which is, I follow my thoughts into my iPhone library of Sinai's songs and play Luciana Souza's version of Leonard Cohen:

> *And here is the dawn*
> *Until death do us part*
> *And here is your death*
> *In your daughter's heart*

The next six days are very harsh. I spend them in a hotel in Malibu, the first three with a bottle of bourbon and an eight ball.

I'm not going to tell you about those days. Fuck you. This isn't a book about me. It's about the Sinais and I am not one of the tribe. I am *not* one of the tribe.

The next three, I spend straightening out.

When I am good, again, or what passes for same, I go back to the Viceroy—I have not let go of my suite, which costs more per night than a week's salary for the average Los Angeleno south of El Pico— and I begin a five-week marathon working on *Cuntmuscle: the Movie*.

The notes I get from the studio I entirely ignore, instead writing the thing from the ground up but, this time, *good* as opposed to *bad*.

I work this one in a very different way. For one thing, I have a huge corkboard delivered to the room and start using Final Draft to produce index cards. For another, I work twelve to fourteen hours a day and in order to do so without my many little chemical friends I go to the gym daily and nightly. And finally, I am relentlessly—and successfully—on the prowl. This last activity is efficiently enhanced when I am introduced to a women's screenwriting group, which, in turn, introduces me through a girl called Teora to a whole circle of lesbians. That helps a great deal.

I so like women.

Everything else wobbles like water in a glass, but women are such a good thing.

They smell good, they feel good, they say things that make you want to be good. Their breasts and their legs and their stomachs and their saline cunts with the various kinds of coiffed hair around them and the mothers and the brothers behind them and the need, the need they have, and the love they need.

Those five weeks, I write a fine screenplay, far too fine, I have little doubt, for my friends at Trident.

October finds me in Palm Springs tanning by the pool at the Parker Meridian with a girl called Elana who edits an AMC series the name of which I cannot get straight which she, in turn, resents. Additionally, she is diagnosed with ADD, which means a Ritalin prescription, and young Elana turns out to be wholly game, now that *Cuntmuscle: the Movie* is done, to joining me in an exploration of the three-dimensional nexus between that substance and several others, depending on the night, and the strong narcotic of long, patient, practiced sex. When she goes back to work, I go briefly up to Monterey where, perhaps I never mentioned this, I am a fellow at the School of International Studies, not a bad gig for a person who writes about the Mideast—have I mentioned I am fluent in Arabic and Farsi, as well as Hebrew and various vernaculars of the above that are spoken in the gutter?—and try to get some work done. But all I really do is use the departmental printer to get a fair copy printed of my magnum suicidus on the Sinai Family. This I look at for a while, sitting on my desk, a pile of paper. Then I print a cover page, which gives an air of finality to it and accents its unlikelihood of ever being punished. Ha ha, see what I just did? I typed "punished" instead of "published." Note the difference. For a few days I sit looking at it. Then I find and print out my grandfather's obituary from the *Times*, and insert it as the frontispiece. That seems to help in some way. It helps a little more when I get the *Times* coverage of Sinai and Mimi's arrests in there too.

Communicating underlying historical context without losing your reader.

The bane of a writer's life.

And perhaps I'd have gone on like that for weeks, months even, but in early November, the *Times* calls and asks me do I remember I have the final piece in my contract with them due? Of course, I tell them, injecting a slight edge of irritation into my voice for effect, though at the time of his call, I am sitting at the bar where they filmed *Play Misty for Me* drinking my fourth Miller Long Neck—yes yes, even dykes fall in love with that fantastic Clint Eastwood—of the afternoon. When am I leaving for Fort Benning? That's a tough one. To answer it, I have to remember where Fort Benning is, why I am going there, and when whatever I'm going there for is happening. To be safe, I say that I am taking the redeye tonight. That, apparently, is the right answer, because I get transferred to some underling who tells me my car-reservation number in Atlanta—so now I know something about where Fort Benning is—and hotel in a place called Columbus and then a ton of details about travel.

When I hang up, I jack in to my iData through my iPhone, planning how I'm going to iYell at Little iLincoln for letting this fucking iSlide, but of course I find that he's done all the research, it's I who have ignored it, and I remember now that I'm going to write for the *Times* about the School of the Americas Protest at the gates of Fort

Benning, Georgia, which is the longest-running act of dissent in American history—which when you think of it also makes it the most pointless. He also lined up the interviews, and sent me everything, along with rather a desperate email about why I haven't been in touch in three weeks.

There's another note in there. It appears that Sinai has slipped an email by my spam filter by sending it to Little L., and Little L. has dutifully forwarded it, and because I am, after all, I am feeling like I'm clinging to a cloud, I make the mistake of reading the fucker.

> Bear in mind, Iz, that Muscogee County is prosecuting for civil disobedience, six months minimum, and that because you're a second offender after your contempt term, you will undoubtedly be in medium security at least. You won't like medium security. So, whatever you do down at Fort Benning, don't get arrested, you dig?

Do I dig? I dig that Little L. is fucking history is what I dig, and I tell him so, immediately, in a terse email.

> I also am hoping that you've made your decision about what you're doing next. I'll be moving down to Bedford Street next week and what can I say? I'm hoping that you'll see your way to coming there to be with me for the next few months. We have unfinished business baby, and I hope, for your sake more than mine, that you won't leave it that way.

I delete Sinai's email, then I power off the iPhone and then, of course, I feel bad. For yelling at Little Lincoln. Poor wee little fellow with his long, unshaven neck. How's he supposed to know? But then I drink another Miller Long Neck—you have to drink them very fast, and very cold, and then slam them down on the bar and you feel just like Clint Eastwood—and a thousand violins begin to play. That amazing woman with the strange libido in his bed right up the road. She gets wet for Eastwood, but into that desire plays possession.

Together, the two make you wet too, and I'm thinking that even if I can't dig up a girl on campus, why, I can get to my room and indulge myself in a couple-three self-induced climaxes.

But aren't you just the little professional? It's a bit like when you reach automatically for the alarm clock while you're asleep. Without really registering what I'm doing, I'm already getting ready to leave. After all, making arrangements to leave somewhere is second nature to me. It's making arrangements to *stay* that so fucks me up. I search and reserve a flight—there's a San Jose–Atlanta redeye at midnight—and change the car—the *Times* has reserved a Corolla hybrid—to a Mustang convertible, which is the highest end sports car available at the airport, which seems rather to favor SUVs. And then I push myself up from the table, take a long, last look at Monterey Bay under afternoon sun and go to pack a bag.

Midnight. Right back where I started. In a first-class seat, the warm throb of marijuana in my stomach. I loaded most of the twelve or so grams of incredibly hybridized Los Angeles pot I had left into a half-pack of Marlboro Lites, then ate the rest in a container of yoghurt—grass, unlike hash, you have to cook first, preferably in butter. By the time I get to the airport to turn in the Mitsu, look at me. I am as helpless as a kitten in a tree! High as a fucking kite, and not just high, but that stupid kind of high where you feel like you've lost half your IQ and the simplest deeds—returning a car, getting a boarding pass, navigating security, and finding the airport bar to order a straight shot of Red Breast and a Miller Long Neck and then another straight shot of Red Breast and a Miller Long Neck and then another straight shot of Red Breast and Miller Long Neck—still wandering through this wonderland alone, never knowing my right foot from my left or, indeed, my hat from my glove—and then find my way, lit like a Christmas light, into my first-class seat with my glass of champagne for the night flight—and this is the part I'm trying to avoid realizing—to an East Coast fall.

See I'm too misty.

And too much in love.

Chapter Thirteen

Isabel Montgomery

November 19, 2011

Fort Benning, Georgia

1.

On November 20, 2011, Isabel Montgomery, née Sinai, née Grant, touched down at Atlanta International Airport on the redeye from San Jose.

She has been flying all night, but that's not really the issue.

She left San Jose drunk and high and is arriving drunk and high, and she has spent the flight staring out the window into, literally nothing.

That's not the issue either.

The issue is that since, six years earlier, she earned a shockingly precocious Ph.D. at the School of Oriental and African Studies in London, and moved on after paying very few dues indeed to take a shockingly precocious byline at the *Economist*, the longest time she has spent *without* crossing the Atlantic Ocean on a redeye was a recent six-week assignment for the *Guardian Weekend Magazine* in Saudi Arabia, from which she was unceremoniously expelled in early spring.

And the issue is that since, ten years ago in Exminster College, she first titrated a glass of good scotch into her slim and strong little body, and felt it rise gently into her capacious brain, she, like her mother before her, knew immediately and with surety that she had just met a very, very important new friend.

And when, shortly thereafter she introduced THC to her strong, lithe little lungs, and felt it enter her blood and go up to massage her brain like a hand inside her skull, she knew she had met another.

And, as fine as those friends were, even they were upstaged in her affections when she met the loves of her life: cocaine, methamphetamine, Valium, Ritalin, Focalin. The glosses on her understanding, ever more, of bliss.

And so the issue is that you cannot fly a hundred thousand miles a year and do so while ingesting a pharmacopeia that would kill an elephant and, along the way, producing a boatload of instantly disposable journalism—which, in fact, you could not have written without the aid of said pharmacopeia—without, sooner or later, hitting a wall.

Okay, enough. Just note a couple-three last things.

Firstly, that for all she has done to her lungs, her heart, her liver, her brain, these ten years and more, there is one thing Isabel Montgomery has never done.

She has never taken an opiate.

You know what that means?

It means that for all her bullshit, Isabel Montgomery knows what addiction is, and how to avoid it. Which, in turn, means that Isabel Montgomery, woman of the runway and of the gutter, is a big fat phony. A well-brought-up, bourgeois, safe little phony.

And there's something else of note in an inventory of her little pharmacopeia. That is, what else is missing? Two key compounds. MDMA, and any psychedelics.

Because those drugs lead to introspection. And Isabel, after her one experience revisiting her childhood on MDMA and acid, has never gone back there again.

And why is that important? Well, it goes a long way to explaining something that has to be understood about Isabel Montgomery. It goes a long way to explaining why, despite all her accomplishments, despite her job that half the world would give their eye-teeth to have, despite her stunning, compact beauty—she so deeply, so completely, hates herself.

And that, combined with a number of other realities of her life, most having to do with her childhood in which the most massive forces of the history of her century, from World War Two to Vietnam, conspired to punish her for when her father abandoned her in a financial-district hotel room in New York, she is now, and has been for a great long time, first a child, then a girl, and now a woman in despair.

Notes from Isabel Montgomery's drive into Fort Benning, Georgia, recorded into her iPhone.

Interestingly, they don't yet show how much trouble she's in.

Title Pawn, Commando Military Supply, Brake Tune-ups, Military Supplies: Buy Sell or Trade, Magnolia Gardens Apartment Homes, Days Inn: 39.95, Day Rates. Total Customizing, Hubcaps, Homer's Lounge: "Welcome to Homer's Lounge, come party with us." Cars out front and it's ten in the morning.

Really, it's not that she's been up one night—that wouldn't bother her. She's up all night all the time. It's that she was up the night before, too, and she's on West Coast time. On the plus side, of course, that puts her about forty-five degrees of longitude closer to cocktail hour. This, perhaps, accounts for the swerve her Mustang convertible takes, as if of its own volition, toward Homer's Lounge. Of course, it's always cocktail hour somewhere. And of course, she's high. Nonetheless she stops herself in the driveway to Homer's Lounge, awkwardly enough to stall the Mustang, which is a standard. She says to herself, out loud: "What am I doing here? Georgia, for fuck's sake. I am so far from home. And I am so alone."

Not three days ago she was walking hand in hand with an MIIS graduate student on Pfeiffer Beach in Big Sur. Now, half-in, half-out of Homer's driveway, it feels to her like she is, in fact, as alone here as she has ever been; that the town of Columbus, Georgia is as enigmatic and empty as the thousands of miles of California coastline; and that here, as there, her GPS is her only lifeline.

Someone honks at her, impatient no doubt to get to the party at Homer's, and Isabel pulls back out into the street, anxiously watching her GPS acquire its satellites and direct her right through the town, if it can be called a town rather than run-down strip mall, too bleak and depressed to have anything but off-brand fast food, and populated entirely by trailer-trash enlisted men and local blacks—the officers and gentlemen no doubt shop at some state-of-the art mall in Columbus. There is no sign of the single biggest protest action in America. And the strip, on either side of a four-lane road, seems to go on forever.

Title Pawn. Pawnshop. Diamond Earrings, 8.95, Play Lotto Here. Uneeda Pawn. Checks Cashed. Checks cashed. Title Pawn. Ranger Joes, Subway, Tattoo Tommy's, Cashwell.

She slows here and looks closer. Her notes read:

Cashwell Title Pawn, lower rates guaranteed. Ten o'clock and lowering, hazy clouds are coming in, a close sun fully risen. The fuck you going to grow a peach in this? And if you aren't going to grow fucking peaches in Georgia, what the fuck is it good for.

Finally, not able to bear it any longer, Isabel pulls over and googles "Title Pawn" on her iPhone, which gives her a site called www.franchisedoc.com. Title pawn, it turns out, is a way to borrow money on your car's title, at incredibly high interest rates, a dozen points over prime, minimum. That makes it the perfect business for a military town, and in fact, franchisedoc.com describes it as "a much needed, high profit, service to the blue collar community."

A much needed service. To the blue collar community. She says to herself, "For fuck's sake." Clearly, the money they can raise on their cars can help to go party with them at Homer's Lounge, or perhaps to memorialize that special evening at Tattoo Tommy's. Then after they spend their money in Homer's Lounge or Tattoo Tommy's—saving $8.95 for some diamond earrings for the hooker they met there— then they can ship out to Afghanistan or Iraq and run a very reasonable chance of never needing the car again.

She can't write this. She knows already, deeply, that she cannot write this piece. It's not that she hasn't known that before. It's that this time, it is true.

She sits back and closes her eyes. For a moment she feels nothing.

Exhaustion, alcohol, THC, and caffeine each on their own little subcutaneous channel running through her little veins.

For a little moment the first wins and Isabel hears her father singing to her and sees the canopies of Molly's maples, rich in green leaf, casting shadow and light over the lawn. In her sudden dream, she wonders why none of it makes her happy. It used to, but something has changed. She stirs, and then the GPS is singing, *You made it there somehow*. That makes her come to with a start.

She puts the car in gear and follows her GPS down another road. Now there's an off-brand supermarket, a barbershop, a Chinese restaurant, and sure enough after a few minutes, the GPS announces: *You have arrived*.

But where?

She actually asks the question aloud, and that she's done so, suddenly sets a little alarm bell ringing inside her.

An alarm telling her that making wry existential comments to her GPS is a very troubling sign.

An alarm telling her, as she pulls into a parking lot where enterprising locals are charging ten dollars a day for SOA Demonstration Parking, and sees a busload of New School college students offloading, that this is risking to be quite a complicated experience indeed.

And soon, her worry is confirmed. Because unless she is very much mistaken, watching those students climbing off the bus, having just driven a thousand miles from New York, in their sandals and T-shirts and shorts and jeans, unloading their protest signs—No

TRAINING FOR TORTURE; US OUT OF LATIN AMERICA; FREE LORI BERENSON—and their sleeping bags and their backpacks and their unshaved underarms and their wrinkled shirts and their *Next Generation Phish* T-shirts and their marijuana-leaf tattoos—that unless she is totally so unfamiliar with the feeling that she no longer really recognizes it, from somewhere entirely unexpected inside of her is the sudden faint echo of a twinge of an emotion she has not felt but twice in recent memory, once with Maggie, once with Molly, maybe not before that since that French girl who thought her too *m'en fichiste* walked out of her *chambre de bonne* onto the rue des Abbesses leaving her alone with herself on a November night in the middle of dark, scary, statuesque Paris—*not feeling so proud anymore more, are you now? Not feeling like such a big girl now?*—and it is unmistakably the desire, sudden and very demanding, to cry.

2.

But remember, this is Isabel Montgomery, girl reporter, consummate professional. Tintin, remember? International correspondent climbing out of her hotshot car and, a crowd of inbred southern fucks staring at her pretty self, walking decidedly toward her assignment. Nothing fazes Isabel Montgomery—never has, never will. Certainly not a crowd of hippies pointlessly protesting the evil of the whole wide world.

And at first sight it appears quite a festive event. The demonstration is held along the approach to the front gate of Fort Benning, perhaps a quarter-mile of dilapidated suburban street where what appears to be a largely black set of residents live in houses of various states of desuetude set on lawns in various shades of drought. America.

Dozens of these residents are running improvised barbecue stops of every possible variety, some as small as charcoal-burning backyard affairs, some huge smokers towed by a pickup. They're doing brisk business, too, and Isabel Montgomery, girl reporter, noting this authenticating detail into her iPhone, asks herself why. Is it that running the gauntlet of the black barbecue vendors between the parking lot and the demonstration itself excited, for the protesters, so much liberal guilt that they feel obliged to abandon their radical vegetarianism and sink their teeth into red meat soaked in barbecue sauce and then burnt to a crisp? Or is it because militating has whetted their carnivorous appetite to such a high degree that they can't stop themselves? This was, she felt, unclear but a huge number of people are stopping to eat. And indeed—perhaps it was that second laced cigarette she'd smoked before she left her car—it smells pretty good, too.

Of course, the whole thing is preceded by a Muscogee County Police roadblock and the twelve tell-tale cameras of a PVI array, and this time, Izzy realizes, she is not going to be able to walk around it. She hesitates, then suddenly she doesn't care, and so she goes on and through the array, feeling computers around the world whirr into life so quickly that by the time she walks past the last camera she knows—knows for a fact—that a Homeland Security officer sitting in front of a computer in Quantico has already ID'd her.

She tells herself that she doesn't give a fuck.

But somewhere under the fact that she doesn't give a fuck, some other thing is apparently happening to her also, and if she doesn't put it into her iPhone, she still notes it, with professional exactitude, as relevant as, at least, to the voice in which she will write this piece, or would write the piece, if she writes the piece, which she won't. No doubt it is because her emotions are exacerbated by her exhaustion—and Izzy actually does *have* emotions, despite what her father liked to say—but that same sudden rise of tears that had come over her when she saw the busload of college students from New York disembarking suddenly returns, this time in force, as she passes the PVI cameras and sees a group of sixty-something men and women in tie-dyed T-shirts gathered round a microphone and singing, a couple playing guitars, a couple more with tambourines, and what they are singing is:

> It's *always* the old to lead us to the war
> It's *always* the young to fall
> Now look at all we've won with the saber and the gun
> Tell me is it worth it all

A song she hasn't heard since her father, then called Jim Grant, sang it to her during their hikes in the Catskills, years and years ago, with her mother, before she disappeared, and Jim Grant disappeared, and this guy called Jason Sinai appeared and told her that somewhere, in this thick substance called history, her entire childhood had been a lie.

Shocked, Isabel stops and listens, and only when she realizes that actual tears are coming to her eyes does she think to turn away.

And all this, all this is just the beginning of the quarter-mile gauntlet of solid protest that she has to walk before she even gets to the stage set up at the gates of Fort Benning, and who in hell knows what she is going to encounter on her way there?

And yet none of this is what she really is noticing as she begins to walk again, the lyrics in her ears—*now look at what they've done/with their soldiers and their guns*—but what she's really thinking is that one day, long after her father is gone, she will have children, too, and who the fuck is going to teach them this stupid song?

3.

Okay, so now the gauntlet to be run is the solid quarter-mile of hippy-dippy bullshit: the booths set up along the side of the road, a tag sale of outmoded idealism no one wants. One after the other after the other: Buffalo State Students for Peace, PeaceWork, Oberlin Peace Activists League, Grandmothers for Peace International, Veterans For Peace Chapter 56, Indigenous Support Network, Buddhist Peace Fellowship, Students for Social Change, International Campaign to Free Lori, American Friends Service Committee, Student Coalition for Action, Council for Peace and Justice, Stop the Madness, Rise Up! Community Collective, Amnesty International, Green Party, Coalition for Global Concern.

Nor is that the complete inventory: after all, Roy Bourgeois, the steadfast organizer of this protest, who lives full-time outside the gates of Fort Benning, is not only a Veteran against the War—a genuine redneck navy boy from Vietnam—he is also a Liberation theologist and an ordained Catholic priest. There is present, thus, a panoply of Christian activists: JustFaith at Church of the Transfiguration, Catholic Workers League, Jesuits, Marymount, Incarnate Word Sisters, Shepherd Progressive Action Committee.

Whether outright hippy-dippy or hippy-dippy and religious freak too, all these folk are displaying their wares, just like the local barbecue vendors, only these wares are either books, or T-shirts, or bumper stickers, or petitions. There are radical feminists, black activists, pacifists, vegetarians, sandal-wearers.

Someone bumps her; she turns to see it is a woman in a Peruvian poncho who doubtless thinks Izzy is what she would call a "narc" because she's looking at Izzy with every appearance of contempt.

As Isabel pushes forward through the crowd, she's feeling rather on the Peruvian woman's side on that one too.

4.

Notes on the central offices of SOA Watch:

Low lying, desperately ugly set of apartment houses, just outside the gates of Fort Benning, can only be meant for the base's civilian custodial staff. SOA Watch is in building 2B. Outside 2C: Maytag dishwasher, rusted clear through at the base, plastic tricycle, bedsprings. Family sitting at 2D like white trash from central casting, wife-beater on father, morbidly obese mother, two kids in diapers. In lawn chairs, barbecue going and a case of Bud, the

King of Beers, the trailer trash evidently enjoying the show. Inside 2B, hand lettered signs on cardboard point to Infirmary (left), Legal Aid (straight), and Press (right).

Isabel is greeted by a young woman who checks off her name on a clipboard—if this is a list of visiting journalists, it is laughably short—and leads her out of the pressroom into a bedroom with a sleeping bag on a mattress, a plastic table, and two very plain white plastic lawn chairs or rather, lawn chairs that were once white. The interviews, apparently, are taking place here. She surveys the room with no happy feeling. The closet, where hangs a single unironed shirt, stands open and on the table the contents of a toilet bag are spilled. Izzy gingerly lifts the less foul of the two chairs and carries it to the window. Sitting, she can see, over the sparse lawn, to the crowds of protesters gathered in front of the soundstage. At the microphone a man speaks in Spanish, with a heavily accented translator echoing.

And today is a special day because yesterday we gained a very great victory in the courts: the Minister of El Salvador was declared guilty of torture.

Listening, she takes out her laptop and puts it on the little table. The screen opens to her face in the camera window; she hits "record" and says to it: "A speech that oscillates between fantasy and trivia." Then she hits pause and redirects the camera outward—this is how she will record her interview, though probably she will not tell her interviewees that she is capturing image too.

There is a knock at the door, Josh Cohn no doubt, but before she answers she shoves the fouler of the two chairs closer so he will be framed in the camera.

5.

Josh sits and Isabel pretends to be looking at her computer to write. Instead she zooms the camera and then squints at his face. He is older than her by a few years. He has a pleasant face, exposed by a heightening hairline and then concealed by a hermit's black beard that grows freely up his cheeks and down his rather long neck. To a certain extent, therefore, he resembles Little Lincoln, and for a second Isabel grows confused, trying to remember if she fired him or not. But only to an extent. His blue eyes are sharp and they wander while he thinks: when he directs them at her, it is only for seconds before they are off again. He does not, she notes, at any point look at her breasts or her legs. She zooms out on the camera to inventory his plaid shirt, buttoned high, showing black hair up on his chest, long sleeves buttoned at his wrists and grey T-shirt. It occurs to her that this, during the height of the protest, must be battle dress. Whether literally or metaphorically. He is, after all, a warrior, of sorts.

But it is time for her explain whom she is writing for and what she wants, and that, for Isabel, means figuring it out to the point of being able to articulate it—something she has been loath to do. She watches out the dirty window for a moment, the soundstage, the Latino speaker, and tries to think. She tries to tell herself that this stuff is easy, isn't it? It is work, after all, and as such, a well of factitious creativity into which she has been dipping with reliable result for years.

But of course that's not it at all.

There is in fact nothing factitious about what she is doing. Not anymore.

She just doesn't know that yet.

So she turns back, shifts in her seat, crosses her legs, and lies.

"So look. What I'm after is a sense of what it means to be an activist nearly forty years and a decade after 9/11. I don't need to quote for you the statistics about progressivism in the United States, the number of Americans in jail under Patriot IV, or the number of un-incarcerated Americans carrying Homeland Security prohibitions, or any of that. You know—you must know—they're running PVI outside. You must know that every soul here is only avoiding incarceration at the government's pleasure."

He acknowledges this with a short nod but without, insofar as concerns his eyes, letting out whether he knew about it or not. He's guarded, in fact, in general, which first makes Isabel wonder if he hasn't had some training in media relations, then second makes her realize that he is treating her as hostile press, and finally, makes her feel unaccountably bad. This, too, sets off little alarm bells behind the part of her mind with which she is still talking.

"So let's start with the question of how you got into this work."

The first part of his answer is clear. He's been a full-time activist since graduation from Oberlin in '02; he is in his early thirties and now a key organizer of the SOA protest; he is the child of people with '60s roots: a physician; mother who worked for the Berkeley Tribe and then was "part of the community in New York who were doing above ground work for people who were underground."

That is any interviewer's opening, and Isabel takes it. "Exactly. Most people your age find nothing but discouragement in the example of your mother's generation."

Having considered this with his darting eyes, he disagrees.

"More people that I know have opted out in response to the draconian law changes and the law-enforcement changes since September 11, 2001." His eyes turn upward. "I think that that was a more discouraging and crushing thing to people than the history"—of Vietnam.

More crushing than Vietnam? Isabel pauses to think about this. Two million Vietnamese died during the war. But Josh is still talking. As an example, he describes his arrest, in '03, for committing "an action" at the protest, that is, crossing the line into Fort Benning military base proper, the culminating act of civil disobedience that ends the protest each year. He served the full six months for what most countries would see as an act of political principle worth a bench appearance and fine.

He is, it occurs to Isabel as she watches his eyes, a little thyroidy.

With a little interior note to return to this shocking statement that the Patriot Act has mobilized more young people than Vietnam—and the consequences such ahistoricism has for her article—she asks him how many people he expects at the protest. He says about the same as the year before, fifteen thousand. Is the protest growing? He answers forthrightly that it had come up three thousand in the past ten years, but "twenty to forty percent there each year are there for the first time."

Aha. Isabel makes a quick note. Here we are at a political movement with a loyalty rate as low as 60 percent and of which as much as 40 percent—nearly half—are brand-spanking new. She considers pointing this out to him, but at the thought it occurs to her that he looks not only slightly like Little L., but exactly like Lincoln himself—a big, bearded, Jewish Lincoln. Lincoln was probably a little thyroidy too. But this guy is the child of Jewish radicals, the whole bit: small-schools New York childhood; then St Ann's or Dalton or Elizabeth Irwin some other such place, because Mother and Daddy might have been peaceniks but they're also educated and beneficiaries of a rising economy from Vietnam to Iraq—indeed, she learns later that Daddy's a doctor and a friend of her Uncle Danny—then Oberlin. Only Josh can't play by the rules and so he takes the whole thing at its word and decides to serve full-time his convictions. Isabel imagines his parents running after his VW van, shouting, *Wait! Wait! We only meant you to* believe *in this stuff, not* act *on it.* His answer is simple, given that chances are his dad did the same in the early '70s. *Why? You* acted *on it. But it was different then.* But Josh, like her father and his little friends, was taking them at their word, wasn't he? It was an act of cruelty. And at the thought, Isabel suddenly stops liking Josh. At the thought, she sees him as one of those hardcore, addicted radicals—like her own father—who would rather be right than kind; who are prepared to do harm to others for their beliefs, as if they can only have a sense of self when the self is feeling the suffering of the other. John Brown, Emma Goldman. The first step of identifying them is that they have really hurt someone in some fundamental way in their path toward a sense of authenticity. For a moment, she regards Josh's image in her computer with something like contempt.

"And what did your parents think of your arrest?"

The answer is not what she expected.

"Really proud of the work that I do and glad that I'm doing this work."

Oh, Isabel thinks to herself: fuck. So everything she has just so brilliantly analyzed is, in fact, wrong. Josh's parents, she understands as he talks, are sincere people and happy to have their son live by the integrity of their principles. And Josh himself is not a *bad*, but a *good* person.

Then what is, she asks herself, the ontological status of her incorrect character analysis?

In a moment, the word surfaces in her consciousness: projection.

Her sense of contempt, now, directed at herself—she changes the topic.

"You seem to me to have given me such convincing reasons to stay home."

Josh directs her a quizzical look, and she goes on.

"I mean, your parents gave a lot of their lives to the struggle. Now you, and the struggle is not any further advanced, all these years later."

Now he understands.

"The faith that I have is in people's desire to do good and the ability to transform their lives. On a personal level I try to follow a guiding principle of reducing the suffering around me and reducing the suffering I do to the world and that owes a lot to a lot of the work I do here."

6.

Okay. Be that way. This is what she is thinking, after he goes, standing by the window, waiting for the next one, her contempt for herself momentarily occluded by what she has just heard. *Be that fucking way. But don't expect me not to go to town on you in print. Because that answer? It's spiritual, and there is nothing that the liberal American press—or what passes for same—hates as much as the spiritual. Maybe because we have to spend so much time toadying to the religious right, that when these soft-hearted spiritual types happen by, we can chop 'em to pieces.*

But then Isabel thinks of what he said about his parents, and a different emotion comes to her. *They're proud of the work that I do and glad that I'm doing this work.*

Out the window, the crowd at the soundstage, where a show of Mexican puppets is taking place, has grown under the thickening sun. *You're just a huge big disappointment to your folks, aren't you? Too right-wing for your father and, as for your mother, for all the time she spent in Laurel Canyon rolling around with whatever groupies were rolling around with Crosby, or Zappa, or whoever the fuck, she still can't stand it when you bring a girl home and God forbid you should be having a second drink.*

Or a third.

Or a fourth.

But her thinking is interrupted now, thank God, by a knocking at the door.

This next one is a different demographic—Christy Pardew, the name kind of gives it away. She's a pleasant woman in jeans and a long-sleeved black pullover—no bra—a freckled, friendly face under sandy brown hair, a pierced nose, and an unaccented American diction.

Soon Isabel knows where she's from (Baltimore); how she was

radicalized (Catholic Workers); what she is working for (societal transformation).

But this time, Isabel's problem seems to be different. Now this flat wa-wa is in her mind, a drained throb as the last of the THC is metabolized. And she is suffering from thinking that none of this seems to be *telling* her anything. It's unfathomable to Isabel that this smart, powerful woman devoted herself full time to this protest. She cannot see what her interest is, nor her ambition, but worse, Isabel can't see how this woman has convinced herself that anything is ever going to come of what she's doing.

When she poses the question, Christy answers simply that she doesn't think that she "could do this work without having hope that we can really make it happen."

As gently as she can—not because she wants to be kind, but because she want to elicit an answer rather than make Christy walk out, like Crown Prince Cuntmuscle did, she suggests that that would be a strong argument, for many, not to do this work. Christy answers after some thought that she gets "a lot of hope from the little victories that I hear about happening all over the world. The ways people are creating new models of being and interacting."

Outside there is more singing, and Isabel realizes that there is an image in her mind of children gathered around the stage.

Smoking that J was a mistake.

Not because she shouldn't be stoned—it's good to be stoned at an interview—but because she's fading fast and she can't re-up: even here pulling out a joint would not go over big, talk about new models of being and interacting. As she comes down, tiredness is pouring over her in waves, actually warping her thoughts, and she finds herself wanting to tell this girl that nothing she's saying makes any sense. New models of being and interacting? Only if that's a phrase in a military procurement bill or a weapons catalog. *Lockheed Martin's Integrated Identification and Interdiction Systems provide soldiers in the field with new models of being and interacting with potentially hostile host populations. When it's boots on the ground in an urban environment with enemy infiltration, Lockheed Martin IHP systems are there.* She realizes that it's a terrible sign, that she is even thinking of expressing herself to an interviewee. So she manages to bring the interview to a close, and in the couple minutes between this one and the next, she leans back and shuts her eyes.

She see her grandfather holding little Brad Flanagan's thin arm—sees him, of course, from Brad Flanagan's point of view, which is how she heard about the whole conversation. He says to her—and she is really dreaming now—that she was coming down here to write about politics, but it seems that the story is really about hope. The thought jars her awake, and she thinks: that makes sense. Given that these people have nothing but hope: no strategy, no vision, no reality, just *hope*. Then she thinks, Oh, you're so, so unfair. They also have *words*. Words, words, words. And everything else was just hope. Outside, a voice accompanied by guitar is singing: *I'm gonna bury that atom bomb, down by the river-side.* As if Bosnia and Rwanda, Iraq and Afghanistan, Lebanon and the two intifadas—as if they all never happened; as if our draftees weren't right now in Iraq and Afghanistan and Pakistan and cruising the Persian Gulf—as if there were any chance in the world of any new paradigm whatsoever bringing new hope to the horrific history of our civilization.

There is another knock at the door, and the usual *pourparlers*, and now a green-eyed young woman with a very pretty, very American face is sitting before her and though her urge to sleep is overwhelming, Isabel shakes herself directly into the interview.

This one explains her roots in grassroots anti-globalization movement. She is a Unitarian and a student at the Universalist Unitarian Seminary in Berkeley. Later she too will describe the influence of Catholic Workers; now she tells Isabel that she "considers her activism to be her life's purpose." She also has been arrested and jailed for six months by Muscogee County, and when Isabel asks her about that, she stops short. "It was hard . . . Gosh." Then she hesitates, long enough that Isabel wakes up and begins paying attention. "It was sad, and terrifying, and exciting, and I wouldn't trade it."

Paying attention, she says to herself, *is a good idea. Sometimes you get answers that mean something.* She doesn't feel so sleepy now, and she decides to try going right to the question she's after—that is, the question of how she persists in doing this protest in the face of the march of history—and this is the response she gets:

"I feel a really profound sense of a belief in the goodness of humanity in general and a respect for life. And out of that grows a lot of my feelings of nonviolence and pacifism and . . . for goodness' sake, my veganism. All of that stuff comes out of it. That's all practice that I've developed out of these profound religious feelings that I've had my whole life."

She goes on to tell Isabel that as a senior in college she fasted for a month in front of the gates of the School of the Americas. A one-month fast, Isabel knows, is another order of business. It is a hard thing to do. Isabel observes the girl, now, with real attention.

"Before I joined SOA Watch Movement I was sort of a good little liberal and I was doing my little liberal things. I was a Sierra Club kid; I worked on raising the corporate average fuel-economy standards for cars, I did campaigns like that, letter-writing campaigns, such as the Arctic National Wildlife Refuge—it was in my freshman year of college that I started that campaign on my campus . . . so I was really into that environmental stuff. But I think that this movement—the coalition building, the really amazing analysis—pushed me to learn more about how the Left isn't really separate . . . there's really such a single vision and my environmental vision went with my human-rights vision, and my human-rights vision went with my anti-capitalist vision. It just all came together, and this movement really helped me to see that."

Oh but my dear. Isabel nearly says that out loud. What she says, though, is that the *entire history* of American activism is a history of failed visions, and she asks her what she thinks about that? The girl nods, ready with an answer.

"Well, I think a lot of things about that. One thing that I think about it is that that's totally true. Really, it's hopeless. We're never going to gain the upper hand. And since we're not trying to gain the upper hand, the people wanting power are going to be the people who keep it, you know, instead of the people who want community or want us all to share power. Since we're not snatching, we're not going to win. That's one thing that I think."

She pauses here, looking at Isabel, who is little less than spell-bound.

"But it doesn't help me to continue my work if I only think of the Revolution as the only win, you know. In order to keep my work going, in order to keep my motivation going, I have to focus on the smaller things that we do win. Like, the labor movement won the eight-hour day. Civil rights. If I think in pieces, I think that, you know, it's not really a history of failure—it's just a history of wins that's smaller than we wish it was. So I have to focus on the small bits that we do win every day, and I also have to focus on the struggles not just in the United States but around the world. I just have to believe in that; I have to believe that it's possible."

Ah. In Isabel's consciousness, one part of her registers that she has just been given her article's peroration. *Where once college students and liberals paraded their dream for a better world before news cameras, now it appears that the hope for social justice has become indistinguishable from the belief in God, and Fox is not covering it. Perhaps, given that history has never offered the slightest proof of the existence of either—social justice or God—this is fitting.* But another part is listening to Sinai speaking. *Revolution happened in Cuba, in Guatemala, in Iran. Never mind what happened after. That's bullshit, saying that nothing can change—always has been, always will. Reactionary visions—even conservatism – are bulwarks of the privileged in any society against the aspirations of the disenfranchised.*

Fuck. Isabel looks at this girl for a long time now. Then she tries to imagine what she, Isabel Montgomery, must look like to her. Her *shoes* cost €00. If she had to, maybe she would have fasted for a month to get them, but not for anything else. Seen from this vantage, the girl has been remarkably open with her, as she is being remarkably open now, looking at Isabel curiously, neutrally.

"Do you know who I am, Becky?"

"Of course I do. Of course. Don't you see? That's why we all agreed to speak with you."

"I see." Isabel finds herself rising now, gathering her things, getting ready to leave. All the while thinking to herself, *Back this fucking interview up the moment you get back to the hotel. Because after you get drunk tonight—and oh my friends, and oh my foes: you, who have just been welcomed by a child who admires you because she admires Sinai, are going to get drunk tonight—tomorrow you will not remember a thing.*

7.

When she walks out into the evening the sky is a blue parabola, a late November in the eastern United States, small-sky country. There is no horizon in this low-lying, ex-urban landscape. An early-rising gibbous moon, pregnant and on the wax, declining sharply to the south, is etched against the sky. Two days later was the night Molly learned that Isabel's grandfather had died. Tonight, it would be her moon, that south-declined moon that seems to peek up into her window from the valley of Saugerties, although of course it's not possible for a moon to shine upwards. The next day, for her, would be the one it rained, when her father was at Huckleberry Point. Then the moon again. On the flagstone path outside the press office Isabel squints up into the sky, then at the protest.

Like the light, the crowds have thickened and slowed, and the direction of movement is toward the soundstage and gate, people still arriving for the last appearances of the evening. For a long time she pushes against the flow until at last, when she reaches the entrance, she finds that in front of the twelve-camera PVI array, a group from Pax Christi has unfurled a long banner reading:

Our God is love, our gospel is peace. No war.

8.

The hotel the *Times* had booked turns out to be an upscale version of a chain with a plush carpet and a swimming pool to justify a price of three times more than even Magnolia's hourly rate. Of course, this is no Homer's Lounge, and by the fact that the staff are wearing these little yellow sports coats and Isabel can see a golf course out the window, she feels very confident that she won't be seeing a lot of people coming to party after their new tattoo from Tattoo Tommy's. Or for that matter, title-pawning—unless, as is likely, the gentleman in the green sports jacket wheeling his golf clubs through the lobby owns a few franchises.

She gets her key, goes up to her room and finds that it's non-smoking. She goes back down and spends a long time at the desk waiting for a party of unrepentant Reaganites in checkered trousers. Then she is told that there is no other room available due to a golf tournament. She tries to imagine coming here because you want to rather than because you have to. Where would you have to be coming from? She goes back up to her room, opens the window onto the golf course, sits at the little phony wood desk, and lights a cigarette. There's a half-bottle of Glenmorangie in her bag, lifted, if she remembers correctly, which is unlikely, from the first-class cabin of her flight from San Jose. She hits this, then closes it and puts it down on the desk next to a Gideon Bible. She finishes the cigarette, throws it into the golf course, shuts the window, lies on the bed.

Isabel doesn't dream, but she doesn't really sleep either. Or if she does, it is a loud, restless activity, punctuated by noises of the hotel, watchful and aware. Perhaps she does dream, a little, toward the end, when she sees her father's face, clean shaven and tanned, under bright sun behind the green of the Catskills in leaf. When she wakes it is instantly, eyes wide open, the picture so real that she is surprised not to have an afterimage of the Catskills sunlight. Instead there is the light from the window to the golf course, a low sky of dusking grey cloud. Without even sitting up she reaches to the bedside table, finds and lights a cigarette—a hash-loaded one—then remembers that she's not meant to smoke here. She gets up and opens the window, ashing the cigarette onto the golf course. On the way, she lifts the half-bottle of scotch off the desk and hits it while she finishes the cigarette. When she puts it back on the desk, her eye falls on the Gideon Bible, and without much thinking about what she's doing, she tosses it out the open window after her ash. That feels good, so she tosses out also the pen, writing pad, and hotel information booklet. She observes, with satisfaction, that they've all fallen on the green of the seventh hole. She closes the window, then goes take a shower, with the cigarette.

When she finishes, she is feeling better. She dresses in jeans—Massimo Dutti, cut for a low waist and good legs—and a sleeveless silk vest, Agnès B, black and buttoned down the middle, its straps as well as its buttons showing a black leotard beneath. She has washed and blow-dried her hair and put on red lipstick and mascara, slowly, all the while smoking the loaded cigarette and hitting the Glenmorangie. When she's done she puts a single credit card in her back pocket and, carrying her cigarettes, walks out into the evening.

The hotel restaurant, the Columbia Inn, is across the parking lot, on the road. This seems intended, Isabel feels, to conceal the connection with the hotel chain and imply some rootedness to the town. But that pretension is belied by the poured-concrete architecture, identical to the hotel, and the fact that the whole thing sits in a development, far from the center of town, where no building is older than ten years. No doubt there is an antebellum heart of Columbia, but out here is newer money, transplants from Atlanta, white-flight, and the drinks menu will more likely have margaritas than mint juleps. It is 7:30. The sun has not yet set.

Inside, there is a long horseshoe bar, lit by low-hanging green-tinted lamps and tended by two very young, very pretty brunette girls, each in a short green skirt and stockings. One is slightly long of torso, which she's trying to conceal with a loose white blouse, and of face, which she's had the good sense not to mess with. The other, who is nearly flawless, wears a sleeveless white top, skin tight, very pretty indeed. This one is cutting lemons, the other loading wine glasses in an overhead rack. Both watch Isabel enter without expression.

Under their examination she stops for a moment, considering. Despite its pretensions, the Columbia Inn has failed to attract the golfing set, which is very revealing about it, and is empty but for a few folk at the bar, of which some seem to be protesters. Beyond sits a series of dining booths, artfully lighted and appointed, entirely empty. On one hand trial by barmaid, the two watching her in blank accusation like a Degas composition. On the other hand the solitude of the mood-lighted dining room. Here the tables are under white cloth. On the walls, framed in polished oak, signed photos of golfers and displays of memorabilia. The style is high Applebees.

Under the influence of the weed, repelled by the barmaids, Isabel begins to make her way to a table, but as she shifts into the mood light the ersatz memorabilia make her feel slightly ill. She stops and sees the study of her grandfather's house. Then she sees that the bar has ashtrays—God bless the Confederacy—the tables not. So she turns back and takes a bar stool and as she attends to the barmaids— who seem to feel that a period of studious indifference is required before they serve her—she realizes that only one of them is out of Degas. The other—the long-torsoed one—is attractive, in this case intensely, rather than pretty—and out of Toulouse Lautrec. When she approaches, Isabel asks for *un absinthe, s'il vous plaît, ma jolie petite laide*, but softly enough so that when the barmaid doesn't hear and asks her again for her order, she can get bourbon and beer.

It is warm enough that she had decided not to—or more precisely, she was stoned enough to forget to—put on a jacket, and so Isabel is bare shouldered, which is a good look for her. She is, she thinks, perhaps not up to the two barmaids, but then, she points out to herself, she can have sex without your partner risking a statutory rape charge, can't she now? Which is not true of the barmaids.

And, furthermore—most importantly, in fact—she has before her now a straight shot of bourbon, cozying up to a beer glass, cute as a button. The first hit sinks straight to her belly and begins radiating heat. Carefully, she chooses a clean cigarette from the pack, lights it, sighs in the smoke, then out. Then she hits the bourbon again.

And here's the way Izzy sees it: she is alone in a foreign country. She can sit right here for the next three, maybe four hours, with a drink, a cigarette, and the ten-yard stare she got from her mother, who before she became an ex-drug addict was a drug addict, and before she was a drug addict was a starlet with quite a little Holly-wood career, and in all three capacities had voluminous call to silence many people with a ten-yard stare. At some point she can add whatever they serve here that has high-fat meat: she is five foot three inches, and she now weighs one hundred and fifteen, despite eating like a horse. Then she can have a few more bourbons. And some-time, sometime late tonight when the restaurant is full and smoky and filled with Garth Brooks or Burt Bacharach or whoever the fuck they play in an ex-urban Georgia restaurant—although right now they are playing for some reason Lennon—she can pay her bill with the *Times*'s credit card, rise carefully and steadily from her seat, navi-gate her way out of the bar and across the hotel parking lot, go up to her room, and if she's not so blind drunk by then that she'll pass clean out without thinking again about Sinai, well then she'll have just enough scotch left for a couple of alprazolam or lorazepam or diazepam or whatever comes first to hand from her copious travel pharmacopeia and then, friend, she will have quite a few hours, won't she just, perhaps longer—perhaps forever!—before she has to think about anything at all.

It is a good life. Isabel is on bourbon two now, and she's thinking, there is of course copious pain available, but it is a good, harsh, peri-patetic life, a world always clean and private. Yeah, hanging behind you somewhere is that crowd of people you belong to, that history-laden, heavy bunch of folk with everything they believe. And yeah, in front of you there is something terribly wrong, something you can't bear to think about, but you are already so drunk you can keep yourself from putting your finger on it, so drunk that you can absorb the pain it generates, the pain you won't think about, into the muscle of your stomach and there let it radiate like rain into a paper cup that slither as they slip away across the universe.

Jai guru deva om, Jesus. It is pulsing through her now, sleeplessness and the fine Los Angeles medical marijuana and ritalin, and coke, and methamphetamine, and ketamine, and alprazolam diazepam Lorazepam whatever the fuck she has been ingesting all these months and above all this deep brown distillation, this silken mother's milk from Kentucky. For an hour, anyway: a good, blissful hour that contains two cigarettes and two more bourbons and a space of images of broken light which dance before her like a million eyes in which everything—Prince Cuntmuscle and Sinai and the girl who said she was *m'en fichiste* on the rue des Abbesses and Molly's dream that comes to her all the time—fail, utterly fail, in her deep, narcotic, alcohol trance, to change her world.

Nothing's going to.

Until, gradually, she becomes aware that someone is talking to her.

9.

He is a medium-sized, very stocky man, perhaps thirty, with a shaved head, directly across from her on the other leg of the horseshoe. The bar is more crowded now, with a couple—a guy with long hair and his girlfriend, both drinking martinis—down and around the bend. To her right there are a few singles—a middle-aged man with something on the rocks, and a middle-aged woman drinking white wine. Next to the man addressing her as buddy, there is another, the same age but taller and with a short-cropped crewcut drinking what appears to be a tall glass of ice water. The short one is drinking tequila shots and chasers, and smiling at her and instantly, unwillingly, as if driven by an adrenal response, she is watching him with the enormous clarity of the very drunk.

"Hey, welcome back."

His eyes are steady under open lids. His face, too, is open as only a bald face can be, and it puts her instantly, instinctively, on the defensive. It is composed and cocked toward her on its neck at a slightly pugnacious angle. His smile is, while belligerent, slightly, just slightly, self-mocking, but it is such in a way that she recognizes immediately as dangerous: once you have implicitly accepted that he is mocking himself, you can't complain when he mocks you, which he will. She recognizes the maneuver. She has used the maneuver. And she is able to see, in it, three things about this guy. First is that he is very, very smart. Second is that he is very drunk, but not as drunk as he plans to be. And third, that he hates himself. That makes him dangerous, and she thinks to herself, You just watch out there, won't you? This man comes on like a wagging dog, but he does not want to make friends. He wants to make someone else hurt like he does.

"Tell me what you were daydreaming about and I'll buy you a drink."

She shakes her head.

This elicits a small smile. Without moving his eyes from hers, he says something sotto voce to his friend. Then he raises his voice.

"Okay, then you buy me a drink and I'll tell you what I just said about you to my friend."

She shakes her head again, still without smiling. But she's lost already, and she knows it. Both barmaids are watching, Toulouse Lautrec more intently than Degas. Toulouse Lautrec, she suddenly sees with clarity, is the one he has already fucked, which is interesting because she's Isabel's pick too. She looks at his left hand and sees a wedding band.

"You got to be from out of state. Turning down a southern gentleman's offer of a drink? You was a man, I'd be handing you my glove."

She tried one last time.

"Nothing personal. Just flying solo tonight."

"Naw, a lady looks like you? That ain't no way to be. Where from, then?"

"England."

"Cor blimey. That's smashing. You hear that, Richie?" He pokes Richie with an elbow. Richie wakes, nods, smiles to her, then looks attentive as his friend goes on. "Let me offer you a confederate welcome. Bygones be bygones, what say? 1776 and all that. Napoleonic wars. The big ones made us friends, didn't it? Plucky little fellows, Battle of Britain, that shit. Then Afghanistan, Iraq, and now you're more or less blowing us, aren't you? What brings you to our fair state? Can I buy you a drink?"

This time, she answers carefully. "Work brings me. I'm a journalist, come down to cover the School of the Americas protest. I got to be back there in the morning. So this qualifies as my nightcap. But thanks."

"Hey, baby, we're just what you need! We're both from Fort Benning. Don't let the civvies fool you—I'm a captain. Richie too. Captains Delaney and Jacobsen at your service. Jacobsen with an "e"—otherwise I'd be a j-e-double yew."

"Captains." She nods. "What unit?"

"Training Corp. We train our boys at the School of the Americas as well as for the Near Eastern theaters. See, this is your lucky day. Formerly of the 32nd Airborne, two tours of duty in Plan Colombia"—he pronounces it Co-lum-beeya—"one in Ko-reea, one in Eye-raq. Detailed to counter-insurgency, staff. Richie here flies a Black Hawk, also counter-insurgency but what we call 'hot ops;' insertion, exfiltration, all that good shit. Been in Eye-raq, Afghanistan, Somalia, and a bunch of places we can't even tell you—Richie's hot shit, man. What you need for your article is an interview with me and Richie."

Does she? Only maybe. She watches him for a moment, as does Richie, she notices, with some care. Then she speaks slowly. "Well, sure, Captains, if you want to talk about Fort Benning, you're very welcome. On the record, though—I tape with this little here thing.

And you'll need to start by a full ID with rank and name for my fact-checkers."

"Why sure." The short one got up right away, Richie's a little slower and, somehow, less willing. To the bartender—Degas, she notes: "Beautiful, set us up yonder and get the 'reporter' whatever it is that 'reporters' drink."

Here, she speaks up. "I pay or we don't talk. No kidding."

"Well then, hey, sweetheart, I warn you, I am not a cheap date. Richie is. He's driving. But not me."

Isabel knows already that she has lost. But that you can't win with this kind of asshole. She is already his date.

As one of the barmaids brings the drinks—tequila and beer for him, bourbon for her, water for Richie, she hands over her credit card and tells the barmaid to hold on to it. She is not so fucked up now. She watches them rounding the bar. Something must have happened earlier between Jacobsen—with an e—and the longhaired guy, sitting to her left with his girlfriend over martinis, because Jacobsen-with-an-e claps a hand on his shoulder and another on his neck, as they pass, and shakes him slightly, all the while saying something that only he, judging by all their faces, finds humorous. To her surprise, though, the longhair brushes it off and goes on with his discussion with the girl. Clearly they are here for the protest. *One of us is misreading this situation*, Isabel thinks to herself: *either I am overreacting, or this guy doesn't understand the danger he's in.*

On balance, though, she is going to stick with her view. She thinks this bald, short guy is dangerous. She thinks he's an enlistee, a combat veteran, an angry little country boy; she thinks he's filled with rage and bent on mayhem. And she thinks that Richie, with his iced water, is designated driver tonight, wing man while Jacobsen-with-an-e gets shitfaced with an a. Later, she's able to confirm this: she overhears Richie telling someone on his cell that he'll be at his local bar by midnight, after he's dropped Hal off because "Hal's up tonight, I'm babysitting."

Hal, meanwhile, sits with her on his left at the bar and Richie on his right and picks up her iPhone to speak his name, serial number, unit, posting. Then he puts it down and hits his drink. He is, she thinks, well on his way.

"So then you're writing about those faggot assholes down here this weekend. You planning on getting our point of view? Or is this just more of your northeast bullshit?"

She doesn't answer. This guy has the knack of posing questions with no right answer. A typical bully. What she does say is: "Are you authorized to speak for the US Army?"

"Why, ah don't need to be, Miss. Ah'm an American citizen, I'se allowed to say whatevah I wants."

Then, switching accents again: "Remember US v. Hernandez, 2008? *A soldier cannot have his First Amendment right to speak to the press abridged even in theater of war.* Supreme Court, baby—a 'super-precedent,' just like good old Roe v. Wade that gives folks like Jewboy shithead here"—he motions down the bar with his head to the long-haired guy—"the right to kill babies."

Now he pauses, this little smile playing onto his lips. "If you don't know the ruling, I'd recommend Haynes Johnson on it in the *Nation*, or even Ronald Dworkin's *New York Review* coverage of the trial. Or you could just read the opinion, if you're up to it: Roberts wrote it, great juridic stylist."

She doesn't respond, which satisfied him no end: "See, you liberals always do the exact same thing. Think cause I'm a southern boy in the forces I'm an idiot, right? Well, the rank and file—Negros, Hispanics, the like—I'm not saying. But you are in the south, young lady, and I'm an officer *and* a gentleman. My daddy was an officer before me, his granddaddy before him. And don't you just know *his* granddaddy fought for the Confederacy. I been through the Citadel, and the army sent me to Duke for my MA in American history. Might just go for the old Ph.D. one day."

By way of response, Isabel raises her eyebrows and hits her bourbon.

"So I can say what I want, see. The only limitation is the self-imposed one. We members of the armed forces keep ourselves from ever criticizing our Commander in Chief. That's why you never hear any of us say anything about Obama, even though we all think that bitchass Secretary of State and all New York Jews that put him in office should all have been sent back to Israel. Until he's out of office, that is. Then I can stop being polite and tell you what I really think."

Thanks for sharing, she says, but only to herself. To him, she says: "So what do you think of the School of the Americas protest?"

He smiles, widely and happily. "Waste of fucking time. Mine, Muscogee County, yours. You know what we do in the camp? We fucking go about our business. This protest isn't a pimple on our lily-white asses. Like this dude here."

He motions at the couple down the bar. "Down from Washington, Christ sake. And his do-good girlfriend. You know that bitch has been giving me the eye all evening? Guess it's free love, right? Pardon me a second, will you?"

While he's speaking, Hal's eyes have several times darted to the couple sitting around the bend of the bar. Now he rises and moves toward them, but before he goes, he orders another round. While he's not looking, however, she covers her glass with a flat hand and shakes her head slightly at the barmaid. Then she looks at Richie, who meets her eyes with an impassive expression. He looks away before she does.

So Richie's the weakest link.

She registers the realization by pronouncing it to herself, several times, hoping that it will survive however drunk she is about to get.

Now Hal has his arm around the guy again, only this time he holds his bicep with his other hand, hard, and edges his body between the guy and the girl. She doesn't know what he's saying, but he says it with a smile. The guy has the good sense, she sees, to look alarmed. Still, when Hal moves away with a last squeeze and a cheery wave, the guy keeps sitting there.

Isabel is thinking: Idiot, you get the fuck out of here while you can, won't you? But she can't, of course, say anything to this clueless bastard, and in any case, who knows? She's not sure Hal would let him leave. Hal, she is fairly sure, is planning on keeping this guy on reserve until later this evening, and, when he's good and drunk, he'll beat the shit out of him. Then Richie'll scoop Hal up and into a car and home. Now, next to her again, Hal notices her half-empty glass and motions to Toulouse Lautrec who, avoiding her eye, serves her. Then he goes on: "All this bullshit out there. Stupid fucks don't realize that the only reason they can carry their dumbass signs around here is because we're getting killed overseas. Free Lori, *sheeee-it!*" He puts on a black accent for that one. "You *seen* that shit? Bitchass aids and abets a communist military group in Peru, and that's a fucking human rights cause? What, you stopping drinking?"

She answers: "Bourgeois has combat duty in Vietnam."

"Yeah, yeah. Exactly my point. Vietnam. Conscript army. Goddamned enlisting one step ahead of the draft. Bullshit. I know all about guys like him. Fragging officers. Doing smack. Throwing their medals back at the White House, just like John Fucking-A Kerry. Then taking their fucking divinity degrees to aid terrorists killing our allies in South America. Hate the war, not the soldiers, blah blah, fuck you. And you wonder why we fucking lost in Vietnam? Bullshit. I *am* Plan Colombia, I *am* Iraq, right here, right now, and so's Richie. I *am* the war."

Which is bad, but the worse thing is, she knows that if she doesn't argue at some point, he'll think she's humoring him, and that will make him even more dangerous. Worst thing you can do with a drunk is humor him, isn't it? Isabel knows that the drunk have a radar for it, and she knows this firsthand. So she says, softly: "I've never heard anyone accuse Roy Bourgeois of anything like that. He's a southern boy himself. New Orleans, you know. And he's an ordained priest."

"Um-hmmm yeah." He agreed readily. "Exactly. A Catholic. So

were the Kennedys. Old Joe with his fuck-buddies McCarthy and Hoover. Jack running around the White House with hookers. Him and Bobby in so deep with the Eye-talians they get their asses shot dead. And Teddy, for fuck's sake. Rudolph the Red Nose Kennedy. You know the real problem here, lady?"

He has ordered again, but this time it's Degas and when she serves only him, he motions to her glass. She gives Isabel a questioning look; she shrugs. Then she motions, with a forefinger, toward the cash register, where her credit card is propped up on the keyboard. This part, Hal doesn't seem to have noticed, because he had bent over the bar, his face right in front of Isabel's, talking not just to her but around her to Richie.

"Richie and me are always talking about this. The problem is we live in a polarized society. Not between left and right or white and black or any of that shit. Right, Richie? We're polarized between the people who sit inside our borders enjoying the privileges of Americans, and those who go abroad to protect them. None of you understand what it's like out there. None of you understand that there's a fucking universe of ragheads out there who want to come here and take your precious First Amendment away from you, for no good god damn reason except that you have it and they don't. Even V. S. Naipaul says it: we're under attack by people who want nothing more than a green card, and he's a damn raghead himself. The rest of us? The ones who go over there to their godforsaken countries, see them with their godforsaken women in veils and kids in rags while they fucking parade around with their endless supply of Kalashnikovs, killing each other, killing us, killing themselves, we understand what we're facing. You know who else understands? The Jews understand. They learn it from Israel. So we end up being the Jews' army, fighting their war, protecting their business. Now that's a good name for a book, huh? 'The Jews' Army.' Want to write it with me? 'Scuse me a second. That reminds me of something I wanted to tell my faggot-ass kike buddy over there. Hey, asshole . . ."

And suddenly she knows—she knows—that it is time to move. As

Hal stands, she stands, pockets her iPhone and cigarettes, and, God bless Degas here, as she brings it, she signs the credit-card slip. "Great to talk to you, Hal, Richie. Good night now."

This pulls Hal up short. "Whoa, now, baby, where you going? We're just getting started."

But, see, he's halfway down the bar. The couple is looking up, as are the bartenders. She raises her voice even slightly, and she can have the whole bar watching. And everybody knows it.

Therefore, a *big* smile, and a raised voice. "No, thanks. I got work to do tomorrow morning. Have a good night."

"Hell, no way. Richie and me? We got so much to tell you. We got so much to tell you about Jew faggots like this guy here and his cunt girlfriend, and your commie buddy Bourgeois, and all those whole-wheat cocksuckers down at Fort Benning . . ."

He's moving toward her, but not quick enough. She steps back again, the heels of her boots on the floor. Now the whole restaurant is watching. She doesn't answer him. Her second step backward had put her right next to Richie, and it is to him she answers.

"Richie? You going to take care of your buddy, or am I going to have the editor in chief of the *New York Times* call your commanding officer tomorrow morning and complain about conduct unbecoming?"

And now Richie is standing, and the guy down the bar is standing, and Hal, getting a hold of himself, is sitting down at the bar again, saying to the guy at the end, "Hey, buddy, don't be alarmed. I'm just letting off steam. Let me get you and your lady a round . . ." And the guy is actually clueless enough to sit down—probably, as Hal says, an East Coast liberal afraid of offending the redneck—and now, feeling slightly guilty, but immensely, immensely relieved, she is out in the night air, feeling sweat drip from under her arm down her side, thinking to herself, Well, aren't you just quick on your feet there, girl, aren't you? And that is her last thought before, although she clearly crosses the parking lot and gets to her room and, by all evidence available the following morning, finishes her bottle of Glenmorangie and has an unpleasant encounter with the telephone, the entire night ends in her memory, unnegotiable, like the absolute silver and absolute black on Molly's lawn in autumn, like a light switch toggling, from on, to off.

10.

She dreams that night about Molly, her green eyes like seawater in sunlight. Her house at night, the lit window when you wake. Then she is in the supermarket, and everyone is stunned because they've announced on the PA system that a girl is dead. She wakes in the morning and realizes that she's been dreaming Molly's dream, when she was in a supermarket when Kennedy was shot. It was the cold aisle in the Grand Union up in Tannersville, near where Molly's husband grew up, where she went to tell her father-in-law that her husband had died, where her father-in-law had, in his grief, made indescribable noises and where, for a moment, the color had drained out of the world. The dream speaks to her across her lifetime, another's dream about experiences before she was born. Like the Internationale spoke to her father. Hers, mine, theirs. The only difference a pronoun, something that only context, not morphology, denotes as subjective or objective. The difference ceases to make sense. That's the heart of activism: *you* and *they*, insofar as the pronouns denote people with different kinds of interests, cease to make sense and your life must be changed in order to change their life. It's a function of grammar, not of existence, and it was invented by novelists. So how is it to be captured, except in a novel? The sun is pouring through the hotel room's window, which she seems to have left open the night before: her memory of yesterday evening stops after leaving Jacobsen-with-an-e. She lifts herself out of bed and goes to the window. Far away on the golf course there is a quartet playing toward her. The Glenmorangie bottle is lying on the green, below, empty, next to the Gideon Bible and ashtray. Also there is the telephone, its cord torn at the plug. It is nine, and she is due to inter-view Bourgeois in an hour.

Fortunately, she has not undressed, and so is able to pee, wash, and check the news on her iPhone while she brushes her teeth. She starts to put on mascara, then she drops it into her toilet bag and turns quickly to the toilet where she throws up, suddenly and dramatically, the slight contents of her empty and abused stomach from the night before. That there is nothing actually to evacuate does not stop the long, powerful, painful paroxysms. For a time she sits, a cold sheen of sweat on her face, on the bathroom floor, trembling. When she can, she shifts slightly to reach her toilet bag on the bathroom sink, and fumbles it down to her. She knows there's Maalox in there, but the bag has gotten wet, somewhere, and the box is broken. Fumbling at the bottom of the bag she finds two white Maalox capsules floating free, which she manages to take, then she rests some more. At long last, she feels able to rise; and washes her face, hard, with soap. Soon she is vir-tually entirely recovered, as quickly as she had grown nauseous. Then she puts on a jean jacket and a baseball cap. She packs and checks out—why not, they're going to kick her out anyway for what she did to the room. Tonight she'll find a plane somewhere. Anywhere.

It is not until she is in the car that she realizes that something is very, very wrong.

It is not immediate. In fact, it is not until she's on the 185 again, fin-ishing the third of the four coffees she carried out of the hotel in four precariously balanced Styrofoam cups—she lost one in the parking lot—and smokes her first cigarette. More exactly, when she finishes her first cigarette. Because as she finishes her cigarette, it occurs to her that she's not sure whether or not it was loaded.

It's not just that she didn't remember to check, or that she can't remember how many she has left.

It's that she can't tell if she's stoned.

She thinks about this for a while. Then suddenly, without warning, she swerves into the breakdown lane and brakes, hard.

First she checks the cigarette pack. It's impossible to be sure, but there are still eight loaded cigarettes in it, and she thinks she smoked two yesterday. So she is not high.

Next, anxiety mounting, she goes to the trunk of the Mustang, opens her luggage, and pulls out the toilet bag. Pushing the bag to the side, she dumps it onto the trunk floor, and looks, very carefully, at what is in there.

Lipstick, mascara, tampons, tweezers, a cornucopia of prescription drugs, an empty Maalox box, broken, and seven pink Maalox capsules, floating free.

Maalox is pink.

And at the very bottom, damp and stuck to the side of the toiletry bag, the empty little envelope that the Rasta dope-delivery man had given her, centuries ago in Bedford Street, containing two hits of pure, pharmaceutical-grade MDMA, with the little red heart, smudged now with moisture, looking at her.

Empty.

Pure, pharmaceutical grade MDMA is white.

For a long, long moment, Isabel stands on the verge of the 185 outside Columbia, Georgia, feeling terror.

Then, with a deep, deep breath, she slams shut the trunk, sits back in the car, and lights a cigarette.

She took the dose perhaps a half-hour ago, on a purely empty stomach. She has, she knows, perhaps another hour and a half of rising high before her brain releases into itself a flood of serotonin, the peak.

I got this. There is a strange, funny calm coming over her. *Fuck this. It's only a drug.*

And that must have worked because the next thing she knows she has parked in the improvised protest parking lot, and is paying her ten bucks, and walking through the PVI cameras, and she finds herself right in front of the Pax Christi banner, which is now swimming slightly in the bright sun:

Our God is love, our gospel is peace. No war.

11.

By now, events are in full swing and there is a palpable difference in the air. At one point she finds herself looking up into the sky for a storm. But it is just a bland, blue autumn sky, a small eastern sky, empty of weather. The drama is on the ground only.

Except for a slight hyper-reality of vision and a distant buzz in her blood, she feels pretty normal. On the soundstage, a roll call is going on in which the names of victims of SOA-trained soldiers are read, one by one, by a procession of protesters, each carrying a small wooden cross bearing a single name. As each finishes their recitation, they take their place in a processional that plants the cross in the chain-link fence, ten feet high, closing off Fort Benning from the protest. Behind the fence she can see a line of soldiers, also equipped with video cameras, waiting to arrest those who cross into the base and, thence, escort them to waiting buses.

Bourgeois's office is in front of her now, the one neat little condo on the property outside of the gates of Fort Benning, where he lives and works. Thoughtfully, she's watching and drinking a cardboard cup of coffee, wheedled out of one of the barbecue men by the entrance and taken, she thought, from his own breakfast pot. In each sip she savors the odors of the interior of his home. The coffee is delicious, life-giving, and she drinks it gratefully.

Of course there is no way she can do the interview. She knows this. The normalcy that she's constituted so laboriously on the flimsy scaffolding of booze and drugs has been proof to everything save this new drug, so long, so sedulously avoided. She may have enough strength left in her, still, to get her up to Homer's Lounge—Come Party With Us—but maybe not even that. In any case, she has no wish to drink, no wish to smoke, no appetites at all. Really, she is growing rapidly unable to do anything, and briefly—but, somehow, confidently—she wonders where she's going to go. But she never will have the chance to find out: as she stands there a man she recognizes as Father Bourgeois, no doubt sick of waiting for her, steps out onto his porch with Christy Pardew, and when Christy sees her, she has no choice but to walk toward him.

Now, for the first time since she took the drug, she feels scared. Still, she begins to walk, on bone and cartilage. No muscle, no heart.

Like Sinai got out of the auditorium at the VALB event.

Like Molly ran the last miles of the eight to Dutcher Notch, that day she paced herself so badly.

Like Danny waited in the bedroom of his Riverside Drive apartment, Passover night of 1996, for Maggie to come.

Like her grandfather climbed, that night after the VALB ceremony, the day he saw Dr. Holmquist, to speak with his wife.

But then, right now, she does not mind feeling scared.

That's a funny difference.

12.

Bourgeois ushers her into a well-ordered office, sits her in front of a desk. He himself sits down at it, his head framed by a poster of Luis Espinal's face, on one side, and four Latin American nuns, on the other. His desk is clear save for an alabaster Buddha and the room, ringed by political posters—all, she notices, of people—is brightly lit with halogen lamps. This is the same kind of hovel that the press office was in. But this one is cared for, lived in, ordered, and put together simply and prettily.

As for Bourgeois, previously, all the pictures she has seen of him are in his cassock, which makes him look old. Now he wears a black cotton sweater over a blue turtleneck and jeans in which he is slim but for a slight middle-aged heft. He is Sinai's age, but he looks younger, partly because he has a full head of hair.

For a time she fiddles with her computer. The camera is built in—you open the cover, launch the camera in the casing, and switch the laptop toward your subject, done. But for the time she fiddles around with the camera, and then with this little external mike she doesn't need.

Because she's trying to cover up the fact that she is crying.

Just a little. Little enough that she can hide it by hunting for a power outlet she doesn't need, and running an extension cord, and plugging in the computer. Or maybe she's not hiding it. Because all the while Bourgeois is sitting at his desk, watching her with an expression of mild curiosity, and who knows what he sees—or perceives. Her throat is so tight she can hear her breath in it. Her chest has turned to lead. And from some recess in her consciousness, awareness is pouring over her that it's not just that there's no way on God's green earth that she's going to interview this man. It's that she is never, ever, going to interview anyone else again ever.

She fiddles as long as she can.

She tries to keep the drug at bay, breathing regularly, deeply.

Then she gives up.

Strangely, once she has started talking, she stops crying. She dries her eyes with a Kleenex from his desk, then, while she searches her bag for makeup, she tells him about how her father is dying. It is not what she meant to say, it is simply what needs to be said. She has no hesitation, further, in saying it: it is, in fact, what she has come here to say, and she knows that. Usually, she tells him, she doesn't read her dad's letters, and hasn't for long time. But she screwed up and read one a few months ago in March on her way between Riyadh and New York and maybe it wasn't a screw up after all because she guesses she needed to know that her father was about to die. After all. The drug is carrying her along on a flood of words; they are coming out of her without thought, directly, unscreened, nearly un-thought, as if the drug had simply removed her mind from its mediating role or, more precisely, her ego. He had been ten years on a cocktail of Velcade, thalidomide, and corticosteroids, wonder drugs that have kept the effects of his blood plasma displagia—commonly known as multiple myeloma—at bay.

Prior to Velcade, he would have been long dead. But he had elected not to do an autologous stem cell transplant, for reasons she didn't understand, and without that treatment this was the limit. He had still the option of allotransplantation, but with a 30 percent mortality he had decided against it, and so, he had decided to die.

She has found her makeup now and, switching the camera on her MacBook to herself, she does her eyelashes, then her lips. All the while telling Bourgeois about how her father had decided to die in the house where his own father had decided to die, the family home on Bedford Street. That Molly would go there with him, as Danny and Maggie had done for her grandfather's death. As she spoke, she was not sure she had even explained who Molly, and Danny, and Maggie were, but that didn't seem necessary either. But she tells him that besides Molly and Danny and Maggie, her half-sister Beck and his husband were in the city, as were dozens of friends. He wouldn't be alone. The question was, would she be there? And that that's what she wanted to ask him about. Not some bullshit about the viability of political protest in this day and age, the possibility of change, none of that.

"See, my dad didn't need to be radicalized, the way you did, down in Louisiana, that's where you're from, right? He didn't have to go to Vietnam and see all the suffering and live through the Tonkin Gulf Resolution and figure out the whole thing was a lie. My grandfather was a Red, a genuine American Red. Fought in the Spanish Civil War, then spent his life as a civil-rights attorney. Lawyers Guild, blacklisted, premature antifascist, all that?"

Clearly, Bourgeois knew who her grandfather was. He nods, shifting slightly at the desk. He has still not said a word. He has, however, somehow summoned someone from an adjoining room, because there is now a tall man in a checkered shirt standing at the doorway, watching her curiously. Like that, Isabel understands how strange she's acting. But at the same time, she understands that the man's presence, like Bourgeois's, is benign.

Everything, in fact, is benign.

"I mean, I could even make the argument that there's something wrong with you, Father. That the fact that you had to go and blow innocent people's heads off before you could realize what was wrong with it all invalidates everything about you. Kill and cry, right? Kill people as a soldier for the US government? Fuck, Father, what were you guys thinking of? One could make the argument that any of you just had to crack a book or two and it was all there for you to understand, that the war in Vietnam was a moral dead end, even more immorally dead-ended than most."

It is hard to tell what Bourgeois thinks of that. Beyond showing comprehension of the point with a little nod, his face still shows nothing but attention. But she doesn't care about him. All she cares about is what she has, so desperately, to articulate.

"But *my* dad knew it. *His* dad knew it. All this political consciousness you've forged since 1963. My grandfather had as astute an analysis of World War II as he had of Vietnam. As *you* had of Vietnam—only you had to fucking go there and shoot people first. And, now, my dad is dying. Maybe a couple-three months, a half-year tops. When I get out of here I'm supposed to go meet my mom in Paris or somewhere, but instead he wants me to go up to New York and stay with him while he dies. And that's my question to you, Father. If I go? What should I tell him? What should be my report from the front of American protest?"

She stops now, not for a response, but because she has just entered into a new level of high. For a second, or what she thinks is a second, she closes her eyes and feels something dissolve in her, some internal capacity, some internal impediment. In its place, against the screen of her closed eyelids, a checkered pattern of sky appears and stretched away forever. It is intensely familiar, and dimly she realizes it is the quilt under which she slept, as a child, in her grandmother's bed. She does not know how long she watches it. But when she opens her eyes again, Bourgeois is still watching her, and she carries on talking as if she had never stopped.

"I mean, there he is, sitting in the house he was born in, looking out not only at his life, but at his father's too. And there's not one damn thing on the landscape that's not a failure. We're at war abroad on two fronts. We remain a segregated society. Huge inequities between the rich and the poor characterize us. The government holds the citizenry in a stranglehold. COINTELPRO? The NSA is Hoover's wet dream. They know where we are every minute of our lives, what we write, what we think, whom we sleep with, what we do. There is not *one* ideal of the mobilization against the war in Vietnam that has not been continuously degraded since 1970."

She is gesturing pretty widely now, sweeping an arm out toward the window where the crowds are milling. And she can't stop herself going on, and she says:

"Isn't that it, Father? They've got the PVI array, the Patriot Act, War Emergency Powers Act, and you? You've got a Pax Christi sign out there. Makes sense, right? Because even though you're a priest and I'm an atheist we both agree that there is *nothing rational* going on *anywhere* in the whole history of the struggle for social justice. There's nothing rational to make people believe that social justice can exist. It's totally without precedent that such a thing can ever occur anywhere, and believing in it is totally senseless. And so that's my question for you, Father. What do I tell my dad, up in New York, except that the whole march of human history, all his life, all your life, proves that everything he's cared about is a failure?"

Isabel is nearly yelling at the guy, now, though she doesn't know it, and he doesn't seem to mind. She lowers her voice and pushes her laptop to the side to lean on the desk, as if to be sure that he can hear: "So this is what I want to know from you, Father. This is what I want to know from you. When I'm sitting up there on the edge of my father's death bed in New York, what should I tell him? What should I tell him that will fight against the thought that the world he's leaving is substantially worse than the world he was born in? That we are substantially less free today than we were fifty years ago? That injustice and suffering have free rein over far more of the globe than ever in the past? That the rich are fewer and the poor are blacker and browner and far more than ever before in human history, and that in any case it doesn't matter because we've unleashed the inevitability of *infinite* suffering, infinite suffering, through the *weather itself*? What should I tell him to disprove for him the certainty that everything he's ever believed in, his whole life, was a waste of time? What should I tell him, Father? That I've just been down to Georgia and I am here to witness that Roy Bourgeois and his handful of the faithful, out of *all of human history*, are going to be the anointed ones who actually make a difference? Because they believe in a Christ of goodness?"

13.

In the hyper-reality of Isabel's vision, a number of expressions have crossed Bourgeois's face while he listens to her.

Number one was a squint with mouth well set, his face fully attentive under his still-red hair, a lot like Sinai's except, of course, much thicker. He is well shaven, clean of expression and direct of eye, which are blue.

The second was the same, but with wide open eyes and raised eyebrows, as if shocked by what she was saying.

In the third, he set his mouth in a thin frown and looks down at his hands, fiddling with something on his desk that she sees to be the alabaster Buddha. In this expression his eyes, directed away, became very focused, and even from an angle you could see his intensity of thought.

And, finally, the fourth: an animated, gesturing discourse in which his face, very alive, constantly sought out her understanding of what he had to say. And this is how he begins to talk.

Outside, on the soundstage, a speaker is exhorting unity with all the working people of Latin America. Inside, Bourgeois talks for a long time.

He talks in a calm, practiced voice, meaning everything he is saying and having said it, and meant it, many times before.

And perfectly silent, perfectly receptive, and—in fact—perfectly content, Isabel lets the drug swirl through her body, which feels more comfortable in this straight-backed wooden chair than anything she has ever felt in her life, and listens.

He talks to her about the huge photograph of Luis Espinal, tortured and killed in Bolivia. He is a bearded, handsome man staring steadily into the camera, above an inscription: "*1932: un justo nace 1980: un justo es asesinado 2005: ¡seguimos contigo!*" He talks to her about Oscar Romero and the rape and murder of four American churchwomen by Salvadorian soldiers, one by one introducing her to the plain-faced women on a painting on his wall: Ita Ford, Maura Clarke, Dorothy Kazel, and Jean Donovan. He tells her about how many of the perpetrators of atrocity in Latin America were trained in Fort Benning, Georgia. Now he directs her eye to the eight Jesuit priests killed on November 16, 1989, their names written on a multi-colored cross on which hangs a rather Mayan Jesus: Ignacio Ellacuría, Amando López, Joaquín López y López, Ignacio Martín-Baró, Segundo Montes, Juan Ramón Moreno, Julia Elba Ramos, Celina Ramos. Under them, there is an inscription: "Christians and all those who hate injustice are obligated to fight it with every ounce of their strength."

He tells her that everyone who has struggled for justice has suffered, many much more than her father or her grandfather. Nothing she's told him is new. This suffering is not a problem to be solved; it is the human condition. He tells her that her father is not measured by his accomplishments, but by hope itself.

"If you're going to hold on to hope you cannot look at the results of your actions," he says. "This is very American, you know, we do something, we want to see results. We work, we want to see what we've accomplished, you know what I mean? The people of Latin America have been struggling for generations and don't see very much progress. Yet their hope is their joy."

*

At that, Isabel nods, and even speaks.

"Um hmm. I see."

She does not close her eyes, but she feels her mindscape a limitless expanse of ice-blue, clear and precise and deeply, deeply angry. It is as if she has been feeling this anger all her life. And yet it is not disagreeable. It is simply there, and has always been there — it's only that she could never, she understands directly, without surprise, let herself feel it.

She couldn't bear it.

Now she can.

She rises, and packs her MacBook and its impedimenta into her bag, and she is done, she speaks quietly, conversationally, without any tears at all.

"Um hmm. But see, in my family, they've been hoping since the Bolshevik revolution. They've hoped their way through two world wars, the Holocaust, Vietnam. McCarthy, Hoover, Eisenhower, Nixon, Reagan, Ford, and two Bushes. They hoped through the religious right, through global warming. And you know what happened with everything they've hoped for? Here it is. Right here. And I'm just not sure that it's enough to die for, Father. I'm just not sure it's a good enough way to die. Surely there has to be something else?"

14.

Surely there has to be something else. It's as if the words are imprinted into her hearing, when she comes out of Bourgeois's office; it's as if they have become the rhythm of her breathing, *Surely, surely, there has to be, there has to be, something else.*

For a time she stands on the porch, eyes closed, letting the sun fall on her face and breathing the MDMA mantra. It seems all she can do, but in fact, as soon as she wills herself to open her eyes, she finds that she has a thorough and immediate command of the reality around her, effortlessly and without any possible negative feeling.

Neither about what is around her nor about the encounter she has just had with Bourgeois. Was that the peak? She checks her watch: one full hour since taking the drug. No, the peak is still ahead.

The porch is flooded in thin autumn sun. Next to her, at a slight remove, she sees the tall man in a checkered shirt, somehow deeply reassuring. Vaguely, she remembers seeing him before, and has the impression that he had been in Bourgeois's office while she was there. Was that possible? She nods at him, and he nods back. Everything—everything—is perfect.

With this effortless clarity, she sees that the pitch of protest has clearly moved to a new level. The long procession of crosses has come to an end, and in the little fenced-off area, to the rhythm of drumbeats, a series of huge, colorful papier-mâché puppets on poles are being marched by the gate of Fort Benning, some representations of soldiers, others representations of the dead. She stands watching and then to her surprise, she finds Josh Cohn at her side, his shirt-sleeves still buttoned at the wrists. To her even greater surprise, she finds that she has taken his bicep in a soft grasp and spoken in a voice that she cannot ever remember using before, but which she has no doubt was hers. "Hey there, Josh. How are you?"

Very surprised, he looks at her. But, she immediately perceives, he has no hesitation in accepting connection. To the contrary, he is totally open to it, even from her.

"I'm good, Ms. Montgomery. And you?"

For a moment she wonders who Ms. Montgomery is. Then she gets it. "Isabel. Or Dr. Montgomery, if you prefer. Not Ms., though, I don't like it. I'm good, really good."

"Isabel. Noted." He smiles, kindly. "Listen, I came to tell you, you may want to go over there to that little area on the other side of the fence. That's where the direct action is going to be."

She may, Isabel thinks to herself, want to find a corner here, lie on the grass, and breathe the mantra of her joy into the sky, that's what she may want to do. But this drug: she hasn't the slightest doubt that that was something she wanted to think, but not say. And she didn't say it. With a nod to Josh—a nod that seemed, to her, to say it all—she looks over and sees that, on one of the lateral fences, a huge opening has been ripped open, allowing direct access to the fence erected in front of the Fort Benning gate. Nearby, on a slight rise, she sees Christy and Becky watching her, and she understands that she has been brought here in her journalistic capacity to see the central act of civil disobedience and arrest. She feels the eyes of the girls, and of Josh, on her for a moment, feels them intensely, and realizes that they are not just now, but always have been, kind. Dimly, she realizes that they were kind even through her hostility, yesterday. But had she been hostile? she asked herself. She had felt hostile. But she had been honest. Didn't that count for something? And yet, why had she felt so hostile?

A sudden battery of drums begins now, beating loudly from a group of perhaps fifteen young people in battle dress, layers of clothes and helmets, now approaching, together, in two lines. The crowd in front of the opening in the first fence parts as the group arrives, and they enter the no-man's-land between the two fences. The crowd hangs respectfully back, except for four young men in work gloves with crowbars who, as if on cue, move forward, lean down to the bottom of the chain-link fence, place their crowbars, and pull the bottom of the fence right out of the ground. This opens a space of eighteen inches or so, just enough for the group of protesters, in pairs of two, to hand their drums to the person behind them, who hands them off until they reach the crowd and disappear, lie down and cross their arms and roll under the fence into Fort Benning.

Nearly without noticing, Isabel has wandered away from Josh and into the crowd, better to see what is happening on the army side of the fence. Dimly, she is aware that the man in the checkered shirt has followed her, but that seems only natural to her. Amazingly, the military police on the other side are watching elsewhere. Perhaps it was a planned diversion, she can't see from here. Five or six protesters are through by the time the MPs see what's going on, and when they do they move swiftly. As a detail of armed soldiers observe, each protester is corralled, has their hands affixed behind them with plastic ties, and is marched off to a waiting school bus.

On the protest side, each time someone crosses, the crowd cheers. More and more people are coming to watch, now, and to help hold the fence up, some pulling the chain link out of the ground, some climbing and rocking on the fence's poles. Clearly, this is a particular faction of the coalition attending the protest: there are no nuns or old people here, now, just college students, many dressed for battle, and they are swarming over the fence, rocking it, pulling it out of the ground.

Two young men, in fact, have set sedulously to work with two pairs of wire cutters, and it is as she watches them that she feels herself shoved forward toward the fence, violently. A phalanx of riot policemen, black clad and helmeted, force their way into the crowd and wrestle the two wire-cutters away from the fence. The boys are cuffed and marched off, the policemen pushing their way through the hooting crowd.

None of it feels bad. It all feels good, and dimly Isabel realizes that this is why Ecstasy is a rave drug. The bodies next to her, the roar of the crowd, the pushing backward, and forward. It is like being a part of an organism. And yet an instinct tells her, surely, that it is time now for her to be somewhere else. Something is changing dimension inside of her, a feeling she has never felt before, and she is not sure how long she can stay on her feet. On this side of the fence, the riot police are at least temporarily gone, and the orderly process of civil disobedience—every few minutes another protester crosses under the fence and is taken off by the MPs. But can she get out of here? For a tiny second, panic comes up. And then she sees, dramatically, how unnecessary it was. The panic. The man in the checkered shirt is standing next to her, watching her with polite interest, as if he knows what she is going through. Now, she is able to see that he is perhaps sixty with a flat belly and an air of strength. And his face, under a bald forehead and with a gap in its front teeth under a thick mustache, is the kindest she has ever seen in her life. She speaks to him without hesitation:

"Can you take me out of here?"

"Where to?"

"Somewhere I can lie down."

"Are you okay?"

"Very. Very. But in a way that makes me need to lie down."

"What is it?"

"MDMA. It's a long story. I took it by mistake. I think I'm about to peak."

"You sure you're okay?"

She realizes suddenly that she has never asked anyone for help before. Ever. Perhaps not since Molly took care of her as a child. She feels herself, in his gaze, a little girl and a grown woman, and realizes suddenly, with crystalline force, that she has always only been one person, the same person, and she is that same person now.

"I'm superb. I'm very, very good."

He nods, once, and then takes her arm and gently leads her out of the thickest of the crowd to an empty space of grass near the interior fence. Along the way he takes her computer bag off her shoulder, which she is intensely grateful for, as her legs are failing her quickly. Or she thinks they are. Maybe they aren't. Maybe she's just that relaxed.

There are many, many fewer people here. For a time she stands next to the man, watching now from a slight distance, as the crowd, young and very angry, face off across the remains of the fence at the MPs on the other side.

And then she is sitting on the grass. He seems to have helped her down, and is now sitting next to her.

And then, although she doesn't know it, he has caught her head as it falls and lowered it gently to his knee while he takes off his coat, with which he makes a pillow, and now she is lying on the grass.

But she doesn't know it.

Isabel will never be able to describe exactly what happens to her next. For the rest of her life it will be a point of reference. On one hand, it is an overwhelming experience of the very strong and very pure chemical given her as a gift by the Rasta pot dealer. On the other hand, it is an absolute, unique experience that is unlike anything she has ever known before or which she will ever have again. An endless expanse of wind is pouring through her, roaring in its enormity; cleansing, corrupt, violent, peaceful, horrible and beautiful, breathing through her with a simple reality that belies any judgment whatsoever. In it everything she has ever considered her identity has dissolved, and whether it is the drug or not she understands with nearly brutal certainty that there is no I or thou or them or us; the concept of pronoun does not exist, nor does there exist any differentiation between the interests or desires of different people. She is not conscious, but she is vividly conscious that this is, simply, reality, and the world of her angst, political and affective, has always been a fantasy, and that is why she has written what she has just written, and what you have just read. She experiences this understanding with immense gratitude but without surprise, as though she has always known it, and always been waiting to feel it, and only had to wait for now to do so. She is not conscious, but she will remember this precisely, and she has no idea of how long it lasts. But as suddenly as it came, so gently does it subside, and slowly, her eyes open to the sky above her. For minutes, she watches it, the captive atmosphere of a revolving globe. Then she says, aloud:

"I didn't know. I had no idea."

The man in the checkered shirt watches her kindly, and says nothing, but she senses his disagreement.

"Okay, that's not true. I did know. I just couldn't let myself."

He nods, once, with approval. "None of us can."

She shuts her eyes again and revisits that perfect awareness for a long, long moment, or at least, the afterglow of it. What a small voice she has. She didn't know. How odd that it should be this drug that should show her this, after all the drugs that have for so long helped her run away.

Then she looks at him suddenly.

"Want to know something?"

"Of course."

"That girl on the rue des Abbesses who called me *m'enfichiste* and then left me alone in her *chambre de bonne*? She was a dear, sweet little person, kind and lovely. All she wanted was to be loved, and to spend her entire life with me. It was the first time I ever was in love, and the last, and standing there, and when she left me in her *chambre de bonne*, after I made her leave me, I ached and I ached, I ached, and I've been aching ever since."

As if he has known her all her life, rather than, as is the case, not at all.

"Okay. So?"

She considered. "So?"

"You don't need me to tell you."

She thinks for a moment. Then she says, deliberately, as if reciting a catechism, what she now understands.

"So love implies loss. Fine. We resist love because we're afraid of loss. And, equally, ideals imply failure. That's what Bourgeois was saying, and Josh and Christy and Becky. Who knows why some people are moved by ideals? But if you are, you're not alone. Millions of people have been. And you can't be afraid of their failure. Nothing's ever going to change and no one's ever going to win, so generation after generation chooses failure. Millions of people have. Billions. That is, they choose to fight for ideals in the face of the inevitability of failure. And if you make that choice, you can do it with despair, or you can do it with hope: the choice is yours. Right?"

He looks away, and again she feels his disappointment. "Almost."

With real curiosity, she asks: "What am I missing?"

A pause. Then: "It's hope. The standard of choice between the two ways one functions in the face of the inevitability of failure isn't hope . . ."

Dimly aware that she is having the strangest conversation of her strange life, on one hand, and that on the other she has never experienced such faultless communication, she literally pokes him with her finger.

"Go on."

"You understand me?"

"Perfectly. Go on."

"The way to judge the choice people make is which one is more informed by love. That's all. It's that simple. You get it?"

Did she get it? Slowly, she asks: "And what about the damage done?"

"What damage?"

"The damage that love does. What I did to the girl on the rue des Abbesses. What my family has done to each other? What my family has done to me?"

He nods now. "Surely you see the difference between wounds inflicted by love and a wound inflicted by hope?"

So that's it. She nods, profoundly.

"Yes. Crimes of love—crimes of family—have victims, but no perpetrators. Right? The consequence is the same, but the intention is different, and that changes everything."

He nods now, profoundly, nearly with gratitude. "So you do get it."

She knows she doesn't need to answer, but she says it anyway, as she turns her head to the parabolic sky of blue in which has floated up all the people she has loved, and all the people she has lost, and is going to lose, and shuts her eyes.

"Yes. If you don't get that, you do terrible things. Like lie to your lover for all of your life. Like marry a person you don't love. Like not read your father's emails for ten years. And then you make more victims."

For a last, long, luscious moment she lets her mind float in the certainty of the sky-blue behind her eyelids.

And then it is time to sit up.

She knows it and in the next second she does it. Companionably next to the man, she actually manages to light a cigarette, and give him one, which he accepts happily and inserts into his lips under his mustache with practiced ease. Her consciousness is returned to the pre-peak purity, but washed clean now of anything like judgment, and anything like fear. Conversationally, she remarks to him:

"It never occurred to me to ask anyone for help before."

"I can see that."

"Stupid, huh?"

"Oh, I don't know."

Smoking together, they see the police are back, having gotten the fence-cutters into school buses, which gives her a precise idea of the length of the peak she has experienced on the MDMA: as infinite as it seemed, it was perhaps fifteen minutes. She also sees what they are doing: that they have managed to encircle this crowd, containing it. They are surprisingly upset, the police, as if this were personal. Every now and again a pair go into the crowd and extract someone in cuffs. Young, large men seem to be their target of choice. One such—one of the pair which first opened the fence—is the object of two cops now, anonymous behind riot face guards, who wade into the crowd to put their hands on him, while he struggles to get away, then goes limp. Two other police have to come help carry him. Someone tries to block them; there is a surge back as more police move in with billy clubs and cattle prods, and the young man is, now, successfully carried off. The cordon continues to form with new police arriving, orderly and slow, and with slight curiosity she realizes that their arrest is imminent.

"Well it sure seems stupid to me now."

"Only if you need to make a judgment."

She looks at him now, in profile, watching the protest. "How do you know so much about me?"

"I don't know anything about you. Except that you're human. Just like me."

This she understands with clarity. Of course she is. She always has been. And with the same clarity she can see that their arrest is now moments away. Indeed, turning, she can see that police vans are being brought up behind the soundstage.

She seems, however, to be the only person here who realizes this.

341

The rest of the crowd, back toward Fort Benning now, is facing off against the MPs on the other side, as more people—here a young man, here a middle-aged woman, here a professorial gentleman in an overcoat—while behind them all the riot police form their cordon. She is, she realizes, about to be arrested and jailed for six months. And now she speaks again to the man in that shockingly small voice, the voice she has never heard from herself before, saying something that is true and has always been true, from the moment she opened her email in Philadelphia to this very moment here, and from which she has been running ever since.

"I can't get arrested. I have to go to New York."

He looks up and around them, with a calculating expression.

"Why?"

Behind, the growing phalanx of riot policemen, and behind them the whole wide world, the wide world in which she has written the work of her life.

"My father is dying. I need to go be with him."

"I see. Well then." He looks around now, and an expression of careful calculation crosses his face. "I wonder what we can do to get you out of here."

The phalanx of police, behind them, is nearly in formation, with arriving cops joining the edge of the cordon on my right.

He speaks now as if to himself. "That looks about the weakest point over there."

She sees what he means. "Maybe we can get through on a press card?"

"Maybe. They don't like press much either."

She nods, and licks her lips. "Then I'm fucked."

"Maybe. Want to give it a try?"

They rise now, the man helping her up with a strong arm. He puts the computer bag over her shoulder. Then, with a hand on her back, he brings her to the right flank of the police cordon, as close as he dares, and stops.

"Ready?"

"Yes." For a moment she stands, staring at him. "How do I thank you?"

"No need."

"At least tell me your name?"

"Ralph."

"I'm Isabel."

"I know who you are. I work with Father Roy. He asked me to keep an eye on you after your interview. Thought something was wrong. In fact, there was something right. Very, very right."

For a time they watch each other, because she so doesn't want to leave him. Then he speaks softly.

"It's time to go now."

"You come too."

"I can't. I'm going to divert them while you try to get through."

"You're going to get arrested."

"I'm always getting arrested. Go now, Isabel. You have somewhere to be."

She nods and, in a flood of regret, turns again toward the police.

And without any thought, I know exactly what is about to happen.

I look back and see Ralph running toward the police, hard. At first they don't notice, so he gives a yell—a loud one—and then they do. At full speed, now, he tackles a riot policeman at shoulder level, knocking him hard to the ground, and is immediately covered in a scrimmage of police.

Now there is a single cop holding a position where there had been five. It is toward him that I point myself. I pull out my press credentials, put my bag over my shoulder, close my jacket, and begin to run.

Can I get by? Almost. I am nearly next to the cop when he turns and blocks me, and I find myself stopped before the matt black of his riot mask, his huge, armored body in front of me, and he is raising his hands to put them on me when I step forward again and push my press card at him, screaming: *"Out of my way goddammit or I'll have you in court so quick you won't know which way is south you fucking trailer trash cracker piece of shit bastard"* —I am, after all, still Isabel, and now I know that I always have been, and always will—and shocked, he makes way, just like that, and I have crossed the line away from the protest.

Face after face, aged, kind, mean, young, soft, harsh, ugly, beautiful face after face after face as if they were all the faces of my life. The soundstage, the religious banners, the barbecue vendors on lawns.

Look at me. I have done the wrong thing.

I have left the protesters I believe in, to go be with my father: I have done the wrong thing, and sent Ralph to jail, and I have done it out of love.

And finally I find myself alone, where it all started, in front of the PVI array with the impassive agents running it.

Standing stock-still as if perfectly suspended, like my father and grandfather before me, like my aunts and my uncle, like my beloved Molly, like everyone I've ever cared about or admired, between what I believe and whom I love.

Just like them.

And realizing that, thinking, Oh my God, oh my God, didn't you just, after all, make it here somehow? Aren't you just, at fucking last, a big girl now?

May 2014
Boulevard Saint-Marcel